SEVEN MINUTES TO NOON

Kate Pepper

A SIGNET BOOK

SIGNET
Published by New American Library, a division of
Penguin Group (USA) Inc., 375 Hudson Street,
New York, New York 10014, USA
Penguin Group (Canada), 10 Alcorn Avenue, Toronto,
Ontario M4V 3B2, Canada (a division of Pearson Penguin Canada Inc.)
Penguin Books Ltd., 80 Strand, London WC2R 0RL, England
Penguin Ireland, 25 St. Stephen's Green, Dublin 2,
Ireland (a division of Penguin Books Ltd.)
Penguin Group (Australia), 250 Camberwell Road, Camberwell, Victoria 3124,
Australia (a division of Pearson Australia Group Pty. Ltd.)
Penguin Books India Pvt. Ltd., 11 Community Centre, Panchsheel Park,
New Delhi - 110 017, India
Penguin Group (NZ), cnr Airborne and Rosedale Roads, Albany,
Auckland 1310, New Zealand (a division of Pearson New Zealand Ltd.)
Penguin Books (South Africa) (Pty.) Ltd., 24 Sturdee Avenue,
Rosebank, Johannesburg 2196, South Africa

Penguin Books Ltd., Registered Offices:
80 Strand, London WC2R 0RL, England

First published by Signet, an imprint of New American Library,
a division of Penguin Group (USA) Inc.

First Printing, May 2005
10 9 8 7 6 5 4 3 2 1

Copyright © Kate Pepper, 2005
All rights reserved

 REGISTERED TRADEMARK—MARCA REGISTRADA

Printed in the United States of America

PUBLISHER'S NOTE
This is a work of fiction. Names, characters, places, and incidents either are the product of the author's imagination or are used fictitiously, and any resemblance to actual persons, living or dead, business establishments, events, or locales is entirely coincidental.

For Oliver, Eli and Karenna
∴ . . again and always

ACKNOWLEDGMENTS

Matthew Bialer, my agent, and Claire Zion, my editor, both worked hard to help steer this novel in the right direction; I offer them my sincere appreciation for all their patience and effort. Thanks also to P.O. Paul Grudzinski of Brooklyn's Seventy-sixth Precinct for taking the time to talk with me and show me around the Detectives Unit. To my intrepid early-draft reader, Gail Barrnett: Thanks, Mom, for your time, enthusiasm and sensitive feedback. Last but not least, my deepest gratitude goes to Oliver Lief for, well, everything.

PROLOGUE

Jen followed her mother to school, earning a *come on* or *hurry up* when she fell too far behind. The early morning air was thick and warm on her summer-tan arms, and Jen wanted to swim, not study; she wanted to play with her friends.

Halfway along the Carroll Street Bridge, she stopped and looked up at the vast blue Brooklyn sky, streaked with cottony wisps: a rabbit, a ship, a baby. She ran her hand along the bridge's iron railing. Someone had painted it blue. Jen liked it. She leaned over and looked down into the Gowanus Canal.

"Let's get moving!" her mother called.

Jen had loved looking for creatures in the canal ever since kindergarten, when she'd learned how a fixed pump had brought the dead water to life. Her teacher had told them all about it. Up until the 1960s the pump had kept the water moving in the man-made canal and all kinds of living things had grown in it. Then the pump broke, and no one fixed it, and the water sat still and festered. By the time Jen's class had come to study it, it was a kind of electric green color, a dead river running between Jen's neighborhood and her school. Some people said the canal was worse than dead, that it was poisonous, and if you fell into it you would get sick and maybe even die. Jen had pictured herself tumbling over the railing and for one brief moment flying, then evaporating the instant she touched the water.

Her teacher had told them that a businessman on Court Street had a dream about the canal and it was this: it could be another Venice, Italy. Instead of factories on its banks, there could be restaurants and parks, and there could be boats on the water. "Gondolas on the Gowanus," Jen's teacher had said, and the class didn't understand what it meant but it sounded so funny they all laughed. But first the canal would have to be brought back to life. So finally, after all those years, the businessman talked to someone who got someone else to fix the pump. Jen's teacher had said that by the end of first grade, they should be able to see life again in the Gowanus Canal.

Now she was starting second grade, and it had happened; it was true. Since last year the color of the water had improved; it was pale green and partly transparent. She looked and looked and looked for something alive. And then she saw it: a turtle the size of her hand, skimming the top of the water.

"Mom!"

"Hurry up. We don't have time for this!"

"I saw a turtle!"

Jen knew she had to move along but couldn't resist one more look. And then she saw something else, and this time, it was magical. She saw a fairy, a woman with a peaceful face covered by the murky water, eyes wide open. The face slowly rotated upward toward the sky, as if looking, then rotated slowly away, and was gone.

"Mom!"

"Jen!" Her mother turned around and planted her hands on her hips.

"I'm coming!" Jen ran. "But Mom, I saw a fairy in the canal! She had long hair and it was flying all around her. Like this." Jen spun around so her own hair would puff and float.

Her mother's breath hissed out like steam. She looked at her watch. "Do you realize what time it is, young lady?"

Jen skipped across the bridge. She would tell her

mother again when she was ready to listen, maybe at cuddle time, right before sleep. She would tell her mother she had seen a lady, a fairy, and it was magical and it was real.

PART ONE

Chapter 1

Alice Halpern waited on a bench in Carroll Park in the sticky heat of early September. She drained the last of her iced decaf from a waxed-paper cup that buckled in her grip. Lauren was late. Her cup, sealed with a plastic top, had formed a skin of tiny droplets. The ice had probably melted by now. She would be disappointed; she liked her drinks icy cold.

The sun shifted and Alice felt its rays burn into her skin, still milky white from months of pampering with sunblock. A redhead, she knew better than to go out without her wide-brimmed hat, which she had left hanging on the coat stand as she hustled to get the kids out the door to school this morning. She moved down the bench into a remaining patch of shade and glanced again at her watch; it was now ten to three.

In a few minutes, the neat brick school building across the street from the park would open its doors and spill the little ones back into the world in a rowdy convocation. Alice took a long, deep breath, savoring the relative calm of these last minutes before the riptide of motherhood dragged her forward until night. She wondered now if she should have stayed in the air-conditioned store, unpacking the latest shipment of autumn shoes. She should have confirmed with Lauren before heading out early into the scalding afternoon. The heat felt like a woolen blanket cinched around her, dark and suffocating. Six months into her third pregnancy—with twins, double the trouble, double the fun—she could already feel the babies pressing against her lungs.

She tried to remember what Lauren had said yesterday about her plans for today: morning errands, then her Pregnant Pause Pilates class at noon in Park Slope. Lauren loved the class and had been urging Alice to join, but she felt she didn't have the time; between work at Blue Shoes and obligations at home, she couldn't squeeze in one more thing. But Lauren was devoted to her Pilates class and always went. Still, she was more than eight months pregnant with her second child and the heat wave may have dissuaded her.

Alice found her cell phone at the bottom of her purse and speed-dialed Lauren's cell. When her voice mail came on, Alice left a message. Then she called Lauren at home and left another message on the machine.

She dropped the phone back into her purse and pulled out the folded, now crumpled letter she was eager to share with Lauren. Flattening it across her lap, she read it again, with its bold, blunt title: THIRTY DAY NOTICE OF EVICTION. She had been served the summons at the store just an hour ago, feeling betrayed that her landlord, Joey—*former* landlord, as of the sale of his brownstone two days ago—had supplied the new owner with her work address. The letter was signed *Julius Pollack, owner.* Why hadn't Mr. Pollack, *owner,* contacted them first? Discussed it? Found out how diligently Alice and Mike had been house hunting lately? Lauren and her husband, Tim, had received a similar notice earlier in the summer—hers signed by a managing agent for Metro Properties—giving them the same thirty days to vacate their apartment before eviction proceedings would begin. Both lawyers, they were fighting it; but they lived in a *multiunit dwelling,* the litmus test of responsibilities and rights that apartments in private homes, like Alice and Mike's—no, Julius Pollack's—lacked. Their lease with Joey had expired and Pollack was under no obligation to renew it. Alice and Mike had hard decisions to make now: should they undergo the exorbitant and exhausting project of moving twice, first to a rental, then to a house they owned? Put the kids, and themselves, through all that? Or dig in their heels and demand the time they needed to move just once to some place they could rightly call their home? Alice needed *facts*. Where was Lauren? Surely she could offer sage legal advice and also commiserate over the shock and humiliation of being summarily tossed out of your home.

As the minutes ticked by, Alice's disappointment grew at the missed opportunity to quietly dissect the new development with Lauren. It would be hard to discuss the notice in front of the kids. She had already spoken with Mike on the phone and they had agreed not to worry the children until it was figured out. Alice and Lauren would have to break their conversation into bits, fitting it into random pockets of privacy during the children's after-school playground time. It was better than nothing.

She carried Lauren's soggy cup of iced decaf with her, just in case she *did* come soon, and walked across the street to the entrance of P.S. 58, where parents and babysitters had gathered in force. The kindergarteners came out first, led single file by their teacher. Peter and Austin were at the end of the line, holding hands; they had been best friends almost from birth and were said to be inseparable in class. Alice knelt down to their eye level and kissed both boys hello.

"How was school?" she asked Peter, shifting forward to plant an extra kiss on her son's irresistibly soft cheek.

"Good."

"How was school for you?" she asked Austin. He had Lauren's light brown hair, cut short, and tufted after a day at school.

"Good."

"What did you guys do today?"

"Good," Peter said, drawing giggles from Austin.

Alice stood up and scanned the crowd for Lauren. It was chaotic; she could easily be missed. Alice didn't see her but there was no point sending up alarms quite yet. She would just stand here until Nell came out, and if

Lauren still wasn't here, then she would decide what to do about Austin.

Nell was at the front of the second-grade line, swinging her purple lunch box loosely from her hand. Alice waved. Nell said good-bye to her teacher and darted away from her classmates.

"Hey, sweetie, how was school?" Alice asked.

"Good," Nell said. "No homework again today!"

Alice figured that by Monday, homework would make its unwelcome appearance. But she didn't want to burst Nell's bubble, so she just said, "Great!" and took her hand.

All of the kindergarteners had been picked up. Peter and Austin stood by the fence, thumb wrestling. Their teacher, Gina, was herself now scanning for Lauren.

"I think I should just take Austin," Alice told Gina. "I have a funny feeling Lauren might have gone into labor."

"Really?" Gina smiled. She was a young woman with long brown hair and tiny but piercing eyes. "How exciting!"

It had already been prearranged for Alice to pick Austin up from school when the baby came, so Gina didn't question the suggestion. She told the boys to enjoy their weekends, and to Austin added, "Congratulations, big brother!"

Alice cringed; she wished Gina hadn't said that. What if Lauren was just plain late?

She took the three children back across the street to the park to wait a while longer for Lauren, just in case. Once on the curb, they bolted straight to the big kids' side of the playground, where the jungle gyms were taller, the slides steeper, and innocence noticeably dampened by age.

Alice sat on the bench and tried calling Lauren again at both her numbers, but again, there was no answer. Maybe Maggie was still at Blue Shoes; maybe *she* had heard something. Alice dialed the store phone but it rang and rang. Strange, she thought; Maggie was either in the bathroom or she wasn't there at all. Five minutes later, Alice tried again. And again, no luck.

A Mr. Frosty truck pulled up at the park entrance nearest to them, and the children hurdled out of play. Nell, Peter and Austin accosted Alice with demands for ice cream money, issuing varied tones of *pleases* calibrated for results. She dug into her wallet, producing dollar bills. The children took them and raced off, returning a few minutes later with beady-eyed, fluorescent popsicles fashioned after action heroes and their nemeses, which may or may not have derived from actual ice cream. Nighttime baths would remove most of the colored streaks from their faces and arms, but Alice knew that a slight fluorescent shadow would still be visible come morning.

The children wove themselves back into the cacophony of play. Phone cradled in her hand, Alice watched them reel from ladder to slide to monkey bars. Then she thought to try Maggie's cell, this time with success.

"Mags! Where are you?"

Somewhere behind Maggie, Alice heard the fading wail of a departing siren.

"Getting Ethan from school. As soon as you left the store, Sylvie called in sick," Maggie said in her crisp British accent. Sylvie, Ethan's babysitter, normally picked him up from his private school in the Heights. "Can you imagine? What about a little advance notice?"

"Do you think she was lying?"

"She said she'd just come down with a stomachy thing, maybe something she ate," Maggie said. "Ethan! *Please* wait for the walk light!"

Alice could picture them: tall, glamorous, blond Maggie at the mercy of her little boy. Ethan was the spitting image of his father, Simon, whom Maggie had summarily divorced last year despite all evidence that she still loved him. They equally shared Ethan, this little boy with his father's haunting good looks, tugging on his mother's hand.

"Mags, did you try Jason? Maybe he can come into

work this afternoon." They had recently hired a young college student to help out at the store, to keep it open later at night and also to pitch in on days like today when child-care disarrangements made the schedule difficult for two mothers sharing what amounted to three jobs.

"He's got classes. I told him after being so late yesterday, he ought to get his priorities straight, drop out of school and work for us full-time!" Maggie's laugh was a high cackle.

"Mags? Why don't I watch Ethan this afternoon so you can work?"

"Righto. And tell Lauren I found that phone number she wanted, the baker on Columbia Street." Alice heard a Mr. Frosty jingle sail by on Maggie's end of the line.

"That's why I'm calling," Alice said. "Lauren never showed up. So I picked Austin up from school. Did you hear from her, by any chance?"

"Not a peep. What are you thinking, Alice?"

"She got held up somewhere," Alice said. "Or maybe she had the baby."

"Have you phoned Tim?"

"I don't have his numbers, do you?"

"I'm pretty sure they're in my Palm Pilot backup at the store," Maggie said. "*All right, but just a small one.* Sorry, Ethan's asking for an Italian ice."

"I'll tell you what, Maggie," Alice said. "I'll meet you at the store and we'll call Tim. Then I'll take Ethan with us to the butcher so you can work. Did you remember the barbecue at our house tonight?"

"Translation," Maggie said, "I don't have to cook. Of *course* I remembered."

Alice gathered the three children and herded them out of the playground and onto Smith Street, tossing Lauren's ruined cup of no-longer-iced decaf into a wire mesh garbage can on the corner. As they waited for the light at President Street, a puddle of paper scraps swirled in a cowlick wind, delighting the children with proof of everyday magic. Alice figured a garbage truck had recently passed, dribbling refuse. New York just couldn't keep clean, though it was partly the grit of the place that was so appealing. Grit and possibility.

She sidestepped the eddy of leftover trash and ushered the children across the street. Two blocks along, Nell made them all stop in a wide swath of shade in front of Smith Home to peer at the window display of silly pull knobs. Nell loved to lure the other kids into the game of choosing which eccentric knob they would buy today if they could. About an inch around, each buffed-pewter knob was a lopsided face, pulled and stretched by some humor or discontent. They reminded Alice of miniature commedia dell'arte masks—pathos, hilarity—and were beautiful in a disturbing kind of way, like two sides of a coin pressed into one exceptional, misaligned image. Scanning the dozens of knobs, Nell announced today's favorite: fat cheeks, eyes skewed directly upward, mischievous grin. Watching her beloved daughter enact this ritual, Alice made herself a silent promise to both please her children and assuage the sizzle of anxiety she was starting to feel like an itch under her skin every time she thought about that Thirty Day Notice. They would never be able to move in time, but if they found something—signed a contract or a lease—any sane housing court judge would give them the time they needed to move, wouldn't they? Alice and Mike would have to immediately step up the house hunt. Raise their price, lower their standards. When they found the right house, she would keep the promise she was just now conjuring and make Nell and Peter a gift of silly knobs for their new rooms, a gesture to a new beginning in a new home.

"Let's get moving." Alice turned into a pool of bright sun and started walking. The children noisily followed. It was just two more blocks to Blue Shoes.

With every step, Alice thought of Lauren and tried to call up her own physical memory of childbirth, its shattering pain, the outrageous joy. Tried to feel herself in Lauren's experience today. Could it be true? *Had* she gone into labor? Alice wondered if Tim knew anything.

Or if instead Lauren had gathered up an amazing story no one had yet been told: birth in the back of a cab, or in the subway, or at home. All frightening scenarios. Alice hoped she had made it to a hospital. That she hadn't been alone. And Alice thought, *Ivy. At last. You are here.*

Ivy was the women's secret, a gift they shared before Lauren would pass it on to Tim at their daughter's birth. As with their first pregnancy, Tim had not wanted to know the baby's gender. He wanted to be surprised. But motherhood had toughened Lauren and the only surprise she wanted was that the baby was born alive and healthy. It was a feeling Alice and Mike shared: they knew their twins were boys.

The other gift Lauren had prepared for Tim, along with the surprise of a daughter, was choosing the name, Ivy, after Tim's favorite grandmother.

Alice and Maggie had kept Lauren's secrets for months. Tonight, Tim would finally know.

Chapter 2

The sun was strong and for a moment the plate-glass storefront of Blue Shoes seemed to float, mirrorlike, against the brick building. Alice was pleased to see that Maggie had remembered to suction the BE RIGHT BACK sign to the front door. She rummaged through her purse for her keys.

The children raced into the dark shop. Alice switched on the lights, instantly brightening the painted-silver tin ceiling, the high gloss of the oak floors, the rich depth of the blue walls. Pinging awake the displays of gorgeous shoes. Blue Shoes had kept its promise and become "Brooklyn's footwear fashion destination," a prediction made by a tiny newspaper article that appeared when they first opened last winter. Alice loved her partnership with Maggie, the bustle of their store. It was a sane, even fun compromise between her former work life as a film editor and her current life as a mother. They had jointly dubbed the store a *midlife reinvention,* an experiment that, blissfully, had worked.

Alice checked the answering machine under the stone counter, its creamy green glaze dazzling in the halogen light. Nothing. Maggie and Ethan arrived minutes later and the four children, lifelong friends, gathered on the center bench to inspect Nell's latest pack of Yu-Gi-Oh! cards.

Maggie, in flowing butter-yellow pants and a cornflower-blue tank top, with her mop of blond hair pinned high on her head, strode through the store like a queen defiant of the heat.

"Anything?" Maggie asked.

Alice shook her head.

They went straight for the computer in the back room and found Tim's numbers. His cell phone went right to voice mail, so they tried his office. His secretary told them he was away on business. When pressed, she explained that he was taking depositions in Chicago.

"When he calls in," Alice asked the secretary, "please ask him to call me as soon as possible. Tell him—" She hesitated to leave an alarming message, but decided spontaneously to follow her instinct. "Tell him Lauren didn't meet me today when she said she would, and I can't reach her anywhere, and being as she's nearly full-term, naturally I thought that possibly—"

"The baby." The secretary summed up Alice's worries so efficiently.

"Yes," Alice said. "The baby."

"I'll get the message through to him."

"Thank you." Alice recited her cell and home numbers, hung up the phone and turned to Maggie. "I'm getting really worried. Do you still have her key?" Maggie had been in charge of plant watering at Lauren and Tim's while they were away recently.

"I do," Maggie said. "I'll tell you what, while you've got the kids, I'll make some calls. I'll start with Methodist, where she's supposed to have the baby, and if she's not there, I'll try other hospitals. And I'll call the exercise place, see if she made it to class. If I don't come up with anything, I'll go over to her apartment."

"Good idea, Mags."

"I wish I could tell you to have a glass of wine," Maggie said, her eyes squinting in a kind of feline smile. "You've had a hard day, darling. Please, leave the worry to me."

"You're not good enough at it," Alice said.

"Well, you're too good at it." Maggie leaned in to kiss Alice on the cheek. Her perfume was light and flowery.

"Don't think about that horrid notice—you'll move when you move. And we're going to hear from Lauren any minute. She probably lost herself at the Barneys warehouse sale. I was there yesterday and I was nearly late back myself."

Alice appreciated Maggie's efforts to distract her from the day's disappointments, but it was no use. "Lauren doesn't shop at Barneys," Alice said. "And she's never been late for anything in her life."

"An impossibility," Maggie countered, "even for the prompt and brilliant Lauren Barnet."

The kids were getting restless; Peter and Austin had already drifted through the front door onto the sidewalk.

"Call me if you find out anything," Alice told Maggie in parting. "I'm stopping at Cattaneo's for barbecue stuff, then going straight home."

Alice ushered the band of children up to Court Street and a few more blocks to the neighborhood butcher. They loved coming to Cattaneo's for a chance to skate in the sawdust that covered the floor and also for the lollipops, which Sal Cattaneo himself doled out to children after every sale.

Cattaneo's was a nice, clean, well-lit store with neat shelves of bottled gourmet sauces that hadn't been there when Alice first arrived in the neighborhood fifteen years ago, pregentrification. She stood at the glass counter and ordered a pound each of ground turkey and beef from Sal, who looked to be in his fifties, with his halo of tousled white hair spilling out from beneath a creased white paper hat.

Sal handed over her order and in his sonorous voice nearly sang to her, "Anything else, young lady?" She adored him for that *young lady*. Thirty-six years old, hugely pregnant, with four children bedeviling his store.

"Not today, Sal, thanks."

He distributed lollipops to the children, who had lined up on cue at the ding of the closing cash register.

Back on Court Street, Alice checked her voice mail to see if she had possibly missed a call; her cell phone's ring was often subsumed by the children's noise. There was, in fact, one message, caller ID *unknown*. She listened eagerly for the sound of Lauren's voice, feeling the first note of buoyant relief as she dialed her code. Then the message played and her moment of hopefulness evaporated.

"Hi, Alice, it's Pam Short returning your call, returning my call, returning your call. Don't ya just love playing phone tag? Now it's your turn. You know my number."

Pam Short was a broker at Garden Hill Realty—where Ethan's sitter, Sylvie, worked part-time as an office assistant—and was supposed to be some kind of miracle worker. Alice dialed Pam back and left her another message. It was a frustrating volley, and all Alice really cared about now was hearing from Lauren, but the house hunt couldn't wait. She marched the children past gourmet shops, antique stores, designer boutiques, spiffy new restaurants and all the real estate brokers who had practically laughed at her request for a house under a million dollars.

They crossed Smith Street and continued along President onto the leafy block of landmark brownstones where Alice had lived virtually her entire adulthood. Up the stoop and back home; well, it was home for now, though clearly *Julius Pollack, owner,* didn't agree. In the foyer, Alice saw that Joey—who had moved out this morning after a lifetime in the house—had left behind some of the miscellany no one knew what to do with after a move: a bag of wire hangers, an old cork bulletin board, a box containing different shades of shoe polish and an ugly picture frame. He had probably left this stuff for Alice and Mike, in case they wanted it. But it was all junk. She would ask Mike to carry it to the curb later.

She turned on the air conditioner and opened the kitchen door to the backyard, into which Nell, Peter, Austin and Ethan eagerly ran. She watched them from the broad window over the sink of her large, well-used kitchen. Nell opened the toy bin and the boys made an eager collection of plastic shovels and buckets and hoes, which they tossed into the oversized sandbox Mike had built.

As she watched the children happily play, unaware that anything was wrong, Alice thought back to yesterday, wondering what she had missed. She conjured Lauren and Maggie to the bench beside her and tried to recall if there was something she had not heard or understood about Lauren's plans.

The day before, Thursday, had been even hotter than today. Alice, Lauren and Maggie had gathered at the playground after school.

Lauren shifted her bulky middle on the bench but couldn't seem to get comfortable. Her blue eyes paled in a flush of sun and she inched closer to Alice, who instinctively slid over to accommodate her. It was an odd sensation that Lauren, who was the smallest among them, suddenly needed so much space. Her long brown hair was coiled atop her head and skewered with a takeout chopstick, but still she couldn't seem to cool down her neck. She fanned it with her flattened hand. A wine-colored maternal family birthmark, roughly the shape and size of a quarter, was visible at the nape of her hairline, just at the nexus of her spine.

Alice remembered the little portable fan she kept in her purse. She took it out, flipped up the yellow plastic blades and held it whizzing at varying angles around Lauren's face and neck. Lauren leaned forward to catch the breeze.

"Joey sold the house yesterday," Alice announced.

Lauren turned to her. "I thought the buyer wanted it delivered vacant."

"He did, but Joey had another buyer lined up, so the first guy gave in. He really wanted it."

When he decided to move to Florida, Joey had asked them if they wanted the house. They had always thought the day would come when Joey moved on and they would take over the title. They knew it wouldn't be cheap, but the price tag awakened them to a shift that had transformed the real estate markets when they weren't paying attention: 1.7 million dollars for a two-family brownstone. Alice was struck dumb when she first heard it. Mike's reaction was to laugh. Joey shrugged his shoulders. He found a buyer in two weeks.

"I still think it's outrageous." Drops of sweat had gathered on Lauren's forehead and she wiped them off with the palm of her swollen hand. Her body had assumed a laden quality, and Alice had a feeling Lauren's baby wouldn't wait for her due date in mid-September. "So much money for a house. People around here are getting pathologically greedy."

It was true. Lately, the streets of Carroll Gardens, Cobble Hill and even Boerum Hill seemed to be turning to gold.

"Any news on *your* housing problems?" Alice asked Lauren.

"Nothing yet." Lauren pressed her hands beneath her belly and lifted its weight off her thighs. "Tim's got someone at his firm handling it. He says if he can prove this eviction's illegal, he'll probably find they're doing it to other tenants too. Metro Properties owns a lot of buildings in the area. Corporate landlords are the worst; we don't even know *who* our landlord is. I think Tim wants to bust Metro and I'm starting to feel the same way. I'm so angry at those bloodsuckers for putting us through this."

"If I were you, I'd get on with it and move," Maggie said. "It isn't worth fighting over scraps."

The remark clearly annoyed Lauren. Her lips scrunched and she looked away. Alice's gaze wandered after Lauren's to a bright red ball that was just then spinning toward their feet. A little boy of about three was chasing it, stumbling over his own chunky sneakers and finally crashing face-first onto the black rubberized mat that covered the play areas for just this reason. He wailed tragically. Alice flinched toward him, about to offer comfort, when a woman raced over and scooped him up in her arms. Young, probably not yet thirty, she wore a scoop-neck purple T-shirt tucked into jeans, and black leather sneakers. Her dark hair was bobbed at her jaw, heightening the contrast of her paper-white skin. The round pink lenses of her sunglasses partially obscured her eyes.

"Shh, buddy. It's okay." Her voice was clear and deep, warmly resonant yet without a ripple of worry for the child. She was not his mother.

To test her hunch, Alice asked, "Is your son all right?"

The woman lifted her face from the boy's thick brown hair. "He'll be fine." She smiled, but only halfway.

Alice found a clean tissue in her purse and got up to offer it.

"My kids fall all the time," she said, "and, oh, the drama!"

The woman accepted the tissue and began to dry the boy's teary cheeks.

"He's adorable," Alice said.

"Yes," the woman said, "my nephew's a doll."

"I'm not a doll!" the boy blurted out. "I'm a person!"

Now the young woman smiled fully. "You're my big boy." She ruffled his hair. As soon as she set him down, he crouched to pick up his red ball, threw it and resumed the chase. His aunt calmly watched him. She didn't wear a wedding ring, Alice noticed. No jewelry at all, as a matter of fact, not even earrings. She was lean and muscular as a gymnast.

"I've seen you here before," Alice said.

"I watch him now and then. It keeps me sane, you know?"

"Funny, being with my kids keeps me crazy." Alice glanced back at Lauren and Maggie to see if they'd caught her joke. They had, and were both furiously nodding.

"I'm Alice."

"Frannie."

"Nice to meet you."

A shriek issued from the other side of the playground, beyond the women's sight. Alice quickly scanned the immediate area for her children but saw neither.

"Excuse me," Alice muttered as she hurried to the other side of the jungle gym.

Someone else's child was fighting for a turn on the tire swing. Alice relaxed as she caught sight of Nell huddled with a girl from her class on a low wooden platform. They were bent over their prized card collections, hands veiled by Nell's long peachy hair. Peter, darkly handsome like his father, was standing at the top of the tall slide, waiting his turn to go down. Flushed with relief, Alice walked back to the bench. Frannie was gone.

"That little jog winded me," Alice said.

"You're telling me. I can barely move an inch without hyperventilating." Lauren stretched an arm along the bench behind Alice. "I'm so happy we're doing this together."

"It'll be nice," Alice said, "to be back at the playground in the mornings with the babies. It's so much more peaceful here when the big kids are in school."

"No offense, ladies," Maggie said, "but I'm thrilled not to be joining you." She haughtily swung one of her tanned, waxed legs over the other. Her beaded flip-flop dangled off her foot. Alice and Lauren ignored the remark; it had long been understood that Maggie's strongest statements tended to be the least true.

"How about a barbecue at my house tomorrow night?" Alice suggested. "We'll say good-bye to summer. Six o'clock?"

"Does the summer really have to end?" Lauren asked sadly.

"Sooner or later, *everything* must end," Maggie said. "Life's like an orgasm, don't you think? The good part's fleeting and the rest is prep or cleanup. Only the perfect shoe can truly elevate the spirit. Right, Alice?"

Alice's burst of laughter drew more laughter from Maggie and Lauren.

Across the playground, Frannie was watching them. Holding her nephew in her lap, she lifted his little hand to make him wave. Alice and Lauren waved back.

"I like her," Lauren said. "I don't know why."

"Me too," Alice said.

After a few minutes, Maggie went back to Blue Shoes. Alice gathered up Nell and Peter and kissed Lauren good-bye.

"Want to meet here tomorrow before pickup?" Alice asked in parting. "Say, two thirty? I'll get us a couple of those yummy iced decafs from the Autumn Café."

Lauren smiled. "It's a date."

Alice opened her eyes to now, today, late Friday afternoon. The children were throwing sand at each other. Why wouldn't the phone ring? She walked over to it and checked again for messages; but there had been nothing before and there was nothing now. She phoned Maggie, who reported no news, saying she was just on her way over to Lauren's apartment. Alice then called Tim's secretary, who informed her that Tim had been given the messages, had been quite concerned, and was on his way back from Chicago. Why, Alice wondered, hadn't he returned her call before heading back? Lauren always said Tim was a poor communicator, and the stab of frustration Alice now felt confirmed it.

She went to the refrigerator and began to assemble barbecue supplies on the counter. Ground turkey, hot dogs, buns, mustard, ketchup, potato salad, lettuce. Practical details to push against the growing current of worry. She could hear the children's voices drifting in through the window, open just an inch to let in sound and a ribbon of hot air.

The phone behind her bleated suddenly into the strange tranquility. She calmed herself with a deep breath, crossed the kitchen, and answered it.

Chapter 3

Alice heard blaring horns on the other end of the phone, clicking footsteps, the layered chatter of too many voices.

"I'm at the airport," Tim said. "Have you heard from her?"

"Nothing," Alice answered. "Which airport? New York or Chicago?"

"LaGuardia." Behind him she heard an echoing announcement about an outgoing flight. He sounded short of breath, talking on his cell phone and walking at a fast clip. "I'll be in Brooklyn in twenty minutes. Is Austin with you?"

"Yes, he's fine. Listen, Tim, Maggie's been calling the hospitals."

"So has my secretary."

"And?"

"Lauren hasn't been admitted anywhere," he said. "Has anyone been to the apartment?"

"Maggie's on her way now," Alice said. "I'm expecting to hear from her any minute."

"Okay, Alice, here's a taxi. I'll see you very soon."

He hung up before she had a chance to ask him if he was coming right over or stopping at home or . . . where? Where do you go when your wife disappears? What do you do?

A few minutes later, Maggie arrived, talking before she was even through the front door. "Hasn't checked into any hospitals *or* been in touch with her doctor. No call back from Pilates. Her apartment's quiet."

Alice shut the front door and followed Maggie through the foyer into her living room. They went straight to the kitchen, where they could keep an eye on the kids. Just now, the boys were revving their toy trucks along the sides of the sandbox. Nell sat on the edge, kicking heaps of sand over her brother's favorite miniature fire truck, evidently trying to bury it but to no avail; his little hand was too quick at digging it out.

"Lauren's such a neatnik," Maggie said. "She's already unpacked and they only got back five days ago."

Alice leaned against the counter. Normally she would have responded with a quip about how long it took Maggie to unpack whenever she went away, but not today.

"What now?" Alice asked instead.

"I'm not sure," Maggie said. "Did you reach Tim? What did he say?"

"He doesn't know anything either. But he's back. Just caught a cab at LaGuardia."

They carried trays of barbecue supplies to the yard and were setting up the grill when Mike got home. He came down the deck stairs in the cloud of sawdust that seemed to swirl around him at the end of every workday. His ripped blue jeans and stained T-shirt gave new life to the idea of distressed clothes; Alice sometimes joked that he'd make more money selling his clothes to a perennially misguided fashion industry (the same one that kept Blue Shoes alive), than designing and building furniture for wealthy aesthetes. It was an argument that held no sway; money was no longer the objective of either one of them. When they were eighteen, young college lovers, they had made each other an idealistic promise to never abandon their dreams. *We'll never sell out to The Man,* they had vowed one midnight, curled together in Mike's dorm room bed. *If we're still together in twenty years, let's stop whatever we're doing and start over again.* It was a precious intention they soon forgot as they forged together into the adult world of life, work, marriage and family. Nineteen years later, Mike was the creative director of a large Manhattan advertising agency, spending long hours of every day at the office, earning big money and never seeing his children before they went to bed. One day, when Peter was a baby and Alice was preparing to return to the commercial film editing business she had built over her own long career trajectory, she remembered the promise. Within a month she decided to sell her business and stay home with her children; she would get to know their every detail and resume work later, in a different way. Mike's memory took longer to ignite, but when it did, it was absolute. They calculated they could afford three years each to pursue a new venture; they would take a stab at ditching the corporate economy for independence, creativity and a more coherent family life. They would honor their own youthful promise to themselves in pursuit of the essential American dream of happiness. Blue Shoes came first, followed shortly thereafter by The Brooklyn Furniture Company, which Mike had established in an old warehouse in Red Hook with one part-time helper. So far, he was doing remarkably well.

"Daddy's home!" Nell and Peter called in unison as soon as they saw Mike. He winked at Alice as he jogged past her to chase the kids in circles around the sandbox—even Ethan and Austin joined in—until laughter buckled them onto the grass. Mike tickled each of the four children, and finally came over to Alice and Maggie at the grill. His sawdust-powdered brown hair was kinked as always by the half-dozen cowlicks that gave him a distinctive appearance of being hyperawake at all times.

He came in close to Alice, sliding an arm around her shoulders, kissing her on the top of her head and divesting her right hand of the spatula, all in one move.

"Me take over grill." He tapped his chest with his other hand. "Me man. Me cook meat."

"Don't you want to shower first?" Alice asked him.

He quickly smelled both his armpits, drawing a loud, shocked laugh from Maggie.

"Oh, *please* go shower *immediately*!" Maggie said.

"It's not too bad." Mike looked at Maggie, keeping his expression as serious as he could. "Have a sniff." He lifted his arm and approached her.

"No!" Maggie backed off.

"Simon coming?" he asked her.

"Well, I didn't invite him," Maggie answered. Then, to Alice, "Did you?"

Alice shook her head. "That's your department, Mags." The truth was, Alice always missed Simon when he was excluded from the gathering of friends, but the right of invitation was left up to Maggie. She was typically inconsistent about it.

"No Simon?" Mike scowled. "No shower! Need man cook meat."

"Give me that." Alice took back the spatula. "Just go take a shower, okay? You can do the grill when you come back down."

"Where Tim?"

"Stop it," Alice said. "It's getting annoying."

Mike leaned in close to Alice and lowered his voice to a near whisper, meant to elude the children's radar. "Seriously, did you hear from Lauren yet?"

He smelled like fresh-cut wood. "Nope," she whispered back. "Tim's on his way back to Brooklyn."

Mike was uncharacteristically quiet a moment, fiddling with something in his pants pocket. "She's okay, though. Right?"

"Right." Maggie ripped apart a sheet of soft hamburger buns.

"So, where's that notice you got today?" A shadow seemed to drift over the natural glint of light in his eyes, and Alice knew he was worried too.

"Upstairs, in my purse."

Twenty minutes later—ample time both for a shower and a look at the bad news of their Thirty Day Notice—Mike reappeared. In clean jeans and a white T-shirt, all scrubbed and fresh, he looked five years younger than his thirty-nine years. Alice watched him as he strode across the yard toward the children, the neck of a chilled beer dangling between two fingers. He settled down on the side of the sandbox, apparently forgetting all about the man-meat equation, and peppered the children with questions and jokes that elicited bursts of giggly disbelief.

"He's good at that," Maggie said.

"He is." Alice flipped a sizzling turkey burger with the spatula. She knew exactly what Maggie meant. "That's partly why I fell in love with him. He reminds me not to take myself too seriously."

"He's sexy too, you know." Maggie raised her eyebrows. Alice turned around to look at Mike with the four children. He had gotten into the sandbox with them. She supposed he was sexy, though volatile pregnancy hormones along with the wiles of time tended to let her forget that.

Maggie took the spatula from Alice's hand and nudged a hot dog along the grill; she liked hers cooked bubbly black on all sides. In the moment they didn't speak, Alice felt the downward shift of the late afternoon sun dragging away whole degrees of heat. A damp coolness settled on the air.

"So?" Alice said suddenly. "Where is she? Why hasn't she called? When will Tim get here?"

"I'm sure she's fine," Maggie said. "I admit it's strange she hasn't called. But she's almost nine months pregnant. I'm *sure* she had the baby today. I'm *sure* we'll hear from her any minute. Aren't you?"

"I'm just as determined as you are to believe that, Mags," Alice said.

Alice covered the long picnic table with a red and white checkered oilcloth she had bought years ago at Manny's Variety, the Dominican sundries shop Blue Shoes had displaced. Maggie counted out enough paper plates to include Tim and Lauren, *just in case*. Mike marched the children into the house to wash their hands while the women served up the food. Alice set down a small tray of hot dogs nestled in buns, then turned to Maggie.

"What do we say to Austin?"

"We tell him the truth," Maggie said. "We say Lauren will call any minute. We say she probably had the baby today and Daddy's with her."

Alice nodded, muttering, "Okay, then."

But Austin didn't ask. He had lived his entire young life with the three families melded in nearly every way, and being without his parents in the Halpern family backyard was not unusual.

Finally, just past eight, Alice's cell phone rang. She pulled it from her shorts' pocket and immediately saw that it was Tim.

"I'm outside. I've been ringing the doorbell but I don't think you heard it."

"I'll be right there." She flipped shut her phone.

"Want me to go?" Mike began to shift himself off the bench, but she stopped him.

"It's okay," she said calmly, though she felt anything but calm. Heart pounding, she walked up the stairs onto the tiny iron deck and passed through the kitchen, living room and into the hallway to get to the building's foyer. In the half-moon window toward the top of the house's front door, Alice saw Tim's sharp profile, looking distractedly toward the street.

She opened the door. Tim walked in and at first said nothing. Medium height, and lean from his weekend hours at the gym, he was dressed in one of the beautiful suits he always wore to work. His thick blond hair was wavy, tucked behind his ears; normally he kept it shorter than this. When he looked at Alice to speak, she saw, in the dimming evening light, that his skin was ashen despite his recent beach vacation.

Tim sighed and lifted his eyes to Alice. For the first time in all their years, she saw how truly green they were. Just like Austin's. Bright, lucid green.

"They said to wait until morning, see if she comes home tonight."

"They?"

"The police at the Seventy-sixth Precinct. I just came from there."

Alice didn't know what to say. What about Ivy? This made no sense.

"I'll go back in the morning," he said, "first thing. I thought it might be better if Austin stayed over here tonight."

"Sure," Alice said. "But I don't understand."

"I think it might make things worse if he comes home and she's not there." Tim's eyes teared up. "Don't you think so, Alice?"

"I don't really know what to think."

"Will you tell him I had to work late? He's used to that. He won't question it."

"But what do I say about Lauren?"

Tim stood in front of her, clearly unable to offer advice. She felt her heart plunge through her body, into the floor, to the center of an ancient earth. Stepping forward, Alice took Tim in her arms. He held her fiercely, crying.

And Alice knew. She just knew.

Lauren was not coming home.

Chapter 4

The next day a dark blue sedan eased up to the curb in front of Blue Shoes. Two people got out, a tall man with a gray-speckled buzz cut, and a young woman. Alice recognized Frannie immediately. Without putting a quarter into the meter, they crossed the sidewalk to the store. Frannie first, the man following. She pulled open the door, which tinkled to announce the arrival of a customer, and he walked in behind her. She stood there looking around at the posh, renovated space.

"So this *is* your place," Frannie said. "When I heard Alice Halpern and Maggie Blue, I wasn't sure."

Alice came around the counter, glad for a diversion from the troubling morning. Maggie stayed behind the counter, distracting herself with receipts, having joined Alice on her alternate Saturday shift. They had spent all morning worrying about Lauren. Making incessant, unanswered calls to her cell phone. Unraveling possibilities until they were depleted. Finally, they had walked the neighborhood, posting MISSING signs they had made at the store and printed on bright yellow paper.

MISSING
Lauren Barnet
36 years old, long brown hair, pale blue eyes,
red birthmark on back of neck. 8½ MOS. PREGNANT.
Last seen on Carroll St. leaving P.S. 58

Friday, Sept. 8, at 8:45 a.m.
Please call with *any* information.

Just above her name, a photo of Lauren smiled beneath the paper's yellow haze.

After posting a hundred signs, Alice and Maggie had returned to the store, unsure of what to do next.

"It's our place," Alice told Frannie. "Like it?"

Frannie glanced down at her worn black sneakers and shrugged her shoulders. "I guess shoes aren't really my thing. It's strange. I don't even recognize this place and I've been coming here my whole life. I always got my Halloween costumes at Manny's Variety when I was a kid. Penny candies. The works." She shook her head.

"Sorry," Alice said, receiving a sharp glance from Maggie, who hated it when Alice apologized. Maggie believed the neighborhood's gentrification was inevitable, while Alice couldn't help feeling guilty for being part of the spit and polish that was rubbing out so many old-timers. Like Manny's Variety. And Frannie's childhood memories.

"Listen, I hate to do this." Frannie dug into her back pocket and withdrew a thin billfold, which she flipped open. "I'm here on business."

Alice was stunned to see the identification encased in the billfold Frannie was showing her. A badge emblazoned with NYPD. And a card reading DETECTIVE FRANCESCA VIOLA, 76TH PRECINCT, DETECTIVES UNIT.

Frannie was a *police detective*?

"This is Detective Giometti." Frannie tilted her head toward the large man who stood behind her. Alice nodded hello to him and was immediately struck by an unusual steadiness in his gaze, a lack of wavering. He had long eyelashes, she noticed, a softness that contrasted with the masklike quality of his skin. Teenage acne, she guessed, though he was attractive despite it.

He opened his own wallet: DETECTIVE PAUL GIOMETTI, 60TH PRECINCT, HOMICIDE.

"Homicide?" Alice blurted.

Maggie hurried around the counter, took one look at Giometti's identification and said, "You found Lauren, didn't you?"

"No," Frannie said. "We didn't. But we're trying to."

"But it says *homicide*." Maggie's tone was accusatory, the mere word breaching a pact that Lauren was, had to be, all right. Alice felt a trickle of nausea worm its way up her throat.

Frannie put her billfold away and stepped forward to gently touch Alice's arm. "We're looking for Lauren, that's all."

"Somewhere we can talk privately?" Giometti asked.

Alice put the BE RIGHT BACK sign on the front door as Maggie led the detectives to the back room. This area had been renovated in a basic way, made clean and comfortable, with a secondhand couch, a small table and two folding chairs. Wall shelves were stacked with shoe boxes. A narrow door led to the small bathroom. Beyond a gated window was an overgrown garden neither woman had time to tend.

The detectives sat at the table. Alice and Maggie took the couch, facing them.

"I'm with the local PDU, the Precinct Detectives Unit," Frannie began, "and Paul's with the Brooklyn South Homicide Unit. He's been detailed to this case." She paused, reading Alice's and Maggie's stunned expressions. "I know what you're thinking. The bad news is that when Lauren went missing yesterday, it resurrected an old case."

Suddenly Alice remembered. "Christine Craddock," she said without hesitation.

"Christine," Maggie echoed. "Oh my lord."

They had never met her but the missing signs plastering the neighborhood two years ago made her seem like a long-lost friend. Christine Craddock had been nine months pregnant with her first child when she vanished. It had been so shocking to consider that anything truly sinister could happen in their quaint village. A local woman, missing? A *pregnant* woman? The case had been a reminder that their community was just a cove in the sea of a vast city. That the city's underbelly, snaking with subways, could belch up any threat at any time. For a few months, Christine became a local obsession. She was sorely missed by a large group of women who had never met her, at a playground she had never visited with a baby that was never born. Alice, Maggie and Lauren had read every news report and discussed the case incessantly on their park bench, on the phone and late at night with their husbands in bed. That haphazard marital chitchat that lulled you to sleep. Only Alice, a lifelong insomniac at the slightest disturbance, had lost hours of sleep over the disappearance of Christine Craddock, a woman whose smiling photo on a missing poster haunted her. Messy short brown hair. Freckles. Three earrings in her left lobe. She had last been seen crossing Union Street over the Gowanus Canal. Eventually, her cell phone was fished out of the murky water; it had been dropped midcall.

"That's right," Frannie said. "There are some overlapping circumstances we feel warrant investigation. But it doesn't mean anything other than that."

"I think that means a lot," Alice said in a quiet voice. "Don't you? Otherwise you wouldn't be here."

"What's the *good* news?" Maggie asked.

Giometti leaned forward, elbows pinioned to his knees. He had lovely, rich brown eyes with wisdom lines fanning at the temples. "We have no reason to think she's dead. No evidence whatsoever. We never found Christine. Truth is, we really don't know what happened to her."

"Years can pass," Frannie said, "before you learn the truth. But that's the worst-case scenario. Mostly we want to crack these right away."

Alice felt a shiver rise through her stomach. She read the newspaper religiously and knew the statistics, that if not found within the first twenty-four hours, a person who went missing was usually either never found or was found dead.

"The husband said you three are tight," Frannie said. "But I already knew that." She smiled more warmly than she had in the park the other day. Now Alice understood the young woman's reserve among the group of mothers; she may as well have been visiting a different planet. Alice understood why Frannie had said her occasional visits to the playground kept her sane; what she saw in her police work had to be horrific. And why she had chosen to pay this visit; a current had passed between them that day, a moment of friendship. Alice understood all that yet had never felt more baffled. All she could see was the word HOMICIDE shining in raised black letters on Giometti's card.

"I'm glad it was me who caught the case." Frannie's eyes were dark as coal, Alice now noticed, with a swallowing depth. "We're going to find her. Together. Okay?"

Alice and Maggie both nodded in agreement. Yes, together they would find Lauren. And she would be fine. Still pregnant with Ivy. Together they would rewind time two days and start over.

"So tell us about Lauren." Frannie looked at Alice, then Maggie. "Tell us everything you can think of about her."

"She's our sister," Maggie said.

Frannie glanced at Giometti, who sat slightly back in his chair, eyes glued to Maggie.

"*Like* a sister," Alice clarified.

"When was the very last time you saw her?" Frannie asked.

Alice's reaction was to assume Frannie already knew the answer—the detective had been with them—but she didn't say that. Instead she reiterated the facts: "That afternoon at the park. When I kissed her good-bye."

"Same for me," Maggie said. "We said good-bye at the park."

Frannie and Giometti listened as Alice and Maggie finished each other's sentences, sharing the story of their last afternoon with Lauren. Where one erred, the other corrected; often they overlapped for emphasis. They were eager to tell the detectives everything they could to help clarify the picture of Lauren's life. Frannie was particularly interested in Lauren's relationship with Tim. Alice felt slightly uncomfortable divulging the details of Lauren's private life, but knew she had to if it might help. Giometti pulled a small pad and pen from his shirt pocket and began taking occasional notes so selectively that Alice cringed each time he leaned over to write.

"They have a good marriage," Alice said.

"He's a solid husband," Maggie added. "She has few complaints."

"What complaints?" Frannie asked.

"Nothing, really," Maggie said. "He works late all the time. Things like that."

"They were happy," Alice added.

Maggie corrected her: "They *are* happy."

Alice held her tongue on the next thought: *Well, they're not happy now, and neither are we.*

"They've been under a lot of pressure lately," Alice said. "Their landlord's been trying to evict them and they've been fighting it."

"Lease?" Giometti's pen hovered above the pad.

"It expired, but they wanted to renew," Alice explained. "Their apartment's rent-stabilized, so they had the right to renew. Their landlord's Metro Properties." She watched as Giometti wrote it down, feeling some satisfaction at having informed the authorities of the offense. "I'm getting evicted too," she blurted out, regretting it the instant Maggie's eyes rolled to the ceiling.

"Let's not get off the point, darling," Maggie said.

"Do you live in the same building as Lauren?" Frannie asked Alice.

"No, I live in a two-family house on President Street. Lauren lives in an eight-unit building on Union."

"It's a coincidence," Maggie clarified to the detectives, in case they hadn't figured it out themselves. "One has nothing to do with the other. Lauren's problem is institutional, so to speak, whereas Alice has the misfortune of occupying the space of someone who wishes to move into his own house."

Maggie's commandeering of the issue grated. "The thing is"—Alice tried to clarify a thought that had barely congealed in her mind—"I'm six months pregnant and I got my Thirty Day Notice yesterday. Lauren was six months pregnant when she got her Thirty Day Notice almost three months ago. Doesn't that have to mean something?"

"Maybe," Frannie said. "Or maybe not. It's kind of stroller city around here. And we've been seeing a lot of forcible evictions. Mostly legal, by the way. No one's ever happy about it."

"It's called gentrification." Maggie reached over to smooth a wrinkle out of Alice's sleeve. "That's really all I've been trying to say. It's why Blue Shoes can exist. There is a price for everything, is there not?"

Neither Alice nor the detectives tried to answer Maggie's rhetorical question. Of course there was a price for everything. But what exactly was the commodity at issue? Shoes? Real estate? A woman's life?

"What's Lauren's due date?" Frannie changed the subject, to Alice's relief.

"September fifteenth," Alice answered. "But Austin was a week early and she thought she might deliver early the second time too."

"Why?"

"Just a hunch, I guess," Alice said. "Bodies follow patterns—you know, habits—in childbirth just like everything else."

"Does she know if she's having a boy or a girl?" Frannie asked.

"No," Maggie answered quickly.

Alice was caught off guard by the lie. She leaned forward to speak, but changed her mind and sat back. She didn't want to bluntly contradict Maggie. But why, she wondered, had Maggie told them that?

There were more questions and more answers until Lauren's life had been outlined and colored in. At the end, Alice and Maggie were given business cards for both detectives.

"Call us with anything you think of," Frannie said.

"Anything at all could be important," Giometti added.

"Don't hesitate, okay?" Frannie reached out to squeeze Alice's hand, then Maggie's, offering both a supportive smile. Alice never would have imagined a police detective to be so friendly, but then she had never known one.

"Thank you so much," Alice said. "We'll help in any way we can." Alice kept her gaze from twitching toward Maggie, whose secretive withholding of Ivy was resonating through every word they spoke. She wondered if the detectives could feel it, smell it, somehow intuit the lie. It didn't seem like it, though, by the gracious, unfreighted tone of their good-byes.

"We'll be in touch," Frannie said. Giometti leaned forward to shake both their hands. They walked together across the store, this time not even glancing at the shoes. Giometti opened the door with a forcefulness that sent a shivering ring through the welcome bell.

Alice watched the detectives' blue sedan pull away. For some reason she couldn't pin down, the fact that Frannie was driving came as a mild surprise. As the car wove into traffic, Alice wondered if she should have spoken up when she had the chance.

"She's too *nice nice* to be a cop," Maggie said, unstacking three boxes that had been delivered earlier that morning.

"What's wrong with nice? Maybe she really cares." Alice removed the BE RIGHT BACK sign from the door and tucked it behind the nearest display case, on which pairs of summer pastel stilettos offered themselves at half price.

"Only *we* care about Lauren." Maggie clicked open an Exacto knife, dragging the blade swiftly across the top of one box and pulling open the cardboard flaps. "You, me and Tim. And Austin, of course. You know that, Alice."

Maggie had a point. There was caring and there was *caring*. Lauren was a Minnesota transplant whose parents had died in quick succession while she was in college, her mother of breast cancer and her father apparently of heartbreak. An only child, she had cultivated her friendships into family. Tim had also lost both his parents and so it was always the Barnets who hosted the holidays for those who weren't going *home* to original families. Their apartment *was* their home and their friends *were* their family. Lauren had once honored her two best friends by declaring them her sisters, which is what Maggie had meant in answer to Frannie's question. Alice and Maggie were Lauren's true, chosen sisters, a declaration that had been both a promise and a bond.

"But Maggie," Alice said, "why did you stop me from explaining about the evictions? You made my comments seem so . . . trivial. And why did you lie about Ivy? What was the point of that? We *know* Lauren's having a girl."

"We can't give away every little bit of her," Maggie said in the too-patient tone of an older sister tired of explaining the obvious. She sliced open the second box, then the third.

"But it's just information," Alice argued. "Ivy is a fact."

"Yes, that's right." Maggie's eyes narrowed. "Ivy *is* a fact. Not was, but is. How will you feel when Lauren turns up with some perfectly sane explanation and we've broadcast her most precious secret?"

"Nothing about this is *sane,* Mags."

"True." Maggie lifted her chin with magisterial confidence. "Nonetheless, I say we hold her trust until we know for sure. Really, Alice, it's the least we can do."

By afternoon the neighborhood was buzzing with the

investigation. A sizable task force had been deployed to canvass the neighborhood for anyone who had seen Lauren Barnet yesterday between dropping Austin off at school that morning, and two thirty when she failed to meet Alice at the park. Everyone who came into Blue Shoes talked about it. All day long, Alice and Maggie talked and talked until they were all talked out.

Even Alice's mother, Lizzie, kept calling from Los Angeles to check in for updates. "So?" she would begin, instead of "hello." Or, "Anything yet?"

"Nothing, Mom," Alice answered. "We're still waiting."

"Waiting's not good, babydoll," Lizzie said in her typically energized voice. "The thing is to find something you can *do*, not just to keep busy but to push things *forward*." Lizzie ran a successful film production studio; she didn't tolerate inaction very well.

"The detectives are working on it, Mom." Alice heard the hollowness of her own voice, its emptiness of purpose from so much talk and hope and fear and, finally, no new information to digest.

"You'll call me as soon as you hear something," Lizzie said. "Stay on the detectives—don't let them overlook anything. And comfort the family."

Comfort the family. The words rang through Alice; all they *could* do, after all, was offer Tim and Austin their physical presence and a stoic refusal to think the worst.

Chapter 5

Lauren and Tim Barnet lived in a gray stone building with double wooden doors dead center, like the node of a spine separating the four A-line apartments from the four B-line apartments. On the building's shallow front stoop, Nell, Peter and Ethan were fighting over who would get to ring the buzzer for 2B.

"I should because I'm the oldest." Nell crossed her arms over her rail-thin body.

"You're the oldest *girl*," Ethan argued. "I'm the oldest *boy*."

"By five weeks, my young man!" Simon protested. "Now let's stop this nonsense. We need a word with you three before going up." His deep voice stilled them; he was a master at registering authority with the under-ten set. Alice had always liked Simon, despite his failures with Maggie. He was a soulful, creative man, an adjunct music professor, freelance pianist and composer of some reputation. He and Maggie had met in London and come to New York together. Alice had always loved listening to them speak, their accents weaving into a kind of exotic song. Poignantly handsome with his clean-shaven, pale face and shaggy brown hair, Simon possessed a strain of sensuality that was hard to contain in a marriage. You could say he was touchy-feely to a fault—as Maggie often had, magnifying the quality into faithlessness.

Simon fell silent and turned to Mike, who turned to

Alice. She wished Maggie were here; *she* would think of some way to tell the kids what was happening without, somehow, revealing their worst fears. But Maggie had gone ahead to Tim's, and Alice had no idea what to tell the kids. Just this: tread lightly. But would they know how?

"This might not be a very happy visit," she said, looking gravely from Peter to Ethan to Nell, who stood above them on the highest step. Her eyes, blue like Alice's, looked skeptical. They always had fun at Austin's.

"But Mommy—" Nell began and was hushed instantly by Alice.

"Let me finish, okay?"

All three nodded; she had this one moment to explain.

"Have you noticed anything different in the last couple of days?"

"School started this week," Peter chirped, drawing a giggle from Ethan and a hearty eye-roll from Nell.

"Right, school started. What else?"

"I know," Nell said. But she didn't elaborate. Of course she knew; little pitchers had big ears, especially when they were seven.

"Auntie Lauren hasn't been home for a couple of days," Alice said, working to keep her tone unencumbered, "and we don't know where she is. I'm sure she's fine—she probably just got lost. But I don't want you guys asking Tim or Austin any questions about where Lauren is, okay?"

"Why?" Peter asked.

Alice glanced at Mike, her eyes imploring him to say something, and he stepped forward with his own attempt to explain what they themselves could not quite comprehend.

"Well, because they might be feeling kind of nervous about it," he said. "Maybe if we don't talk to them about it, they'll forget. Maybe that way they could have a little more fun tonight. Okay, guys?"

Fun. Suddenly such a foolish-sounding word.

Nell raised her hand with an earnestness that brought a wave of love to Alice's heart.

"Yes, sweetie?"

"What is *missing,* Mommy?"

And then her heart, which had swelled with the profoundest affection, became desiccated, inept. Of course Nell had noticed the yellow signs on the way over.

"That's the big question," Alice said. "We don't really know what it means right at this moment."

Peter jumped up. "*Now* can I ring the bell?"

"No, me!" Ethan followed him to the strip of doorbells too high for them to reach.

Simon jogged up the stoop and pressed the buzzer for 2B, eliciting staunch objection from all three children.

"Done," he said.

As soon as Simon pushed open the heavy door, Nell, Peter and Ethan battled past each other to get in first, then ran up the flight of stairs. Maggie greeted them at the apartment door, letting the kids hustle past her, then stepped into the hallway to whisper, "It isn't good at all in there. Just a warning."

The apartment was eerily quiet with no sign of any of the children, which meant they had already sequestered themselves with Austin in front of the TV in Lauren and Tim's bedroom. Alice abruptly decided they would order Chinese food from the place whose number she had memorized. They would hobble through the night as best they could, together.

Alice, Mike and Simon followed Maggie into the living room, where Tim sat hunched, strangely, on a tiny chair at Austin's little art table between the street-side windows. Both were open, inviting bursts of warm air through the sheer white curtains. The diaphanous fabric Alice remembered Lauren choosing and fitting to the long windows now billowed dramatically. Billowed then sucked hard against the screens with the breeze's sudden evacuation. Alice noticed a crinkle of dust, the kind of small accumulation Lauren never would have tolerated, under the art table at Tim's feet.

There he sat, with stringy hair that had been neither washed nor brushed, inhaling deeply on a cigarette. Not once in all their years had Alice known Tim to smoke.

Alice was the first to approach him. Then Maggie. Mike. Simon. The friends huddled around Tim, who remained on the little seat as if pressed down by an unbearable load. When the long ash of his cigarette threatened to fall, Simon caught it in the cupped palm of his hand and held on to it, refusing to move.

"The police were here," Tim finally said. His voice was thin, exhausted. "They were here all afternoon. But why? *Why* did they ask me all those questions?" He looked searchingly at Mike, who responded by settling a hand on Tim's shoulder. They said nothing. These men, who grilled together; painted each other's homes; hefted each other's cartons; shared hours of debate on politics, art, movies and sports; and routinely traveled together to the Bronx to see the Yankees or to Coney Island to see the Cyclones, could find between them not a single word. Nothing to bridge Tim's private anxiety to the fact that they were now all gathered together in the single physical body of their friendship.

"They came to us too," Alice said.

Then Maggie: "They came to all of us."

Tim squashed the bright ember of his cigarette into one of Austin's open paint jars. White, now darkened with oily streaks. Three other butts had been squashed in the paint.

"They were here for *hours*." His voice rose. He ran his hands through his unkempt hair then let them flop to his sides. The skin beneath his eyes was dark purple. "Do they actually think I had something to do with Lauren's disappearance? *Could* they?"

"Of course not." Mike stepped up next to Tim. "They're just doing their job. You're the person closest to her, so they need to ask you questions."

The person closest to her. Was he? He worked such long hours that, other than weekends, he was hardly home. Who *was* the person closest to Lauren? Austin, Alice decided. And the *sisters,* of course.

"They're treating me like a suspect," Tim nearly whispered. "I'm a lawyer. I know what's going on. This is a nightmare. They want answers from *me.*"

One thing that was clear to Alice was that Tim did not deserve this. How could he? He was a good man who worked hard, cared for his family, *loved* them. Alice and Mike had known Tim for five years; they *knew* him. If the police suspected him of anything, they were looking in the wrong direction, losing time.

"They want answers," Simon said in his most soothing voice, "from everyone and everywhere."

"That's right, Tim darling," Maggie chimed in. "It seems to me they're casting a wide net. That's all. You needn't worry."

Her lead-footed remarks could usually be ignored, but not this one. Tim looked at her so fast and so hard, all possibility of conversation ended right there. Alice was startled by the intensity of his eyes, which held on to Maggie in a merciless, desolate glare.

It was awkward after that, but they stayed. As the night darkened, Alice became aware of a blossoming nub of mourning for the close friendship of the three families. But she reminded herself that with Lauren missing, with each word and glance a grain in the quicksand of possibility, there was no way any of them could find their equilibrium. Still, something was lacking between the friends tonight, a kind of cohesion they had grown lazily accustomed to.

Alice and Mike stayed until just before midnight, finally lugging home their sleeping children and climbing into bed, desperate for sleep.

Alice lay awake next to Mike under their soft, light blanket. The house was so quiet she could hear its nuances, its hollow sighs, every creak and moan of the wooden beams hidden behind plaster walls, the swish of each car that passed outside the closed windows. She put in her earplugs and strapped on her eye cover, creating a private capsule of sensory deprivation. The quiet now was exquisite, the darkness total. She waited for sleep. Time passed awkwardly through her mind like an ill-gaited runner, and she waited, but sleep was nowhere in her body. The dissonant resonance in her mind became deafening, until finally she gave up and got out of bed.

As with most of the area's lower duplex apartments, the bedrooms were downstairs, keeping the high-ceilinged parlor floor above for the business of daily life. Wedding-cake moldings traced the edges of the large living room, with its ornate marble fireplace and floor-to-ceiling windows. Wide wooden planks creaked under Alice's feet as she tried to move carefully, quietly, above her sleeping family. She passed through the saturated darkness, under the wide arch joining living room to kitchen. When she turned on the overhead light, the kitchen sprang into focus. Mahogany cabinets, buttery Formica counters, workhorse appliances from the 1970s all clean and ready to service a new day.

It was 3:00 a.m. She could feel her babies moving inside her body and wondered if she had woken them or if they were normally awake at this hour. She would find out soon enough. After rummaging through the fridge, she spooned some peanut butter from the jar and poured herself a glass of orange juice. She moved the laptop from the shelf by the garden door to the kitchen table and plugged it in. As she waited for it to boot up, she looked out into the dark backyard, silvery with moonlight. Her lush summer garden was as still as a photograph. She would miss it when she moved.

Once she had the kettle on the stovetop and a peppermint tea bag waited in her favorite mug, she sat down and Googled Lauren's name. It came up a few times in association with her former life as an attorney but there was nothing about her now. No mention that she was missing. Next Alice Googled Christine Craddock. She clicked on www.christinelost.com and instantly the screen was filled with a picture of the young, pregnant woman proudly displaying her immense belly. The Web site's pages were neatly listed down the left side, offering different views into the lost woman's life.

Christine Craddock had been an unmarried mother-to-be. Her baby's father had been her graduate school professor and thesis adviser; married with a family of his own, David Jonstone had denied any personal relationship with Christine. She was preparing a paternity suit at the time of her disappearance, to be delivered to Jonstone upon their baby's birth. It was unknown whether the professor had been aware of this. The morning of Christine's disappearance, which was also her baby's due date, she was overheard arguing with someone on her cell phone—the cell phone that had been found buried in silt at the bottom of the canal. The call was traced to a pay phone, so there was no way to know who had been on the other end. Christine Craddock was last seen crossing Bond Street, walking in the direction of Park Slope.

One page of the Web site was devoted to the police investigation, headed by Detective Paul Giometti of the Brooklyn South Homicide Unit. Other pages were lighter: Christine's Family; Christine's Favorite Movies; Christine's Pets, A-Z; Christine's Hopes for the Future. There was even a page called Christine's Politics, which mostly explained her decision to become a single mother.

Alice searched every strand of the site for mention of where Christine had lived, if she had owned or rented, if there had been any trouble. But there was nothing beyond the fact that she had been in Carroll Gardens for three years.

The last time anyone had posted any comments was over a year ago. Alice closed Christine's site and moved on to the next listings, a few old newspaper articles and a link to the National Center for Missing Adults. *Case still open.*

Alice sat back under a swell of exhaustion, thinking

about how someone had cared enough to take the time to build a Web site for Christine. In the turmoil of her disappearance, someone who loved her had stayed focused on the single most important thing: finding her. Sipping the last of her tea, Alice leaned over the keyboard and Googled *Web site building*. Within half an hour she had secured a domain name: www.findlauren .com. She had a year's worth of downloaded photographs from her digital camera, and by sunrise had put up a home page showing Lauren in July, seven months pregnant, laughing as Austin tugged a book out of her hands. It was Alice's favorite recent photograph of Lauren because it showed so much of what was important to her: love, family and intellect. Lauren had a good life. That she had vanished felt wildly out of sync.

At the sound of the morning paper thumping against the front door, Alice knew it was time to stop. Her eyes stung from staring at the computer screen. She flipped shut the laptop, moved it back to its place on the shelf and put her mug in the sink.

The newspaper was sitting on the stoop in its blue plastic sleeve. She brought it inside and turned immediately to the Metro section. There it was, front page, above the fold.

CARROLL GARDENS WOMAN MISSING, NINE MONTHS PREGNANT read the headline. Not quite nine months, Alice thought, wishing she could correct the detail. In a half column, a reporter named Erin Brinkley summarized Lauren's disappearance, listing facts and circumstances that Alice already knew.

She put the paper down and swallowed a knot of anxiety. It was only six o'clock. She dressed in clean clothes pulled from the dryer, wrote a note for Mike and left the house. Walking down President Street, she saw the yellow MISSING signs everywhere. Lauren, summarized on paper, imploring help. Alice had always liked being out early in the morning in the sleepy lull before the world began to stir, but there was no peace in it today. Her eyes trailed a bronze Mini Cooper that zipped past her and turned onto Hoyt Street. Then, once again, she was alone.

She crossed Hoyt, turned right and took the next left onto Carroll Street. Without having consciously decided to, she found herself heading toward the Gowanus Canal. It was where Christine Craddock's cell phone had been found. And presumably it was one of the last walks Lauren had taken on her way to Pilates. Although Lauren lived on Union Street, which had its own canal overpass, she had once said she preferred the older Carroll Street Bridge, which took you through a slightly less industrial area.

It was downhill all the way to Bond, then leveled off for the half block just before the bridge. On the left was a concrete office building with a blue awning that read BOND STREET LIMO. A large man with neatly trimmed gray hair stood outside, smoking a cigarette. He nodded to Alice as she passed. She nodded back, assuming he was a limo driver even though he wasn't in uniform. He had creepy eyes—one blue and one green—that stayed on her as she moved toward the bridge. His attention felt intrusive and she walked faster, away from him. She saw the flare of his flicked cigarette butt as it cartwheeled into the street. Moments later a long black limousine slid past her, but every window was one-way glass and she couldn't see if he was driving.

To the right was a round building, an artist's house. Alice remembered hearing about a whimsical fountain with jets reaching a hundred feet, misting passersby, but had never seen it. Lauren had complained about being sprayed by toxic canal water. She hadn't liked it.

Alice walked onto the bridge and stopped midway. She set both her hands on the blue-painted iron railing and looked out. She knew she was facing the ocean, though it was blocked by the industrial silhouette of Third Street. Beyond that was the Buttermilk Channel, into which the canal emptied through its filtering grate. She looked down into the thread of dull green water, which undulated only slightly in the tranquil air. For years the water had been too murky to see into, like a solid mass, or a long, old secret. Alice stared into the canal until its drab surface seemed to shimmer awake. She wanted to see the crabs and turtles and trout that had supposedly reinvigorated the canal since the old pump was fixed two years ago. For a moment she thought she saw a small, swimming creature. But it was just a passing shadow. She stared and stared until the water seemed to have collected every last bit of ambient light and reflected it back at her, making it impossible to see beneath the surface.

The morning was gathering heat when Alice turned around and headed back up the steep hill into Carroll Gardens. She could not look at the yellow MISSING signs as she walked along Hoyt Street, past her own block, and turned up Union. Allowing herself just a quick glance at the front door of Lauren's building, Alice kept moving. Going. Walking. One step at a time toward the Seventy-sixth Precinct.

The detectives had urged them to come forward with anything. *Anything at all could be important,* Giometti had said.

It seemed as if the canal and the streets and the neighborhood had simultaneously sealed Lauren in and spit her out. But there was one thing Alice could do. There was one seal she could break in an effort to find the truth, and that was Maggie's lie about Ivy.

Chapter 6

Alice climbed the steps of the Seventy-sixth Precinct, a squat concrete building with a blue-tiled facade, and was struck by its incongruity on a block of antique brownstones. The faded modernist precinct building on western Union Street had the visual impact of a broken promise, a husk that resonated with vacated architectural and social ideals, yet housed a vital civil service.

Just inside the entrance, a bleached-blond older woman in a purple leisure suit sat at a small desk. She greeted Alice impassively: "Yeah?"

"Is Detective Viola or Detective Giometti in?"

The woman picked up her phone and dialed an extension, averting her eyes from Alice. Just beyond, three uniformed officers sat at a counter, fielding phone calls and a constant frizzle of police dispatches. On the wall was a chalkboard logging the precinct's squad cars and vans.

"Okay," the woman told Alice, without specifying exactly whom she had reached this early in the morning. "You wanna wait in there?"

Alice walked through a swinging half door and entered the large common area. She stood next to a group of tables in the center of the room, glancing over bulletin boards displaying crime statistics charts and wanted posters. Her attention landed on the mug shot of a man whose face sagged so deeply that it seemed pulled by an extraordinary gravity. Across the room, a large fish tank sat on a low wooden cabinet. There was one very large fish in the tank, and beneath it, a handful of small ones swimming quickly in circles. The walls were lined with snack and soda machines, the sight of which sent a bolt of queasiness through her. Never in three pregnancies had she suffered morning sickness, which was supposed to hit you in the first trimester, though she knew as well as anyone that there were exceptions to every rule.

Someone tapped her shoulder and she turned around.

"You're up early," Frannie said.

"I couldn't sleep."

"I hear you." Frannie looked tired, like she'd been up all night too. "I pulled the graveyard shift on rotation last night. You want to talk?"

Alice nodded. Why else would she be there?

She followed Frannie past a glass door that read AR-REST PROCESSING (NO GUNS BEYOND THIS POINT). A glance in showed an industrial metal desk, a chair and two unoccupied cells. They walked through a doorway just to the right of Arrest Processing and up a flight of worn stairs, at the top of which a bulletin board announced the precinct's annual Labor Day picnic, already outdated. Frannie pushed open a door announcing PDU. Alice followed her in, past a short hallway crammed with old file cabinets hand-labeled COLD CASES, WARRANTS PENDING, M/E REPORTS. The tiny hallway blossomed into a large room packed with clusters of mismatched desks. Light filtered weakly through the closed venetian blinds on a row of windows. Toward the back of the room a young Hispanic man pecked at the keys of an old typewriter. Alice noticed that for every computer in the room, there was one of these old relics.

"I haven't seen a typewriter in years," Alice said.

"Old habits die hard. We have a state-of-the-art database but we still type our reports. Maybe they printed up too many forms, like, twenty years ago." Frannie stopped at a desk near a long, shallow cell whose black iron bars covered half the expanse of one wall. A skinny, pallid-looking man was draped across the cell's single bench. She glanced at the sleeping man, then spoke to the other detective. "Hey, Jose, anyone in the interview room?"

Jose glanced up, smiled and shook his head. "Nope, baby, it's all yours." He continued typing.

Frannie sucked back a little hissing sound. *Baby.* Alice got the feeling the PDU wasn't used to *girl detectives.*

"Let's go in there. It's more private," Frannie said. She picked up her mug of half-finished coffee. "You want some? We've got decaf too."

"No thanks. I'm good." The mere thought of coffee made her want to throw up.

"Come on, then."

Frannie and Alice wove between desks to cross the room. The interview room announced itself as such with a computer-printed label affixed with yellowing tape to the door. Inside was a drab box of a room, with a table pushed against one wall and four uncomfortable-looking straight-backed metal chairs. Again, the blinds were fully drawn, giving the space a cramped, murky feel. A small, rectangular window sat three-quarters of the way up the opposite wall. One-way glass, Alice guessed by its dull, mirrorlike glaze.

They sat across from each other at the linoleum table, scarred across the middle by a deep, jagged scratch. Alice wondered who had done it and how. With a key? She could see it. Left alone in this suffocating room, staring at the blind eye of the one-way glass, you would be desperate for something, anything, to do. It was an awful room, she decided. Or maybe the myopia of her exhaustion was plunging her mood into darkness.

Frannie reached across the table and touched Alice's hand. She hadn't realized how cold she was until Frannie's touch sent a jolt of warmth through her. Alice took a deep breath and began.

"There's something I need to clear up."

Frannie's face was free of expression, the dark swaths

beneath her eyes the only indication of strain on her pale skin. No smile or furrowed brows or clenched jaw. Just the open channel of her listening.

"Yesterday, at the store, we told you Lauren didn't know the sex of her baby."

"Maggie told us that, yes."

Frannie was giving her a little out, nudging her off the hook. It was true, Maggie had said it. Alice simply hadn't contradicted her. She felt herself begin to relax, the words now flowing a little more easily.

Alice looked squarely into Frannie's black eyes. "It isn't true."

Frannie waited. Listened. Reached out for Alice's other hand.

"Lauren's known for months her baby's a girl."

"A girl," Frannie repeated softly.

"Her name's going to be Ivy. Or is Ivy. Or—" Alice pulled one of her hands away to cover her eyes.

"Thank you, Alice. It might help to know."

Alice wiped her eyes dry and finished. "There's one more thing."

Frannie nodded.

"Tim doesn't know."

"About the name?"

"The name or the sex," Alice said. "He didn't want to know. He wanted to be surprised. That's why Maggie didn't want to tell you."

"I can understand that," Frannie said, her gaze sweeping from Alice's face to her fingers. Alice now realized she had been tracing the scratch in the linoleum, back and forth, for at least a minute.

"Are you going to find Lauren?"

"Yes." The deep confidence of Frannie's voice was an island of hope. Irrational, but necessary, hope. "I won't give up on her, Alice, no matter what." Frannie's lean arms tensed as she shifted her chair closer to the table. This woman was strong, Alice thought, stronger even than she looked. "The task force is going out again today. They're knocking on every door, talking to everyone. There's a transient element to the area, a lot of young people moving in and out, folks coming for the restaurants. You never really know who's going to turn up one day to the next."

"You should go home and sleep," Alice said, not meaning it at all. She wanted Frannie out there every minute of every day and every night until Lauren materialized back into the world.

"I can't sleep anyway," Frannie said. "I don't know about some of the guys around here, but when women start disappearing in my neighborhood, it bothers me. I'll be pitching the case at roll call this morning and working the rest of the day."

One of Alice's babies began to move, and soon both were shifting inside her. She stood up. "I should go. My family's waiting at home."

"I'll walk you out."

In the precinct lobby, the women shook hands.

"Thanks again," Frannie said. "I'll call you if anything happens."

Alice walked alone into a morning whose sleepy quiet had bubbled awake while she was inside the precinct. A little girl in a flower-power helmet raced by on a hotpink two-wheeler, her father trotting steadily beside her. An old woman in a cotton day dress swept her front stoop. Alice couldn't wait to see Mike and the kids. Maybe, she thought, she could manage a nap this morning. Maybe today things would turn around. Lauren would safely return. Frannie would call with good news.

But that, it turned out, was wishful thinking.

Frannie never called. The day passed. By evening, Alice's agitation was unbearable. Finally she phoned the precinct, expecting nothing, and was surprised when Frannie told her there was, in fact, something to report.

Chapter 7

"We've got a witness," Frannie said. "Our first lead."

The children's melodious voices floated from the backyard through the screen door into the kitchen. Alice sat at the table, watching Mike at the stove, where he patiently stirred his special risotto. It was her favorite dish. Dense, creamy rice, ham, onions, carrots, peas. A hint of lemon.

"He's an artist," Frannie continued. "Lives right there on the canal, in that round house with all the skylights. He had his easel set up on the Carroll Street Bridge Friday morning. He saw Lauren at quarter to twelve, crossing the bridge."

Quarter to twelve. On her way to Pilates.

"This guy," Frannie continued, "he didn't know about Lauren going missing. He's one of those people who hates the news, doesn't watch TV, won't read the paper. Travels a lot. Only likes the pretty picture, if you know what I mean."

Alice heard sounds of shouting behind Frannie.

"What's happening?"

"Some idiot's blocking the box." *Traffic fools* was what Mike called drivers who lamely jammed an intersection.

"Frannie, did he talk to Lauren?"

"They smiled at each other. Lauren seemed 'pleasant and civilized,' the guy said. She did not appear to be in labor."

"Then?"

"He went back to his painting. Stayed another three hours, packed up and went home."

The kids barreled in from outside and Mike indulged them in an extra round of TV so Alice could concentrate on the call. He turned off the flame under the risotto and sat next to her at the kitchen table, wiping his hands on his floral-and-stain-patterned apron. A trace of dirt darkened his fingernails. He had been working so hard lately, preparing for his booth at a big furniture expo in Las Vegas next month, dust and grime finding every exposed fissure of skin. She reached over and pressed her fingers between his; for twenty years, a perfect fit.

"So now we've got a more focused area to search," Frannie said, "between the canal and the Pilates place, where she never showed up."

"What?" Alice said. "She never got to her class?" The instructor had never called Maggie back; the storefront classroom hadn't been open since after the Friday class, and presumably no one had heard the message.

"The teacher saw the article in the newspaper," Frannie said. "She called us. Alice, I know this doesn't sound like good news to you, but it's going to speed things up. You'll see."

Alice closed her eyes and summoned an image of the canal and its scant neighborhood. The limo place on the corner. The parking lot with all those Mr. Frosty trucks. The place that made cast plaster reproductions. There was at least a block before it really got residential again.

"Listen, Alice, I've got to get going," Frannie said. "I'll call you if there are any more developments. And if you think of anything, anything at all, call me or just stop by. This morning was good. We're going to find her. Together."

Together, Alice thought, just as Frannie said the word.

Alice hung up the phone and told Mike everything.

"So that's good," he said in the same encouraging tone he used to placate the children when they were being irascible.

"You think it's a bad sign, don't you."

"I don't know. It's just so specific. It makes me feel . . ." He shrugged his shoulders, clearly trying to slough off a sensation he didn't wish to share with Alice.

"Say it," she told him, fixing her gaze into his. "It's creepy knowing someone actually saw her, and then she fell off the face of the earth. It's bad news. Say it."

"Okay." He planted his hands on his waist, suddenly reminding Alice of Buzz Lightyear in the frilly apron at Mrs. Nesbit's tea party, having given up the ghost of his identity. The lines of Mike's face succumbed to gravity, vanquishing the essential yang of his personality. "It scares me."

Alice nodded, grateful for Mike's honesty in acknowledging that this could turn out to be something even his good humor couldn't fix. She didn't like to deny him the presumptions of his natural happiness, but she also didn't like to pretend. The discovery of a witness might have been hopeful, but in truth it felt foreboding, pinning Lauren down in a specific place at a specific time heading in a specific direction. Her disappearance now seemed more tangible. Now they knew that between eleven forty-five that morning, when she was last seen, and noon, when she failed to arrive at Pilates, something had changed her plans. Possibly her life. In just fifteen minutes' time.

"What do we do now?" Alice asked, surprised by the warble that had entered her voice.

Mike reached out to touch her belly and watched his own large, squarish hand circle their twins. Then after a moment he looked up to face her. Brown eyes, bright with a golden flint.

"I'll tell you what I really think."

She had seen this troubled mix of regret and resolution in him only once before, nine years ago when she had miscarried their first child. He had refused to let her believe they would never have a family, and had energetically rallied her back to the cause, even though, at the time, having a child was more her wish than his.

"What do you think, Mike?"

"I think—I *know* there's nothing we can do about this." His eyes narrowed, darkened. "And worrying won't help."

Alice felt a stab at that; it was one thing to joke about her nervous edge and wholly another thing to identify it as a weak link in their life's overall perspective.

"Worry is normal," Alice countered, "in a situation like this."

"Yes, it is." His lips seemed to stiffen and stretch into a forced, almost professional smile. She didn't like it. "How much did you sleep last night, Alice?"

She looked away from him, at the linoleum floor, a sea of off-white squares nearly impossible to keep clean. "Not much."

"Did you sleep at all?"

She shook her head. Counted the squares.

Mike leaned forward, raising his voice, forcing her eyes to acknowledge him. "You're pregnant," he said. "Not that I need to remind you."

She smiled a little. "No, you don't."

"Try not to indulge in the anxiety, sweetheart, okay? That's all I'm saying."

Alice nodded.

"I love you," he whispered below the loopy refrain of SpongeBob SquarePants that sailed in from the living room. "We don't want this to become worse than it needs to be."

"I wish I knew what it needed to be."

"So do I," he said. "But we can't know until we know. Even Tim can't know. I called him this morning after I read that stuff in the newspaper. He's a total wreck. We've got to hold ourselves together for Tim and Austin, okay? We have to keep reminding them that at this very moment we know nothing for sure, that Lauren is probably out there somewhere, that there's still a good chance she'll be back."

"We don't know—"

"It's all we *can* know right now, Alice." He laid his

hand over her stomach again. "I'm telling you, don't go to that other place. Okay?"

Alice placed her hand over his, stilling the restless babies under the weight of both their hands. This was the real Mike she married, not the comedian, not the hyperactive creative director, not the humble carpenter, but the man who cared and felt deeply, who for better or worse never let her slide.

"Okay."

Mike ran a hand through his hair, dislodging his largest cowlick. "The risotto's gonna be mush if I keep turning the heat on and off."

"Go cook, then."

"Are we square?"

"I don't know about you," she said lightly, "but I'm pretty round."

"Ha ha ha." His tone was sarcastic, but his smile was pure love.

"I'll try not to worry so much," she said.

He nodded. "We should concentrate on finding a house."

"Right."

"Getting out of here."

"Right."

"The police will find Lauren," he said. "That's their job." He got up and resumed his place in front of the stove. Relit the flame, knocked the glob off the spoon, gently stirred.

After a minute, Alice asked, "Do you think a person can be too nice?"

"You mean Tim?"

"I was thinking of Frannie. Did I make a mistake going over there this morning?"

"No. Definitely not. It's always better to be honest."

"Frannie said it wasn't me who lied."

Mike smiled. "That *was* nice of her!"

"It made me feel better, you know, less guilty. Because Maggie was the one who spoke the words, told the lie, not me."

"Lies of omission," Mike said, "are probably just as bad."

"Anyway, Maggie thinks Frannie's much too nice."

"Maggie would." Mike twisted around to look at her, the spoon now stilled in the risotto. "If a person's really nice, there's not enough margin of error to mess with their head later."

Alice believed Mike basically liked Maggie but had grown to distrust her since she walked out on Simon for his alleged unfaithfulness. That was why he taunted her whenever he got a chance; if he spoke his real mind, it would be too painful.

"Then why does she like *me*? I'm nice."

The habitual glint in Mike's eyes snapped into tight focus. "You're not *that* nice, sweetheart."

"Asshole."

"See?"

For the rest of the night Alice's thoughts wandered through the mirrored corridors of what *niceness* really meant. She considered the merits of intention versus deed, unable to decide on the value of plain honesty, no matter what the fallout. She, for one, chafed under the yoke of dishonesty; lies made her deeply uncomfortable. She didn't know whether she *should* tell Maggie about the betrayal to the police of her well-intentioned lie about Ivy, but Alice decided she *had* to. The proverbial chips of friendship would have to land . . . wherever.

On Monday morning, when Alice pushed open the door to Blue Shoes, the tinkle of the welcome bell didn't register over The Blind Boys of Alabama playing on the stereo. She had expected a quiet morning, alone at the store, figuring out how to confess yesterday's visit to the precinct. She had given Ivy up, against Maggie's judgment, delivering the *sisters'* secret to the world. If Lauren came back—no, *when* she came back—it would be Maggie who had kept strong and true, and Alice who had buckled.

"What are you doing here?" she called through the

noise to Maggie, who was perched behind the counter at the back of the store, rifling through a shoe box of receipts.

When Maggie raised her eyes, Alice saw they were badly bloodshot; so Maggie hadn't slept well either. For Alice, a second night in a row of insomnia, drifting between half sleep and worry, had propelled her out of bed again to work on Lauren's Web site. Now, faced with a new day and business that would never be as-usual again, she was feeling mildly delirious.

Maggie reached below the counter to switch off the music, creating a sudden, welcome quiet. "We have Martin at noon for our quarterly taxes. Did you forget too?"

"Shoot!" Alice *had* forgotten. "Can't we put it off?"

"We've already rescheduled twice. I sensed he was annoyed last time, and we don't want to lose him. He's a good accountant."

"But—"

"Shh. Darling. We must go forward."

Maybe Maggie was right. Lauren had been missing three days now, three endless days and nights of waiting and hoping. But hope, it seemed, had a diminishing return, its potency devoured by the passage of time. They had to move forward, over the quicksand, grabbing on to the simple, necessary guideposts of their routines.

"I don't suppose you want me to go alone to Martin's?" Maggie asked. It was a ridiculous suggestion given her dysfunctional relationship with numbers, hard facts beyond dispute.

"Definitely not," Alice said. "I'll go." She pulled the shoe box of receipts across the counter. "We'll split it in half and get it all categorized before I have to leave."

They sat together behind the counter, building neat piles of receipts in broad categories of expense, and sub-categorized by vendor and account. Every now and then Maggie glanced at Alice and Alice thought *now,* now I'll tell her. But each time Maggie's gaze slid away, she sighed or rubbed her eyes or made some gesture or remark that underscored her special fragility today, and Alice couldn't bring herself to speak.

Forty-five minutes later, not a single customer had come in, allowing them to burrow in the details of their task until Alice's stomach rumbled so loudly, even Maggie heard it.

"Hungry, are you?"

"Starving. I didn't realize it until now."

"I could use a cappuccino. Why don't I run out and pick us up something?"

Maggie reached under the counter for her purse, unsnapped it and rifled inside for her sunglasses.

Now, Alice thought, and began, "Mags—"

"Let's don't forget *this.*" Maggie pulled a pair of dinosaur-festooned pajamas out of her purse and shoved them onto the shelf under the counter. "Ethan's. It's Simon's night, and Sylvie's coming by for these." Distress gripped Maggie, and her bloodshot eyes seemed to ignite. "Can you believe he phoned me this morning to say he didn't have any clean pajamas for his son? Of course, he couldn't get to the washing machine. Oh no, not Simon. Probably too busy boffing Sylvie."

"She's been *sick,* Mags."

"Yes," Maggie sniffed. "So she says. Her claiming sick time these past few days has made all this with Lauren so much harder for me."

Alice couldn't think of what to say. Lauren's disappearance and Sylvie missing work were not comparable; linking them was almost beyond belief. Alice took a deep breath, and another, before finally swallowing frustration at Maggie's histrionic jealousies along with her own urge to confess the possible lapse in friendship. She was glad she hadn't blurted her confession to Maggie; chances were it would have been misunderstood.

"Try not to think about it." Alice stood to give Maggie a few dollars from her purse to buy her customary yogurt smoothie. "Strawberry-banana, please."

"Oh, shoot, look at the time. If I don't hurry up, you'll

be late for Martin." Maggie slipped Alice's money into her purse and hurried out, the welcome bell jangling behind her.

Sitting alone in the shop, in a growing silence, Alice thought the floor seemed oddly shinier, the walls bluer, the ceiling more reflective. She didn't like the heightened sensations. For a few minutes she didn't want to *feel,* didn't want to *think.* She loved Maggie, they *were* sisters, but she had to be managed and it could be exasperating, especially now.

Alice reached down to put on more music, slipping in a Norah Jones CD. Maggie had had the volume so high, the opening guitar riff blasted. Alice dialed down the volume, and only then, in the ebb of noise, did she realize someone had come into the store.

It was Sylvie. She smiled when she saw Alice and crossed the store with her casual, lilting walk. As always, a deft line of kohl accentuated her smallish, dark eyes and by contrast brightened the blond hair that frizzed and kinked to her shoulders in stylized chaos. She wore charcoal capris with a short white blouse that revealed a glimpse of belly button pierced by a ruby stud. A tattoo bracelet wrapped around her right ankle. Red leather flip-flops encrusted with rhinestones brought attention to her fresh pedicure, red to match the shoes.

She kissed Alice on both cheeks.

"Feeling better?" Alice asked.

"Ah, yes, it was stomach flu." Sylvie grimaced, but even that sounded pretty in the French accent that lay like golden sunshine over her otherwise fluent English. "Any news about Lauren?"

Alice explained about the witness and Sylvie, of course, was very interested in this.

"Maybe she ran off with an Italian lover," Sylvie suggested.

In the direction of the Gowanus? Doubtful. It was well known that Sylvie consumed romance novels and the suggestion of an *Italian lover* was straight from that fantasyland. Sylvie's hopeful youth and lightheartedness were suited to expatriate nannyhood. But not to this conversation. Alice decided to let her off the hook.

"Let's hope she did."

Sylvie smiled a little sadly, as if she knew she had misspoken and was grateful for the forgiveness implicit in Alice's answer.

"How are our babies doing today?"

"Kicking like mad."

Sylvie blew two kisses to Alice's flourishing tummy. Maggie was crazy to doubt her, Alice decided; the girl was pure charm.

Alice reached down for Ethan's dinosaur pajamas and put them on the counter.

"Need a bag for these?"

"I'll just put them here." Sylvie folded the pajamas neatly into her canvas purse with its long shoulder strap and large blocks of color. She had been in Brooklyn four years and had mastered the look of the New Local woman—understated clothes, easy hair, a casual bag slung across her middle.

"Are you going over to Garden Hill today?" Alice asked. "I've been playing phone tag with that broker you recommended. I can't remember who owes who a call, I've been so distracted. But she must know what's going on."

"Oh yes, if it's happening, Pam will surely know about it. But no, today I'm not working there. I'm taking a walk and running some errands. It's such a lovely morning."

Alice glanced at the window. The sun was out in full force. "Enjoy it," she said, just as Maggie appeared on the sidewalk out front and charged through the door. She was breathless, her forehead speckled with drops of sweat.

"Did you hear?" Maggie asked.

"Hear what?" Alice leaned over the cool stone of the counter.

"Over at the canal," Maggie said. "They found a body."

Chapter 8

"Come on," Maggie said. "We'll call Martin later and explain." She set the brown paper bag on the counter. "Sylvie, can you watch the shop?"

"Yes, of course."

Alice and Maggie left the store. Maggie started to run, then slowed down so Alice could keep up.

"It could be nothing." Alice's head had begun to throb.

"It can't be nothing," Maggie said, "but it may not be her."

By Degraw Street Alice's lungs were burning. They turned the corner and from two blocks away could see the chaos. There were four blue-and-white police cars, two dark sedans, a dented white van with its side door gaping and an ambulance, lights revolving in eerie silence.

Alice and Maggie had both slowed to a trot by the time they crossed Bond Street, where the blunt end of Degraw quickly turned derelict. Bands of hastily strung yellow police tape separated a cluster of onlookers from the area surrounding the bank of the canal. People were gathered on the sidewalk by a strip of dried earth that strangely boasted a plaque announcing a Parks Department urban renewal project; another good intention unfulfilled. Police and plainclothes detectives swarmed the garbage-strewn landing overlooking the end of the canal. Men and women wearing tight plastic gloves were collecting things into paper bags. Evidence. Alice remembered reading once in the newspaper that evidence was collected in paper bags, not plastic, to avoid the damaging effects of moisture.

Alice and Maggie stood with the onlookers, attention fixed on the low metal fence at the crest of the canal's muddy bank. The fence was covered in graffiti and malformed as if someone had rammed a truck into it.

Frannie stood in a deep bend in the fence. Hands jammed into her pockets, she seemed to be watching something below. Her face, tilted toward the canal, showed a case-hardened weariness that jolted Alice. Frannie's forehead was clenched tight, eyes skewered on some new, ugly truth.

Maggie squeezed next to Alice in the crowd. Together they struggled to look where Frannie was looking. In the distance, Alice saw nothing but a blur of refuse: a shopping cart tipped out of the muddy water, a kid's bike wheel covered in algae, a deflated pink condom hanging off a craggy branch jutting from the bank. Staked into the ground just next to Frannie was a yellow traffic sign in the shape of a diamond. END, it said, with awful simplicity. Someone had felt the twisted need to add to that sentiment in black marker: *boned a bitch here.* Alice wanted to cry.

"What's happening?" Alice asked a police officer who was just then coming toward them.

"Crime scene," was all he said before turning his back on the gaggle of curious citizens.

"Wait! Officer!" Maggie shouted.

Frannie turned around and saw them, then twisted back to face the canal. Alice now noticed Detective Giometti down on the muddy bank with his brown work boots toed into the water. His hands were planted on his hips and he too was staring at something.

"What's happening down there?" Maggie called to the officer, who glanced back to answer.

"Divers."

There was no shade and the sun grew hotter over them, as hot as deep summer.

Divers. Alice felt her stomach rumble, an onslaught of nausea threatening to force itself up.

Finally, in the distance, the water eddied and the back of a dark dry suit emerged. About five feet farther out, a second diver's head surfaced. Facing each other, the swimmers appeared to be synchronizing their efforts toward the bank of the canal. Alice watched them move slowly against the weight of the water, goggles fogged over, breathing apparatus strapped to their backs. Then, with a surge against gravity, she appeared.

Lauren was bloated and her skin was mottled gray and blue. Her eyes were open, filmed with algae. Her long brown hair had been chopped off. Her face looked plastic, masklike, strangely serene. A riotously colorful tent of a maternity sundress clung to her stalklike body. Her belly appeared to have reversed itself; instead of pregnant, her middle looked scooped out, emptied.

The divers dragged Lauren onto the craggy incline that served as shore. When they shifted her body to keep her from buckling into the canal, Alice saw the back of her head. It was crushed. Two officers hustled over and covered her with a bright yellow plastic tarp.

Alice collapsed forward at the waist, falling to her knees. The palms of her hands caught the concrete and she held herself up on shaky arms. The sour smell of her own vomit hit her in waves. Weeping, Maggie knelt beside Alice, holding her hair out of her face.

Finally Alice collected herself, drawing a breath of the fetid air. She knew Maggie had to be thinking the same thing.

Alice summoned her voice and said it first: "Where is the baby?"

Chapter 9

The effort to dredge the canal and find the baby became furious in the hours to follow. Dental records confirmed the body to be Lauren's. The media latched on to the possibility that Lauren's baby—*it*—might have been spontaneously borne of the underwater phenomenon known as *coffin birth*.

It. Ivy was not an *it*.

Last spring, Alice had bought two tiny dresses, one with a matching bonnet. They were Ivy's dresses and Alice would hold them for her, for when she was found. Lauren's death was confirmed, but Ivy could still be out there somewhere, alive.

The canal was an enclosed water system with a grate at the ocean end. Nothing as big as a full-term baby could possibly get through. If the baby was there, they would find her.

Alice learned many things that awful Monday, three days after Lauren disappeared. The day her wrecked body was found. She learned about the steep incline of grief. She learned how to stay alive in a state of half consciousness, barely breathing. And she learned that loss, violent loss, was merciless. Merciless and hungry, devouring hope and future and love in a single gulp.

Simon had heard the news around the neighborhood and hurried over to the canal to bring Alice and Maggie to his house. Mike was summoned home from his workshop. The store was closed. All the children were put under Sylvie's care at Maggie's apartment while the adults gathered at Simon's and prepared themselves to visit Tim and Austin, whose teacher had personally brought him home.

The men silently bolstered the women as they walked numbly through the neighborhood to Lauren and Tim's building. Alice felt deeply, wrongly contradicted by Lauren's death, herself obliterated, floating through an everyday world she had no right to inhabit as if things were normal. Through her numb heart she felt exploding droplets of poison anger. She wished she could fly backward through time to just that morning, when she was firm in her refusal to believe the worst. She wished she could turn to Mike and tell him, *You were right. There was no reason to worry.* If anyone tried to make her accept this new truth, she would shut her eyes. Tell them *no*. She would *not* embrace this thing she had seen for herself. There would have to be two worlds, two truths. Before and after. The problem was right now.

Alice had no idea what time it was when they got to Tim's. There was daylight. Warm summery air. He met them at the door himself, pale and automatic. Let them in without speaking. He exhaled, as if he had been holding his breath waiting for them, and allowed each friend to hug him in turn.

Gina—Austin and Peter's teacher—was sitting on Lauren's favorite antique wingback chair. The purple one in which she used to read. Austin was sprawled on the floor playing with his blocks, building them higher and higher with Gina's gentle encouragement. Her long ponytail hung lazily across her shoulder in a way that inexplicably broke Alice's heart. Gina was being so tender with Austin. Austin with his thick sandy brown hair looked more like Lauren than Tim. Alice wanted to run to him but wasn't sure how much he understood. She didn't want to frighten him. Instead she offered him a faint smile.

"No!" he shouted and smashed his tower. He must have seen something else in her face, in all their faces.

He was only five but he had to feel the disproportion of everything that was happening around him. He jumped up and ran out of the living room, refusing to look at the grown-ups who had gathered before him like ghosts to ruin his perfect sleep.

Tim's haggard face contracted, squeezed like a fist. Draining him. Completing his desolation. "I have to tell him," he said in a voice broken into gravel.

"I'll go," Alice offered.

"Yes," Maggie said. "Let us."

"No." Tim breathed deeply, as if trying impossibly to pump air into waxen lungs. "I have to do this."

Tim followed Austin down the hall and a door clicked shut behind them.

Gina sighed and stood up. "I'm so sorry," she said.

Simon thanked Gina for bringing Austin home and, gallant as always, showed her out. When he came back into the living room, Alice suddenly remembered that Mike, Simon and Tim had Yankees tickets for a game that night. She saw the three empty seats, midway up the stands. Heard the roar of a crowd that would gather without them. Saw a hard white ball swallowed by a candy-blue sky, disappearing into a rapturous silence.

All the windows of Tim's apartment were shut and no one bothered to open one, a detail that occurred to Alice as a kind of out-of-body observation. She was vaguely aware of the possibility of walking over and opening one of the windows. Instead she sat pressed against Maggie on the couch Lauren had recently reup-holstered in raw eggshell silk.

Mike positioned himself behind the purple chair, run-ning his hand back and forth across the nubby fabric. Simon walked over to one of the windows, posting him-self there as if on lookout.

Above Alice, the glass pendants of Lauren's antique chandelier threw brilliant slivers of sunlight across the room. The sudden rain of refracted light galloped over them, dizzying Alice. Lauren was everywhere all at once, ricocheting off the walls and ceiling and floor. Talking up her love for Austin. Asking favors. Planning projects. Detailing hopes for Ivy.

Lauren. Echoing. Resonating. Everywhere.

Alice pressed her hands against her ears and shut her eyes. She couldn't take it in. But the cacophony of Lauren didn't stop.

"What should we do?" Mike said, glancing toward the hall down which Tim and Austin had fled.

"Leave them alone a little while, I think," Simon answered.

When the doorbell rang, Simon and Mike both jumped to the intercom. Moments later, Frannie and Giometti appeared in Lauren's living room. They strode in with the perfect mixture of sympathy and confidence; it was as if, having often visited scenes of such crises, they were buffered from the raw shock. All of a sudden Alice saw the detectives, these people, in a new light. The way they stoically walked in, joined the friends, *handled the situation*. Alice felt suddenly reduced, childlike; irrationally reassured.

"We'll need to talk," Giometti said in a tone that was both sad and determined. He glanced around the living room, those soft eyes beaming regret from his toughened face. "Where's Tim? He'll need to hear this too."

"Right," Simon said. "I'll go." He went down the hall, returning a few minutes later behind Tim, who carried a limp Austin over his shoulder. Tim settled himself and Austin uneasily in the purple chair, stroking the small back as sobs alternated with deep, reflexive breaths. Simon stood behind them, his fingers playing lightly in Austin's hair. Giometti helped Mike bring extra chairs from the dining table.

Frannie sat next to Alice on the couch, bringing with her a faint scent of rosemary.

"We're sorry," Frannie said softly to Tim. "We know this is a terrible, terrible thing for you. For all of you. We were hoping to find her—"

Alive, Alice thought, and began to cry. She could still feel Lauren's warmth on the bench beside her. Hear the precise way she formed her words. As Frannie spoke, everyone surrendered to tears. Maggie, Mike, Simon, even Frannie, all of them. Tim's green eyes were roiling oceans of sorrow.

"You were her family," Frannie continued. "We honor the love you feel for her."

Then Giometti carefully said, "We have some information to share with you. We've found that it can help the family to know the facts."

He waited a moment for the rest of them to still their emotion. Alice understood now that this was his role in the partnership: he was the left side of the brain, always sober and pragmatic, to Frannie's intuitive, emotive right side. They were perfectly tuned to each other. Choreographed, almost.

"The medical examiner finished the autopsy and I'm going to tell you what he found. Can you hear this now?" He looked at Tim.

Tim nodded, stroking Austin's heaving back.

"You might want to take the boy into another room," Giometti said.

"Let me." Maggie got up from the couch. Her eyes were swollen and Alice knew she just couldn't take any more right now. She leaned over Tim and took Austin into her arms, carrying him out of the living room and down the hall, whispering, "Shh, baby, shh, shh."

Outside, a shadow passed over the sun. The room darkened and the chandelier's glass pendants emptied of light. Frannie put an arm around Alice's shoulder, bracing her.

"It's important for all of you to know the details in case any of it rings a bell. We're going to find Lauren's killer, and all of you could play an important part in helping us." Giometti glanced carefully at each face, making sure they felt his regret at having to present them with the facts. "There are things a body tells, final messages you might say. Are you ready?"

No one answered. How could they possibly be ready for this?

"Lauren was shot in the cranium with a .22 round-nose bullet that went in right here." He twisted around and pressed a finger into the hollow nook at the base of his head. "The bullet lodged itself in the front of her skull. This kind of injury tells us she died instantly. She felt no pain, none at all, other than—" He stopped himself.

The moment of fear.

"Following her death, the attacker removed her dress."

Tim cringed and sputtered, "Oh no."

"There was no evidence of sexual assault."

Giometti let that statement hang a moment in the air, meager balm, and then continued. Frannie tightened her grip on Alice's shoulders.

"A crude Caesarean section was performed. The placenta was left inside her body. An attempt was made to close the incisions with electrical tape. Her dress was put back on after the procedure, which we know due to the condition of the dress. At some point, probably right away, she was transferred to the canal."

Alice's attention snagged on *transferred*. The word had a technical quality, removed from emotion; it wasn't violent enough for what had happened to Lauren. *Thrown. Pitched. Dumped.*

"The crystal of Lauren's watch was smashed, probably after she was shot. This tells us two things: that she fell against a hard surface, and the exact time of the attack. Her watch stopped at eleven fifty-three. That's the official time of death."

Eight minutes after the artist smiled at her. Seven minutes before she was to have arrived at Pilates. Lauren's life ended at exactly seven minutes to noon. A shadow passed through Alice's mind, and stopped, as on a sundial separating darkness from light. Before from after. Halting time at one precise moment. Halving her consciousness of reality—love, friendship, trust, honor, truth, and *this*—into two incompatible parts.

"Our major liability now is that we haven't found the

crime scene," Giometti continued. "There should be a lot of blood somewhere but we haven't found the spot, and if it's outdoors, then time is against us. Time and weather. If we're lucky, the crime scene will be somewhere indoors."

Lucky. Alice's stomach lurched and she clamped her throat against it.

"The medical examiner's already signed off on his ruling. It's murder, which is going to give a lot more magnitude to the investigation. The baby is now officially missing. Because a pregnant woman disappeared once before in the same area, the feds are deciding if they're going to put the FBI behind us. It's not an interstate crime but there's a possibility the baby might have been moved, crossed jurisdictions, which is when the feds normally come in. Basically we've got three intersecting cases here. The pregnant woman who disappeared two years ago by the canal. Lauren's murder. The missing baby. They've been dredging the canal all day and they're going to keep dredging it until they've covered every square inch of it. But so far, nothing."

Frannie disengaged her arm from Alice's shoulder, leaving her cold. Leaning forward to look squarely at Tim, she said, "Someone took great pains to separate your baby from Lauren. There's a good chance it's still alive."

It. Suddenly Alice understood the usefulness of the generality. And she understood how the media was working with the police in agreeing to leave out the detail of the baby's gender. They were holding something back, one remaining morsel of truth. A single secret, to tease out Lauren's killer.

PART TWO

Chapter 10

The next morning, Alice huddled in bed, listening to the sounds of her family upstairs in the kitchen. A chair scraping across the floor. Footsteps. Dishes clanking. The ebb and flow of familiar voices. Mike was getting the kids ready for school, a respite for which she had not needed to ask him.

A bright seam of light joined the curtains where they fell loosely together. Alice felt starved for darkness and quiet and rest. All night she had lain here, her brain grinding up the spent truth of Lauren's brutal death. Assembling and dissembling it. Adding lurid colors and dimensions that couldn't possibly exist in the real world. Seeing the knife and the bloody fleshy parting of Lauren's skin and muscle. The exposure of her bone. *Seeing* it. Ivy curled inside her mother for the last time. Shocked by the sensation of air against her newborn skin. The ratchet of her first cry as it hurled into a deaf universe. Without love, who would hear her?

What did they suffer, those two females, as they were forced out of and into the world?

And Alice asked herself: *If fear was a giant wave overcoming me, what would I do? Dive into it or turn and run away? Fear the fear, or surrender to it?*

She lay on her side, caressing the taut capsule of her twins. They were quiet—sleeping, she presumed—and she didn't want to wake them.

Close to eight thirty, a cascade of footsteps carried

Mike, Nell and Peter out of the house. It was quiet. Alice closed her eyes and tried to sleep but could find no bridge out of her misery. She missed Lauren so badly it hurt; it was the worst and strangest pain she had ever felt in her life.

The phone began to ring and Alice tried to ignore it, but it wouldn't let up. Finally she reached for the bedside extension.

"It's all set," Lizzie said.

"Mom?"

"I'm on the plane right now." She spoke in the crisp, bossy tone with which she had nudged and guided Alice through childhood. "I'll be at LaGuardia at ten past one."

"You're coming today?"

"Babydoll, I canceled four meetings but who cares? Mike called me. First comes first and that's you. Big kiss. Don't get me—I'll take a cab."

"No, Mom, I always pick you up."

"Not today, you don't. I'll—"

Alice hoisted herself to sitting and put some strength into her voice. "We're not opening the store today, and if I sit around the house, I'll go crazy. Let me do this for you. Give me your flight number. I'll get there early."

Alice showered and dressed. On the kitchen table she found a note from Mike: *Call me when you wake up.* He had probably gone to the workshop and would leave as soon as she phoned him, rush home to try to protect her from her own anguish. She didn't want him to save her from this, nor did she want him to use her as a distraction from whatever he himself was experiencing. She would leave him, for now, in the quiet of his workshop, where he didn't have to smile or talk or comfort her, where all he had to do was sand a single piece of wood to perfect translucence. Discover and enhance the direction of the grain. Understand it for what it was. What Alice needed right now, she knew, was her mother. Lizzie was coming; that was enough.

Alice forced herself to eat something, for the babies,

but had trouble getting down even a single piece of toast. She drank a few sips of milk, which immediately triggered the queasiness she was growing to dread.

Because traffic on the Brooklyn Queens Expressway was wildly unpredictable, she decided to leave early. She could already feel the distraction of the journey prying her back toward the mundane bliss of the everyday world. The one from which people didn't vanish and weren't murdered. The one that used to be so real to her and now seemed ephemeral. The one where her children lived and to which she needed to find a road back.

She locked up the front door and turned down the stoop into a wash of sunshine, wishing she had thought to bring her sunglasses. Still on her own block, she encountered the first yellow sign. MISSING. Lauren's smiling face, inviting a search. MISSING, not DEAD. Alice ripped the sign off the light post and crumpled it up. She threw it in the garbage can on the corner of President and Smith. Across the street, she could see the little kids' side of the playground, bustling with prenap toddlers, mothers building new friendships and nurturing old ones. She didn't know how she would ever be able to go back there. But she would; her children would demand it. The playground made her cry again so she looked away, down Smith Street. Horns were blaring. Up ahead an intersection was blocked. Yellow rectangles glared from light posts, tree trunks, electric junction boxes. MISSING transformed into FIND MY BABY PLEASE FIND IVY DON'T WASTE A MINUTE FIND HER SHE'S OUT THERE ALL ALONE. Alice ripped down every sign she saw, crying more uncontrollably with each removal.

Where was Ivy? Where *was* she? She needed a mother and Alice could *be* that mother. Without a mother, Ivy could know nothing about herself.

Alice was glad not to run into anyone she knew. Only strangers witnessed her fury as she ripped down the signs and crushed them and threw them in the trash. Weeping. Destroying. Raging against what had happened to her *sister*. Every block had at least one storefront under construction and twice she tore signs from their temporary plywood fronts. She couldn't remember taping them here; it must have been Maggie.

Finally the punctuation of yellow signs stopped. She walked steadily forward, dizzy from fatigue. Degraw Street between Hoyt and Bond, where they parked the family car in a cheap lot—Mike kept his pickup truck on the street since he used it all the time—was deserted. Almost deserted. A gray-haired man turned around and walked in the other direction as soon as she stepped onto the block; he looked vaguely familiar from behind but she couldn't place him. She undid the parking lot's padlock with her key and pulled open the massive iron double doors. The sound of gravel underfoot was oddly reassuring. She opened all the windows of their old green station wagon before squeezing into the driver's seat. The air conditioner hadn't worked for two years; it was an '88, not worth repairing. Sweat glued her thighs to the vinyl seat.

It was a relief to be driving, moving, *going*. On Bond, where she had to drive for a block before turning left up Douglass Street, she caught a fetid whiff of the canal just to her right. She hated that smell and drove faster. The farther she distanced herself from the canal and Bond Street and Hoyt Street and Smith Street the better. She couldn't wait to get onto the highway. When she turned left onto Court Street, she knew she should have slowed down as usual—with so many cars and trucks double-parked in front of stores, the driving was always a nerve-wracking zigzag—but she didn't slow down. The yellow signs were everywhere and she couldn't get to them, rip them down. Erase what had happened to Lauren, to Tim, to Austin—and to her. She felt suddenly that she had to get out of Brooklyn and for a moment, when she pictured the airport, she considered the possibility of getting on a plane. She could do it, buy a ticket and leave. Maggie could run the store. Mike and the kids could join her wherever she went. They could go to France, Italy, Greece, Mexico—forget about everything. Her mind was just capturing the aqua clarity of water, broad pale beaches, an endless horizon, when up ahead she was jolted to a near stop by a knot of traffic. She had to get out of it, to keep herself focused on the vast ocean with its quiet promise that nothing really mattered but the turning of the earth. A shaft of sunlight exploded against her windshield. She squinted into it, veering sharply right at the next corner.

She felt the scrape and jolt of her collision with the bus before she even saw its hulking form. The impact threw her against the steering wheel and a spasm passed through her middle. *Her babies.* Her hands flew to her belly, which had contracted against the shock. Hardened in a Braxton Hicks contraction, or just hardened.

Panic saturated her, making her almost drunk, unable to think. She tried to drive forward. Backward. Nothing worked. The side of her car was locked against the front corner of the bus, which had squealed to a complete stop.

A tall black man standing on the corner was waving to her. His ragged clothes seemed to be draped over a too-thin body. An absurdly large cross made of bumpy aluminum foil hung around his neck.

"Lady, lady!" he called to her.

Alice looked up at the bus. The driver, a stout woman with short, metallic red hair, was eyeing her fiercely through the broad windshield.

"Lady!"

The man was now walking toward her. Was he deranged? Alice didn't know what to do. She wasn't even sure what had happened. As he approached, she saw that his eyes were strikingly white around soupy brown pupils.

"Just take some deep breaths and calm yourself down," he told her. "Do it now, lady. One, two, three." He breathed for her, showing her how, and for lack of a better plan she followed his direction. She felt the hard sheen of panic begin to ease off her. Her mind loosened. His face was now all the way up to her open window.

"You know something, lady? Twenty years I drove a city bus. Retired. One time I did the same thing you just did. Let me give you some advice."

But what exactly had she done? All she knew was that for one brief moment, she had escaped. Maybe her brain had shut down. She didn't know.

"Every time you get ready to make a turn, check and check again until your strategy meets up with reality. You can't get too familiar with the one-way streets around here. Always make *sure*. You hear me?"

Horns were blaring behind the bus. Alice could see the stream of cars backing slowly down Union Street toward Clinton, trying to reverse into the flow of traffic. She took one more deep breath and got out of the car.

Now, shading her eyes against the glare, she saw the one-way sign pointed in the opposite direction. So she had tried to turn the wrong way onto a one-way street. Glare or not, she should have known better; she *knew* these streets. She had vacated reality at just the wrong moment.

"Holy lord!" the man exclaimed. "When you due?"

"December." Alice touched her belly; the babies felt still and heavy inside her. "Before the holidays."

The bus driver had descended to the street and was now shaking her head at Alice and the man. Faces had gathered in the bus's windshield, staring at her. Voices spilled from the bus onto the street.

"Get a driver's license!"

"You're making me late!"

"Wear your glasses when you drive!"

Alice had never felt so foolish. She stepped forward to the bus driver.

"I'm sorry. It was my fault. I turned the wrong way. I take full responsibility."

The woman seemed shocked by Alice's lack of argument. This was New York City. This was *Brooklyn*. A pregnant woman with no fight was just not someone you could argue with. The driver shook her head again and turned to assess the damage. Alice joined her as if they were comrades in the same assault. A long dent had buckled the passenger's side door of Alice's car. The bus was unscathed except for a heavy rubber bumper that was hanging partly off, but nothing was broken.

"That dent was already there," Alice lied; the dent was *her* fault.

"Oo-we," the man said, shaking his head at her.

Alice followed the bus driver onto the bus, aware of all the agitated eyes on her. She turned to the passengers and repeated what she had told the driver. "I'm sorry. It's my fault. I'm sorry if I made you late." She could feel the deflation, as if the bus itself had lowered hydraulically to let on a disabled person. It had. It had let on Alice, one badly damaged soul.

The bus driver took down all of Alice's license, registration and insurance information. She continued to apologize and the driver continued to nod and say nothing, but Alice felt her compliance was appreciated. She couldn't fight this. It *was* her fault. Then something else happened, something even more unexpected than the accident or the retired evangelical bus driver who had sprung to her aid. One by one, some of the passengers began to forgive her.

"I did that before. Twice."

"Don't worry honey. You're human."

"Take care of that baby, okay?"

"Don't worry about us. We'll just catch the next bus."

Alice nodded and looked into the eyes of every stranger who spoke to her. Even the ones who didn't, who held on to their resentment for the delay, eyeing her sullenly. She shrank from none of them.

Finally she got back into her car and the man, her savior, stepped into traffic to pause it while she backed up and pulled out. She drove slowly and carefully down Court Street, turned on Degraw, and parked the car back in the lot.

She was terrified of the car now, of the day, of what she may have done. She speed-dialed her obstetrician's office, explained that she had been in a minor accident, and was told to come in right away. Then she called Mike and waited for him to come get her. Eyes squeezed shut, she prayed to any god that would listen. Begging for the well-being of her babies.

Chapter 11

Alice climbed into the passenger's side of Mike's black pickup truck. Thick slabs of oak were strapped onto the uncovered back.

"What happened?" The engine was revving but Mike didn't drive. A streak of black grease ran haphazardly from his wrist halfway to his elbow, stopping abruptly. "Are you okay?"

Alice nodded, pulling the seat belt as long as it could go and buckling herself in. The truth was she didn't know if she was okay. She was afraid to speak; they had lost an unborn child once before; she was twice a mother now; she should have known not to take any risks.

"Dr. Matteo's waiting for me," Alice said, stilling her voice against a strong undercurrent of distress.

"What *happened*?"

She waited until he began to drive. She wanted to get there, not talk. As they wove through the quiet morning streets of their neighborhood, she explained. Mike listened, his forehead taut, but he said nothing until she had finished. Then he reached out to gently touch her knee before sliding the stick shift into a higher gear for a green-light cruise along Clinton Street.

"I could have gotten your mother from the airport," was all he said before they fell to silence. They both knew that. Alice had *wanted* to go. She shouldn't have. It was that simple.

Dr. Sally Matteo's waiting room at Long Island College Hospital on Amity Street, where she kept morning hours once a week, was packed. Alice sat with Mike in a pair of unoccupied chairs. The dry warmth of his hand locked into hers had an almost narcotic effect on her, making her calm, sleepy.

They kept quiet in the high chatter of the crowded waiting room. It was a different crowd from the Pierrepont Street office where Alice always went for her scheduled appointments. Here the faces were darker, *people of color,* a description that always made her think of the red patent-leather Mary Janes she had insisted on wearing to parties as a little girl instead of the white ones she despised. She realized instantly that this was a different Brooklyn from the one where she lived. There were two Brooklyns and they were superimposed over each other, sometimes contradicting, sometimes obliterating each other, rarely in agreement. Here, girls and boys didn't get many choices, people didn't live in renovated brownstones or buy hand-sculpted pewter knobs. Here, poverty simmered on the streets, a breeding ground for common tragedies that were not reported by the media. Here, naivety like hers—to have expected so much from a greedy world—would be laughed at, ought to be laughed at. She saw herself white, shimmering, vacant in a sea of color. Pale and fading.

She couldn't help hating herself, though she couldn't say exactly why. It was just that Lauren was *gone* and she was still here. It made no sense at all. And what about Ivy? Was she alive? Was anyone caring for her?

Alice rubbed her eyes and exhaled.

Mike put his arm around her shoulders, pulled her close to him and kissed her lightly on the side of her head.

"We should call your mother," he said.

"Right." Alice dialed Lizzie's cell number and listened to the slightly too-loud voice intone: "Lizzie Taylor here. I'm probably out buying diamonds. Leave a message." She was nineteen when she married Alice's father, Richard Taylor, and had eagerly taken his name, transforming herself from Elizabeth Liptutz to Elizabeth Taylor with one gold ring.

"Better take a cab from the airport, Mom. I can't come," Alice said. "Everything's all right. But take a cab and I'll meet you at home." She regretted saying everything was all right. It would only trigger her mother's antenna since it was so clearly untrue.

A nurse appeared and brought them into an empty examination room. Alice was told to undress while they waited for Dr. Matteo, who arrived quickly. Mike sat in a chair against the wall at Alice's side as she lay on the paper-covered padded bench. The doctor leaned over her, searching her eyes, checking for signs of concussion.

"I'm okay," Alice said. "I think."

"Let's just find out."

Dr. Matteo was an elegantly handsome woman who had once outlined her complicated lineage to Alice as Puerto Rican, Greek, Irish, French, Spanish, "and a few drops of Native American." She was a true, rainbow-blooded American and a vintage New Yorker. The night Alice was in labor with Peter, Dr. Matteo had charged into the delivery room in a sleeveless black gown with a red-satin-lined black cape flung over her shoulders. She had been at the opera, and had been beeped for an emergency that had been contained. "I heard you were here," she told Alice and Mike, then left the room, returning a few minutes later in her green surgical garb to take over the show.

Up close, Alice noticed the soft pucker of skin around the doctor's mouth and realized she had rarely seen her without a smile.

"Tell me what's going on," Dr. Matteo said in a calm yet studied tone. "You got in an accident?"

"It was my fault," Alice said, though here the statement had a different effect than on the bus. Dr. Matteo's expression of concern broadened, pulling the lines farther across her face.

"Kids in school?"

What she was asking, of course, was if Nell and Peter had been with her in the car.

"Yes," Alice answered. "I wasn't going very fast. There really wasn't any damage except a little bit to the car."

"Wiggle back a little, okay?"

Alice inched back on the bench, her feet high in the dreaded stirrups, and held her breath as the doctor gently examined her, feeling and listening and peering. Her stethoscope searched the expanse of Alice's stomach. Then she asked the nurse to bring in the ultrasound machine.

"Did you hear their heartbeats?" Alice asked.

"Shh," was all Dr. Mateo said.

Alice closed her eyes and let the paper gown fall open. She heard the scrape of Mike's chair as he arranged himself at a better angle to view the screen. The doctor squeezed cold gel onto Alice's abdomen and smeared it around with the plastic-covered ultrasound wand. The nurse meanwhile switched on the machine and set the program to the correct attributes. She typed in the date and Alice's name. Then she pressed a button and nodded.

Dr. Matteo slowly moved the goopy wand over Alice's tummy, her attention fixed on the screen, which the nurse had swiveled toward her. She continued to shift the wand over the vaporous forms of the twins. The doctor remained thoughtful as she searched for heartbeats. Alice wanted these babies, had wanted them every day since the initial shock of twins had worn off. She could not be deterred from wanting them, even knowing all the work that lay ahead of her, because she also knew of the expansion of love that came with the bargain. And now, as the cold, gelatinous wand roamed her skin, she *needed* these babies as much as she wanted them. She needed their hope and their promise, needed to see their eyes smile at her for the first time, to feel their tiny hands squeeze her fingers. It was *their* forgiveness she needed most of all; the forgiveness implicit in the fact of their life.

"Yes, the babies are fine," Dr. Matteo said. "But you are not."

Alice breathed in those words, *the babies are fine*. She looked at Mike and they shared a smile at the reprieve.

"I can't sleep anymore," Alice said. "I shouldn't have been driving at all."

"How long haven't you been sleeping?"

"The last three nights. And I've been feeling sick, which is new for me."

"You're also a little dehydrated," Dr. Matteo said. "Your amniotic fluid needs to be maintained. Have you been thirsty in this heat, not drinking enough?"

Alice didn't know. Maybe she had been thirsty. Thirsty and hungry along with sick and tired. Maybe her body's revolt these last few days had been stronger than she had even noticed. Strong enough to shut down her brain today, midtraffic, and steer her into a wrong turn.

"We lost a close friend of ours this week," Mike said. He explained everything that had happened since Friday. Dr. Matteo listened gravely.

"Yes, I heard about that, but I didn't know the woman was your friend. I'm sorry."

"Lauren was my sister." Alice began to cry. "Like a real sister."

Dr. Matteo scrawled a prescription, tore it off the pad and handed it to Alice.

"You take this tonight and get into bed. Let's start by sleeping; then we'll see about the nausea."

"Sleeping pills?" Alice looked at the doctor's black scribble on the small white page. "Is this safe?"

"Perfectly safe. It's very mild. It'll make you and your babies sleepy, that's all. But for you, Alice, it could make all the difference."

As Alice's eyes focused, elements of the scribble became decipherable. The doctor was right; she was delirious and had to sleep. She would take just one pill, she decided, then put them aside unless she really needed them again.

Dr. Matteo tucked Alice's file folder under her arm. "Alice, your job is to rest. Mike, you're on duty tonight, dinner, kids, everything."

"Aye, aye, Captain." Mike took the prescription out of Alice's hand, folding it with a sharp edge down the middle and slipping it into his T-shirt pocket. Beneath the stripe of grease on his forearm, Alice now noticed a thick, pulsing vein.

"My mother's coming today." Alice struggled to sitting and pulled the paper gown closed over her swollen middle. "She loves to take over."

"Now would be a good time to let her." Dr. Matteo leaned forward and placed a hand on Alice's belly. "Maybe you can't hear this right now, Alice, but I'll say it anyway. Dealing with grief when you're pregnant is a terrible thing. But please, let's see if you can find a way."

Alice and Mike left the hospital arm in arm, he detaching to open every door for her, she thanking him quietly each time. But beneath his gallantry and her appreciation of it, a silence loomed between them. They had always been good—too good—at politely avoiding tension, keeping it to themselves until its elements had formed into digestible nuggets. They held their silence on the drive home, until Mike suddenly veered the pickup around a pothole, startling Alice.

She looked at him, his sharp profile edged in sunlight as the pickup passed from under a shade tree. "How are you feeling, Mike?"

"Fine."

"No, I mean *feeling*, about Lauren. Not 'do you have a cold.'"

His response was strange, she thought: sad eyes, a self-deprecating shrug of his shoulders as he steered them onto Court Street. "Kind of numb, I guess," he finally said. "I don't know what to feel. I mean, it's kind of terrifying, Alice, isn't it?"

"Kind of?"

He turned left down Union Street and stopped at a red light. Looked at her. In the harsh noon sunlight that poured through the windshield, his skin looked rich and imperfect as handmade paper. Raw, without color. He hadn't shaved that morning.

"Are you going back to work today?" she asked him.

"I don't think so," he said, glancing at the back of the truck with its load of oak.

"You just picked that up?"

"It doesn't matter."

But she knew his deadline for the furniture show was looming; she knew how much it meant to him to do well there.

"Go," she said. "I'll be fine. Mom's on her way."

"No, Alice, I don't want to leave you alone." He turned onto President Street and found a parking spot on their block.

"I'm okay. I'll rest until she gets here."

In his moment of hesitation, she knew she was giving him what he wanted: to be alone with his inchoate sadness.

"You sure?"

"I think it's better if you work."

He took a long breath. "Maybe just for an hour or so. I could deliver the wood, and Diego could get started on the table."

She kissed him good-bye and got out of the pickup. Walking along the sidewalk, up their front stoop, she could feel him impatiently waiting for the click of the front door. She turned and waved to him. He waved back. As soon as the door closed behind her, she heard the truck drive away.

She went straight to the bedroom and lay down in the quiet early afternoon, waiting for time to pass, grateful to have been forgiven by blind luck for causing an accident that could have cost her and others so much. She lay there, wishing Mike had chosen to come inside with her, but glad she hadn't made him. She lay there, missing

Lauren and realizing it was an ache that would not soon disappear. And she lay there, searching her mind for avenues to Ivy, any thought or memory or clue that might help the police track the baby down. Was there anything, any small detail lodged in her mind—a memory, a remark—that might hint at such greedy brutality? Who could have done such an awful thing? Was it someone who knew Lauren? Or a random snare of evil she had stumbled into? Alice lay on her bed, wishing she had never left her dark bedroom this morning. Through the open curtains she watched a lush green tree juggle coins of sunlight outside her window. Only when the doorbell rang just before two o'clock did she get up.

As soon as she opened the front door, Lizzie put down her suitcase and stepped inside. She had lost weight, cut her hair very short and bleached it white-blond in her quest to appear younger than her sixty-one years. She wore new calico rectangular glasses and bright red lipstick. But she didn't look young; she looked like herself. Beautifully real and consistent under the layers of effort and California glitz.

"Come here, babydoll."

Stepping into her mother's arms, Alice smelled the familiar perfume and felt her face screw up reflexively. A lurching breath threatened more tears.

Lizzie drew Alice against her, murmuring, "Come here, come here, come here."

Chapter 12

Nell and Peter were ecstatic to see their grandmother waiting for them outside school at three o'clock. Bypassing Alice, they flew at Lizzie, who fell to the knees of her white slacks and embraced both children at once. They doused her in a rain of chatter all the way to Sweet Matilda's, where they were being treated to a "fancy snack." Alice phoned Mike's cell to let him know where to find them, leaving a message on his voice mail. She didn't really mind that the delivery had taken longer than expected, but she had begun to miss him and to entertain a tiny, unfamiliar sense of abandonment at his decision not to stay with her that morning.

High tea arrived on a tiered tray of crustless sandwiches, petit fours, droplet cookies, muffins and scones. Alice and Lizzie shared a pot of chamomile tea. The children snuggled on either side of Lizzie on the wall bench while Alice sat alone in a chair, facing them. In her heart, she wanted to be over there in her mother's lap too. But this was good enough. Just being here together. Every now and then Lizzie sent Alice a kiss through the air.

"How long are you staying, Gamma?" Nell asked. Lizzie was *Gamma* to both children, starting with Nell's early attempts to say *Grandma*. When Peter learned to talk, he had automatically adopted the nickname.

"Just two nights, sweets. Gamma's got business in

LA." She kissed the top of Nell's messy strawberry head, then stayed fair by kissing Peter's chocolate mop.

"Really, Mom?" Alice said, failing to hold back her disappointment. "You came so far."

"This is nothing," she said. "I'd travel to China for just one meal with my family."

"Can't you stay a little longer? You could help me look at houses," Alice said, thinking a project might attract her.

"How's that going?" Lizzie nibbled off an edge of lemon poppy muffin, leaving a batch of crumbs stuck to her lower lip.

"Two new businesses and now a new house," Alice said. "If we'd kept our old jobs, it'd be a cinch to afford whatever we wanted. Almost."

"You two did the right thing, changing your lives." Lizzie cleaned the crumbs off her lip with a napkin, leaving behind a lipstick kiss. "This tragedy with Lauren just proves it. It can all change in one second"—she snapped her fingers—"just like that."

Alice's heart began to sink, again, at the thought of Lauren. Why had she mentioned the house hunt? There was no way she could traipse around looking at homes, chatting with brokers, running calculations through her mind for the perfect, winning numbers. Not yet. Mr. Pollack, *owner,* would have to understand.

"What about that broker Maggie's babysitter hooked you up with?" Lizzie asked. "You had such a good feeling about that one."

"Never mind, Mom." Alice broke a corner off a scone, then returned it to the plate. "I can't deal with it right now, anyway."

"How can you not deal with it?"

"Mom—"

"You have a family. Do not allow this to turn into yet another crisis." Lizzie tilted her chin proudly up, the angle briefly magnifying her eyes behind her narrow glasses. "Anyway, how long did you think you could last in that apartment? Were you planning to put all four kids into one room?"

Yes, Alice thought but didn't answer. It was a large, beautiful room. Alice had envisioned two sets of bunk beds; people in the city did it all the time. But she had to admit that, put so bluntly, it sounded like a patently bad idea.

"*Please,* Gamma," Peter begged, nuzzling closer into Lizzie's armpit. "Stay."

"I wish I could." Looking squarely at Alice, Lizzie added, "I've got a few more things to tell your mother that don't carry on the phone. Two days should do it."

The voice that was too loud over the phone was pitched perfectly for Lizzie in person. As a teenager, Alice had once accused her mother of thinking of herself as larger than life. "Wrong," Lizzie had countered. "I'm as big as life. I match it. When you grow up, you'll learn the difference."

By now Alice knew. The difference was in the choices you made, how you calibrated your reactions. Her mother had always dived into the wave when it overtook her.

Just before five o'clock, Mike finally called Alice, offering to pick up some Middle Eastern food on his way home. Alice agreed it was a good idea. Strangely, he said nothing about his long absence or his failure to return her earlier call.

"That was a long hour," she said, wanting to hold on to her understanding of him, with its implicit forgiveness, but instead succumbing irresistibly to resentment. Why had he needed to escape her today? Why hadn't he been able to forgive her for the accident? Why was work and not home a balm for his pain?

"It was the longest hour of my life," he said quietly. "It's over now."

She wondered if the wood ever got to the workshop. If the table had taken shape.

"I was getting a little upset—" she began.

"You don't have to tell me, Alice. I know."

They stayed on the phone, saying nothing. Finally she let go the strand of her irritation; it was useless and almost arbitrary in the context of everything else.

"It's okay," she told him. "Just come home. We're all waiting for you."

Half an hour later Alice, Mike, Lizzie and the kids were seated around the kitchen table, eating paper plates of humus, baba ghanoush, skewered lamb and fresh pita. Mike seemed okay, Alice thought, considering. Today had been painful; she had missed him more these hours than she had thought she could since their first bloom of love. She *was* glad he had taken some time, since he needed it. And glad he was back home.

Lizzie was to sleep on the foldout couch in the living room. Mike took the kids downstairs to put them to bed while Alice arranged the sofa bed. Lizzie got changed in the bathroom, emerging in a lavender spaghetti-strap nightgown with feathery trim at her knees and matching slippers that looked like powder puffs. Her skin was loose and tan, but not from lying on the beach; Lizzie worked long hours, and her tans were purchased at a salon.

Alice pulled back the covers and got into the sofa bed, laying her head on the pillow. Lizzie slid in next to her, running her fingers through Alice's short peachy hair. Her mother's soft skin was still heaven to Alice.

"I never knew where you got this red hair," Lizzie said. "It didn't come from Rich and it didn't come from me."

"Do you remember you used to tell me my freckles were fairy dust?"

Lizzie's laugh was throaty. "Oh yeah, that one. Sure, I remember."

"I believed you."

"Well, babydoll, it was what you needed to hear back then." Lizzie traced Alice's face with her fingertip: forehead, nose, cheekbones, chin. It was what she had done to help Alice relax at night when she was young, troubled by insomnia even then.

"I took the sleeping pill the doctor gave me," Alice said, "but I don't feel it working yet."

"It will. Just wait. You'll see."

"Thanks for coming, Mom."

"Mmm hmm."

Downstairs, the bedtime clatter quieted. Peter was always put to bed first, being the youngest, then Nell. Mike was probably lying in Nell's bed right now, telling her a story.

"Tell me a story, Mom."

"Do you remember your father?"

"A little, not much. I was eight when he left. Shouldn't I remember him better?"

"He was a bastard, a real loser, but when he dumped us for that bimbo, my heart was broken," Lizzie said. "I mean *broken*."

"She was a marine biologist, I thought. Didn't she work in Daddy's lab?"

"She was a *bimbo*. It works better for me that way. Do you remember what I did when he left?"

"I remember you were kind of quiet. It scared me."

"It scared me too." Lizzie's fingertip lingered on Alice's forehead. "The first thing I did was I went shopping, for both of us. Then I sold all our old stuff. Then I sold the house. Then we moved to California."

"I remember all the new clothes—that part was fun. But I was mad at you for selling my old stuff because I wasn't finished with it."

"I figured that out later. Sorry. But we humans make mistakes."

Alice propped her head on her hand and faced her mother. Lizzie was lying flat on the scant mattress, staring at the ceiling, having let Alice take the whole pillow. The intensity of her eyes betrayed her irreverent tone.

"The thing is," Lizzie said quietly, "he never came looking for us. I made a lot of noise leaving and he never noticed."

Now it was Alice's turn to trace a fingertip along her

mother's face. Free of makeup, a web of fine lines mapped her skin. She was still so beautiful to Alice.

"Another thing." Lizzie turned onto her side to face Alice. "Even though I might have still loved him in a certain way, he was *over* for me. I left him behind in Long Island. He did not come to California with us in any way, shape or form. I refused him in my heart."

Alice had always wondered how her father could just leave them like that. As a wife, she found it painful to imagine. As a parent with a daughter nearly the same age, she found it shocking.

"Alice," Lizzie said, "when that bastard-whoever-he-is murdered Lauren, when he took her from us, he took you too. Don't let him have that power over you. Don't!"

The force of that last word startled Alice into tears. "I don't have control over my feelings, Mom."

"I'm here to tell you you're wrong. You do. You have got to steel yourself against the pain. Make yourself some armor and wear it, just like I did. You have children—falling apart is not an option." A tear rolled onto Lizzie's lower lash and she ignored it, but Alice couldn't; she reached over and flattened it with her fingertip.

"You make it sound so easy, Mom."

"I never said it was easy, did I?"

Alice fell asleep next to Lizzie and slept there all night long. A solid twelve hours, nearly a good sleep.

What ruined it was waking up to today. Lauren's funeral was at one o'clock. Alice squeezed shut her eyes, trying to press away the anguish. She wanted to take her mother's advice but didn't know how. After a while, Nell and Peter crept upstairs and burrowed under the sofa bed covers in a crowd of wiggling limbs and kisses. Alice knew she would have to learn her mother's lesson. Lauren's killer could destroy many lives, if Alice let him; but how to cast him out of her soul?

Chapter 13

Lauren's funeral was held at the Scoletto funeral home on Court Street. Tim stood in front of the double brownstone, smoking under the leafy branch of a magnolia long past its bloom. Austin hovered nearby in a little dark suit and striped clip-on tie, struggling to control a squishy lime green yo-yo ball that veered in all the wrong directions. Nell broke away from the family to join him.

On their way over, the sky had suddenly darkened, and now Alice found herself shivering. Lizzie pulled her close.

"What a good girl she is," Lizzie said as Nell showed Austin how to handle the yo-yo ball. Peter stood with them, watching.

"It's good for Austin we brought them," Mike said.

Alice hoped it had been the right decision. Maggie and Simon were bringing Ethan too. The adults had decided it was best to expose the children to the truth up front, answer questions they may not have known how to ask. Show them the stark wrongness of Lauren's death so they wouldn't grow up thinking she had simply gone away. "Lauren is dead," Lizzie had told the children that morning when Alice and Mike couldn't bring themselves to. "She was killed. Today we're all going to say good-bye."

Lizzie had made it seem so simple, but Alice knew what response that notion would get. *Whoever said it was simple? You do what you have to. These children need to know.* But they didn't cry and Alice suspected they didn't really understand, that it would hit them later—days, months, maybe even years later. They had asked a few obvious questions: who, where, when, why. To all that, there was still just one answer: she died at seven minutes to noon on Friday. It was all they knew.

Mike walked over to Tim and drew him into a long hug. Tim seemed slight and deflated in a dark gray suit that now hung off him. The burning end of his cigarette was squashed between two yellowed fingers that dug into Mike's navy suit jacket. From where the children were clustered—now including Ethan, who had arrived with Simon—Alice saw Austin's glance at his weeping father. There was such anger in the little boy's eyes; it was as if he had been brought to some dreaded event against his staunch objection.

It *was* a dreaded event, Alice thought; it was the worst possible thing. Austin's anger was absolutely right. She stepped in front of the children and looked at him, not smiling, and let his green eyes fight her. Then she crouched in front of him and held him in her arms. It was a mother's complicity, a plain acknowledgement that life was a beast. It was the best and only thing she could give him. He did not push her away for a full minute, a long time for a child with friends and a toy within easy reach.

When she stood, Alice found Tim watching her with bloodshot eyes that looked sunken, almost bruised. *Thanks,* he mouthed, as Mike drew an arm around his shoulders and led him into the funeral parlor. The double doors had been opened; the service was about to begin.

Just then Maggie ran up, panting, and immediately spun Austin into a hug. "Aunt Mags has got you now!" she said in a tone that Alice found too buoyant. Grating, almost. But then Austin laughed and Maggie's onslaught seemed, on the contrary, perfectly tuned. She carried

Austin through the front door. Lizzie ushered in the other children. Alice, Mike and Simon followed.

They were led through a large lobby into the first floor chapel. It was a wide room, painted taupe and slate blue, with an aisle separating two banks of pews. There was an absolute symmetry to the chapel, Alice noticed, with two large urns of white nasturtiums whose spicy sweetness could not overcome an odor of mothballs and formaldehyde. The huge flowerpots sat on pedestals at the foot of a shallow set of stairs leading to a platform where, set behind the urns, was Lauren's casket. The golden-hued oak wood was highly glossed, with large brass handles at either end. The casket was closed.

Alice saw Maggie's back collapse as soon as they came into view of the casket. She held herself together long enough to set Austin down on the floor. He slid along the first row bench until he was pressed against his father, then coiled into a ball, tucking his head between his knees. Lizzie, Alice, Mike, Nell and Peter slid in next to Austin. Maggie, Simon and Ethan were behind them in the second row. Muffled sobs floated around them like remnants of a cloud that had lost its foothold in the sky.

Soon the chapel was full. Friends from the neighborhood had come, but mostly Alice didn't recognize anyone. It seemed as if everyone who had ever known Lauren was there, from her childhood through her college days through her early years in New York before settling down with Tim. Alice was part of Lauren's motherhood life, and it struck her now what a small slice of time that had been. She felt a thin vapor of loneliness, sitting there among so many strangers who had loved Lauren or at least cared enough to see her off. Alice suspected, though, that some of the mourners hadn't ever met Lauren but knew her story and had come out of curiosity. The ones standing at the back of the chapel were clearly reporters, with their casual clothes, notepads, and cameras slung over their necks.

Alice spotted Frannie standing among the reporters. She was dressed in a black skirt suit and black high heels. Her hands were folded behind her back and she leaned against the wall. She nodded, smiling sadly, when she noticed Alice looking at her.

The service lasted over an hour, with Tim following the rabbi as the first speaker. Alice had never known Tim to have trouble with words—as a lawyer, persuasion was his strong suit—but now he struggled to find something to say. "I can't really believe this is happening," he began in a voice that was tinny and thin, scratched from too many cigarettes. From crying himself to sleep or just crying. Alice wanted to rush up to the lectern and save him from the necessity of burying his wife. But she didn't. Couldn't. It had to be done. She stayed in her place on the bench, an unofficial sister, listening as Tim struggled to define—and conclude—a marriage, a woman, a love, a life.

"I met Lauren in law school," he began. "We were married eleven years. . . ."

Then his face seemed to fall apart, shattering like a broken mosaic. And he just wept.

Pressed next to her mother, holding hands, Alice felt her fingers suddenly pressed in a steely grip. She turned to see Lizzie staring intensely at her and realized she had stopped breathing. As soon as she took a breath, Alice found she couldn't swallow enough air. How her mother had known this was beyond her but it became clear Lizzie was worried. She hovered and tended Alice like a child throughout the reception, bringing her plates of food just as Alice and Maggie brought Austin food, though he wasn't interested in eating.

Alice wished she could unleash her mother's doting onto Austin, who stood in the corner and played with the other children. They were taking turns with the yo-yo ball, jointly blocking out the roaming visitors they didn't know and all the voices they didn't want to hear. When a reporter snuck up to take Austin's picture—the stark image of a gaggle of overdressed, smileless children fixated on a single toy—it was Simon who stepped forward to block the shot. Alice was relieved he interceded, preventing one more misrepresentation by the press. She could just see the caption, *An American child at his mother's funeral,* leaving gaping holes for the reader's imagination to fall into. None of the tragic stories Alice had read over the years in the daily papers had come close to the truth. The truth was *this*. And there was no explaining it.

"Off with you," Simon ordered in his deep voice.

The reporter, a skinny young woman, skulked away as Simon crouched among the children. He took the yo-yo ball from Ethan, who was just starting his turn, and squeezed the gelatinous ball, warping it to reveal a hidden eyeball.

"Gross!" Austin said, and all the children giggled.

Simon stood to his full six-foot height and yo-yoed the ball up and down; it jerked with a rubber spasticity that returned it every time.

"What are we going to do about Austin?" Maggie had snuck up behind Alice and Lizzie.

"We'll take care of him," Alice said. "*We'll* be his mothers."

Not wasting a minute to begin her quest to win the little boy's love, Maggie marched over and pressed herself between Simon and Austin. Simon raised his eyebrows and smiled hugely before draping an arm around Maggie's waist. She wiggled closer to him. Austin blushed. All the children knew about Maggie and Simon's bitter divorce, having lived through it at the side of their good friend Ethan. Alice had once eavesdropped on Ethan mimicking his parents' arguing: "I said I was at the chemist's!" "Who spends three hours at the chemist's?" "A devoted father getting medicines for his child. Who do you think?" "Well then," a hearty Maggie-esque laugh, "it must be another one of your children, because ours isn't ill!" During his performance, Ethan postured in vivid mimicry of both his parents' sublime dramatic personae. He had perfectly captured their absurdities and the impossibility of agreement. Every marriage had its own unwinnable argument and theirs had been simple but enormous. SHE: You are unfaithful. HE: I am not. They had parted over this irreconcilable difference.

Mike came up with a small plate of finger foods for Lizzie, who pinched his cheek, then dug in hungrily. "You're a mensch, Michael," she said. "Screw the diet. I'm *starving*."

Alice didn't bother asking, *What diet?* There *was* no diet. This was one way her mother had come to match life: by refusing its petty denials in advance.

"Wow, will you look at that." Mike spoke through a mouthful of bagel and cream cheese, having just noticed the Maggie-and-Simon show playing to the children in the corner.

"They're doing what they know how to," Alice said.

"Power to them," Lizzie said through a bite of mini quiche.

Tim seemed to float across the room like a lone boat seeking familiar mooring. When he saw Lizzie, he nodded politely. "You must be Alice's mother."

"You don't have to make small talk," Lizzie answered.

Tim nodded again, a small, tight nod, as if to stopper an onslaught of emotion.

"Tim, I want to help you," Alice said softly. "Let us take care of Austin as much as you need. After school when you're at work, evenings, weekends, anytime."

"Thank you," he whispered. "I appreciate it."

"We're here for you." Mike patted Tim's shoulder. "Anything at all, just say the word."

Without responding to Mike's comment, Tim's foggy eyes pinioned themselves to Alice's face, as if there was something he needed to say but couldn't. Not because he didn't have the words, this time, but because he couldn't bring himself to issue them. It was a strange, chilling moment in which the unbearable weight of his grief momentarily evaporated. Alice glanced from face to face to see if anyone else had seen it. She wouldn't have been able to explain what had happened, but something, in that moment, had changed.

Then, finally, he spoke. "I don't know if she told you, but it was my idea to have another baby. I wanted that little girl so badly. Now I'll never be able to hold her in my arms." His face grew paler as he spoke, his voice more vaporous. "I don't know what to do."

Alice's heart pounded heavily.

That little girl.

Chapter 14

Alice followed Frannie out of the funeral parlor onto Court Street, into a heavy rain.

"Frannie!"

She turned around. Her black suit was getting soaked.

"Can I talk to you a minute?" Alice stood in a dry strip under the awning.

Frannie nodded but stayed in the rain.

"Come under," Alice said. "Don't get wet."

"I have to be somewhere." Frannie hesitated. "But I guess I can take a minute." She stepped onto the strip of dry pavement, next to Alice.

"Did you hear that?"

Frannie nodded. "I did."

"Tim didn't want to know the baby's sex when Lauren was—" Alice couldn't say it.

"Was alive," Frannie finished the sentence.

"He *refused* to know. He wanted to be surprised. Lauren would have told me if that had changed." This was something Alice felt sure of, they had discussed Tim's *not* knowing so often.

Frannie cocked her head to the side. Her dark eyebrows clamped down. Only now did Alice notice the detective's bright red lipstick.

"Alice, I hate to say this, but don't you think it's possible there are things about your friend's life you didn't know?"

"No," Alice answered, realizing her absurdity even as she spoke. "It isn't possible."

"Alice . . ." Frannie shook her head, gently touching Alice's arm.

"Lauren said that only Maggie and I and Dr. Rose, her obstetrician, knew the baby's sex and her name. The doctor promised not to tell Tim."

Frannie was listening. "And?"

"I don't think Dr. Rose told Tim about the baby being a girl," Alice said, "and I don't think she told him Ivy's name. And neither did you. You never told him the baby was a girl, Frannie, did you?"

Frannie's face was stony, pale. Alice knew she was getting somewhere.

"The doctor didn't tell him anything. If she had, she would have also told him the baby's name. He would have used Ivy's name just now," Alice said.

"How do you know that, Alice? There really isn't any *way* to know that."

The funeral parlor door creaked open. Alice glanced behind her to see Lizzie standing in the door and felt herself shivering again, suffocating almost. She took a deep breath.

"It's just a feeling, I guess," Alice said.

"I thought Tim was your friend."

"He was. I mean he *is*."

"Then why the misgivings?" It was a strange question coming from a detective. But Frannie always somehow derailed Alice's expectations, reminding her she had no reason to expect anything in particular.

"When he said that just now," Alice answered, "how he wanted his little girl, it just hit me. And now I need to know."

"Okay." Frannie lightly touched Alice's shoulder. "I'll ask Dr. Rose. I'll see what I can find out."

"Thank you, Frannie."

"Now I really have to go or I'll be late. I'll call you tomorrow."

Frannie turned down Court Street, walking slowly in the rain, her heels clopping along on the wet sidewalk. Under cover of the angry clouds, the afternoon was darkening prematurely. Alice watched Frannie swerve around a puddle made visible by the wavy, upside-down letters of a flashing blue neon sign.

Turning to her mother, who looked as if she was about to speak, Alice said, "Don't. Please, Mom, just *don't*."

"I wasn't going to say anything," Lizzie said. "Just come inside. You can still catch a cold in summer."

Even without speaking, Alice knew what Lizzie would have said. Something about the dangers of friends turning on each other. Well, Alice didn't suspect Tim of anything. All she needed was an answer to one simple question, which she held back, tucked behind her tongue. They proceeded in a string of cars, through the pouring rain, to Greenwood Cemetery, where Lauren's broken, robbed body would be given to the ground.

Lizzie took Alice, Mike and the kids out to dinner that night. But no one, not even the kids, had much of an appetite. There was little to say; they were all deeply exhausted. As soon as they got home, everyone went right to bed. Alice slept without pills, thoughts or dreams.

In the morning, Lizzie made French toast for everyone, directed conversation over breakfast, then let Mike clean up the mess. Alice went downstairs to shower, and when she came back up, she found Lizzie parked at the kitchen table with a pad of paper and the phone.

Alice caught Mike's attention and rolled her eyes at her mother's irresistible urge to micromanage her production office from afar. But instead of responding in kind, he lifted his eyebrows and conspicuously shifted his gaze to the lined yellow pad.

Alice walked over and looked at her mother's list. In Lizzie's loopy scrawl, she was stunned to see an outline for Alice's own life. *Smith Salon, Saturday 3 p.m., spa package (massage, facial, pedicure); Monday, 10 a.m.,*

Pam Short, Garden Hill Realty, meet @ office, see 3 houses.

Alice's first reaction was outrage. But then, as soon as she thought of both Mike's and Lizzie's imminent departures—he was going to the workshop "for a little while," meaning all day, and a cab was coming in just over an hour to take Lizzie to the airport—she was overcome by gratitude. Lizzie was steering Alice away from pain to her own version of California, away from the longing that had turned her the wrong way into traffic two days ago. Away from the anxiety that had made her follow Frannie out of the funeral parlor yesterday, chasing ghosts and pointing fingers at friends. Lizzie had come all this way to build her only child an entrance ramp back into her own, sane life.

It was a good list, Alice decided, and she would follow it. But it was incomplete. Another scheduling item that neither Lizzie nor Mike knew about yet hovered invisibly between the lines.

When Alice was downstairs just now, Frannie had called her cell, the house phone's call-waiting going ignored.

"I want you to come in tomorrow," Frannie had said. "Mike too. Everyone. We need to go over things again."

Chapter 15

Alice sat down on a stoop across the street from the precinct and waited her turn to be interviewed, again, by the detectives. There were still ten more minutes before her noon appointment. She didn't want to wait inside, knowing that Tim was in there with Frannie and Giometti. They were being stacked into hour-long time slots—Simon, Tim, Alice, Maggie, and Mike—undergoing a mandated evaluation as if to find out what had gone wrong between them. As if they, as a group, had swallowed up Lauren and her baby.

Alice propped her elbows on her knees and lowered her face into her hands, breathing deliberately, deeply, willing her mind to unwind a notch. The sounds of the street began to dissipate and she was transported thirty years backward into her mother's bedroom. Scrunched into her mother's bed, under the covers, eating a bowl of ice cream and watching *Laugh In* on TV. Her father had left them two weeks earlier for *the bimbo* with a doctorate degree. Pressed against her mother's skin, in her parents' bed, in her family's house, Alice drank in the cruel loss, and held in her own pain as a policy against her mother's dissembling. Alice's ice cream that night was strawberry and sweet, and when it dropped from her spoon onto her mother's pillow, nothing was said. The fear she had felt at that moment thirty years ago, in that awful silence, bloomed into her mind now as she sat on the stoop on Union Street. The sticky blossom of memory intruded on her brief rest and her mind sizzled awake.

She thought of the risks people took with lives constructed of fragile compromises, pulling a favorite colored thread out of a whole tapestry, pulling and pulling, destroying years of well-earned love. The denuded aftermath. Her father leaving, just like that. Her mother's pain hardening into a tough, glamorous Hollywood shell—a persona who nevertheless remembered what mattered, and cherished the love of her family.

Alice shook her head, scattering the burdened memories.

It was 11:55. She crossed the street and went into the police station. The attendant at the front desk checked her name off a list and pointed her to the waiting area. This time, she didn't look at the wanted posters; she couldn't bear to see those awful, twisted, needy or, worse, average faces because every one of them was Lauren's killer. Every one of them had held Ivy in his arms. Or had not held her. The possibilities were too cruel to consider.

Alice stood in front of the fish tank and watched the big fish circle the little fish, darting through a miniature landscape of neon coral. One fish hid behind a sunken plastic pirate ship. Someone was keeping the tank meticulously clean.

A familiar voice snagged her attention and she turned to see Tim pass through the lobby. He was with a tall man in a suit and tie, presumably a lawyer. As soon as Tim noticed her, he fell silent. She waved and he waved back, but that was all. The man with him glanced her way, then at Tim, then lifted his chin toward the door and directed them out of the precinct.

Alice watched her friend leave, chilled by his cool departure. What had just happened? Had Frannie and Giometti told him *she* was the one who had pressed the issue of his baby's gender? Had they told him she couldn't be trusted? Was it true? Could any of the friends trust each other anymore? Were they all suspects in Lauren's death?

"Alice." Giometti's soft voice startled her. "Com
with me."

He led her upstairs to the interview room, where Fran
nie sat at the table, waiting.

"Hi, Alice," she said warmly. "Have a seat."

Alice resisted the feeling they were friends. They wer
not friends. She reminded herself that she had been sum
moned here for what basically amounted to a
interrogation.

The light in the room was gritty and dim. As before
the blinds were closed. Giometti sat down next to Fran
nie, who leaned forward to switch on the tape recorder
She stated the date and time, and listed who was in th
room. Then she looked directly at Alice.

"The questions today are mostly routine."

"Okay."

They started with her whereabouts last Friday, when
Lauren first disappeared. Alice repeated everything they
already knew, retold it all until she was emptied of de
tails. She recalled that day as if it were a jewel in
spotlight on a dark stage. She remembered waiting in
the park for Lauren, her growing conviction that Lauren
had had the baby, her excitement about Ivy. She remem
bered all of it with incredulity at her hopefulness that
afternoon. She remembered walking along Court Street
with all four children. The story of her day ended with
the recollection of lying in bed and not sleeping that
night or the next night or the next, the nights rolling
over her in sleepless redux, until finally she crashed the
car. But Alice didn't say any of that; she simply said, "I
went to bed," and eased into a pause that ended the
interview. Frannie's eyes flicked to the wall clock, then
announced the time into the tape recorder and turned
it off.

"Thanks." Giometti half stood and leaned over the
table to extend his hand to Alice.

"That's it?" Alice asked.

"You're done."

"All right if I ask you a question?"

Frannie smiled. "Shoot."

"What just happened in here with Tim?"

Giometti tensed up a little. He glanced at Frannie before answering. "I'm sorry, but that isn't a conversation we can have with you."

Alice looked at Frannie, into her dark eyes. "What did he tell you about the baby? How did he know she was a girl? What did Dr. Rose tell you? Did you even speak with her?"

"We spoke with Dr. Rose," Frannie said, "if it makes you feel any better."

"And?"

"I'll tell you what." Frannie stood up and came around the desk to guide Alice to the door. "If you want to know how Tim found out the baby was a girl, ask your friend. Ask Maggie."

Alice walked out of the police station into the bright afternoon and saw Maggie walking slowly up Union Street, late for her one o'clock appointment. She was wearing a tight yellow skirt that flared just below her knees and a pair of the dove-gray suede shoes with spiky one-inch heels that had come into the store just yesterday. Alice felt a quick bleed of irritation.

"I hope you paid for those," she called down the street.

"What?" Maggie kept her slow pace.

Alice came down the steps. Maggie stopped three feet in front of her.

"What is it, Alice?"

"I'm a little confused." Alice plucked a dime from her sundress pocket and ran her thumb along its ridge. "I saw Tim walk out of here an hour ago, with a lawyer."

"I see." The sun hit Maggie's eyes, washing them out. "And if I pay for my shoes, that becomes easier to bear?"

Alice gathered herself. She couldn't shrink from this. "Mags, did you tell Tim about Ivy?"

"Being a girl?"

Alice nodded.

The sun shifted, and in the sudden clarity Maggie's gaze swung from Alice's face to her own elegant feet. "Wonderful, aren't they?" She leaned in to kiss Alice's cheek. "And yes, I paid my full discounted rate, as agreed." She winked and headed up the stairs.

"Well?" Alice asked.

Maggie stopped and twisted to look behind her. Her face became serious. "That's a long conversation. I'll be with Ethan the rest of the day. Meet me at the shop in the morning, okay? We'll talk while we finish up receipts. Did you know Martin's left us three messages to reschedule quarterly taxes?" She walked through the open doorway and disappeared into the precinct.

Chapter 16

Walking along Smith Street the next morning, on her way to Blue Shoes, Alice heard her mother's voice ring through her mind. *Flowers,* she thought, recalling one of Lizzie's silly yet forceful statements when Alice had been dumped by her first teenage boyfriend. Lizzie had come home from work with an armload of African daisies, declaring, "Flowers *will* mend a broken heart." Alice turned into the spiffy new florist just past Butler Street, smiling as she approached the counter.

"Good morning!" A man with shoulder-length brown hair tucked behind his ears stepped out from a back room. "What can I do for you?"

"Peonies," Alice said, overlooking the stylishly presented offerings of exotic bouquets. "I know they're out of season, but do you have any?"

"They're not out of season in the hothouse." He led her into a nook toward the back of the store, where a green plastic bucket was crammed with whitish pink peonies in various stages of bloom. "I just got them this morning—haven't had a chance to separate them yet."

"Don't," Alice said. Peonies had been Lauren's favorite flower. "I'll take them all."

Ten minutes later, she left the store, arms loaded with two dozen peonies wrapped in clear cellophane with a sky-blue ribbon tied at the bottom. She had also selected an oversized glass vase and placed a standing weekly order for peonies, which had delighted the man so much he gave her the vase for nothing. Alice inhaled the gentle perfume of the flowers as she walked three more blocks to Blue Shoes.

Maggie was already there, reorganizing piles of receipts along the counter into the same stacks that had been hastily dissembled five days ago, just last Monday, when Lauren's body was found.

"Lovely!" Maggie ran over to take the large bag with the vase. She poked her nose into Alice's armload of peonies. "Ah, yes, I see."

"We'll always have them," Alice said. "For her."

"It's a perfect idea, Alice." Maggie looked like she might cry. "You're the most marvelous friend and I've been truly awful." She collected herself and faced Alice, who felt some kind of betrayal coming and needed to settle in first. She hated having things thrown at her the minute she walked in a door: greetings, news, confessions. She had always felt that if she was prepared, she could handle anything.

"Help me with these," Alice said.

Maggie filled the vase with water in the bathroom at the back of the store, then returned with it, straining under its weight. "Where do you think?"

"The counter, for now," Alice said. "Maybe we'll get a pedestal made at that cast iron place on Bergen Street."

Maggie set the vase carefully on the pale green counter. Together, they cut the bottoms of each peony and arranged them in the vase. They were lush and glorious. Their perfume triggered Alice's queasiness but she didn't care. She pressed her nose into the soft petals and breathed. She felt a maternal swing toward the burgeoning life in her womb, and sensed her old happiness like a river at her feet.

"I'm still in love with Simon."

"Well, that's no surprise, Mags. But I thought you made a decision."

"I did."

Alice stood back and looked at Maggie and waited. She could tell there was more.

"Look, Alice, we sleep together now and then."

This *was* news. "But you're divorced!"

"Not exactly." Maggie's face creaked open with a naughty smile.

"But you said—"

"I told you the papers had come through. We simply never signed them."

Suddenly Alice understood. With Maggie's typical lack of discipline, in the rush of her irreverence, she had shared secrets with Simon, little offerings to bind him to their endangered intimacy. Things he probably didn't even care about, like the gender of Lauren's baby, providing him with a blip of amusement or interest. Like a spy Maggie had passed Ivy on to Simon, who had passed her on to Tim. Now that Alice realized what had happened, it made sense. Maggie and Simon's passion had always spilled over their ability to contain it, messily invading the space of innocent bystanders.

Alice stood across from Maggie. The peonies loomed beside them.

"I understand," Alice said quietly.

"I couldn't help myself. I didn't mean to tell him. It just slipped out. And I certainly never imagined I'd be questioned by the police about it."

The thought of Maggie explaining herself to the detectives seemed punishment enough.

As the morning progressed, Alice felt a bubbling of anger at Maggie for having withheld such a significant piece of information, not that Maggie and Simon were lovers again, but that Tim had known the baby was a girl. No wonder Frannie and Giometti kept hashing over the same stories, having been given reason to question the friends' reliability.

Maybe they were right, Alice thought, as she headed home just after one o'clock. She walked down Smith Street lugging groceries in several plastic bags whose handles cut into her fingers. The labor of carrying the heavy bags and the pain it caused her felt deserved. She had pushed Frannie to investigate Tim, her friend, when all along another friend had held the answer. Alice felt betrayed by *herself*, but also by Maggie for the lie of omission that had led her to the misstep. Much as Maggie had felt betrayed by Simon for never explaining his hours-long absences, and as Frannie had undoubtedly experienced a betrayal, hidden beneath the friendly veneer, when Alice marched into the precinct to announce her own lie of omission.

Alice turned onto President Street, and felt the draining force of her pregnancy. She took a deep breath and marched forward.

As she walked toward their house, past summer gardens lush with impatiens and marigolds and no Lauren—everywhere she went, *no Lauren*—she became aware of an incessant honking. She noticed the jammed traffic, then the moving truck two-thirds down the block, its girth blocking the flow.

That was right, she remembered now: their new landlord was moving in today.

She walked up the stoop into the shadowy front hall, set her bags down on the floor outside her own entrance and called up the wide stairs.

"Hello?"

She immediately heard a rumble of footsteps and a large man came down the stairs. He was wearing gray sweatpants that had been cut off into shorts, but his legs didn't merit them; they were heavy and pale, with sparse black hairs. He was sweating in a white sleeveless undershirt through which his stomach bulged. His curly pitch-black hair was obviously dyed, and his face was flaccid, jowly. But what most struck Alice, truly surprised her, was his glasses. They were trendy in a way he clearly was not, minimalist rectangles in plastic lilac frames. He hadn't shaved that morning, but it was his moving day, so it was understandable. Alice decided she would force herself to accept this man, if only out of a survivor's instinct.

She offered a hand. "I'm Alice Halpern."

He shook her hand without bothering to wipe off the sweat. She held her smile.

"Julius Pollack," he said in a syrupy voice that reminded her, strangely, of yellowed lacquer.

He made hard, immediate eye contact and seemed to wait for her to speak.

"Mr. Pollack," she began, bolstering her tone with confidence, professionalism; holding herself still against his keen stare. "I don't know exactly how much Joey told you about our situation. We asked him to explain. We—"

"He told me you were still here." Julius Pollack smiled stiffly. A plastic smile to match his lacquer voice. He gave her the creeps. "And now I'm here. We're here together."

Once again, he stared at her and waited.

"Buying a house takes time," she told him.

The smile. He knew that; she felt foolish for having said it.

"We have children," she explained. "We need a certain kind of space. And as you know, the market right now is—"

"I don't want an explanation." His syrupy tone had gone chokingly sweet. "Just a date, in writing, before the end of the month. Telling me when you'll be gone."

"I'm sorry?"

"No you're not."

Bloodsuckers, Alice heard the snap of Lauren's voice. *I'm starting to hate those bloodsuckers for putting us through this.* A strong emotion curled through Alice's mind, a hybrid feeling of deepening and unrequitable love for Lauren merged confusingly with loathing. Already she detested this man, this Julius Pollack, and they had only just met. This was the man who had signed the Thirty Day Notice. The man to whom she needed to explain their situation; to politely ask—no, *beg*—for more time. What *was* their situation? A sealed-tight real estate market and now this, *this,* the unbearable loss of her beloved friend. Lauren's loss was like a bag over her head, incapacitating her, heightening her senses. She wanted to tear off the bag, find herself somewhere in the mush of this last week, strip off every raw iota of pain and throw it at this awful man for insulting her. Scream at him, *This is for Lauren. She would not have tolerated your arrogance. You wear the bag, you asshole.*

But Alice wasn't Lauren; her words did not spark as nimbly off the flare of emotion. Alice stood in the hallway, struck dumb, unable to react, while Julius Pollack, *owner,* turned away from her and stepped into a slant of light at the front door. His voice cloyed at the movers: "*Please* be careful with my things!" As he walked onto the front stoop, Alice noticed the hulk of his back rising in two hairy flanks from the neck of his undershirt.

She carried her bags into the apartment, where on the kitchen table she found a note from Mike. He had taken the kids to the movies. Without them the apartment felt empty. Hollow. She put the groceries away and sat in the quiet of her kitchen, only it didn't feel like her kitchen anymore. After fifteen years, it suddenly didn't even feel much like her home. It was Julius Pollack's house. The Thirty Day Notice had made that perfectly clear, and now the man, in person, more than anything an *owner,* had *owned* his right to begin eviction proceedings if they weren't out in, now, twenty days.

Glancing at the notepad on the table, scribbled with notes and lists and phone messages, she thought of the appointment her mother had made for her to meet with that real estate broker. Alice peeled back the two top sheets and felt a pang of comfort at the sight of her mother's rounded script: *Monday, 10 a.m., Pam Short, Garden Hill Realty, meet @ office, see 3 houses.* Pam Short was the one Sylvie claimed could find a house for anyone. Alice had not planned on keeping the appointment—the idea of house hunting in her emotional fog had been impossible—but now she knew with certainty that she had no real choice.

A date, in writing, before the end of the month. Telling me when you'll be gone.

Creep. *Bloodsucker.* But Alice knew she couldn't fight him. They had no lease and it was his house. She picked up the phone and confirmed her appointment by leaving a message on Pam Short's voice mail, deliberately making it harder for herself to change her mind.

Chapter 17

Garden Hill Realty was on Court Street next to the monolithic Old St. Paul's Church, where you could play bingo on Saturdays, pray on Sundays, attend AA meetings on weeknights and shop for organic produce on Tuesday afternoons in summer. Through Garden Hill's gated storefront window, Alice could see a gold etching of the Brooklyn Bridge with trees blending into the words YOUR GATEWAY TO BROWNSTONE BROOKLYN. LICENSED BROKER: JUDITH GERSTEN. The window postings of house sales showed prices upward of two million dollars. They couldn't possibly have something in Alice's price range, she thought, but regained herself quickly; she wouldn't let the high market deter her. There *had* to be something out there for them, even if it was just another rental.

Alice looked at her watch. It was ten past ten; Pam was late. She looked as far down Court Street as she could, studying faces for one that might be Pam Short. But it was, of course, from the other direction that the woman arrived, startling Alice.

"Hello!" Her voice had the tonal clarity of a bell. "I'm *so* sorry I'm late!"

Pam Short was in fact not short at all; she was a good three inches taller than Alice's five foot six, and at least fifty pounds heavier. Pam's caftan, with its swirling pink and orange print, reminded Alice of things her mother used to wear in the late sixties, when she had seemed so *cool* to a very young Alice. Pam's shoulder-length brown hair shone with the bright red patina that had recently come into fashion. Her pink lipstick matched a predominant shade in her caftan. Lastly Alice noticed the woman's shoes: her feet bulged out of the same red, rhinestone-encrusted leather flip-flops that had looked so dainty on Sylvie's slender feet. As a foundation for Pam Short's large, magnificent persona, the sandals were a sly wink. Perfect, Alice thought, for how they defied expectations.

Pam rattled a large keychain out of her purse and unlocked the long metal box on the wall that contained the storefront gate's chain pull. With a few deft tugs, the gate scrolled up. Inside, Pam brushed a hand upward on a panel of switches and the lights came on all at once, opening the room like the page of a pop-up book. The walls were pale pink, and what looked like an original tin ceiling had been painted cream. Two antique ceiling fans slowly turned. On every wall, pinpoint lights illuminated photos of Old Brooklyn with its pastures, farms and shanties, paired with photos of New Brooklyn with its gracious homes and gardens. An oriental-carpeted aisle separated two rows of four desks each, all with tidy desktops, except for one at the far end on the right side. That desk alone was busy with knickknacks, and behind it were three framed needlepoint legends Alice couldn't read from the distance.

Pam sat at the very first desk on the right, the one with the best view of the street. Alice sat in a chair at the side of the desk. Folding her pudgy hands together on top of a white binder, Pam faced Alice squarely.

"Before we start, I've just gotta tell you how sorry I am about your friend. Sylvie told me about her and I've been reading about it in the papers. You must be a wreck, and in your state. I *feel* for you."

"Thank you," Alice said. "I appreciate it. My mom thought I should get back on my feet, so she made this appointment, but—"

"We can do this another time," Pam gently interrupted. "We can reschedule."

"No, I have to do this now. My mother's right. Our new landlord already served us a Thirty Day Notice. He wants us out, no discussion."

"Don't tell me you have the lower duplex."

"We have the lower duplex."

"I hear you, honey."

Pam booted up her computer and started flipping through the white binder. "Your mother said you were looking for a house, minimum two-family, but frankly we'd be idiots not to look at three. The double income makes a big dent in the mortgage, and she said you could look in the eight-hundred-thousand-dollar range, but I think you could start higher. Hell, you'll *have* to start higher in this market, but don't worry, we'll do the math and you'll see what I mean."

As Pam spoke, she stuck hot pink Post-it notes on the edges of some of the notebook's pages. She wore four rings on each hand, including a wedding ring that was almost lost beneath a red plastic sphere.

"Do you want to look at rentals too? Give yourself time to find the perfect house to buy?"

The perfect house. Was there such a thing? Alice saw herself surrounded by towers of boxes, her lungs filled with dust, her muscles aching through and through from shuffling all their stuff from one place to another. Two demanding children and, soon enough, two crying babies. "I am not a gypsy," Lauren had said to Alice just three weeks ago, accepting half of Alice's bagel at the Autumn Café. She could see Lauren biting down into the dense bread and taste the cool, rich cream cheese on her own tongue. "In America we have rights," Lauren had said. "That's the whole point."

"No," Alice told Pam. "We just want to buy. I don't want to move twice."

Pam nodded. Alice was sure she saw the quick pull of a dimple in Pam's cheek, the suppression of a smile as she flipped the pages of her notebook, sticking on Post-its.

"It looks like there actually might be a few possibilities," Alice said.

Pam stopped turning pages and fixed her eyes on Alice. "Honey, there are always possibilities. I'm in the business of making things happen. I've never failed a customer who seriously wanted to buy."

Pam quickly lined up appointments to show Alice houses: two first thing the next morning, one later in the afternoon, and one the day after.

The next day Alice dropped the kids off at school and then wandered slowly toward the address Pam had given her on First Place between Court and Clinton Streets. Because she was early for the nine o'clock appointment, she took a circuitous route up Carroll Street and all the way to Henry, basking in the long shadows of the houses on the north side of the street. Each brownstone facade was a cipher of history and tumult and the passions of lives that had passed through it. Most of the houses in the neighborhood were built in the 1800s, back when babies were born at home, deeds were kept in the family, and grandparents died in their childhood beds. She turned the corner at Henry onto First Place, passing tall, wide houses with their gated front gardens abundant with roses.

A glance at her watch told her to hurry. She quickened her pace to the corner of Clinton, where she waited for a small burst of traffic to pass. It was then, in that brief pause, that she noticed the large gray-haired man with the mismatched eyes, the limo driver from the other morning by the canal, sitting on a stoop across the street. He seemed to be watching her, and as soon as she noticed him, he nodded. Just like before. This time, she didn't nod back. He was weird, and she didn't like him; sometimes this urban village could get too small. If that eerie-eyed man on the stoop lived in the house it was attached to, it was one strike against the block.

She kept walking, almost there.

Pam had told her that the owner was asking only seven hundred thousand dollars. Only. Alice wondered when she had joined the ranks who thought that was a bargain. But for this neighborhood, it was. "Heart of Carroll Gardens," Pam had read from her sheet. Four floors, owner's triplex, one rental, unusually narrow at fourteen feet wide, and only twenty-five feet deep, lots of potential. Available immediately. Before even getting to the house, Alice had spun a fantasy about fulfilling the abundant potential of her unseen, centrally located, bargain home. It would be their quick route away from Julius Pollack. But as soon as she saw it, her stomach dropped.

Lots of potential, she learned in the instant her eyes fell on the lean, brick husk, meant *gut renovation required.* Pam was waiting for her outside, scribbling in her notebook. When she saw Alice, she started walking.

"I'm *sorry,*" she said with such conviction Alice believed she really meant it. "It's a new listing and I never saw it. Can you believe this crap? I couldn't even show it to you if you wanted to see it. It has no floors! Come on. We'll grab some coffee before the next stop."

They went around the corner to La Traviata Café, stood at the counter and ordered cappuccino for Pam and an orange juice for Alice. Stock photos of Frank Sinatra competed with a life-size poster of Placido Domingo on the rear, brick wall. It was a funny hodgepodge of a place, offering the *Post* and the *News,* a few women's magazines, a single rack of paperback books and an eclectic assortment of opera and rap CDs. Candy and gum were arranged on slanted shelves beneath a counter that held both cash register and huge, gleaming espresso machine. The air was rich with the smell of strong coffee and by the time Pam's arrived, Alice felt ill. She regretted ordering juice; it would be too acidic on her queasy stomach.

They picked up their drinks and sat at the single outdoor table. Pam blew craters into her milky foam and stirred in a packet of sugar.

"That place," Alice said, thinking about the house and the limo driver as if an ill-willed cloud hovered over their shared territory.

"Forget it." Pam sipped her coffee. "Every house is a blind date. It's hit or miss, mostly miss. You move on."

"I'll remember that."

"You never looked before?"

"We've lived in the same place for fifteen years. Before we changed careers, we could have bought something easily. We *should* have, then. But we had a great apartment that was a great deal, so why bother?"

One side of Pam's soft face puckered. "You wouldn't believe how much I hear that. Back when nobody knew about this place, that was when you should have struck. Now?" She shrugged her shoulders. "Never mind. You've got a down payment and good savings, and your store's a keeper. I just feel it in my toes." Pam let out a burst of laughter and kicked one foot out from under the table. Alice recognized her shoes immediately: round-toed fawn-colored wedgies.

"You're the one who bought those?" They were among the most recent arrivals in the store, expensive ditties at three hundred dollars apiece. "Why haven't I ever seen you at the store?"

"I go late in the day, after work."

Maggie's shift. Perfect alchemy: Maggie's charm, eager feet and an open wallet.

Pam looked at her watch.

"Do we need to go now?" Alice asked.

"We've got a few minutes still." Pam pushed her empty mug across the table and sat back. "So you might as well tell me about this new landlord of yours."

A city bus pulled up, let out two women and a diesel burp, then groaned back into traffic. "He's a nightmare," Alice began. "The timing couldn't be worse. Between the twins coming and Lauren's . . ." She became dizzy at the memory of Lauren's ruined body being hauled out of the canal. "I'm having trouble just getting out of bed in the morning. But we can't live under the same roof as that man. Lauren was fighting an eviction. She was a *fighter*. But not me." The flow of words unlatched something in her and she found herself talking, pouring out. She told Pam all about Lauren and their friendship, describing Lauren's disappearance and discovery in detail, along with her hopes for Ivy. She even told Pam what Ivy looked like, or what Alice imagined her to look like: small, light brown hair, Lauren's pale blue eyes. As she gushed, Alice began to feel embarrassed, realizing that what she really needed wasn't a real estate agent but a therapist to listen to her winding recollections, disturbances and unanswerable questions. Pam Short might have made an excellent therapist, Alice was just thinking, when Pam suddenly interrupted.

"She lived where?"

Alice repeated Lauren's address. "Her husband's there alone now, with their son."

Pam's eyes narrowed. "You said they have the second floor on the B side? Three bedrooms, lots of details, great kitchen, deck to the yard?"

"How do you know all that?"

"That listing just came in to us. We were given an October one occupancy date. I guess he's giving up the fight."

Alice was shocked. Tim was moving? Where would he and Austin go? Would they stay in the neighborhood? Why hadn't he said anything about his plans?

"Well, you won't have any trouble renting it," Alice muttered, "since it's stabilized."

"Stabilized, hell! That place is at the top of the market. They're asking thirty-two hundred for it, if I remember right."

"But Lauren and Tim only pay eleven hundred," Alice said. "It's *stabilized*. It can't go up that much, can it?"

"Only if the rent hits two thousand or there's been significant renovation." Pam shook her head. "I hate it when the landlords lie to us. What do they think we are, idiots?"

"But you can't be responsible for knowing something's stabilized, can you?"

"If it's registered, I am. *Shit.* Sorry—I can't curse when I'm at home. Ray hates it." Pam drummed her fingers on the table. "No point worrying about that now, right? I'll look it up when I get back to the office. Ready to rock and roll?"

As they walked to their next appointment, Alice considered that if Lauren's apartment could go for that much money, hers would go for even more. Because their apartment was in a two-family building, it wasn't covered by any rent controls. It seemed they were paying only a third of its market value, and it hit her that Julius Pollack might want their apartment not for himself but for its potential income. Maybe he wasn't motivated by a desire to live in the building's better space but by the same money lust that was dogging so many of the new local owners. Of course, that was it. That was *always* it. Julius Pollack didn't care about the Halpern family *or* the space from which he was evicting them; he cared about money, lusted after it in the same contagion that had wiped out most of the neighborhood's old-timers since Alice and Mike had first arrived.

The next house was better than the first, but still depressing. Alice came away from her first bout of house hunting feeling flattened. She walked along Court Street with Pam, hearing a pep talk that must have been well worn by now.

"See you later," Pam said, pumping her fist in the air. "Upward and onward. The next one is much better, I promise you. Kiss those gorgeous shoes hello for me."

"I will," Alice promised. It was after eleven, already late to open Blue Shoes. But Alice had something she needed to do first, something she just couldn't get off her mind. She needed to make a quick stop by Tim's apartment to find out what was going on, if it was true that he was leaving.

Chapter 18

Tim hesitated a moment before telling Alice, "Come on up," and buzzing her into the building. That catch in his voice was the first bad sign. The next was the stack of bulging plastic garbage bags accumulated in the hallway outside his front door. *Lauren's* front door. Was he throwing out her things?

The door was cracked open, so Alice walked in. Austin was playing on the living room floor in his pajamas. She bent to kiss the top of his head.

"Where's Daddy?"

"In the kitchen." He didn't break his gaze from his toys to look at her. She wondered how long Tim would keep him out of school.

In the galley kitchen off the living room, Tim was in the midst of an excavation of appliances, dishes, pots and pans. The mini food processor Alice had recently given Lauren as a prebaby present—for pureeing baby food—was in a pile on the counter, still boxed. Tim stood in the middle of the kitchen looking enervated, beyond exhaustion.

"What are you doing, Tim?"

"I was going to tell you and Mike tomorrow." Tim reached into his shirt pocket and pulled out his pack of cigarettes. He slipped one out and was about to light it.

"Tim," Alice said, "I'm pregnant. Please don't." She was surprised by her own assertiveness. They had crossed a boundary: she had caught him at something he was no longer to be pampered so gingerly. He laid the cigarette on the counter and slid the pack back into his pocket.

"Sorry." He opened his hands beseechingly. "Alice, I *am* sorry. I don't want to go. I don't want any of this. I don't want it! But I can't go back to work and I can't stay here."

"We'll help you, Tim. Please let us—"

"You don't understand." He moved to the sink and brusquely turned on the cold tap, rinsing his hands and drying them on his shirt. "It isn't about money. I can afford to stay home in terms of *money*. I just can't be here. Do you understand? I can't *be* here anymore."

Yes, Alice understood. How could she not understand the desire to flee the places that resonated with Lauren? Every minute of every day Lauren shimmered around her. She knew. But there was more than just herself to think about; she had a family. And so did Tim.

"What about Austin?"

"He'll be fine. We'll take a break, go somewhere new."

"You're taking him out of school?"

"It's kindergarten, Alice. He'll be fine." In a burst of irritation, Tim picked up his unlit cigarette, twirled it in his fingers, then put it back on the counter. "We'll be back, I'll get a new place, I'll go back to work, but nothing will ever be the same."

"Where are you going?"

Tim shrugged deeply and with such finality that Alice knew it was a question he couldn't answer. But how could she just let them leave? How could Austin, especially, be taken from the people he'd known as family his entire life?

"Out west probably. For the winter. We'll come back in the spring."

Alice nodded slowly. "How will we reach you?"

"I'll call you when I have an address, okay? Alice, we won't forget any of you. We're not leaving *you*. We're just . . . leaving."

Alice thought of something she had to ask, even if it pained him. "What about the investigation? Do the police know you're going?"

"I cleared it with them. They're done with me, Alice," he said with such bitterness that she knew, she just knew he believed she no longer trusted him. He picked up his cigarette and abruptly lit it. "Listen, I've got movers coming in two days. All this stuff's going into storage. I've got to get back to packing or . . ." He didn't finish the sentence but he didn't have to; Alice knew the ending: *or I'll go crazy.*

"Don't leave without saying good-bye, Tim. Please?"

His eyes, green as moss, considered her. He balanced his burning cigarette half off the counter, crossed the narrow kitchen and took her in his arms. This close, his smoky smell was pungent.

"Of course we'll say good-bye."

"I'll miss you and Austin so much," she whispered into his coarse blond hair, feeling Lauren well up inside her, burying her own face in her husband's neck for the last time.

Alice stopped on her way through the living room, where Austin had circled a tiny cowboy with a ring of brown plastic cows. She bent down to kiss his soft cheek.

"You smell like cinnamon." She kissed him again, then added in a whisper: "I love you." Austin froze as she ran her fingers gently over his face, memorizing every curve and swoop of bone and flesh.

She let herself out, deliberately not turning around for final glances. Walked slowly down the stairs, through the building's front door and into the hot, noisy neighborhood. Walked steadily toward Blue Shoes. She would open the store, late. Sit there. Serve customers. Go through the paces. There was no place she felt she could easily be today, so it didn't matter where she was. The life of the street continued and she felt soaked by a sensation of helplessness. In less than two weeks, one third of her life—the Barnet family—had spun into oblivion like an extinguished star.

She stopped in front of a corner deli whose window was papered with magazine covers. A sidewalk rack held the day's newspapers. Lauren had become a subset, a little box in the corner of the dailies. POLICE HUNT FOR MOTHER'S KILLER, NO CLUES. UNBORN BABY STILL MISSING. LADY KILLER STILL LOOSE IN BROOKLYN. Moment to moment, Lauren's death was fading from the front page. Tomorrow, would it even be there?

Alice picked up the *New York Times* and looked at the Metro section. For the first time in days, the reporter who had been following Lauren's case did not have something on the front page. Alice searched her memory for the reporter's name. Erin Brinkley, that was it.

She wondered if she should call Erin. Talk to her. Give her the forbidden nugget of held-back fact: that Ivy was a girl. Alice fished her cell phone out of her purse and flipped it open. Slowly, she dialed Information. She could call the newspaper and be connected with the reporter in minutes. Splash the news of Ivy over the front pages so people would know what they were looking for, not just a baby but a baby *girl*. Alice could tell Erin Brinkley everything.

But then she thought of Frannie and Giometti. Ivy's gender was being held back on purpose; the detectives had to know what they were doing. Alice flipped shut her phone; making secret calls was not for her. She would not be the one to jeopardize the case. Instead, she would stick to what she could do: care for her family, run her business, find a new home.

After three hours at Blue Shoes, tending the shelf life of beautiful, overpriced shoes, chatting with browsers and watching street traffic pass from her side of their sparkling plate-glass window, Alice still couldn't get her mind off Tim and Austin's leaving. For the hour they overlapped, from two to nearly three, she and Maggie analyzed and deconstructed Tim's decision and discussed how to tell the children that Austin would be gone for a while.

"It's going to break their hearts," Maggie said. "For them it'll be another death."

"Mags, that's too extreme. He'll be back."

"I think Tim's leaving for good. I think he's had enough."

"I hope you're wrong," Alice said.

"I only know that if it were me, I'd be gone. This whole place would be too painful." Maggie dinged open the cash register drawer for no reason other than dramatic effect, then pushed it shut.

Maggie had a point. The more Alice thought about it, the more she wondered why she and Mike were staying in the neighborhood. Why didn't they let the situation with Julius Pollack eject them not just to another house but to another city? Another state? *Why live here?* she wondered as she walked to school to pick up Nell and Peter. Why not move south, where it was always warm? Or north, where they could ski in winter and enjoy cool summers? Or overseas, away from their roots, where they could raise sophisticated, multilingual children far from the crass commercialism of American culture? Why stay here at all?

Because, Alice thought as she turned right onto Carroll Street and stopped in front of the school, *because this was their home. It was where they lived.* Having come to Brooklyn via a childhood in Long Island, then California, Alice had long felt that this little neighborhood was the true home of her soul. She also knew, from her mother's flight from pain, that there was no real transportation away from the loss of Lauren and Ivy. That would linger anywhere, everywhere. By the time the children appeared with their classes at the door, Alice had stopped even considering the possibility of leaving town. They were here and they would stay.

Nell and Peter held Alice's hands and chattered about their days as they walked over to Maggie's apartment. Sylvie had agreed to watch them, with Ethan, for an hour or so; she was always happy to double up the babysitting, both to earn extra money and provide Ethan with a built-in play date. And Alice had decided it would be better to house hunt as much as possible without the chaos of little voices. There were enough voices causing conflict in her mind as it was.

The next house was a wide Clinton Street brownstone with single-pane windows that ran from floor to ceiling and were so clean they reflected the shimmering light that played on the leaves of a big sycamore tree out front. It was a large, five-story house with fancy iron-work and carved wooden double doors that looked re-cently varnished. It even had an indoor garage—a rare amenity in Brownstone Brooklyn—with a driveway lead-ing down to the half-submerged basement level. An old rosebush, covered with masses of yellow roses, leaned against the house. Alice loved the house the minute she saw it. She sat on the front stoop, waited for Pam, and imagined herself coming home here. It felt right, perfect even, and she knew in the same thought that it couldn't possibly be within her reach. She wouldn't even go in-side, she decided, if the price was too high.

As soon as she saw Pam trundle up the street in her neon orange caftan and new wedgies, Alice got up from the stoop and went to greet her. They kissed each other on the cheek like old friends.

"How much?" Alice asked.

"See it first."

"How much?"

"You're going to love this one. We can work the numbers."

"I knew it."

"Just come inside."

Alice shook her head. "Tell me."

"One point nine." Pam sunk her gaze onto Alice's. "But everything's negotiable. Let's go in."

Alice knew it couldn't be that negotiable, but the temptation was too great and she felt her resistance drain away. She would see it as a voyeur, she decided, not a potential buyer.

"Are the owners home?" Alice couldn't bear to face

them, whoever they were; they would know the minute they saw her that this wasn't her level of house.

Pam jangled a set of keys out of her pocket. "Both at work."

Alice followed Pam up the stoop.

The front hallway was spacious, with a white marble floor and a glittering crystal chandelier. The living room was huge and ornamented, without all the layers of paint that ruined the details of so many local homes. Everything about the house bespoke wealth.

"What do they do for a living?" Alice whispered, as if they might hear her from their vast distance.

"Who knows?" Pam winked. "Yada yada yada."

They made a quick tour through the restaurant-quality kitchen, the master suite upstairs with its renovated bathroom and closet-lined dressing room, and three bedrooms upstairs. Alice didn't have the heart to enter the landscaped backyard; she only glimpsed it from a top-floor window.

"Why did you bring me here?" Alice asked Pam, when they returned to the parlor floor.

Pam put her purse on the dining room table. "Because I wanted you to see what was possible."

The women stared at each other.

"This house isn't even for sale, is it?" Queasiness rose into Alice's throat.

"No."

"Is this your house?"

"You bet it is. Wanna know how much I paid for this place?"

"One point nine, I guess." Alice's tone was hard but she didn't correct it or try to apologize. "I'm leaving."

"Wrong!" Pam followed her to the front door. "I paid one hundred fifty thousand dollars for this house, seventeen years ago. At the time I thought it was way overpriced. I said forget it, but my husband showed me the math and I knew he was right."

"There's no math that could convince me I could ever get a house like this, Pam."

"Wrong again! Come here. I've got something to show you."

Alice put her hand on the knob but didn't turn it. She hated real estate, hated this whole thing. Maybe she was wrong; maybe she *could* wrest her soul out of Brooklyn.

"Give me five minutes of your time!" Pam delivered the ultimate salesman's pitch with such enthusiasm that Alice burst out laughing.

"All right," Alice said. "Five minutes."

Pam set them up at her dining room table with a legal pad and a calculator. Twenty minutes later, Alice was convinced that she and Mike could afford to pay one point two million dollars for a house, so long as it came with two rental apartments and was in a good enough area to command high rents. She was flabbergasted.

"Your one point two today," Pam said, "was my hundred-fifty thou yesterday. And another piece of good news. I did a little research this afternoon. Even though your friend's apartment was stabilized, it wasn't registered with Housing, so the ball's in the landlord's court if anyone decides to play him." Pam threw up her hands, showing Alice the backs of her bloated fingers, pinched by their rings. "But when I saw who it was, I knew it wasn't going to be me, no way. Julius Pollack is the worst scum landlord I ever saw. I wasn't one bit surprised."

Chapter 19

Alice was stunned by the news that Julius Pollack had been Lauren's landlord. All these years Lauren's landlord had been Metro Properties, a cold, corporate entity. Now, with a name attached—and not just any name but that of a man whose callousness Alice could personally vouch for—the vitriolic fight at the other end of Lauren and Tim's eviction made perfect sense. Alice was so upset by the revelation that, by the time she turned the corner onto Warren Street, she had broken into a near run.

Her mind spun with questions. Hadn't she mentioned Julius Pollack's name to Pam at the coffee shop that morning? How could she have left out that crucial detail? Should she have recognized the importance of his name? *Julius Pollack.* It was just a name. It had never occurred to her until this moment that there could be such a thing as a real estate tycoon in their little neighborhood; that the tenants of Carroll Gardens might be puppets; that above them, one man held all their strings, twitching them to his own purposes. Alice ran faster, her babies jostling within her, a heavy sweat collecting on her face. By the time she reached Maggie's, she was so exhausted she could hardly climb the stoop.

"What's wrong?" Sylvie opened the door and stared at Alice.

"I was afraid I was late." Her breathing was labored and she forced a slow, calming breath. "The kids okay?"

"Fine. They haven't stopped playing since they got here. Come in, let me get you something to drink."

"Water would be nice."

Alice followed Sylvie into Maggie's all-white kitchen and sat on a counter stool, catching her breath, while Sylvie poured her a glass of ice water. The sudden coldness on her tongue and its wash down her throat calmed her. She drank another long swallow.

"I just found out," Alice said, "that my new landlord and Lauren's old landlord are the same man."

Sylvie's eyebrows rose. "Oh?"

"Pam told me. Apparently the man's even worse than I thought."

Alice drained her glass and set it on the marble counter. Sylvie sat on the stool next to her. Small, sharp voices rose from the downstairs bedroom level, approaching the pitch of trouble before unwinding suddenly in laughter.

"I feel like there's some relevance," Alice said, "but I can't put my finger on it."

Sylvie picked up Alice's glass and crossed the kitchen to refill it.

"Thanks," Alice said. She drank only half the water this time, finally sated. "Pam said she's going to check him out for me. She's really something, isn't she? Thanks for introducing us."

"Please," Sylvie said. "Anything I can do."

The kids came streaming up the stairs, locked in a three-way battle over a single toy. They all had their hands around it and moved in a clump, unraveling at the top of the stairs to reveal the point of contention: a tiny Lego astronaut with a visor that moved. Nell had the prized toy in her steel-tight grip, with both boys clawing at her hands to get it.

"Ethan," Sylvie commanded, "share your toys with your guests!"

Alice walked over to pry the children apart. "Nell, let it go. It's Ethan's. I said let it go."

"You see?" Ethan's voice rose triumphantly. "It *is*

mine." He stood apart, apparently satisfied with that fact having been established.

"Give it to me, Nell," Alice said, pulling Peter off his sister. "Now."

Nell handed over the one-inch plastic toy. Alice held it up and shook her head.

"You guys are friends," she said. "And you're fighting over *this*?"

"But—"

"No," Alice interrupted Peter. "No little plastic toy is worth that much fuss." She handed it to Sylvie, who slipped it into the pocket of her striped bell-bottoms.

"But it's *mine*," Ethan said.

"Now it is mine." Sylvie pronounced each word like the strike of a piano key, accentuating the prettiness of her French accent.

"Thanks, Sylvie." Alice led Nell and Peter to the front door. "Sorry it ended like this."

"It's nothing." Sylvie pursed her lips. "He'll forget it in two seconds."

Out on the street, Nell and Peter chattered about the little Lego man. They went home to a simple dinner of rolled cold cuts, leftover pasta and carrot sticks. After their baths, Nell and Peter lay with Alice on her bed and snuggled against her sides. She read to them from the original *Winnie the Pooh* by A. A. Milne, whose quirky prose sailed over their heads but still lulled them. They fell asleep in Alice's arms. Mike was working late, so she left them in bed for the time being, brought the covers up to their necks and switched off the light.

Dishes done, Alice brought the laptop to the kitchen table and booted it up. She couldn't resist the temptation to Google Julius. When she plugged his name into the search engine, she was astonished by what came up.

Voluminous complaints filed with the Better Business Bureau. Archived articles detailing lawsuits. The Web page of a tenants advocacy group listing nearly a hundred properties owned or co-owned by him. In all the listings or articles, only Julius Pollack's name was ever mentioned: "Julius Pollack and his partner in Metro Properties."

Alice looked at the time. It was nearly eleven o'clock, too late to call Pam and ask her who Julius's partner was. She sat back, away from the keyboard and the blinking laptop screen, and listened to the quiet. She was rarely alone in the evenings when the kids were asleep. The current of her ongoing dialogue with Mike, or the television, typically blotted out this depth of silence. Such stillness. She heard a key struggling in the outside lock. Finally, Mike was home.

She got up and crossed through the living room to their apartment door. Her hand was on the knob and she was just about to turn it when she heard footsteps tramp up the stairs. She cracked open her door and watched Julius's back labor upward. He was wearing a pale pink raincoat and—were her eyes deceiving her?— silver high heels. She crept into the hallway and peeked up after him, glimpsing the coat as his door shut and locked.

How had the infamous Julius Pollack come to buy this house, her home? It was a beautiful house on one of the best, old blocks in the neighborhood. He was rich, and he wanted respectability, but he also wanted privacy. He could have afforded a penthouse anywhere in Manhattan. He couldn't possibly want her apartment for the income; he wanted to hide out alone in this big old house in Brooklyn. Why? Because he cross-dressed? These days even that wasn't so shocking. There had to be more.

Standing in the common foyer, in the dim overhead light, she knew she shouldn't be there—not in the hall and not in this house. She crept quietly across the foyer to her front door, then stopped. Upstairs, she heard a high, thin crying. She walked back to the bottom of the staircase, put her foot on the first step, and pitched an ear forward. The crying was distant, but she heard it escalate. She was sure of it: there was a baby up there.

She walked halfway up the stairs, slowly, leaning her

weight into her hand on the banister to help blunt the sound of her steps. She stopped and listened. It was utterly quiet. She moved farther up the staircase as it curved toward the upper landing.

The squeal of a door opening nearly detonated her heart.

"Alice!"

Mike stood in the foyer.

"What are you doing?"

"Shh!"

She quickly padded down the stairs. She heard footsteps in the apartment above, but no crying. The baby had quieted down.

"What's going on?" His tone was weary, almost plaintive. It was nearly midnight and he had been at the workshop all day.

"Come inside," she whispered.

He followed her into the apartment. She closed the door and locked it.

"Mike, listen to this," she said, and told him everything: Julius Pollack, Metro Properties, the crying baby upstairs.

They sat at the kitchen table with the dark night quilted around their windows, diminishing the room's size, increasing the impact of the overhead light. The middle-of-the-night space was off balance, its proportions rearranged.

"Well," he finally said, "it's definitely strange."

"We should tell the detectives, don't you think?"

Mike got up, walked quietly through the living room and opened the apartment door. The hinges screeched into the quiet.

"Shh!" Alice followed him. "What are you doing?"

Mike froze, then quietly edged himself into the front hall. Alice stood behind the partially open door, watching him. He kept perfectly still in the middle of the foyer, listening. After a minute, he looked at her and shook his head, mouthing, "Nothing."

It was so quiet Alice could hear her own breathing.

Her body suddenly felt unbearably heavy. She turned into the living room and picked up the phone and her address book on her way to the couch, into which she sank. Mike came back into the apartment, issuing creaks and snaps and clicks as he closed the door and turned the lock.

"I didn't hear any baby," he said. "Are you sure you heard it?"

"Positive," she said. "I *think*."

"Alice—"

"Mike."

"You're really calling the detectives?"

She nodded. Yes, she was calling Frannie, despite the uncertainty that now trilled vaguely through her.

"It's midnight," he said.

"They work odd shifts." Alice flipped through the pages of her address book until she came to *P* for *police*. "They'll either be there or they won't."

Mike angled himself next to Alice on the couch, watching her as she requested Detectives Viola or Giometti and waited on hold. Alice held Mike's eyes, listening to the Muzak on the precinct's line. The saccharine melody, meant to calm and distract, only increased her nervousness. Finally a detective Alice didn't know came on, explaining that Frannie would be on the morning shift starting at eight, and Giometti usually got in a little after her.

"Is there anything I can help you with?" the detective asked.

Alice hesitated. "No, thanks," she finally answered. "It can wait until the morning. Could you please tell Detective Viola I called?" She recited her name and number, ended the call and looked at Mike. "Maybe I should have told this other guy. What do you think?"

"I think you're probably right. It can wait until morning." Mike leaned forward and took her hand. "Let's go to bed, okay? One of them will call us back tomorrow. Remember that thing called sleep?"

They went to bed and Mike drifted off immediately.

But Alice couldn't sleep with the sounds, the distant cries, that echoed through her mind. *What if,* she asked herself, *Ivy is right here in this house, and all I have to do is walk upstairs and get her?* She eased herself off the bed, crept upstairs and laid on the couch, listening for a thread of sound. One more cry, she promised herself, and she would call the precinct back, get a detective over here.

Hours passed; a gray mist began to infiltrate the darkness outside. She didn't know what time it was but it must have been close to morning. Convinced she would never sleep, she dreamed of her exhaustion, of her *desire* for sleep. When Lauren appeared in her dream, nursing newborn Ivy, who sucked greedily at an overflowing breast, Alice snapped awake. With relief she realized she had indeed slept. And then, with plunging despair, she remembered Lauren was dead. She was *dead.* She remembered Ivy and the crying baby last night.

Alice was desperate to know one way or another whether Ivy had survived Lauren's murder. She needed to *know,* to have something to grasp so she would know what to believe and how to feel. Was she mourning or hoping? Images of Ivy plagued her. The supersoft newborn skin, the ripe smell. For a moment, sitting up on the couch, Alice closed her eyes, cradled her arms over her own bulging middle and held Ivy. She felt Ivy startle, flinching her limbs open in an inchoate certainty of free fall, and rocked her, whispering, "Shush, shush, shush." But this Ivy, the one in Alice's arms, didn't cry; she had no voice. She was a vapor.

Alice let her arms fall to her sides. The crying she'd heard last night, *was* it real? She had been so upset about Julius Pollack, she couldn't stop thinking about Ivy, it had been late at night, and she'd been all alone. *Had* she imagined it?

She got up and walked over to the front door. Cracking it open, she listened and listened, but there was nothing, just the heavy silence of early morning.

* * *

Eight a.m. came and went. The phone didn't ring. Nell and Peter were making noise downstairs, getting dressed, when Mike appeared. He stared at Alice a moment as she sat in front of the laptop, an empty teacup at her side.

"Take a sleeping pill tonight, *please,* Alice?"

Since she had known him, his skin in the morning had a special pliability, like warm clay. She always wanted to touch him then. Crossing the kitchen, she raised her face to kiss him. His lips were soft.

"I will."

Alice gave the kids frozen waffles, fresh strawberries and glasses of milk for breakfast. Mike quickly constructed their idiosyncratic lunches. He threw on the work clothes he had arrived home in last night, and in twenty minutes they were all three out the door. She began to clear the breakfast dishes and was just about to load the dishwasher when the phone rang.

"I'm not calling too early, am I?" It was Pam, not Frannie; but even so, Alice was glad for the call. "I just heard from our morning appointment. The owners don't want us until later today. Can you do two o'clock?"

Alice had forgotten she was supposed to meet Pam to see another house.

"Sure, that's fine," Alice said. "Pam? Who works with Julius Pollack at Metro Properties?"

"He's got a staff—"

"No, I mean his partner."

"What partner? Pollack works alone as far as I know."

Alice told Pam what she had read on the Internet.

"I'll see what I can find out. If I get any info before two, I'll call you. Otherwise I'll just see you later, okay?"

"Thanks, Pam. See you at two."

Alice hung up and looked at the glowing-green rubber buttons of the phone, realizing she hadn't yet tried Frannie's cell number. The detective answered after two rings.

"What's going on, Alice? I got your message from last

night. I had to run out but I was going to call you back in a few minutes."

In Frannie's background, the rumble of an engine crescendoed, then suddenly stopped. Something clacked together rhythmically. Voices.

"I heard a baby crying last night." Alice heard the errant hiss of anxiety in her own voice, and heard Frannie hearing it, the warble of disbelief.

"A baby."

"Right here. Upstairs, in my new landlord's apartment. Julius Pollack. Does that name ring a bell?"

"It rings a symphony," Frannie said. "Go on."

Alice described everything in detail: her encounter with Julius in the foyer when he was moving in, her continuing search for a house, Pam Short's discovery that Lauren's landlord—Metro—was owned by Alice's new landlord, her visit with Tim as he packed, the crying baby upstairs last night. The pregnancies, the evictions, the coincidences that were twisting a knot in her mind.

"Did you know he was Lauren's landlord?" Alice asked.

"We knew," Frannie said, "but we didn't know he was moving in there."

"What about Christine Craddock? Was her landlord Metro too? Was *she* getting evicted from her apartment too?"

In the pulse of silence that followed, Alice heard the voices behind Frannie collide in argument.

"Alice, I have to go," Frannie said, "but it's good you called."

"Do you think he's got Ivy up there?" Alice gripped her tea bag's paper tag, folding it with a sharp crease. The string detached and went sailing into what remained of her hours-old tea.

"It's doubtful, but we'll check it out."

"What do I do about Julius Pollack? What if I hear the baby again?"

"Call us right away."

Chapter 20

There were so many things to *not* think about—Ivy, the baby crying upstairs, Metro's heartless evictions, Julius's shoes, Tim's leaving, Maggie's secret life, Lauren's corpse buckling back into the canal—and they all floated like slivers of glass beneath the surface of Alice's consciousness. What saved her from drowning in the ebbs and flows of memory and implication was the immediate goal: finding a house, getting away from Julius Pollack and the mysterious partner. And the bigger goal, the hard one, that lurked in the back of her mind: locating Ivy.

As she walked the five blocks to Blue Shoes Wednesday morning, Alice felt a trickle of nausea work its way up her throat. Exhaustion and nausea seemed in collusion, one triggering the other. Despite her promise to Mike to take a sleeping pill tonight, she wasn't sure she would. It worried her. Thalidomide was once called safe; how much did they really know about the chemical environment of a developing fetus? She promised herself another sleeping pill only when she really needed it. Did she need it now, or would this get worse? She sensed her loose foothold on the slippery slope of panic. But she had summoned the detectives, told them about Julius, about the baby. She was doing everything possible. And now, today, she was seeing another house with Pam, trying to get her family out from under Julius Pollack's roof.

A date, in writing . . . telling me when you'll be gone. Julius's tough words boomeranged inside her head.

And Lauren's: *bloodsucker.*

She had the law on her side, Alice reminded herself. And if Julius did have Ivy, if he was in any way involved in Lauren's or Christine Craddock's deaths, it was too late now for him to elude detection. They were watching him.

She moved tenderly along Smith Street, slowing as a tidal wave of dizziness gave way to an avalanche of nausea. The next thing she knew, she was hinged over, kneeling on the dirty pavement.

She looked down to see if she had vomited; she had not. Having never fainted before, she was just as surprised by the acute embarrassment that overcame her next. Her stomach inexplicably settled and she carefully stood up. She looked around to see who had noticed her. An old man in a doorway across the street nodded soberly and waved. At the corner, a teenage girl with huge gold hoop earrings and dramatically outlined eyes in the style of a hip-hop Cleopatra stared blankly at Alice. In those eyes she saw that she had become the woman every teenage girl disavowed, and she wanted to call out, *No, you've got it wrong. Just you wait and see.* She pulled her purse in close and walked carefully to the corner, where she waited for the light to change. She crossed without looking at either of her witnesses.

As she walked, she felt a shadow of the nausea materializing over her. Not again. She stopped in her tracks, to let the feeling pass. Footsteps abruptly halted behind her. It was like the sudden quiet after a refrigerator's buzz cycles off; only then do you realize how loud it had been.

Alice turned around and saw him. The limo driver was right there, so close she could touch him. Deep creases sagged the skin on a once-handsome face, and those eyes: one green, one blue. He nodded and passed her at a crisp pace. He smelled of unwashed clothes and cigarettes. She watched him cross the street, huddled into his shoulders.

A cloud moved and the sun spilled down, blinding her just as it had before she steered the car into the bus. Everything flashed white, and for a split second the beach reappeared—she could *smell* its salts and mildews, it was so real—with the limo driver walking in his dark city clothes on the shifting sand. Smoking his cigarette, flicking his butt into an ocean that instantly absorbed it.

A horn blared. The limo driver disintegrated. The beach vanished like a pulled veil.

The teenage Cleopatra had come up close and was staring at Alice now with a mixture of indignation and concern. Under all the makeup, her eyes were a gentle brown.

"You okay, ma'am?" the girl asked.

Alice rubbed her eyes, refocusing herself on the concrete and the buildings and the natural music of everyday urban life. This she recognized clearly, and was grateful for; it was more vibrant than the beach dream that endangered her whenever it came.

"I didn't feel well for a minute," Alice said.

"That guy knocked into you," the girl said. "I saw him, the a-hole didn't even notice you."

So he *was* real. Alice had started to wonder if the limo driver was part of a hallucination that was edging out her hold on reality.

"Thanks," Alice told the girl, and resumed walking. As she moved forward along Smith Street, each step hit the pavement with resolve—banishing the beach, the limo driver, the dream of forgetting and escape, even the girl.

She *would* take another sleeping pill tonight, she decided. In the morning, with a clear mind, she would sort all this out.

She arrived at Blue Shoes just before eleven and switched on the lights. The gorgeous colors Maggie had chosen for the store, the blues and silvers and pale woods, coaxed Alice away from the swallowing sensation that had grabbed her just now on the street. She opened the cash register and answered a few e-mails. Jason arrived soon after, more or less on time.

With his wiry build in a T-shirt and jeans, pale gaze and close-cropped blond hair dusted with silver glitter, Jason reminded Alice of Peter Pan: young and sweet and ridiculously hopeful.

"Morning, boss." He smiled his most cocky, man-at-twenty smile and checked his watch. "Made it on time today!"

If ten minutes late is on time, she thought. But what she said was, "Boy, am I glad you're here."

He came around the counter and kissed Alice on both cheeks, taking her by surprise. He smelled sweet, cologny—thoroughly un-American. He must have been spending time with the local French transplants who had lately claimed the neighborhood. *Little France,* Maggie called it. She enjoyed the affectation of his perfumed kisses for a moment before her stomach reeled. Then she ran into the bathroom, slammed shut the door and threw up.

She spent the rest of the morning hiding out in the peaceful, shabby back room, feeding herself toast and ice water and lying on the couch. She listened as Jason politely served a customer. Three times he came back for different shoes in the woman's size. Then, without the sound of the cash register—no sale for all that fuss, though that wasn't unusual—the customer left.

It was quiet for a while before Maggie arrived. The welcome bell dinged immediately after, announcing another arrival, and the hum of business out front tightened to a buzz. Women's voices spun furiously around quick punctuations of Jason's quasi-sardonic laughter. The bubbling tone of Maggie's enthusiasms was like boiled sugar to Jason's quick stirs. Alice was sure she heard Pam Short's voice. She had to find out what was happening out there.

Pam was seated on the center bench, queenlike in a

flowing magenta caftan with uneven green stripes. Her hair was tied up in a magenta and green polka-dotted ribbon.

"Alice!" Pam opened her arms but didn't rise. "Come here. Let me have a hug."

Alice leaned over and put her arms around Pam. She smelled like baby powder.

"Did I miss an appointment?" Alice asked, wondering how badly her inner clock had been thrown off by her escalating nausea.

"Nope," Pam said. "We've just got the two o'clock. Can't I visit my favorite shoe store? I'm taking an early lunch hour."

"Slow morning in real estate?" Maggie said.

"You got it, honey."

Maggie was just then putting away the last customer's try-ons, nestling a burnt orange autumn pump against its mate in a bed of pearl tissue paper. She placed the lid carefully on the box and handed it to Jason.

"Hold it a minute," Pam said. "I'll take a look at those lovelies."

Maggie opened the box and presented it to Pam as if offering a selection of the most delectable chocolates.

"Shall we find your size?"

"Please," Pam whispered. She lifted one of the shoes out of the box and ran her fingers along the suede toe.

A minute later, Jason came out of the back room and announced, "We don't have a nine."

"Can you order it?" Pam asked.

"Of course we can," Maggie answered.

"Tell you what," Alice said. "Find me the perfect house by the end of the week and the shoes are on me."

"You have got yourself a deal!" Pam stood up, flouncing the wrinkles out of her caftan. "How about throwing lunch into the bargain? Doesn't look like they need you here." She winked at Maggie, who gamely nodded.

"You go on, darling," Maggie said. "Jason and I can handle the hordes."

Alice collected her purse, said her good-byes and left her shift early to treat Pam to lunch. She *was* hungry, though skeptical of her ability just now to hold anything down.

Walking arm in arm with Pam along Smith Street, Alice asked, "What do you feel like eating?"

"Julius Pollack." Pam stopped walking and pivoted to face Alice.

"Excuse me?"

"He just paid me a little visit at my office. I had to get out of there. I wanted to tell you, but I didn't know how much to say in front of the others, so I bit my tongue."

"Just now?"

"Yup. He walked into the office and kindly asked me to stop snooping around. The look in his eyes." Pam approximated a forced-pleasant squint. "He's gotta be the most passive-aggressive person I have ever met. I see your special fondness for him. He's a major piece of work."

"But why did he go see *you*?"

"Beats me. I only made a couple of calls. Someone must have gotten back to him. They all know each other." Pam shrugged her hefty shoulders, creating a wave of fabric across her massive breasts. "He's something, isn't he? Those glasses."

"I think he cross-dresses," Alice said. "I think I saw him wearing silver high heels. I think I heard a baby crying in his apartment last night, but he lives alone, and—"

The look on Pam's face stopped Alice. She wasn't sure exactly what Pam was feeling—incredulity, pity—but there was enough concern on the woman's face to float a charity.

"Never mind," Alice said. "I slept for about ten minutes last night. I'm probably imagining things."

"No," Pam said, weaving her arm back through Alice's. "If you heard it, it's real."

They walked in silence for a few minutes before deciding to eat at the French bistro on the corner of Dean Street. When they had settled at an outdoor table, Pam said, "Guy in our office used to cross-dress but he didn't keep it a secret. Told anyone he felt like, so it seemed like nothing."

"I think Julius hides it," Alice said, steadying her tone, "except for the glasses. And at night."

"He's a freak, in or out of ladies' clothes." Pam reached into her purse, withdrew a small tube of hand cream and squirted a dab onto the back of one hand. "I haven't found out who his silent partner is, but I will. Someone from the Buildings Department who owes me a favor is getting back to me." She rubbed her hands together and smiled, satisfied. "Learn to work the ropes, my mother used to say, and you'll go far."

"You must have had quite a mother."

"Still do. She's conquered Florida, says she'll only leave the state in an urn, which will never happen, because my mother intends to live forever."

After lunch they walked up to Hicks Street for their two o'clock house.

"Well, here we are," Pam said.

It was another 1.5 million-dollar house, this one overlooking the twin lanes of the Brooklyn Queens Expressway, and across the street from the emergency-room entrance of Long Island College Hospital.

"What a noisy corner," Alice said.

"It's always something, isn't it?" Pam rolled her eyes conspiratorially. Alice wondered if Pam managed this same camaraderie with all her clients, or if she was special. She remembered how much energy it used to take to please and appease her commercial editing clients.

"Well, let's take a look."

Alice marched up the front stoop ahead of Pam, who followed with the keys. The stoop, Alice noticed, was crumbling, but she didn't mention it. She was depleted, without patience even for her own complaints.

"One-bedroom rental on the ground floor," Pam said, pushing the front door open into a dim corridor with stuccoed walls. Only one weak bulb illuminated the entrance but Alice could see the cracked brown linoleum lobbing up the stairway, its edges curling off the ancient steps. "Cosmetics," Pam said. "A little lipstick makes all the difference, my mother used to say."

As had Alice's mother; it must have been a generational thing. Alice could still see the image of Lizzie's partial face reflected back to her in the rearview mirror, stretching her lips taut for the dark shade of red she always wore.

"We enter here." Pam singled out another key and put it into a door on the first-floor landing. They entered another narrow hall off which five separate rooms clustered like starved peas in a withered pod. Each room was small and dark, except the last room that faced the street, which was larger than the rest and was the only one that got any light.

"Picture how nice this could be," Pam said, "with all the walls knocked out. If you took all three top floors, you could open the whole parlor floor to the staircase. It would look like a different place."

"Is there an upstairs to this apartment?"

Pam shook her head, clearly embarrassed. But Alice knew the woman was doing her best in a ridiculous market, showing Alice what was available both above and below her target price. Driving home her point to strive upward, take a risk, and come out happy at the other end.

"This is a two-bedroom unit, and the two floors above are also two-bedroom units. That's a lot of rental income for someone who wants to ease into their mortgage payments."

"Or a big gut renovation for someone who doesn't," Alice said. She looked around and tried to see the *potential* here. The building was wide and deep, and while the ceilings weren't high and had no detail, they weren't exactly low either. But after a few minutes of thinking it over, she knew she fit neither of the profiles they had mentioned, neither the income hoarder nor the gut reno-vator. She and Mike were willing to pay their share of the mortgage for a nice house, but weren't up for much more than a paint job and maybe sanding wood floors. Plus they had to move quickly; there would not be time for major work.

"Let's keep looking," Alice said.

"You're the boss." Pam followed Alice out and locked the apartment door behind them.

"I'm sorry—" Alice started.

"What did I tell you?" Pam held up her hand. Today's rings were shades of green to match the stripes in her caftan.

"I know, but still." Alice wove her arm through Pam's and felt a warm tug closer. "I appreciate your pa-tience, Pam."

"Good. I'm the most patient person I know. That's why I always succeed."

Up close, Pam's skin looked slightly translucent in the midday sun. Alice noticed a dusting of powder on the folds of Pam's neck, the baby-powder scent. They stood on Hicks Street in front of the house, next to the buzzing highway. Pam opened her green patent-leather purse, pulled out her overstuffed date book, removed the rub-ber band that held it together and flipped through the pages until she found what she was looking for.

"Tomorrow, we've got a ten o'clock."

"We do?" Alice came around to look over Pam's shoulder at the page scrawled with pencil and various colors of pen. She couldn't discern her appointment in the scribble.

"Didn't I tell you?"

"Not that I know of," Alice said, "unless Mike forgot to give me the message."

Pam rummaged for a pen, scrawled the time and ad-dress on a blank page at the back of her address book, ripped it out and gave it to Alice.

"Anything else to see?" Alice was just asking when

across the street, on the highway side of Hicks Street, she spotted the limo driver walking slowly along the curb.

"That man!" Alice kept her voice low but couldn't contain the pitch of hysteria. "He's been following me all week!"

"Him?" Pam pointed at the man, who had become aware of the attention and was now walking quickly away. "That sucker? Are you *sure*?"

"Positive."

"Hey!" Pam shouted at the top of her voice. "You! Where the hell do you think you're going?"

Alice watched, dumbfounded, as Pam rushed across the street after the large gray-haired man, shouting all the way. "Get over here, bozo! Mama wants to talk to you! Stalker!"

The man broke into a trot, then a run, and to Alice's surprise actually jumped over the waist-high fence separating Hicks Street from the highway. Pam leaned over the fence, her caftan catching the gentle breeze like a sail, inflating her beyond all natural proportion.

"Come back here, asshole!" she called to the buzzing thread of highway below. Then she turned to face Alice, across the street, and shrugged. "Gave it my best shot."

Pam's grip on each moment terrified and thrilled Alice. Suddenly there was no doubt in her mind. Yes, if she heard it, it was real. And the limo driver *was* following her.

Chapter 21

"Are you sure, Alice?" Frannie's voice sounded tinny. Their cell phone connection was breaking up.

"Frannie? Are you there?"

"Who's Frannie, Mommy?" Nell had walked into the kitchen and was searching the refrigerator.

Alice shushed her, whispering, "I'm on the phone. What do you need?"

"Apple juice, please."

She poured Nell a cup of juice and left her alone in the kitchen to hide out in the bathroom, where she could talk in private; she didn't want the kids to hear her talking about being followed.

Alice put down the toilet seat and sat, listening to the swoosh of traffic on Frannie's end of the phone. Where was she? Finally her voice materialized.

"Hello?"

"I'm still here, Frannie. Where are you? Are you driving?"

"Paul's driving. We're entering a tunnel. If I lose you, I'll call you back."

If they were in a tunnel, chances are they were heading into New Jersey. Why were they going there?

"Alice," Frannie said, "tell me exactly what you saw."

"I first noticed the man a week ago, over by the Carroll Street Bridge. Then I saw him again on Clinton Street. And I'm starting to think he was the man who turned around and walked away on Degraw Street on the block where we park our car. The way he ran away today, I'm sure he was following me. He's creepy, Frannie. He smells like dirty laundry."

"He came that close?"

"This morning, the first time," Alice said. "I thought I'd have a heart attack when I turned around and there he was."

"Describe him."

Alice told her everything she could remember about the limo driver. Thick, steel-gray hair. Mismatched blue and green eyes. Tall and beefy, the reek of tobacco, badly dressed.

"Well," Frannie said, "we can see if we get a hit on him in the DMV database. Not too many people have two-color eyes. We'll start by finding out who he is."

"Thanks."

"Try not to go out alone if you can help it. Walk on busy streets if you have to. Okay? If you've got a real stalker, we'll get him."

"Frannie?" Alice had to ask this. "What if he's the other half of Metro Properties? What if he's the one who killed Lauren? What if he's after me now?"

There was a pulse of silence.

"There are so many assumptions in what you just said, Alice, I wouldn't know where to begin."

"Right. But what if—"

"Do you think you're in danger?"

"I don't know. He never tries to talk to me."

"Here's what we're going to do." Frannie's voice was breaking up again and she spoke quickly. "If you see him again, you'll call us right away. You'll keep telling us everything. *Everything*. We'll do the rest."

Then her voice evaporated into whatever tunnel had swallowed the car she was in.

The next morning, Mike dropped off the kids at school, then returned home to wait for Alice to get ready for the ten o'clock appointment with Pam. She found him at the kitchen table, wearing clean but torn work clothes, his eyes fixed on a single spot of the morning paper.

"Mike?" Her presence seemed to startle him. "You okay?"

"Fine." He pushed the paper away and stood up. "Ready?"

"You weren't actually reading the newspaper just now."

"Can't concentrate," Mike said. "Didn't sleep much last night."

"That's not like you." They locked up their front door and passed together through the shadowy front hall. "We can't both be insomniacs. That'll never work."

He smiled a little but didn't laugh.

Alice reached up to tuck the faded tag back into the collar of his forest green T-shirt as he locked the building's front door behind them. As she was about to move down the front stoop, he caught her wrist. "From now on, when I can't go see houses with you, you'll have Pam meet you and take you over. Okay?"

"Yes," Alice agreed. There was a wisp of cool breeze in the air, a hint of the autumn chill that would soon swallow the last of summer.

"And we'll get Maggie to bring you to work, or that Jason of yours—"

"Mike, I don't need a babysitter! Frannie said to stay on busy streets and I will."

"I don't get it." He was walking a little too quickly for Alice, who struggled to keep up. "How can I not worry? Worrying doesn't belong only to you."

"Mike, slow down."

Quickness, a call to action, had always been his response to anxiety when upon rare occasion he succumbed to it. She wished he *would* leave the worry to her; she was better at it.

He walked faster.

"Mike, I've only told you what I've seen and heard. The facts. You're the one always telling me not to embellish." She wished now that she hadn't told him every nuance of her thoughts and fears, that she had trusted her instinct to hold things back.

She hooked her arm through his to keep him from racing ahead. "You're the only person I know who gets more energy with less sleep."

After a minute he allowed himself to fall into an easier pace. Arms linked, the two walked south along Court Street. It began to feel more like the old Carroll Gardens than the shinier, gentrified one that had taken hold the closer you got to Atlantic Avenue. Here, there were still unprepossessing storefronts, plain-vanilla hair salons offering discounts on ladies' weekly styling, independent video stores, publike eateries with five-dollar hamburgers.

"It's kind of nice down here," Alice said. "Calm."

Mike hummed agreement; the shift in neighborhood was having a good effect on them both.

They arrived early at the house on Third Place between Clinton and Henry Streets. It was a lovely, quiet block lined with simple brownstones set back behind the front yards that had given Carroll Gardens the second half of its name. The address Pam had scrawled on the page was a corner house with a flowering front yard that turned around the side of the house, connecting seamlessly with a backyard. It was an unusual layout. Massive clusters of antique red roses spilled over the front fence.

"Get a whiff of this," Mike said, leaning in to smell the blossoms.

Alice stepped into the yard and leaned toward the delicious roses, whose scent indeed was a tonic. "You could really look forward to springtime here." She pictured herself inside the house, standing behind one of the gleaming windows, waiting out winter for spring to come.

They stood in front of the three-story house, observing and discussing what little they could tell from the outside. It had the tidiness of recent renovation, they decided. The full-pane windows looked new, with wood frames painted slate blue. The house's facade was a rich, chocolaty brown. The front stoop was wide and solid with freshly painted black banisters in scrolling ironwork that led to an arched front door of polished oak. There was an air of peacefulness to this well-tended house.

"I like it more than any of the other houses I've seen so far," Alice said.

"It looks good from the outside." Mike turned a mischievous smile on her. "Which means it's got to be a total wreck on the inside. Right? Poetic justice."

"I hope not."

"We should probably take it anyway," he said. "Take it no matter what. Just move."

"You sound like Maggie."

His eyes shone and she knew what was coming. Mike did voices, impressions, and was very good at it. " 'Twas an annus horribilus, 'twas." With a hand on Alice's lower back he tugged her closer. They melted into a hug and shared what felt like well-deserved laughter.

Half an hour later, Pam still hadn't arrived. Alice called her office number but her voice mail came on, and the machine answered at her home. Alice left messages in both places. Then, as a last resort, she tentatively walked up the front stoop and rang the bell. She could hear its faint chime behind the door, dissolving into silence.

As soon as Alice got home with the children that afternoon, she picked up the phone and dialed Pam's office. All day at Blue Shoes her calls to Pam had gone unanswered, routed through Garden Hill's voice mail system to Pam's mailbox. She never called, as hoped, to describe some scheduling mishap. An errant alarm clock. Crossed appointments. Run-down cell phone batteries. Something to explain her absence at the Third Place house. As she listened to the phone ring, Alice assumed the voice-mail system would answer again. Instead, this time, she was greeted by a human voice, "Garden Hill Realty."

"I'd like to speak with Pam Short."

"Hold on, please."

Another woman's voice, this one deeper and a little coarse, came on the line. "This is Judy Gersten."

Alice recognized the name from the storefront's window: JUDITH GERSTEN, LICENSED BROKER.

"I'm filling in for Pam today. May I ask who's calling?"

"Alice Halpern. She's been showing me houses. We had an appointment this morning at ten and she didn't come. I was surprised—"

"Yes, Alice, Pam mentioned she was showing you the Third Place house. I couldn't find your number. I've wanted to call you all day."

"Is Pam sick?"

Judy didn't answer. Then, "She had an accident."

"Is she all right?"

There was another pause, this one longer, and Alice knew in that instant that something was terribly wrong.

Chapter 22

"What happened? Where is she?"

"Alice, dear." Judy's voice lowered to a grainy whisper. "Pam was fond of you—she told me that."

Was.

"I heard your voice mails today. I'll help you with the Third Place house."

"Please tell me what happened."

Judy sighed deeply. Alice could see her sitting at the far right desk, the one cluttered with knickknacks, beneath the framed needlepoint legends that might have read OFFICE SWEET HOME or TODAY IS A NEW DAY, reminders not to mourn what couldn't be changed.

"A neighbor found her in her car this morning, with the motor running. The man smelled gas coming from behind the garage door."

Alice could see the black-painted scrolling door of Pam's garage, an urban rarity for which she had seemed remarkably lucky.

"But that's impossible," Alice said. "Pam *wouldn't.*"

She saw Pam's lips curling in humor, heard her shout of laughter, smelled the baby powder wafting off her skin. The woman had so many projects and plans. She never would have sent Alice to the house this morning, if she had known. . . .

Unless. Had Pam sent her to that house, knowing she wouldn't be there, knowing Alice would love it and be on her way? Was it a parting gift?

Alice had no experience with the parameters of suicide, neither the slope toward it nor the promise of its obliteration. All her assumptions aside, she had no real idea if one approached it logically or blanked out by despair. She recalled the illegible scrawls on today's page from Pam's date book; there was no way anyone but Pam could have discerned her intentions for the day. Alice reminded herself that she barely knew the woman; everything she believed about Pam was based on assumptions.

"We're all in shock," Judy said softly. "Pam's at Long Island College Hospital, if you want to send flowers or a card."

"I don't understand," Alice said. "Do you mean she's alive?"

"Barely. We're hoping."

Alice jotted down the hospital information on her kitchen calendar, which reminded her that it was Thursday. A simple fact. Another Thursday.

She felt suddenly sick, as if two opposing currents were at war in her body, one surging up from her stomach, the other pressing down from her mind. She quickly said good-bye to Judy and hung up the phone. Peter was playing on the rug with his little fire truck, guiding it through a maze he had built of boxes and wooden blocks. Grateful for his concentration, Alice rushed past him en route to the bathroom, where she flung up the toilet seat in the nick of time.

She called the hospital three times that night and each time was told that Pam was in intensive care and could receive no visitors other than family. It would have to be enough to know she was alive.

Alice decided she could appease her desire to help by doing the neighborly thing. She would bring a chicken stew over to the house for Pam's husband, Ray; after all, the man still had to eat. She pulled a chicken out of the freezer and put it in the fridge to defrost overnight. Then she assembled ingredients on the counter and went into the garden for a sprig of fresh rosemary.

She could hear that the kids were out of their bath downstairs and were busily getting themselves ready for bed. Alice had been on dishes duty tonight, Mike on bedtime. In a lull of activity, Mike came up the stairs into the kitchen.

"Any news?" he asked.

"Nope."

He stood back and watched Alice finish her preparations, finding the last can of crushed tomatoes at the back of the cupboard, pulling carrots and potatoes out of the fridge.

"Are you cooking *now*?"

"I thought I'd get it started right after the kids go to school in the morning." She took two onions out of the fridge drawer.

He squatted in front of the corner cabinet, reached in for the big, heavy soup pot they had received as a wedding gift, and carried it over to the stove. Then he came over to hug her. "All of this," he whispered. "It's going to be all right. It has to be. Okay?"

Was he reassuring her? Or asking her to reassure him?

"Okay," she whispered into his salty-smelling neck. "And if it doesn't, we'll just take the kids and go, okay? Anywhere. We'll just leave."

He nodded. And so it was agreed. They wouldn't fight this battle for long.

"I'll get the kids into bed," Mike said.

"I'll join you," she said, and turned off the lights.

Pam's brownstone looked just as imperial and peaceful as when Alice had first seen it, the basement-level garage door shut tight as a sleeping eye. The roses out front were a sea of fragrant yellow that made Alice's heart weep. She still couldn't believe Pam had tried to take her own life. They had been together just two days ago and Pam had seemed better than fine. She had seemed utterly, perfectly herself.

Alice rang the bell and waited with Jason on the front stoop. She had requested his help carrying over the heavy stew, without mentioning Mike's insistence that she go everywhere now with an escort—or, more precisely, a bodyguard—until the limo driver was picked up by the police.

A very old woman answered the door and squinted at them from behind thick glasses that magnified her eyes to twice their normal size. She was so thin her veins were visible beneath her skin, wrapped tight on sinewy muscle. Her hair was teased into a 1950s-style beehive, and she wore thick blue eye shadow. The psychedelic retro Mary Mekko dress was the real giveaway.

"You must be Pam's mother," Alice said.

"Do I know you?"

"I'm Alice, a client of Pam's, and this is Jason."

"I'm Esther. That looks heavy. Give it over."

Esther took the container out of Jason's hands and carried it through the living room and into the kitchen. Alice followed, understanding where Pam got her determination but not her size. Jason, meanwhile, waited in the vestibule for Alice to complete her errand.

"You know Pammie's husband, Ray?" Esther slid Alice's stew onto the kitchen counter next to a small mountain of other pots and pans and containers of neighborly food. A diminutive man with a shaved head, wearing baggy olive-green shorts and a black T-shirt, sat on a stool at the marble-topped island.

Sitting across from him were Frannie and Giometti.

It was a shock to see the detectives out of context, in Pam Short's kitchen where they couldn't possibly belong. Alice stood dumbly at the kitchen threshold, not knowing what to say. Ray twisted around to look at her, the stranger in his kitchen, and she knew she had to explain herself.

"I'm Alice. Pam was helping me find a house. I've been spending a lot of time with her lately and I was just shocked when I heard—"

"Oh yes, she mentioned you!" Ray lit up, and turned to the detectives. "Pam was hell-bent on finding this lady a house. She never gave up on anyone. You see? That's what I mean. It never made any sense to me that she would do such a thing to herself."

Alice's expression must have shown her confusion, as Ray now turned back to her and spoke as adamantly as he had to the detectives.

"It's not Pam's style," he said. "She isn't repressed enough to kill herself."

"You mean she didn't do this to herself?" Alice asked, understanding in that moment why the detectives were there. They were homicide detectives; they didn't investigate suicides. They must have thought that someone had tried to harm Pam.

"Is Pam all right?" Alice asked Ray.

"She's in a coma. Someone put my baby in a coma." He began to cry.

Esther came up next to him and draped a thin arm around his shoulders. "Shh, we're gonna get our baby back. You'll see."

The fingers of Giometti's right hand drummed the marble counter one time, quickly, as if practicing scales. Frannie was quiet and still, not smiling; her gaze rested on Alice but gave nothing away. Alice felt she was intruding on something. She hardly knew Pam, not really, and had a strong feeling no one would argue her out of cutting her visit short.

Glancing at her watch, she said, "I'd like to see Pam when you think she's ready for visitors."

"Tell me your number," Esther said. "I have a perfect memory."

Alice recited her phone number. Esther listened closely, nodded, then began unloading the containers of food from the counter into the refrigerator.

"Good luck," Alice told Ray.

Though he was still crying, he slipped off his stool. He was quite short, she saw now, about five foot four. Joining Esther at the counter, he pushed aside a few containers until he found a tray covered with aluminum foil cinched around the edges.

"Brownies," he said. "Esther's watching her figure

and I'm on a heart-healthy diet. Pam mentioned you had kids. We tried, but for us it never happened. Here." He handed Alice the tray. "If I eat these, she'll kill me. That she would happily do."

"Thank you. Nell and Peter will love these." Alice leaned over to kiss Ray's cheek, then left him with the detectives.

"Go straight home," Frannie said, causing Alice to turn around in the kitchen doorway and look at the young woman with her rose-colored sunglasses perched atop her black hair.

"But I have to open the store."

Frannie leaned forward on her elbows. "Have your guy out there take you home. He can open the store himself."

"Why?" Alice asked.

But Frannie didn't answer. The tense set of her expression made it clear there was more, but it would have to wait.

PART THREE

Chapter 23

KILLER ON LOOSE IN CARROLL GARDENS, by Erin Brinkley. Alice's pulse jumped when she read the headline, the first thing she saw when she pulled the morning paper out of its blue plastic sleeve. It had been such a busy morning, hustling the kids off to school, cooking and getting the stew over to the Shorts', and she hadn't had time to look at the paper until now.

The lead article was not long, but there were associated articles and she wanted to read them all so she wouldn't miss anything. She sat down at the kitchen table and forced herself to read carefully, not to skip ahead.

A Brooklyn real estate broker who was found Thursday by a neighbor asphyxiated in her car was a victim of foul play. Pam Short had in fact been shot in the neck and left in the car by her attacker, who turned on the engine and abandoned the fifty-year-old woman to die in her private garage. But in the botched murder attempt, the .22 round-nose bullet that had meant to kill Ms. Short bounced off her jawbone instead and lodged in a pocket of fat on the side of her neck.

Alice read the details in horror, forcing her mind to slow down as she scrambled for new information between the cramped lines of the newsprint, which resonated with truths—some unproven, some plainly chilling—from her own small life.

Pam Short appears to have no enemies in the tightly knit community in which she has lived and worked for over twenty years. She has been married to her husband, Ray Short, an antiques dealer, for seventeen years. Nor is there any record of mental illness or suicide attempts in Ms. Short's history.

Although the location of the gunshot wound might have indicated self-infliction, attempted suicide has been ruled out by a forensic pathologist. Ms. Short's hands were free of barium antimony, lead deposits that collect on the fingers and palm of someone who has recently shot a gun. There was also no sign of the blood spatter or tissue particles, known as blockback, that are found on ten percent of suicides.

In a related development, the New York City Criminalistics Laboratory has determined that the bullet used in the attack on Ms. Short was shot by the same gun used nearly two weeks ago to kill Lauren Barnet, also of Carroll Gardens. Ms. Barnet was nine months pregnant at the time of her murder. Her unborn baby has not been found, and is currently being treated as a missing person by Brooklyn's Seventy-sixth Precinct.

The article continued toward the end of the Metro section, and this was where Alice found the related pieces on Christine Craddock and Lauren. The sight of Lauren's photograph, a straight-on glance at the photographer, had the effect of a final valediction. *Over,* it said. Gone. Lauren had become a stepping-stone in the path of a madman. Alice couldn't bring herself to read the article, not yet. She went first to Christine Craddock's.

Christine's story had advanced since new interest had been turned on it by Erin Brinkley. Alice imagined the reporter as young, *hungry* as they said in the trade, willing to go farther and faster than the police, unencumbered by doubt or due process. Ms. Brinkley had found someone who had spoken with Christine the morning of her disappearance. Alice was sure this was new information; she would have remembered reading it on Christine's Web site or the older articles. The last person to see Christine was not the man at the local deli, where she had bought a small bottle of water just before she vanished, but Andre Capa, the artist who lived in the round house on the Gowanus Canal.

Andre Capa—so now he had a name. The artist whose sculptures awed and entertained passersby, spraying them with toxic water. Who sat on the bridge with his easel, from time to time, painting the rough horizon. Andre Capa. The last person to see Lauren alive, eight minutes before her death. And now, the last person to see Christine Craddock.

Andre Capa had been standing on the Carroll Street Bridge, photographing his latest fountaining sculpture— a twisted-wire angel spewing canal water from her mouth—when he saw a hugely pregnant woman stop on the Union Street Bridge about a hundred feet down the canal. He saw her bend forward in apparent pain, stopped taking pictures of his angel, and turned his lens on the woman who he assumed was in labor. One of the pictures was printed next to the article. It showed a distant bridge on which a blurry woman leaned into the railing. Her head was tilted forward, her elbow bent, as if she was trying to stop herself from falling. Asked if she did fall, Capa said that no, she pushed herself back up and slowly continued across the bridge. Asked why he hadn't come forward with the information at the time, he explained that he never read the news, didn't own a television, and within days after Christine's disappearance had left the country for Bali where he kept a second home.

"I called to her," the article quoted Capa as saying, 'and asked if she needed help. She said no, she was in labor and was on her way to Methodist Hospital." Ms. Brinkley answered the reader's next potential question about why Christine hadn't called herself a cab to get to the hospital, stating that new wisdom advised pregnant women to walk in the early stages of labor.

Alice remembered her own early labor, doubling over in excruciating pain every couple of minutes. Eventually, walking became impossible. How far, she wondered, had Christine made it before she was unable to go on?

She turned back to the article about Lauren—her peaceful photograph—and with a stab at her heart read what amounted to an obituary. *A graduate of Harvard Law School, Lauren Barnet suspended her career to stay home with her children. She leaves behind her husband, Tim Barnet, and five-year-old son, Austin.*

Leaves them behind.

Yet they too were now gone, having left behind everything they had known of their life with Lauren.

Alice pushed the newspaper across the kitchen table in disgust. How was this happening to people she knew? In her own neighborhood? In her *home*?

The house was eerily silent. Even Julius didn't seem to be home, or if he was, she couldn't hear him moving around upstairs as she sometimes did. Outside, a car rumbled past. The bones of the house creaked and moaned.

She picked up the phone and called the precinct, leaving a voice mail for Frannie: "Please call me back. I'm sitting here going crazy. Did you read the paper today? I think that artist is after me." She hung up, feeling part angry and part ashamed. She knew her message made her sound paranoid, but why shouldn't she be?

She pushed a spray of breakfast crumbs into a pile on the table in front of her. She had to think this through

Andre Capa.

Maybe he was the limo driver. Maybe he worked for Metro. Maybe ridding Julius Pollack of his more stubborn tenants was his day job. But what would they want with the babies?

To get her mind off the gruesome details of Pam's attack and everything else—*everything*—she took a pad of paper and a pen and started a shopping list. *Milk, bread, oranges, graham crackers,* the simplest of things. Then, without meaning to, she started a new list, and another, jotting lists for anything that came to mind. *Moving. Baby Prep. Kids/School. Blue Shoes.* She needed a way to unknot and streamline her goals and thoughts and worries and plans. Then she decided to try listing the things that kept her up at night, not just what needed to be accomplished during the day. *Lauren/Ivy. Phantom Baby. Pam. Julius/Partner. Capa/Stalker. Investigation. News. Fear of Being Next.*

She called Frannie's numbers, then Giometti's, and left more messages. "Call me." Mike's voice mail answered. "Call me. Please." She sat with her hand heavy on the phone and thought: Mags.

Maggie answered her home phone right away.

"Have you read this morning's paper?"

"Alice? No, I haven't. What's wrong?"

She described her morning to Maggie, who listened in uncharacteristic silence. Within fifteen minutes, she was at Alice's front door.

"If Mohammed can't come to the mountain—" Maggie brushed Alice's cheek with a kiss as she walked in without invitation, but then she didn't need one.

"Jason's opening the store," Alice said. "I can't go out. I've been ordered to stay here and wait, but I don't know what I'm waiting for. I—"

"Slow down, darling." Maggie sat Alice at the kitchen table, brought her a glass of water, then settled in close enough to touch knees. "I'm not worried about the store, I'm worried about you. You're a complete mess. Haven't you slept?"

Alice shook her head. "Not much."

"But the sleeping pills."

"I'm pregnant, Mags—"

"Didn't your doctor say they're safe?"

"Thalidomide was safe too, remember?" It was the

first time in days Alice had voiced that particular concern, it having slipped beneath so many others. She brought her hands to her face, rubbed off a new grip of anxiety, set them back in her lap. "All those babies born with partial limbs."

"That was decades ago." Maggie touched Alice's cheek with a soft fingertip. "And the car accident. Your insomnia is dangerous. You must keep some perspective."

"I'll take one tonight," Alice promised halfheartedly. "I will."

"Tell you what." Maggie uncrossed her legs. "I'm taking you out to lunch." She stood up. "Come on, get your purse. It's a lovely day outside. Let's go."

"I'm already out to lunch." Alice tried to joke but her effort fell flat. "Anyway, Mags, I can't leave. Frannie told me to stay home."

"Right. Well, then, let's see what I can rustle up here." Maggie got up and began to search the refrigerator and cupboards. "Personally I've never understood the American obsession with tuna fish, but when necessity calls, one makes do." She opened two cans of tuna and began mixing in mayonnaise, washing lettuce, toasting bread.

"Maggie, I have a confession to make," Alice said to Maggie's back as she worked.

Maggie swiveled to look at Alice briefly enough to say, "Yes?" then returned to her lunch making.

Alice told her everything: her visit to Frannie, the crying baby, the stalker. When she was finished, she felt tremendously relieved. "I don't know why I didn't speak up sooner, Mags. I've been getting tied up into knots. I'm sorry."

"Oh, nonsense," Maggie said. She delivered two plates with sandwiches to the table, along with a small bowl of carrot sticks, which she placed between them. "I am, after all, the queen of nondisclosure. But really, Alice. You've been hearing a *baby*? And you have a *stalker*? You *are* discreet."

"Not really," Alice said. "Just tired and overly hormonal."

"I think you're doing beautifully," Maggie said, "considering." She reached across the table and patted Alice's hand.

"What do you mean?"

"This thing with Lauren has been a nightmare for me too. I can't sleep much either, knowing little Ivy could be out there somewhere. But Alice dear, you are six months pregnant and living under the same roof as Lauren's evil landlord. Frankly I don't know how you do it, why you don't just pack up and move *anywhere* this instant."

Alice knew Maggie's comments were fair—Mike himself had voiced the same idea—yet she felt a swell of defensiveness. She remembered Maggie's words to Lauren on their last afternoon together. *If I were you, I'd get on with it and move. It isn't worth fighting over scraps.* Maggie didn't really comprehend the costs of Lauren's battle, or Alice's for that matter. Thanks to an inheritance, she had always had anything she wanted; nothing was ever hard-won.

"Actually, Mags, we're trying to move," Alice answered, aware of the sharp cut of her tone. "I'm trying not to get too hysterical about it, though obviously I'm not succeeding."

"Listen," Maggie said, pushing aside her sandwich. "I say a lot of things I don't mean, just for a laugh, but don't let it fool you, darling. I know what you're going through. You and Lauren had a special friendship. Your mutual American seriousness, I suppose. But I *am* here for you now. I *love* you. You're my very best friend and if I say anything to hurt you, a pox on me! Agreed?"

It was the straightest Maggie had ever been and there was no possible argument, nor did Alice wish for one. Maggie was right—bottom line, once you weeded through the tangles of her sharp-edged commentary, Maggie usually *was* right—it was just the two of them now.

They finished their lunches and waited together for the phone to ring, for Frannie or Giometti to call and explain Alice's house arrest in light of everything broadcast in the morning paper. It calmed Alice immensely to have Maggie there as a comrade in her obsession, defused it somewhat, and she was grateful. Maggie made some herbal tea for Alice and strong coffee for herself, and they settled into old conversations.

"Will you and Simon get back together, do you think?" Alice asked.

Maggie's face burst into ridicule. "He's much better as a lover. Why ruin it with domestic bliss?"

"Does Ethan know? Is he there when you're together?"

"Isn't it funny? One of us hires Sylvie to watch him if we see each other in the evening. We don't want him to get his hopes up, poor darling. He'd be at me nonstop to move back into the house."

"Maggie." Alice leaned forward and lowered her voice. "Do you ever wonder if you only *imagined* Simon was unfaithful to you back then? I mean, he still denies it, doesn't he?"

"Yes, he does, the bastard."

"Do you?"

Maggie hesitated, probably trying to avoid the question more than consider it.

"I have entertained the thought, yes."

"And?"

"There was evidence." Maggie also leaned in, bringing the women's faces close together. "There was the button—"

"A button, Maggie!" Alice would never forget that button, a red plastic rose the likes of which Maggie had never owned. She had discussed it at length with Alice and Lauren, displaying it in the palm of her hand like the nugget of gold an ancient miner always knew he'd find if he just kept looking. The possibility Maggie would never entertain was that the button could have been brought into the house in the pocket of any of Ethan's friends. Alice herself was always amazed at the things she found in her children's pockets: wads of tape, miniature wheels, broken pencils, food, money, ticket stubs for movies they had never seen. She had watched them pick things up from the street and try to slip them into pockets, always with her objection. It was when she wasn't looking that the secret agents of miscellany made their way in.

"Yes, a button. And all those errands that took hours." Maggie's eyes shimmered with the effort it took to maintain her belief that her dignity—her *soul,* as she'd put it—had demanded her decision to end her marriage. "Listen, it's no big deal if I want to have sex with him, or even if I'm in love with him. I don't want to *live* with him. I don't *trust* him. It would happen again, all of it, for whatever reason."

"Right," Alice said. "I see what you mean."

It didn't matter whom the button belonged to. It was what the button had stoked in Maggie's imagination that really mattered; her jealousies and fears were what she had ultimately run from.

Sitting with Maggie, Alice began to wonder just how much her own imagination had been playing with her fears. Had Pam been wrong in her generous assurances that there *had* been a baby upstairs in Julius's apartment, simply because Alice believed she had heard it? That if she was convinced she had a stalker, he *was* real? One thing was clear: Maggie was more comfortable than Alice with the ambiguity of her own assertions, and maybe it helped keep her this side of sanity. But Alice didn't know if she could tolerate the indefinite twilight of not knowing the truth.

Alice's cell phone began to simultaneously vibrate and ring. She fumbled it open and caught the call just before it reverted to voice mail.

"Alice, it's Frannie. Sorry it took me so long to get back to you. It's been crazy. We've got some time now. Where can we find you?"

Chapter 24

Giometti was driving the blue sedan when they pulled up in front of the President Street house. They hadn't wanted to talk inside, once they heard Maggie was over, and insisted on picking up Alice. They would take her to her children's school for their three o'clock pickup. Frannie reached back from the passenger's seat and popped open the back door for Alice. She slid awkwardly in—her growing bulk was making it hard to move gracefully—and the car glided into Smith Street traffic.

Alice could see Giometti's calm, steady eyes suspended in the rearview mirror. They shifted briefly to her, then back to the road. Frannie twisted around and began the conversation Alice had been waiting for.

"So you've read the papers," Frannie said wearily; it was only midafternoon and already it had been a long day.

"Yes."

"So you know."

"Is it him?" Alice shifted forward, closer to Frannie. "The man who's been stalking me? Am I supposed to be next?"

Frannie seemed to hesitate before answering. "We can't be sure."

"Haven't you found him yet? You've had enough time! Is it Andre Capa?"

Neither Frannie nor Giometti responded to Alice's outburst and she almost regretted it, but not really. She was afraid. They were keeping something from her.

They traveled the length of Smith Street in silence, turning up Atlantic Avenue and heading toward the ocean, which now swelled into view; Alice was always surprised by any reminder that they lived on an island.

"He's been arrested," Frannie finally said.

"Arrested for what?" Alice asked. "Murder? Stalking? Bad manners? *What?*"

"Alice, please, calm down." Frannie's tone had lost any pretense of patience. "There's a lot going on here. I'm telling you what you need to know."

"Which is?"

"To answer your question, yes, Andre Capa *was* following you. We've run him through forensics in every possible way, and right now we're waiting for the results. If it's him, Alice, we're hoping he'll lead us to the crime scene."

"If it is him," Alice asked, "are you thinking he might have Ivy?"

"We don't know."

"What about Julius Pollack? The crying I heard?"

The car sped along Hicks Street now, all the way to Hamilton Avenue. They veered left under the shadowy highway overpass.

"We're waiting on a warrant, search and seizure, home and office. We can't do anything until we get it."

"Why is it taking so long, Frannie? Do you think this Capa might somehow be involved with Metro? Could *he* be Julius's partner?"

"I'm telling you," Frannie said, "we don't know yet."

Giometti drove the car along the leafy shade of Clinton Street, past multimillion-dollar brownstones, into the heart of Carroll Gardens.

"What this means for you, Alice, is that you don't have to be so afraid." Frannie found her old, warm smile. "Okay? We figured it would help you to have this information. But please don't spread it around. We don't want any attention on this, not until we can figure it out."

Alice nodded. They pulled up to the school, where parents and babysitters were clustering around the entrance.

"The main thing is for you to know we arrested your stalker. We know his name. We know where he lives. We don't know why he was following you, but we've got him. You're *safe,* Alice."

Alice wondered where Frannie got the confidence for the assertion of her safety. Frannie reached over to pop open the back door so Alice could exit onto the sidewalk, back into her life. Peter was just then coming down the stairs with his lunch box trailing from his hand. When he saw her, his face blossomed in smile.

Chapter 25

A careful scan of the Saturday morning newspaper and also the Internet convinced Alice that the detectives had succeeded in keeping the information of Andre Capa's arrest secret.

"I'm surprised that reporter, Brinkley, didn't find out about Capa." Alice folded the newspaper and turned to Mike, who was stooping to wipe syrup off Peter's face with a damp paper towel. "She found out everything else."

"She found out what we've read about," Mike said. "There could be other stuff we don't know."

"Right." Of course, Alice thought, there would be. The police always held things back, crucial facts like Ivy's gender and name. Maybe there was more. "But at least the detectives told us," Alice added, "so we don't have to worry anymore."

"Go brush your teeth, and tell Nell too." Mike shooed Peter toward the stairs. "We're leaving in five minutes."

"We don't need to worry anymore, Mike, right?"

"Are you asking me, or telling me?" His smile was slightly mischievous, bubbling with some nascent humor he wasn't yet ready to let loose. He *was* feeling less worried, she realized with relief.

"A little of both, I guess."

"We better boogie if we're going to make it on time," Mike reminded Alice, who was the only one still not dressed for their ten o'clock appointment with Judy Gersten to see the Third Place house.

She got ready as quickly as she could, though she was beginning to notice that with each passing day it was harder to move around. As the twins grew, her physical capacities seemed to shrink; going through the simplest routines could feel like walking through water.

She joined the family out front, where Nell and Peter were enduring the wait by decorating the stoop with chalk drawings.

"Oh, Julius is going to *love* that," Alice said.

Mike grinned. "More color, kids!"

They began to energetically fill in hollow outlines: a pirate ship, a miniscule Captain Hook, crazed bolts of lightning.

"We really have to get going," Alice said, earning a pair of raised eyebrows from Mike.

"Well, excuse us for keeping you!"

"Yeah, Mom, excuse us!" Nell had her hands splayed on her hips, sassing Alice with squinted eyes.

"Excuse us, Mommy," Peter said, missing the sarcasm altogether, reaching up to Alice for a hug.

Judy Gersten was standing in front of the rose-covered fence when they came down Clinton Street and turned the corner. She was a prim woman in her middle fifties, Alice guessed, with neat iron-gray hair cut at an even length at her jaw. She wore a navy skirt that fell to just below her knees, with a crisp white blouse and a blue blazer that nearly, but didn't, match her skirt. She clutched a large canvas shoulder bag tightly to her middle. When Alice got up close, she was surprised by Judy's extra touch of bright blue mascara on an otherwise plain face.

"You must be Judy." Alice offered a hand to shake and Judy lightly squeezed it. Their eyes locked for a moment, acknowledging the innate discomfiture of their appointment, resulting as it did from the attack on Pam. "This is my husband, Mike, and our kids—"

Just as she tried to introduce them, Nell and Peter ran

past the cascading roses, up the path and onto the front stoop. Sated by pancakes and television, they were ready for some action. Peter sat down in front of the door and revved his fire truck along the stone step.

"I spoke with Pam's husband this morning," Alice told Judy. "He said she can't have visitors yet, except for family. Have you seen her?" Knowing Pam had worked with Judy for many years, Alice wondered if she fell close enough into the family category to have been permitted a visit.

"Yes, this morning."

"How is she?"

"Same, I'd say." Judy pinched her lips into a truncated smile clearly meant to end the conversation. Alice wondered whether the refusal to share details had any significance, if the visit had caused her some pain, or if the woman was simply a poor conversationalist.

"By the way," Alice asked Judy as they started up the stoop together, "did Pam ever get a call back from someone in the Buildings Department?"

"Didn't you ask me that once before?"

"Did I?"

The same pinched smile, revealing nothing.

"Yes, I'm sure you did." Judy frowned in thought. "No, she didn't get any messages from Buildings, not that I know of."

Just as they reached the top of the stoop, Peter began to vigorously drive his fire truck up the gleaming oak door, running it back and forth, oscillating his voice in mimicry of a siren on high alert.

"Hey hey hey, Peter!" Mike said. "Not on the front door."

"Daddy said to stop!" Nell tried to wrench the truck out of Peter's hands, but he resisted.

Mike pried the children apart. "One more problem with the fire truck, Petie," Mike said, "and I'll have to put it in my pocket for the whole day. Okay?"

Peter became still, clutching the truck tightly in his hand, and nodded.

Judy rang the buzzer and waited a minute to make sure no one was home before opening the door with her own key. She was very still, Alice noticed, hardly any movements for each action, a tight perfection in every choice. She stood aside for the family to file in after her.

"There's a two-bedroom rental unit on the ground floor," she said. "They have their own entrance. We can go down there later if you're interested. The rental income's pretty good."

The kids raced ahead of them, right through the living room and into the kitchen. Alice heard their chatter studded with *wow* and *what's this* and *that's my spot*. At the table, Alice presumed. She wondered if they had already seated themselves, if they had served themselves a snack from a fruit bowl or even the refrigerator.

They followed Judy into the living room, a parlor floor with separation walls removed, except where an archway offered distinction from the kitchen. Wide planks gave the floors a farmhouse feeling that was contradicted by an ornate marble fireplace. A simple but beautiful chandelier hung from a round molding in the center of the ceiling. Two windows stretched from floor to ceiling and let in a gentle light that seemed to dance across the room. The current owner had draped the windows with fabric the color and texture of parchment, twisted loosely around leaf-patterned curtain rods.

In the kitchen, the children had indeed placed themselves at the table, but the snack they were eating was imaginary. They looked natural in this modest but efficient kitchen. It was a good kitchen, not fancy, renovated once, though not recently. It had every appliance, modern enough, with plenty of blond wood cabinetry, and pink counters in a style of Formica whose interlocking triangle pattern had recently rebounded into fashion. Everything looked like it was in good shape; either someone had reconstructed an older-style kitchen or never much used the original. It was cozy enough to work in without getting lost and spacious enough to easily accommodate two or three cooks.

"Not renovated," Mike said in a tone more sober than any of his usual voices. It was a new voice: the cautious buyer.

"This house has been very well maintained over the years," Judy said. "Plumbing and electric are in excellent shape. You have a dry basement, new windows. The kitchen isn't new, but it looks like it's in good condition."

Alice wanted to shout, *Yes!* but held herself back. She was glad the kitchen wasn't renovated and hoped the bathrooms weren't either. The potential she saw, no *felt*, in this house was not about fixtures but her family's daily life, their happiness. New fixtures were an added pizzazz that looked great and probably were a dream to use but also tended to inflate the price beyond reasonability. They didn't really matter.

A glass door to the right of the table looked out on a grassy backyard bordered by gardens. An iron scrollwork table with four matching iron chairs sat in a slate circle at the foot of the stairs that led up to the kitchen deck, where another table and chairs sat under an umbrella.

"A good family house," Judy said, though she needn't have.

"Can we see the upstairs?" Alice asked.

Nell and Peter abandoned their pretend tea party and followed the grown-ups to the staircase.

Judy went up first, followed by the children, then Alice and Mike. When no one was looking, Alice nudged Mike's shoulder. He looked at her and she raised her eyebrows and nodded. He winked, and she knew they had found themselves a house.

Upstairs there were three bedrooms, two average in size, the third very small but with its own window. Everything looked neat and clean and newly painted. Nooks cradled built-in shelving that had a civilizing effect on the space, with things and stuff tucked into their places.

"Closet." Judy opened a door in the hallway, revealing a narrow linen closet next to the bathroom. "Another closet." She opened a door in one of the larger bedrooms. "And there's one more big closet upstairs."

"There's another upstairs?" Mike asked.

Judy smiled. "Follow me."

They trailed her up another flight of stairs to the top floor. There was no hallway, just two large rooms joined together by a doorway without a door. One of the rooms was being used as an office, the other as a sewing area. Alice looked around and saw, in her mind, another bedroom and a play area.

"I can show you the basement if you'd like," Judy offered.

"Sure," Mike said, nodding. "Definitely."

Judy started down the stairs and they all followed her. Mike went all the way into the basement but Alice stopped halfway as a buffer to keep the kids from following into whatever hazards might be harbored down there. It looked like an average, stony, cave of a basement. Utility shelves were stocked with kitchen overflow, bikes were lined up against one wall, a large hot-water heater occupied the opposite corner.

"The technicals are all good," Judy said. "But of course you'd get an engineer to inspect. I can give you some names if you'd like."

She was doling out the crumbs and Alice was devouring them. Yes, they would like the name of an engineer. And a real estate lawyer to close the deal. And a mover to make it final. She couldn't wait to move out of Julius Pollack's house. Maybe they wouldn't even tell him they were leaving. They could let him begin eviction proceedings, agitate himself, under the watchful eye of the police. They could steal the final word; after all, he didn't own *them*. But before allowing herself the satisfaction of victory, there was one more thing Alice needed to know.

"Judy," Alice asked from her perch on the basement stairs. The kids pressed up against her, but she held fast. "Pam never told me the price."

Judy nodded and didn't smile and that worried Alice. She could hear it coming, some astronomical asking price for this sweet jewel of a house. If they could pay one point two, as Pam had showed her they could, then of course this house would turn out to be one point seven or eight or nine, bringing it well past their reach. She could feel the disappointment wash over her before Judy spoke.

Judy reached into her purse for the property listing and consulted the top of the page. "The asking price seems to be nine ninety-five." She looked at Alice. "But there may be room for negotiation."

"Mike." Alice summoned him up the stairs. "Can we talk just a minute?"

He nodded, and together they ushered Nell and Peter back into the kitchen. Judy stayed behind in the basement, waiting for her cue.

"What do you think?" Alice whispered. "Believe it or not, that's a really good price."

Mike glanced around the kitchen. "I like it a lot."

"This house is perfect."

"Okay," he said, "let's do it."

Alice called Judy from the top of the basement stairs. She came up, making an effort not to smile, Alice thought. She was good at this in a different way than Pam was. Judy was controlled, seasoned, whereas Pam would have been howling in delight. Pam wouldn't wait to be told what Alice thought; she would know, and would insist they grab the house while it was still on the market. *Honey, don't be an idiot. Take it.*

"We want to offer the asking price," Alice said.

"Well! I'll be happy to pass that on to the seller."

They left the house, Judy locked up, and they said good-bye standing in the front gardens.

"I'll let you know as soon as I hear," Judy said, then went to the corner, where she waited alone for a car to pass.

Alice just then had a thought and turned around to walk back toward Judy. "Maybe *you* know who Julius

Pollack's partner is?'' Until now it hadn't occurred to her to ask Judy directly.

Judy's expression was blank, a sky without clouds or horizon lines, surreal.

"Julius Pollack,'' Alice explained, "who owns Metro Properties. You must handle some of their apartments.''

"Yes,'' Judy said. "Of course we do. As far as I'm aware, he works alone.''

"Are you sure? I've seen a few mentions of a partner but no one seems to know who it is. I thought you might.''

"No, dear. Sorry.'' The light on the opposite corner switched to the white WALK signal, but Judy didn't seem to notice; her eyes stayed on Alice. "Why the interest in a partner? If there even is one?''

It seemed the strangest question, Alice thought, considering recent events. Why *wouldn't* they want to know the identity of the silent partner behind Lauren's and Alice's evictions? The identity of the person Pam had been trying to unearth when she was attacked?

"The house where you live is owned by Julius Pollack alone,'' Judy said, suddenly well informed. "Not Metro. It seems to me, dear, that your eviction is a very personal matter, not connected to Metro Properties, not really.'' Judy finally released her full smile, broad and steady, surprising Alice with neat rows of tiny, white teeth.

"Alice!'' Mike called. He was already half a block along, keeping up with the restless children.

"I was just wondering,'' Alice said.

Judy's attention moved to the flashing orange DON'T WALK sign; the traffic signal was about to change. She stepped into the street, preparing herself to cross. "I'll let you know about the offer. It's a wonderful house, isn't it?'' She walked away, not waiting for an answer.

Alice eventually caught up with her family as they were entering Carroll Park. Nell and Peter ran down two separate paths to the park's center. Almost immediately, Peter ran back toward his parents, weeping.

"Where's my fire truck?" He pressed his face into the side of Alice's belly.

Alice stroked his hair. "Did you put it down just now? Is it in the park?"

"No!" His crying escalated.

Nell walked casually over, with the special authoritative expression that meant she knew something they didn't.

"He left it in that house," she said, "in the way upstairs."

"Did you know he left it there?" Mike asked, trying to control the annoyance in his voice.

"I *saw* him put it *down* but I *didn't* think he'd *leave* it there." Nell planted her hands on her skinny hips and waited for a rebuttal. There was none.

"Okay, sweetie," Alice said. "I'll call Judy and ask her if she can help us get your truck back, okay? It isn't really lost—we know where it is. You'll get it back, I promise."

Reassured, Peter ran back through the park and into the big kids' side of the playground, chasing Nell up a ladder and down a slide. Alice pulled out the business card Judy had given her, figuring she'd find a cell phone number and could catch Judy before she got too far, but there was just an office contact. A little bit relieved not to have to speak with that strange woman again, so soon after their awkward conversation at the corner, Alice left a voice mail about arranging to go back to the house to get Peter's lost toy.

The call wasn't returned until the next night, Sunday. Judy's voice sounded muted, almost slurred, Alice thought, as she delivered two messages:

"Congratulations, they accepted your offer! Also, I've got your son's fire truck. It's in my purse. I'll be home all day tomorrow waiting for the dishwasher repairman as if I have nothing better to do with my time than wait for the dishwasher repairman between the hours of eight and five. Eight and five! As if I have nothing better to do!''

Alice wasn't sure, but before Judy ended the call with her home address, her voice seemed to spiral out of control. Was she actually weeping?

Chapter 26

Judy Gersten lived on Douglass Street just off Court, in one of the blue clapboard houses scattered around the neighborhood that stood out from the typical brown-stones or brick townhouses. Alice climbed the front stoop, rang the front bell and waited. It was only a quarter to nine but Judy had specifically said she was expecting the dishwasher repairman some time after eight, so it couldn't have been too early. Even so, no one came to the door. It occurred to her that she knew nothing about Judy, whether she lived alone or with a large family, a husband or a lover, male or female. And she had been so upset last night; maybe something had changed her plans. Alice rang again.

Finally the front door cracked open and one of Judy's watery blue eyes squinted at her visitor, registering what appeared to be a total lack of recognition. Alice was tempted to apologize and leave, but she had promised Peter the fire truck when he got home from school today.

"Is it too early?" Alice asked. "I came by for my son's toy."

Judy swung open the door. She was wearing a champagne-colored satin robe that fell open over a pair of old drawstring pants and a man's undershirt with no bra underneath. Without the second skin of her composure, Judy seemed raw and comfortable. Oddly, she looked both older and younger. Alice found herself more drawn to this Judy than to the professional Judy who had shown her the house. Until, that is, she spoke.

"It's right over here," Judy said. "I'll get it."

Alice was hit by the oaky twang of whiskey. So that was it; Judy was drunk. But Alice wanted Peter's fire truck and so followed Judy inside. The living room was a comfortable mess, French provincial, and well used.

"I'll just take the truck and get out of your hair," Alice said.

"Oh, my *hair*!" Judy sounded like she would weep. "What do I care about my *hair*?"

It was even worse than Alice had thought. "Maybe I'll come back later."

"Just wait, will you?" Judy's voice sounded weak, pathetic.

The morning paper was spread open on a divan in front of a tall window with a rose-scattered ivory sconce. Next to the divan, on the floor, was a mug with Judy's *coffee,* an oily, amber liquid anyone would recognize as booze.

Judy rifled through her purse while Alice's eye caught something in the newspaper that gave her a jolt. She inched closer to the divan. It looked like a photograph of Julius, a strange picture because he was smiling and she had never seen him smile before. He had his arm around another man. There was a headline above the article, but Alice couldn't read it upside down before Judy came up beside her.

"Thanks." Alice turned away from the newspaper and took the little red truck. Up close, Judy looked more than drunk, she looked distraught. Alice wondered if it was not the whiskey that had upset her, but something else. "Are you okay?" Alice asked.

"Oh, I'm just fine!" Judy said dramatically. She walked over to a couch against a brick wall and crumpled onto the soft cushions. Alice remained where she was but her eyes stayed with Judy. Poor woman. It was always the ones with the tightest surfaces, the highest sheen of control, who contained the most turmoil.

"Something happened," Judy sobbed into her hands, "and now it's all over."

"I'm sorry," Alice whispered. And she was, though she didn't know what for. She stood there waiting for an ebb in the tide so she could say good-bye and leave.

Glancing around the pretty, disheveled room, Alice saw the true impact of the handiwork samples she had noticed around Judy's desk at the office. The woman seemed to have crafted every soft surface in the room except the rug and possibly the sofa's silver jacquard upholstery. The seats of two antique armchairs were meticulous canvases of needlepoint gardens. The chairs straddled a small, scallop-edged table holding a framed eight-by-ten photograph of Judy and a man who looked vaguely familiar to Alice. They both smiled broadly, arm in arm, linked together in a happy moment like an old couple. But nothing else here spoke of marriage; it was so completely feminine a room. An antique hutch was draped with an elegant, hand-sewn runner with midnight-blue tassels at either end. On the couch where Judy sat was a collection of needlepoint and bargello pillows, all but one with symmetrical patterns of minute flowers creating the effect of a kind of garden fireworks. The exception was a single pillow whose minutiae had in effect been reversed. Instead of an abundance of flowers, it showed a single bloom in perfect detail, with the tight focus and burgeoning sexuality of a Georgia O'Keeffe painting.

Alice must have been staring at it because Judy's sobbing eased suddenly. "It's supposed to be a peony," she said, "but like everything else I probably got it wrong."

Now Alice saw that it *was* a peony.

"It's beautiful," Alice said.

Judy picked up the pillow and ran her shaky fingers on its nappy surface, keeping her eyes on Alice. "It was the French girl's idea." Her voice was rough from crying. "Sylvie. She told me about the woman who loved peonies, the one they found in the canal. A woman thrown away like garbage." Judy began to weep again. "Here."

She threw the pillow to Alice. "Sylvie told me the woman was your friend. This means more to you than me."

Alice caught the pillow. "I can't take this."

"It doesn't matter to me." Judy took a deep breath in an effort to control herself. She lifted her rheumy eyes to Alice in what looked like both abandonment and plea. "I only make them because I need something to do with my hands. Sylvie backs them for me and takes them over to the Women's Exchange. I sell them because they mean nothing to me. I don't need the money. Take it, please."

Judy got up and walked over to the divan. She stooped down for her mug and immediately drained it, her eyes avoiding the newspaper.

"Thank you," Alice said. "I know just where I'll put it."

Judy waved her off with a nonchalant wrist flick. Holding Peter's fire truck and the pillow, Alice found the front door.

As soon as Alice got home, she slid that day's newspaper out of its plastic sleeve and spread it out on the kitchen table. She flipped directly to the Metro section and quickly found the photo of Julius and his cohort on page three beside the headline BROOKLYN SLUMLORD INVESTIGATED IN BROKER ATTACK, *Realtor in Coma, Possible Connection to Missing Pregnant Women,* by Erin Brinkley.

Alice was amazed at the speed with which Erin Brinkley had discovered Julius Pollack. Recently it seemed as if the reporter was reading Alice's mind. The man in the photograph was identified as his partner, Sal Cattaneo. He was in his fifties, Alice guessed, with a tousled halo of prematurely white hair, and smile lines extending from his eyes. He looked friendly, unlike Julius, who even in this picture, with his smile, appeared hardened. Alice took another look at Sal Cattaneo, the man Pam, with all her connections, had tried and failed to unearth.

How had Erin Brinkley discovered him so easily? Sal Cattaneo. Both the name and the face were familiar to Alice but she couldn't place either.

Sitting at her kitchen table, she read the article.

In a convergence of three unsolved cases, local police have begun to scrutinize notorious slumlords Julius Pollack and Sal Cattaneo, longtime partners in Metro Properties, in connection with the death of Lauren Barnet and the disappearance of her full-term, unborn baby. The two men are also under investigation in connection with the disappearance two years ago of Christine Craddock, who was also pregnant. Ms. Craddock vanished on her baby's due date. Both Ms. Barnet and Ms. Craddock were Metro Properties tenants who, at the time of their disappearances, were fighting Metro's efforts to evict them from rent-stabilized apartments in the Carroll Gardens–Cobble Hill area. In addition, sources report that police have questioned Mr. Pollack and Mr. Cattaneo about the recent attack on Pam Short, a Brooklyn realtor who may have uncovered information about Metro Properties that put her at risk. Ms. Short remains in a coma at Long Island College Hospital.

According to the police, previous suspects, including Ms. Barnet's husband, Tim Barnet, and Ms. Craddock's boyfriend, David Jonstone, are no longer considered lead suspects. When the three cases appeared to be connected, it was necessary to broaden the search.

In an investigation rampant with theories ranging from a lone serial killer to a real estate conspiracy to a black market for babies, there appears to be a growing sense of puzzlement.

"It's starting to seem obvious someone out there is playing with us," said Detective Francesca Viola of the Seventy-sixth Precinct. "We're looking at all the common denominators, and right now they're two pregnant women who went missing, their land-lord Metro Properties, and a real estate broker who may have been onto something."

Alice read the article through two more times. There was still no mention of Andre Capa; Frannie and Gio-metti were holding tight on to that piece of information. But *why?* For a moment Alice was tempted, again, to contact the reporter herself, fill in a few blanks. But as before, she decided against it. She had promised Frannie not to tell.

As if the brief temptation to betrayal had summoning powers, the phone began to ring. Caller ID announced the Seventy-sixth Precinct. Alice reached to pick up the phone when something else became clear to her.

She remembered where she had seen Sal Cattaneo before: it had been just half an hour ago, in Judy Gers-ten's apartment, in the eight-by-ten frame on the pretty table. Standing by Judy's side with the complicity of a husband or partner or lifelong friend.

And then Alice remembered where else she had seen the smiling man in Judy's photo; suddenly she knew ex-actly who he was.

Chapter 27

The dear friend of Judy Gersten and partner of Julius Pollack was also the local butcher. In Alice's mind she saw the blue awning over his Court Street shop announcing CATTANEO & SON in white script. Only there never seemed to be a son. And now, there were at least three Sal Cattaneos. The one she knew was always so nice and friendly, but what about the other two?

She picked up the phone, hoping to catch Frannie's call before she finished her message. A long dial tone told her it was too late.

She pressed the down arrow on her caller ID to recall Frannie's number and was just dialing it into the phone when she heard the first crash.

Someone was standing outside her door, pounding it with tremendous force.

"You!" Julius shrieked. "You fucking bitch, open the door or I'll break it down!"

"Stop it, Julius!" Alice screamed back.

She brought the phone with her through the kitchen to the garden door, just in case she needed to escape, though once she was out there, she didn't know where she could possibly go; she'd be trapped. He slammed the door again and again. The wood vibrated, then seemed to bend inward.

"Stop it! I'm calling the police!"

The moment she said it, the banging stopped. It was suddenly as if he wasn't even there.

"Seventy-sixth Precinct," the receptionist answered.

"Fran Viola, please. Tell her it's Alice Halpern."

She waited. The kitchen seemed to fill with quiet. She began to feel dizzy and realized she was hardly breathing. She took a deep breath, then another, listening to Julius's heavy footsteps plodding up the stairs.

"Alice," Frannie said.

Alice quickly explained what had just happened.

"Where are you now?" Frannie asked.

"In the kitchen."

"Is he still outside?"

"He just went upstairs."

"Stay where you are. Don't answer the door and don't even answer the phone. We'll be there in two minutes."

Time stretched long and thin as Alice waited, frozen next to the garden door. Julius must have thought she had something to do with the article in the newspaper. Had he connected her with Pam Short? Did he know Pam had been digging around on Alice's behalf? Did Andre Capa work for him? Had Capa reported back before being arrested?

Alice remembered the old man with the foil cross, saw his bright insistent face and heard him telling her, *Take a deep breath lady, one, two, three.* Standing there now, pressed against her kitchen door, Alice rubbed her belly and breathed. *One, two, three.* Her heart was still racing but she could feel a trace of oxygen entering her brain. The deep breathing was working. *One. Two. Three.*

With shaking fingers she dialed Mike's cell phone. After three rings, voice mail answered; he must have been sawing, or instructing Diego, or maybe he was blasting music through the workshop as she knew he often did. Frustration clumped in her throat. "Mike!" she whispered on his voice mail. "Julius was trying to get in! Come home! *Please!*"

Alice listened as Julius's footsteps thumped back down the stairs. She clutched the phone so hard her fingers went numb. Where were Frannie and Giometti? As he reached the foyer, just outside her door, she dialed 911 and listened to the phone ring and ring. Then she heard Julius open the building's front door.

She crept across the kitchen, into the living room. He was talking to someone. Pressing her ear against the door, she felt the vibrations of his voice, its low pitch, its arrogance. Then she heard a higher, more insistent voice. A voice she recognized.

Frannie.

A tinny, distant voice beckoned from the phone in Alice's hand: "Hello? Hello? Is there an emergency?" Alice pressed the END button.

Julius was arguing with something Frannie was saying, arguing but managing to hold his temper. The next voice to speak was Paul Giometti's and whatever he said seemed to rein Julius in. Alice held her breath. They were negotiating something. She heard Frannie's voice rise with the words "restraining order."

"All right," Alice heard Julius say. "How much?"

There was a hushed conversation that ended with Julius's voice tightening, getting higher. "You do that and you'll regret it." He marched back upstairs with crisp, angry steps.

Alice waited where she was and kept listening. Quick footsteps told her Frannie and Giometti were approaching her apartment. At the first knock, she swung open her door. They stepped inside and shut the door behind them. Both the detectives' expressions were taut, concerned.

"You okay?" Giometti asked Alice.

"Just scared, but I'm okay."

Frannie angled her sunglasses off her face and used them like a headband to push the dark hair off her forehead, which was misted with sweat. "We want you to file a restraining order."

"But he lives here."

"Yes, he does." Giometti's voice was gentle, in contrast to the sharp squint of his eyes, holding her to a simple certainty: "But you don't. Not anymore."

He was right; she couldn't stay here with her children.

"But he'll find me, won't he?" Alice said. "He's angry about the newspaper article this morning. He thinks I had something to do with it. Won't a restraining order make it worse?"

"We don't know," Giometti said.

If they said *we don't know* to her one more time, she would scream.

"Listen." Frannie stepped close to Alice. "If he does it again to you or anyone else, it's on record, that's all. It doesn't mean he'll stop, but it gives us a paper trail. It helps the lawyers if he ends up in court one day."

"If he hurts someone," Alice said. "If he hurts me."

Frannie looked steadily into Alice's eyes. "That's right."

"Let's go." Giometti put his hand on the doorknob.

"Wait," Alice said. "I need to get a few things first."

She hurried downstairs, where she packed an overnight bag for the family. They didn't live here anymore, after fifteen years. Just like that.

Giometti drove the car. Frannie, in the passenger's seat, twisted around to face the back. Alice told them all about her visit to Judy Gersten, and the prominent photo of Judy with Sal, and Judy's anguish. Frannie and Giometti had already seen the *Times* article but apparently hadn't been surprised by anything they had read. They pulled into one of the precinct's parking spots. The detectives got out of the front seat and Frannie opened the back door for Alice.

She was taken to a room behind the reception desk. Giometti and Frannie stayed with her while she answered questions to an officer who filled out a harassment report on the spot. There was an air of seriousness in the room, with both the questions and answers simple and direct. It took only about ten minutes. Alice was asked to sign the bottom of the report.

The detectives then drove her to the courthouse, where they double-parked their blue sedan on Adams Street with an assumed immunity that Alice found strangely thrilling. It was a gesture of power, of protection. They hurried up the courthouse steps, ushering Alice through a revolving door and down a long, drab hallway. They veered into a room sectioned into judges' chambers. It looked nothing like the courthouse dramas on TV. Instead of a lofty dais, each judge occupied a grim cubicle in which a battered wooden counter separated them from the complainant. Alice's judge was a woman in her sixties with the restless air of someone who had waited too long for promotion, or retirement, or any transfer out of here.

"Keep it simple," Frannie whispered when Alice was called to the bench.

She stated her case as succinctly as possible, details swirling around her in a sea of glittering omission. "My landlord is Julius Pollack. He has recently begun to harass me. I'm frightened for my children."

There was some back and forth about her relationship with Julius, and whether or not she would have to bring criminal charges against him before requesting the Order of Protection. Giometti stepped into the procedural line of fire, lobbing back answers Alice understood as little as the questions. Finally the judge nodded, signed a Request for an Order of Protection, banged her gavel, and it was over.

Alice felt dizzy, swept into the current of a bureaucratic system she had never imagined she would need to tap. She had always felt secure knowing the justice system was there, but now wondered how stacks of offices and reams of paperwork could protect her, or anyone, from the cracked seed of human potential. She had always figured everyone contained elements of good and bad. Life threw obstacles in front of you, challenging you to choose a reaction. She now knew one thing in her bones: she could kill Julius Pollack if she had to. She didn't *want* to, not really, but what if something happened to coax her to it? She imagined Lauren in her final moments, put a gun in her hand. *Shoot,* Alice silently cautioned Lauren, gathering fixed images of noontime Brooklyn from the backseat of the police car as they drove away from the courthouse. *Shoot first.*

In the squad car on their way back to the precinct, Mike finally called.

"I'm at home," he said. "What the hell is going on?"

Alice explained. "I already packed for you. If there's anything else you want, grab it now. Call Simon, okay? See if we can stay there."

"This is unreal, Alice." She could hear the twist of agitation in his voice. "Let's get out of here, okay? Get on a plane. Go."

It was a compelling thought, and for a moment the infinite stretch of heat-wavering pastel beach filled her mind. Yes. They could go. For a week, two, maybe more.

"They're taking me back to the precinct," she said. "Just call Simon. And will you pick the kids up from school? I'm not sure I'll be done in time."

Alice, Frannie and Giometti crossed through the lobby and climbed the stairs that led to the Precinct Detectives Unit. The low-ceilinged room hummed with detectives talking to each other or on the phone or tapping their keyboards or just sitting at their desks thinking. Alice and her detectives settled in around Frannie's desk, and in the bubble of their conversation it felt like just the three of them alone in a lens that was finally being put into focus.

"We're going to be square with you now, Alice." An uneasy shadow passed over Frannie's face as if she was not quite certain it was time to remove a veil, reveal a truth, but she was going to anyway.

"Good," Alice said. "I really need to know what's going on." Across the room, Alice heard a spate of typing, then the ding of a typewriter's return.

Giometti took his hands out of his pockets and shifted in his chair. Frannie's gaze slid to his face, then back to Alice.

"Andre Capa wasn't following you," Frannie said. Her eyes were round and dark, fixed on Alice, drinking in every reaction. "Andre Capa is an artist who lives near he Gowanus Canal. He has nothing to do with this case."

Alice was confused. Andre Capa was the last witness o Lauren's life. Erin Brinkley had written about him eeing Christine Craddock cross the Gowanus Canal. Alice herself had seen him watching her that early morning on her solitary walk. She had seen him so many imes. She had *smelled* him, he had come so close. Unless . . .

"Who was following me, then?" Alice felt a swell of panic at the thought that the limo driver—whoever he was—might still be out there.

"He's one of our men," Giometti said.

"A cop?" Alice was stunned. "What do you mean?"

"Alice." Frannie leaned forward and softened her oice. "We've been keeping an eye on you since Lauren lisappeared. First Christine Craddock, then Lauren, hen . . ."

"Me?"

"We didn't know." Viola picked up a paper clip from he surface of her desk and bent it out of shape. "We ouldn't take any chances."

"*Have* I been in danger?" Alice asked. "Am I now?"

"We've been covering every possible base," Frannie aid. "We're getting closer, we think. But there's more work to do."

"Why did you lie to me about Andre Capa?" Alice elt a rise of indignation; after she herself had tried so hard to share the truth with them, they had outright lied o her. "Why did you tell me that he was stalking me and that you arrested him? *Why?*"

Giometti uncrossed his legs and leaned toward Alice. "You read the newspaper."

"Yes."

"All those articles about the cases?" he said.

Alice nodded.

"Some of the stuff that writer's been reporting has been undisclosed information," he said. "We talked to Erin Brinkley, the reporter. She said a woman's been calling her anonymously, feeding her tips. Some of them are just wrong."

"We needed to know if you were the leak," Frannie clarified. "I'm sorry, Alice, but we had to test you."

It began to dawn on Alice now. "You mean you deliberately lied to me to see if the story about Andre Capa stalking me and being arrested would turn up in the newspaper?"

"That's right," Giometti said.

"And it didn't." Frannie dropped the twisted paper clip into a wastepaper basket at the side of her desk. "So now we can work with you, if you're willing."

"How?" Alice felt very cold, as if someone had cranked up the air-conditioning. She glanced around the room at all the detectives, sweating in their shirtsleeves. One guy, at the neighboring desk, had a small fan pointed at his face.

"We have a plan, Alice," Frannie said. "We think you might be in danger. We're going to help you, and we're hoping you'll agree to help us too."

Chapter 28

"This is Dana," Frannie told Alice. "She's been detailed to the case."

Dana was a light-skinned black woman whose hair was a waterfall of miniature braids. Medium height, with a lithe, elegant build, she was a colleague of Giometti's from the Homicide Unit at the Sixtieth Precinct and a stranger to Carroll Gardens, which was exactly the idea. Here, she could pass as Alice's friend, unrecognizable to the neighborhood as a cop. You never would have suspected Dana was a detective with a gun holstered to her ankle under the flowing red batik pants.

"You'll need to keep Dana's identity private," Frannie said. "You can't tell anyone. It could get around and really screw things up."

"What about Mike?" How disappointed would he be, Alice wondered, to learn that Alice had agreed to help the investigation—which meant they wouldn't be able to leave town after all?

"Only Mike."

"The kids?"

"Do them a favor," Dana said in a smooth, mellow voice, "and don't tell them. They'll be more comfortable with me if they think I'm some long-lost friend of yours. Kids who know secrets, they feel like they'll explode if they don't tell someone."

"Okay," Alice said. "Are you a long-lost friend who's

with us? Or one who stands outside our front
or all the time?"

Dana and Frannie both laughed. "That's a good one,"
Dana said. "I like this one."

"Don't get too cozy," Frannie warned. Then, to Alice,
"She won't be staying with you. She's an old friend from
college who's visiting and spending time with you. When
she's not with you, someone else will have the eye."

"The eye?" Alice looked from Frannie to Giometti to
Dana, her new triumvirate of protection.

"Watching you," Frannie said.

"Okay, college friend." Alice held out her hand and
Dana shook it.

"So, where did we go to school?"

"Sarah Lawrence College in Bronxville, New York."

"Got it."

"What did we major in?"

"I majored in film. You majored in . . . dance."

Dana nodded. "Sure, dance. Why not?"

"We're going to stay with our friend Simon," Alice
said. "Maggie spends time there, even though they're
separated—"

Frannie and Giometti chuckled; they knew.

Alice felt a flush of defensiveness on Maggie's behalf.
She knew how it sounded—it sounded like just what it
was: confusing and contradictory—but Maggie was her
best friend.

"My point is," Alice continued, "that Maggie won't
buy the old friend story. I've known her way too long."

"I don't know about that." Frannie sat back and
crossed her hands behind her head. "You'd be surprised
what people are willing to believe."

It was nearly four when the police finished with Alice.
She walked with Dana in the dappled shade of Clinton
Street toward Simon's house, carrying the overnight bag
she had packed earlier. Ribbons of humidity were beginning to choke what had started as a cool day. They
climbed the stoop of the house Simon had shared with
Maggie predivorce, rang the bell and waited in front of

the double door flanked by large Italian clay planters overflowing with red geraniums and slips of ivy.

"Nice place," Dana said.

Mike flung open the door with Nell and Peter by his side. Peter clenched a fistful of popcorn. Alice noticed a dribbled trail of popcorn up the blue carpeted stairs that led from the foyer to the second-floor family room, where Simon and Ethan spent a fair amount of their time.

"Mommy!" both kids shouted at once, assaulting her with hugs. The ardent grasping of their soft arms around her legs and bulging middle felt heavenly.

"We're having a sleepover!" Nell announced.

"Me too?" Peter asked.

"Everyone," Mike said, winking at Alice.

She handed him the overnight bag.

"Do you have pajamas in there for me?" Nell demanded.

"What about for me?" Peter seconded.

"Yes and yes," Alice said.

Mike opened the front door wider, letting Alice slip in past him as the children fled back upstairs. She heard sounds of cheering coming from the family room; the television was on.

"Is Ethan home?" She couldn't remember if it was Simon's night or Maggie's.

"Sylvie's got him over at Maggie's, but they're all coming over here later for dinner. I have to run out to the store. I've been waiting for you." He kissed Alice, then extended a hand to Dana. "Mike Halpern."

"This is Dana," Alice told Mike, raising her voice to add, "my old friend from college." She winked, and leaned in closer to Mike to whisper: "Homicide. She's working with Frannie and Giometti. No one else can know."

"Oh boy," he said. "This is going to be fun."

Dana had a warm, ready smile. "Nice to meet you, old friend."

"Coming in?" Mike moved aside to clear the doorway.

"Love to." Dana stepped into the house and stood in the archway that separated the foyer from the living room. Alice recalled the first time she came here, for a playgroup with Maggie, Lauren and a couple of other mothers when the boys were babies. It was impossible not to be overcome by the richness of every detail in every room, though by now Alice had spent enough time here to have noticed flaws.

There were few changes to the house since Maggie had moved out, leaving behind her stamp of oversized furniture, extravagant colors and even some original art commissioned for the walls that had failed to hold in the passions of a marriage. Simon's baby grand Steinway dominated the living room, beneath an ornate crystal chandelier Maggie had bought in Austria. White walls, oriental rugs on glowing walnut floors, modern light fixtures recessed into the ceiling's ample Victorian detail. Maggie had loved this house. In a dramatic gesture, she had insisted Simon keep it, underscoring her ability to afford her own condo in a frothy new set of houses on Warren Street, and his inability to pay for much of anything.

Shouts and more cheering emanated from upstairs.

"What's happening up there?" Alice asked Mike.

"Yankees and Red Sox, four-four, top of the ninth."

"So close," she said, "but do you really think—"

"Nuh uh, sweetheart. Today we squash the Evil Empire."

Mike was a lifelong Red Sox fan, having grown up just outside of Boston. Simon, however, was an ardent Yankees fan, having dubbed himself a born-again New Yorker as the father of an essentially American child who he felt needed a team affiliation.

"Mike, listen—" Alice began, but before she could complete the thought, he interrupted in a whisper:

"I called the travel agent. We can get flights out tonight—"

"We can't," Alice stopped him. "I have to explain this to you. Come."

She took his hand and led him into the living room, where Dana had seated herself at the piano. Hands cupped over the keyboard, she began to play lightly and beautifully. A sonata, Alice thought, possibly Mozart.

"Impressive," Alice said after.

"I wish I'd taken my lessons more seriously." Dana lowered the keyboard cover and ran her hand gently over the gleaming wood. "My mother told me I'd regret it, and I do."

Mike and Alice sat together on the emerald-green velvet sofa. Dana got up from the piano and faced them in a sapphire-blue wingback chair with tassels dangling off the seat. She sat with her feet planted on the floor, Alice noticed; the ankle holster would show if she crossed her legs. Alice filled Mike in on her visit to Judy Gersten's house, the articles in the newspaper, Julius's attack on their front door, the restraining order, her meeting afterward with the detectives, the true identity of her stalker. Everything. Dana chimed in only when it came time to describe the plan.

In the morning, they would return to the precinct to prepare for Alice's visit to Cattaneo & Son to try to find out where Sal Cattaneo was positioned in the web that had swallowed three women and a baby girl.

Chapter 29

Mike and Alice held hands as they walked with Dana through the increasingly sultry morning to the Seventy-sixth Precinct. Mike had insisted on coming along and Alice was grateful, her sense of heroism vanquished by yet another bad night's sleep. "I can't go to the workshop," he told her, "when you're going undercover." When he said that word, *undercover,* it really sank in. What she was about to do could be provocative, even dangerous. She had agreed to wear a wire on her visit to Sal Cattaneo, the local butcher—and what else?

Down in the precinct's basement was a small room that was empty except for a table and a tall metal cabinet with double doors padlocked together in the middle. Giometti undid the lock and opened the metal doors. Inside were shelves neatly stacked with electronic devices Alice didn't recognize. Frannie and Giometti selected equipment from the shelves and laid it out, piece by piece, on the table. Dana meanwhile foraged through another cabinet for an assortment of fresh batteries. Long thin wires were attached to a two-inch-long, rectangular transmitting device. At the end of one wire was a tiny black microphone, the size and shape of a button.

Giometti squatted down and rummaged around the bottom shelf. "Found the tape." He stood up holding a roll of black electrical tape, which he handed to Frannie.

"The department's got a requisition in for fully wireless, you know, *modern* equipment," she said to Alice and Mike. "But this being New York City—" she shrugged. "Maybe next year."

"Something to be said for the tried and true, though," Giometti said. "We know this set *works*."

As the three detectives proceeded to assemble the listening device on the table, separating wires and testing batteries, Alice began to think about the last two weeks. She felt like she had passed through a lifetime in fast-forward, uphill all the way, carrying a ton of stone on her back. Though she was nervous about today, even scared, it was a relief to have been deemed not only sane but able. Tired and scared. But not insane.

Sitting on two chairs the detectives had set up for them, Alice was surprised by the sudden warmth of Mike's hand slipping into hers. She squeezed his hand, greedily drinking in the rich warmth of Mike's skin, the solidity of his bones and muscles. He leaned closer, twinning himself to her until it would be time for her to go the next step alone. She wished he could go with her but knew it was impossible; a woman alone was vulnerable, and that was the whole idea.

"Okay, ladies," Giometti finally said. "It's showtime."

Mike smiled and almost pulled a voice, a *lady's* voice Alice guessed by the hitch in his expression the moment Giometti called them all *ladies*. Who would it be, she wondered? He did a fierce Julia Child and Katharine Hepburn. Alice herself began to smile in anticipation of a little levity. But as quickly as Mike's humor rose, it now fell, and instead of speaking he seemed to deflate against the back of his chair. Alice squeezed his hand.

"Get out of here, Paul," Frannie said.

Giometti left the room and Dana shut the door behind him.

Alice took off her dress and stood there, exposed, as Frannie placed the transmitter box between her breasts and Dana taped the wires securely against her skin. The little black button would be hidden just beneath the neckline. When she was all rigged up, Frannie stood a few paces away and in a casual voice—as if in normal conversation, or shopping for dinner at the local butcher's—said, "Testing, testing, Mary had a little lamb." She circled Alice, reciting nursery rhymes. The same rhymes Alice lulled her children with at bedtime or to pass long hours in the car. Here, the poetry lost its innocence, like a bouquet of lollipops held by a lurking, parkside stranger. The candies and the words, stripped of their promise to anoint the sweetest of dreams, became beacons of every mother's worst fears.

Giometti knocked three times on the door. "All set," he called in.

Apparently, he had been testing the remote end of the device, heard the nursery rhymes, and now they were ready. *Ready.* Alice would never be ready for this but she would do it anyway.

Dana opened the door. Giometti was standing on the other side, hands jammed in his pockets. He glanced at Alice, issuing a smile that abruptly turned him handsome through the mask of pocked, toughened skin. His tiny gesture was the warmest he had offered her yet and it fortified her immensely. If cool Giometti was on board, then the plan was right. Maybe her errand *would* somehow advance the search for Ivy and slow the danger to herself and her babies. Maybe, in the end, no one else would come to harm.

Frannie assessed Alice, who took a deep breath, feeling the wires cinch her skin.

"Ready?" Frannie asked.

"Ready."

Chapter 30

Alice moved along Court Street's concrete sidewalk feeling like she was in another body, another life. Dana was with Frannie, Giometti and a technician in a white Van Brunt Bakery van that had parked at a meter across the street from Cattaneo's. Alice sharply missed Mike, who was back at the precinct, reading wanted posters or staring into the fish tank or just sitting there, waiting.

Humidity cloyed at her skin and she could feel sweat dripping down the wires taped under her dress. She wanted to puff out the fabric around her sore, swelling breasts, to create a little breeze, but was afraid she would disturb the transmitter. So she did nothing, simply willed herself to walk forward along this familiar yet suddenly foreign street. Nothing looked real; it was like a movie set with flat fronts whose simple signs and offerings misrepresented the true stories behind them. Not even the people seemed the same. As she walked, she waved to old Mrs. Foglia across the street, plodding along with her shopping bags. Alice said hi in passing to an acquaintance from the park, as she would on any day, trolling Court Street, running errands. *Going to the butcher shop to find out if her landlord's secret partner wanted her babies or her blood.*

Alice kept walking.

She was a survivor. She had survived abandonment by her father, she had survived the film industry and she was surviving motherhood. She had cleared every hurdle so far, despite obstacles, and she had to continue. Put aside her fear.

Nothing could happen to her; she was protected.

The wires clung to her damp skin.

She kept walking.

Two small boys she recognized from the playground zoomed toward her on their bicycles. Their babysitters, jogging to catch up, smiled at Alice as they passed.

She crossed Warren Street, past the locksmith, an antique store, and the old vegetable place. The front door to Cattaneo's was closed to seal in the air-conditioning. She pulled it open, feeling suddenly faint. Taking a deep breath, she stepped inside and let the heavy door fall shut behind her.

The rotund young man behind the counter smiled. "How can I help you?"

"Is Sal around?"

"In the back."

Alice braced herself. "Could I see him a minute?"

The young man pushed through the swinging door that separated the shop from a back area. A moment later, Sal Cattaneo appeared, looking more like a butcher than Alice had ever seen him. His white apron was saturated with dark red blood and his clear plastic gloves oozed with something yellowish and thick.

"How can I help you?" Sal offered his usual bright smile.

"Could we talk privately?" Alice asked.

Sal hesitated a moment but never lost his courteous smile. "Come on in the back."

She followed him through the swinging door into a back room that was both an office and a dry-goods storage area. The room had a rough, comfortable, old-world feeling, with a poster of Sicily tacked to the wall, and completely lacked the gourmet luster of the front shop. To the left was a metal door with a long handle that Sal pulled. He held the door open for Alice, who hesitated a moment before going in. Three feet out of the refrigeration room, she could feel the chilly draft.

Sides of beef and pork hung by their back legs from the ceiling. Clear, heavy-duty plastic bags in bins on the floors held massive clumps of chickens. Even the free-range pesticide-free kind Alice bought—displayed so neatly in the refrigeration case in the front of the store, flagged by their high-end price—were lumped together in the bins. There was a raw, tangy smell in the air. Two stainless-steel butchering tables stood in the center of the space, one of them holding the partially butchered carcass of a skinned pig. A bloody cleaver lay next to it on the table.

"After you," Sal said.

Alice held her breath and walked in.

The cold slammed her. Sal shut the door behind her and she turned around, wondering, suddenly, if there was a latch to let you out. For a split second she thought he might have shut her in here alone, but he hadn't. He walked slowly over to the center butchering table and picked up the cleaver. And yes, Alice noted, there was a latch to open the door from the inside.

Sal picked up his job where presumably he had paused to greet her, slicing off the pig's second ear. He tossed it into a stained white bucket, where Alice saw the feet and a long, yellow coil of intestine.

She thought of the homemade apple pork sausages she sometimes bought here—they were delicious grilled—and realized she could never touch them again.

"What can I do you for?" Sal kept his eyes on his slicing blade, which parted muscle from bone at the shank. Droplets of blood collected in the cleavage of the pig's flesh. Alice noticed blood caked under Sal's wedding ring.

She gathered herself to the moment. This was the man they had been looking for, the silent partner in Metro Properties. Lauren and Christine Craddock's landlord. Julius Pollack's cohort. Someone special in Judy Gersten's life. This was the man who seemed to be the common denominator. The man inside the black hole that had stolen Lauren, swallowed Ivy and put Pam in a coma.

"I was hoping you could reason with Julius Pollack for me," she began.

He snickered, but said nothing, didn't even lift his eyes from the long, smooth cut he was making along the pig's breastbone.

"Julius is my landlord."

He put down his knife and forced his fingertips into the front seam of the breastbone. With two hands, he pulled apart the rib cage.

"Not through Metro," Alice said. "I live in his house."

Sal scooped out the pig's heart and tossed it in the bucket. Then he laughed.

"I don't envy you there!"

"Sal, I've lived in this neighborhood a long time—"

His eyebrows rose, and she knew what that meant: she was still an outsider.

"—and I want Julius to understand that he doesn't have to worry about us vacating. We've already found a house. Our offer's been accepted, but it's going to take a little time. His impatience has been . . ."—she was going to say *cruel,* but caught herself—". . . unnecessary."

"I've got nothing to do with that." Sal picked up a smaller knife and gouged out the pig's right eye, then the left, and tossed them into the bucket.

Alice wished the pig could scream, run, anything. She wished her wire could pick up the subtext, not just the talk, because Sal was communicating beyond words.

"The thing is, we know Julius doesn't want us there and we *are* moving. We just need a few more months," Alice said, knowing she would never live in the President Street house again, no matter what. She mustered her best acting skills and continued. "He doesn't need to start eviction proceedings when the Thirty Day Notice expires. We're moving out. I was hoping you could reason with him."

"Who says Julius won't be reasonable?"

So they had discussed it. A chill zippered up Alice's spine.

"He acts as if—"

"He's an old actor," Sal cut her off. He looked at her and winked, but what did it mean? Was there something she was supposed to implicitly understand, and didn't?

"We're buying our new house through Garden Hill Realty," Alice tried, thinking maybe *that* would get through to him.

Sal brought the edge of his cleaver down along the pig's haunch.

"I was at Judy Gersten's house just yesterday."

The knife stopped moving. Sal's eyes crept up to Alice's face. She had never seen his expression so still, and as every shred of civility dropped off his face, he became a different man. He stared at her with eyes that had transformed from blue to steel gray, and seemed to wait.

Alice knew in that instant that Judy was not Sal's wife. She also knew that Judy was more than just a friend. They were lovers, or she was part of Metro, or both.

"She was in bad shape," Alice continued.

Despite the frigid room, a new sweat gathered on her skin. She felt the wires tracing a map on her body.

"She was drunk," Alice said. "It was first thing in the morning. I think she'd been reading the newspaper, it was lying open. It was that long article in the *Times*."

Sal put down his knife.

"Don't go there again," he said calmly.

Alice nodded, then remembered she had to speak for the wire. "Okay."

"I'll talk to Julius. Don't worry about the notice. You take your time."

He crossed the room without looking at her and pulled the latch that opened the door. Alice stepped out of the freezing room into the cool back office, then passed through the shop into the respite of summertime heat.

She headed back toward Union Street, to the Seventy-sixth Precinct. The Van Brunt Bakery van passed her and drove slowly down Court Street to Union, where in the distance she could see it make the right turn and disappear around the corner.

Chapter 31

Mike, Frannie, Giometti and Dana were standing together in the precinct lobby when Alice walked in. Mike hurried over to her, his hair such a frenzy of mismatched direction that she knew he had spent the hour worrying it with nervous fingers. He stared into her eyes, assessing her mood, then pushed a strand of sweat-plastered hair off her forehead.

"How did it go?" he asked.

Alice cringed. "Let's give up meat."

His face lifted in smile, crinkling his eyes at the corners, where his wisdom lines seemed to have deepened in the last two weeks. She wanted to tell him everything, recount every detail and nuance so he could *see* it, rewind time half an hour and be there with her. She could still feel the deep chill of the meat locker, the goose bumps on her bare arms. Yet the humidity in the precinct was stifling.

"It's so hot," she said. She began to feel dizzy and a little sick. With an arm at her back, Mike led her to a chair at one of the center tables. He joined Frannie and Dana where they stood at a vending machine, drinking small bottles of water. Giometti was banging his fist on the soda machine.

"Let it go, Paul." Frannie opened her wallet and pulled out a dollar bill. "Here, try something else."

"Thanks." He threw up his hands. "But it's the principle of the thing. Excuse me, people." He left them for the front desk.

Frannie used the dollar to buy Alice a bottle of water. She tried to refuse but Frannie insisted. Alice realized how thirsty she was when she drained the bottle in three gulps.

"You did good," Frannie said.

Mike and the women gathered around Alice, pulling chairs close, leaning in.

Dana reached over to rub Alice's neck. "Excellent."

Alice felt her muscles begin to relax. Suddenly, she began to sweat in earnest.

"Delayed reaction to stress," Dana said. "Come on, let's get you into the AC." She stood, and the rest followed with a quick scraping of chairs. Mike helped Alice up.

"Paul, we're going in," Frannie said. They passed him at the front desk, retrieving his lost dollar from the officer who controlled the petty cash.

They went back to the small basement room where Alice had been wired earlier. The technician was there, unloading equipment.

"Got everything, Eddie?" Frannie asked him.

"Yup. All set."

"Can't leave anything in the van." Frannie rolled her eyes. "Even in our own parking lot."

"So, *was* it good?" Alice asked.

"It was good." Frannie turned to Eddie. "Okay, buddy, scoot."

Eddie left the room and Dana plucked the tiny microphone out of Alice's dress.

"Carefully," Dana said, as Alice lifted the dress over her head. The cool air on her clammy skin felt exquisite. Frannie carefully removed the wires and placed them on the table for Eddie to sort out when he returned.

"What we learned," she told Alice, "is that Garden Hill Realty is involved. As soon as you mentioned Judy Gersten, Cattaneo tensed. We don't know why exactly.

But I have a hunch things are going to start shaking up in the local real estate markets just about now."

"What next?" Alice asked.

"We wait," Frannie answered.

"You mean we just go back to our regular life, except that nothing's regular about it any more?"

"What I mean," Frannie said, "is you go back to normal as much as you can. And then we'll see."

"What if we got away for a while?" Mike asked. "I'd like to take Alice and the kids and go somewhere."

In the heavy pause that followed, as Mike looked from woman to woman, Alice felt the pinch of his helplessness. He hadn't told her in so many words, but she pretty much figured he had abandoned his plan to go to the furniture expo in Las Vegas. Day to day, they were both redefining priorities, and she knew that when he said *away,* he meant *far* away. Not just across state lines. To another country.

"We'd rather you didn't." Frannie sat down, leaning her elbows on the tabletop. "It might help to have you around."

"Why?" The jugular vein pulsed in Mike's neck. "So this psycho can butcher my wife? So you can catch him in the act this time? When it's too late for us?"

Frannie sighed deeply and sat back in her chair, the hinges of which let out a loud moan at the sudden weight of her body. She closed her eyes. Her lashes were very long, Alice noticed. And she knew: Mike's accusations were unanswerable because they were partly true.

"Just tell us," Alice begged Frannie in a voice buried in whisper, "what's going to happen next, so we can know. We need to *know* so we can decide."

Frannie opened her eyes. After a moment's pause, she said, "We've got a few ideas, but we can't share them right now."

So they were back to that. Alice pressed her lips shut against a vitriolic surge of frustration, helplessness, fear and grief that was threatening to erupt from her stomach to her mouth.

"I want to go home," she whispered to Mike.

"Me too," he whispered angrily. "But we can't."

Alice missed her old home on President Street and yearned for her new home on Third Place. But living in Simon's house, even just for one night, she had developed an awareness that home was not so much a place. Home was Nell and Peter and Mike, and it was her twins. Home was the dark hole in her existence where missing Lauren still hurt. Home was a good meal, a hot shower, a clean bed. Home could be anywhere.

But still, she missed home. Even though it scared her a little, she slipped forward to the edge of her chair to make a single demand.

"I need to get into the President Street apartment." She looked Frannie squarely in the eye. "I need to pick up a few things."

And she needed to say good-bye.

Frannie nodded slowly, thinking, and finally said, "All right. Tomorrow. I'll arrange it."

Chapter 32

Mike dropped the kids off at school, then went to his workshop. Alice, with Dana, opened Blue Shoes at eleven o'clock. And then at just after two—when they had been alerted that the coast was clear—they headed over to the President Street house to gather clothes and toys and a few other things. Sylvie had agreed to pick Nell and Peter up from school in case Alice couldn't get there in time.

"That's him," Dana whispered to Alice as they passed a man wearing a Yankees cap, sitting alone in a gray Ford parked in front of the house. Meaning, he was the cop surveilling the house. He was reading a newspaper, or pretending to. They passed him without so much as a glance in his direction and entered the house with Alice's key.

They had only been gone a few days, yet the house felt eerily abandoned. Things were just where they had left them in the rush of their lives. Dishes were in the sink and Alice's half-finished mug of tea sat on the counter by the phone. Toys were scattered where the children had left them before school that last morning.

Alice checked her watch. "How much time do we have?"

"Just what you need." Dana sat at the kitchen table and waited.

Alice forced herself to ignore the dirty dishes and the trash that was starting to smell. She went directly downstairs, where she collected clothes for everyone, a stack of books Nell hadn't yet read and a small bag full of Peter's favorite trucks and action figures. When she came upstairs, Dana had a funny look on her face.

"What?" Alice asked.

"Shh." Dana tilted her ear toward the ceiling. Footsteps. Alice now heard them clearly.

"He's *home*," Alice whispered. "He wasn't supposed to be home."

"He just came in. Come on—we gotta go. Quietly."

Padding through the living room, Alice noticed Judy Gersten's peony pillow where she had left it on the couch. Veering slightly off course, she stooped to pick it up and jam it into her overflowing bag. Dana cast her a frustrated look—why was Alice stopping to get even one more thing? But this could be her last chance to take the pillow. Since bringing it home, Alice had wanted it for Blue Shoes, where with the flowers it would live as a constant reminder of Lauren. It could be a kind of shrine.

Dana opened the apartment door as carefully as possible and Alice followed her into the hallway. Except for the footsteps, all was silent. And then the footsteps stopped and Alice heard it. The baby was crying upstairs, again.

She looked fiercely at Dana, widening her eyes and angling her ear toward the stairs as if to say, *Do you hear it too? You must hear it! A baby is crying, right now, right here.*

Dana mouthed, *Not now.* She shook her head and walked to the front door.

Yes, now, Alice thought. If not now, when? Whatever the police knew about Julius and the phantom baby, if they knew anything at all, they hadn't shared it with her. They hadn't found a crime scene. A search warrant for Julius's apartment hadn't even been issued, as far as Alice knew. Unless there were still things they hadn't told her. She didn't know and right at this moment, she didn't care.

She was here now. Right now. And right now, a baby was crying. Upstairs. In this house. Just above their heads.

Alice set down her bags and turned to the stairs.

"Stop!" Dana hissed. "You go up there now, you could screw up the whole case. Let us do it the right way."

Alice hurried, climbing the stairs quickly, taking them two steps at a time. By the top of the stairs, she was panting for breath. Her belly contracted hard over her twins—a Braxton Hicks. She ignored it and continued on. Dana flew up the stairs behind her, saying, "No, Alice! Let us—"

But Alice couldn't wait anymore. She knocked hard on Julius's apartment door. The footsteps came loud and fast, and the door swung open. Julius stood there in his sleeveless white undershirt, flesh bulging out. His hair was a mess and his face looked haggard. The rectangular lilac glasses rested halfway down his nose.

His eyes went instantly hard. "What are you doing in my house?"

Behind him, the baby's cries were louder but somehow less real. Alice heard a woman's voice humming a lullaby. The baby's cries calmed, then petered out.

Dana stood next to Alice, gun in her hand, aimed at Julius Pollack's shabby kitchen. A white Formica table was piled with mail and newspapers. Boxes were everywhere. Behind the table, next to an old, deep porcelain sink, was a life-size sewing model with the curvaceous shape of a large woman. It was dressed in lavish but mismatched women's clothes, as if someone had decided to bring out a favorite element of different outfits. At the foot of the model were the same silver shoes Alice had seen Julius wearing that night she first heard the baby cry.

A plate with a half-eaten sandwich sat in an uncluttered niche on the kitchen table. Julius had been eating, his chair haphazardly pushed away to answer the door. On a counter directly across the room, facing the table, was a television. He had been watching something while he ate, and now Alice saw what it was.

Moving gently across the screen of Julius's TV were scenes from a home video. The tiny pink face of a baby in the arms of a woman who studiously ignored the camera. A close-up of her fingertip caressing the baby's face as it calmed. The sound of Julius's own voice, sounding unruffled and satisfied, speaking from the video: "She'll sleep. Let her be."

Alice recognized the baby's cry as it slowed to a whimper. It was the sound she had given Ivy. It was the sound of her own babies calming themselves to sleep. It was the cry that had haunted her since she first heard it. A sound she had inflated and mistaken for something it wasn't.

It wasn't Ivy. It was a different baby. Possibly Julius's own baby, for whom he pined in his solitary apartment.

"What the *fuck*." Julius's tone was low and controlled.

"We apologize," Dana said edgily, her gun held taut. "Alice, apologize to the man, please."

"I'm sorry," Alice said.

"No, you're not," Julius said in the same tamped-down tone, holding back floods of . . . what? Alice noticed a speck of mayonnaise glistening on his top lip. "But you will be."

Chapter 33

Alice and Dana walked quickly up President Street. The stifling afternoon was growing darker; the air felt almost wet. Leaves shivered in a staccato of quick breezes.

"What were you thinking?" Dana's tone was stern; gone was the soft posturing of friendship.

"I was thinking there was a baby up there who needed someone to find her."

"What if there was? Why does it have to be you?"

"If I'm the one who hears her," Alice said, "then I'm who she gets."

"You could have just seriously jeopardized the investigation. Do you know that?"

Walking beside Dana, Alice shifted her heavy bag from one hand to the other. "I couldn't help myself."

"Why not? I was standing right there. I *told* you not to go."

"I'm a *mother,* that's why."

They turned onto Smith Street where the playground came into view. She could see Nell shooting down the slide and Peter on the swing being pushed by Sylvie. She wished she could turn into the park, kiss her children, discuss trivialities with Sylvie by the swings. But she had to finish this; she had to make Dana understand. And she had to absorb a new understanding herself: the crying that had haunted her had not been Ivy or any other living child, but a memory cherished by a man she loathed. A man she had thought incapable of warmth.

A man who it seemed had left behind a past that included love and, presumably, some kind of loss. There was so much Alice needed to think over.

"Someday," Alice's voice calmed, "when you're a mother, you'll understand."

"Oh, *please* don't start that shit about how no one can understand who doesn't have kids."

But it's true, Alice thought, though she didn't say it. Motherhood was a transformation in your humanity and you simply could not fully understand it without experiencing it yourself. She couldn't explain it to Dana; this was a hopeless debate.

"I shouldn't have gone up," Alice said, stating the simple, official fact. "You told me not to, and then I did."

"Damn right," Dana said. "You filed a restraining order against Julius Pollack and you just went into his apartment! Frannie's gonna be pissed."

"But I got something for her," Alice said.

Dana stopped walking and looked at Alice. "What's that?"

"The baby I heard crying upstairs wasn't even real."

Dana smirked. "We knew there was no baby up there! Did you think Frannie didn't check that out? This just proves you weren't hearing things."

Alice was stunned by this news. "But she *knew* I would keep listening for a baby. It was making me *crazy.* Why didn't she tell me?" Alice could still feel the seepage of exhaustion all those nights she lay awake listening for the distant cries.

Dana seemed to consider her words carefully. Alice watched her, waiting for an answer, feeling the humidity cramp around her.

"Julius Pollack had a wife and baby daughter," Dana said. "They were killed in a car accident two years ago."

Alice could see the tiny face squeezing out whimpers, calming under her mother's touch. Julius's half-eaten sandwich in the lonely apartment. The tsunami of his anger.

"It would have helped if she had told me," Alice said quietly.

"Helped *you,* Alice," Dana said. "We talked about that. Frannie *wanted* to help you, but she's a detective. The investigation comes first."

"Right," Alice said, remembering Frannie's words. *We had to test you, Alice.*

They stared at each other in silence. Alice knew she was the one who had to surrender her point of view. Despite her rage at the manner of Lauren's death, despite her pained frustration at the utter disappearance of Ivy, despite the possibility that she could be the next target—despite all that, she knew quite simply that Dana was right.

The women locked gazes, and then simultaneously took a breath.

"I'm sorry," Alice said.

Dana half smiled. "I'd keep it to myself, but Hank saw you go in."

Hank. The man in the gray Ford.

"Do you think he'll tell her?"

"I know he will," Dana said. "He probably already did."

A quick call to Frannie confirmed it. But by the look of alarm that swept Dana's expression, it wasn't professional reproach she was hearing. After the call, Dana took Alice by the elbow and led her quickly along President Street toward Court, away from the playground.

"Wait a minute! I have to get my kids!"

"That sitter have a cell phone?"

"Yes, but—"

"Call her. Tell her to bring the kids to Simon's. We're going straight there."

Dana took Alice's bags so she could get her cell phone out of her purse. She could actually hear Sylvie's phone ringing inside the playground. Twisting back to look, Alice saw Sylvie answering her phone, her eyes trailing Peter as he ran in front of her.

"Sylvie, it's Alice." She tried to control her voice,

keep it calm, but the tremor of anxiety was unmistakable. "Change of plans. Can you bring the kids over to Simon's house?"

"Sure," Sylvie said. "Shall I bring them now? It looks like rain."

"I'll meet you there." Alice ended the call and dropped her phone back into her purse. "What's going on, Dana. *Tell* me."

As they crossed Court Street against the light, the sky quickly darkened.

"Frannie said Pollack's on a rampage. He's been calling people, telling them the cops entered his apartment unlawfully. Then he ran out of his house."

"Where is he?"

Dana clenched her jaw and shook her head; she didn't know.

"Wasn't Hank watching him?" Alice hurried beside Dana the best she could; her body felt heavier than ever, slow, uncooperative.

"His assignment today was you," Dana said. "We're understaffed, Alice. We're doing our best, trust me."

"Can't you arrest Julius?" Alice struggled for breath; they were moving too fast. "He threatened me. Isn't that enough?"

Dana's hesitation was Alice's answer. Julius Pollack couldn't be arrested without a solid, verifiable reason.

"Frannie's got a call in about that, but Alice, you broke the restraining order when you ran up those stairs."

As the image of an enraged Julius Pollack blossomed in Alice's consciousness, the sky opened up and a deluge began. Hurrying forward along President Street, toward Clinton, Alice fought an urge to turn back to the playground. Nell and Peter were going to get wet. She wanted to go to her children, usher them safely home.

"I'm going back for my kids." Alice turned around. "They'll get soaked."

And what if Julius Pollack sought them out at the playground? *What if?*

"Alice!" Dana shouted. "Let the sitter bring them home; they're probably on their way already. Frannie's gonna meet us there as soon as she can get back from Jersey. Come on!"

Having ignored Dana's advice to such dramatic ill effect just half an hour ago, Alice decided to follow orders. Dana was right; Sylvie was perfectly capable of bringing the children home and it would be smart of Alice to be there when they arrived. Then they could lock the doors and huddle inside, waiting for Julius to be located. Waiting for all of this to finally end.

"Why is Frannie in New Jersey?" Alice asked as they hurried through the pounding rain. "What's she been doing there so much?"

"Later," Dana answered.

Lightning and thunder raged overhead. It was the kind of flash storm that hit so ferociously on summer afternoons, then dissipated like a forgotten drunken rage. The sidewalks had cleared, with only a few people running through the storm for shelter; otherwise there was no one around. By the time they reached Simon's brownstone, the storm was starting to clear, leaving behind an eerie silence draped in heavy fog. And the shadow of a message finger-drawn on Simon's front window:

STOP OR THEY'RE NEXT

Dana had the keys and was opening the front door. But Alice couldn't move. She stood on Simon's stoop, staring at the lopsided note scrawled on the wet glass, and pried her hands beneath her soaked shirt to massage the tight skin of her belly.

PART FOUR

Chapter 34

Within minutes a squad car arrived, followed by a battered silver van from the Criminalistics lab. Forensics technicians scrambled over the window, isolating it, analyzing elements invisible to Alice's eye. All she could see was STOP OR THEY'RE NEXT.

She huddled on the couch, petrified and shivering under a red fleece blanket, caressing what she could reach of her twins. She had always felt her unborn babies were safe inside her body, safer than they would ever be once they were born. It was when her children left her—disappeared into their school every morning, or worse, went on a field trip to places Alice didn't know—that she most suffered their vulnerability. It was when they were without her, not within her, that they had always seemed unsafe. She ran her hands along her skin, still tacky from the rain, and silently promised the twins her protection. But watching the technicians crawl over the front of Simon's building, she knew it was a promise she might not be able to keep.

With shaking hands, she reached into her wet purse for her cell phone. She would call Mike, summon him home. Once Nell and Peter made it back to the house, Alice would have all she needed. She would talk to Mike about leaving. *Insist* on it. Whatever was happening now was too confusing and too dangerous. And she, huge with her twin sons, was a sitting duck.

It took a few rings for Mike to answer. Before she

even spoke, she heard the tension in his voice. "I'm stuck in traffic in the Bronx. We had this delivery in Westchester. I should have had Diego do it but I wanted him to get some stuff done at the shop."

She told him about Julius, the crying baby, the note on Simon's window.

He began to blow the pickup's horn, over and over. Each wail drove Alice's anxiety deeper.

"Mike, stop it! That won't get you home any faster."

"But I need to get to you!" A long, final wail of the horn. "I can't be stuck here like this!" She heard a rustling and the slam of a car door. "Screw it. I'm taking the subway."

"You can't just leave the pickup, Mike!"

"Let them tow it. I'll pay the fine."

"I'm not alone, Mike. The police are here, a whole bunch of them, and Dana—"

"Where are the kids?"

"With Sylvie. She's bringing them home."

His breathing was labored and she could see him, walking quickly, cell phone pressed to his ear, hair electric, somewhere in the Bronx. She had never been to the Bronx, she realized, and didn't know how it looked. Thus her mind conjured looming concrete canyons, the street an urban valley through which Mike strode alone.

"Mike, honey, get back in the pickup."

He sighed and the motion around him seemed to quiet.

"Rushing back won't change anything," Alice said. "Dana has things under control."

"You're probably right."

"I love you." She heard another slam of a car door. "Are you in the pickup now?"

"Yes."

"Is traffic moving?"

"No, but I guess it will."

"Call me if you're worried, Mike. I'll be right here."

They ended the call and Alice held her phone in her hand. She surprised herself by feeling less frantic now having called Mike for support, then being called upon for encouragement, she had actually calmed herself. Yes, the police were there, *handling the situation*. Trying to determine what the situation was. Alice pulled the blanket over her lap and watched the impressive sight of Dana running the investigation in Frannie's absence.

A lab technician sprayed something on the windows to evaporate the water, then painstakingly examined every inch of glass. A photographer took pictures of each stage of the process and every aspect of the building's exterior. He even photographed the inside of the windows. "Just in case," he casually told Alice, who hovered in the living room, waiting.

In case of what? Her momentary calm began to dissipate as quickly as it had gathered.

When would Frannie arrive?

Nell and Peter—where *were* they?

Standing in the middle of the living room, Dana surveyed the work. Finally, when she wasn't answering a question or issuing an order, Alice spoke to her.

"Obviously Julius did this."

Dana's keen eyes slid to Alice but showed no reaction. "Nothing's obvious," she answered. "We collect the evidence and look it over. Whatever's there, that's what we work with. The facts."

But it *had* to be Julius. Who else? He was out there, plotting against Alice, against the police, against the world for stealing his family. A man with so much money and power, badly misusing his assets. *You've been punished,* Alice caught herself thinking of him, *punished for your vile nature and the pain you cause other people.* Unless he wasn't always this way. Unless the loss of his family created the misanthrope that was Julius Pollack. Unless . . .

"Yup," Dana briskly said. Alice had not realized Dana was on the phone. "See you in twenty minutes if the tunnel isn't blocked."

"Why is Frannie in New Jersey?" Alice shifted positions on the couch, unable to get comfortable.

Dana now turned fully to Alice. "They found the crime scene. Forensics just got there. Paul stayed behind to supervise."

They found the crime scene. The very place where Lauren lost her life—no, had it stolen from her—at seven minutes to noon two Fridays ago.

"What about the baby?" Alice asked. "Did they—"

"No." Dana sat beside Alice on the couch. "No baby. Just a lot of blood."

Staring across the space of Simon's living room, Alice saw dust dance in a poststorm shaft of light. "What else did they find?"

Dana pulled the blanket over Alice's shoulders. "You're wet. You should change your clothes."

"Tell me," Alice said. "What else?"

"Forensics is collecting everything. Frannie will give us a better idea when she gets here. Any minute, Alice. She's on her way."

Then Alice thought of something. How could Lauren have crossed the Carroll Street Bridge in Brooklyn at eleven forty-five, and died in New Jersey at eleven fifty-three? Sitting forward, she faced Dana and asked how such a discrepancy could be true.

"It happened in Brooklyn," Dana answered, "inside a vehicle that was moved to New Jersey."

"A vehicle?" Alice closed her eyes and pictured it. Cars had windows, anyone could see in. It had to be one of those minivans with tinted windows. They were everywhere. Or a van with *no* windows. She had read the much-circulated e-mails warning you to keep away from vans; they were the vehicle of choice for serial killers. A door could slide open and snatch you up before anyone noticed. Never park next to one, you were told. If one parks next to your driver's side, get in via the opposite door, then drive away as fast as possible. Now Alice could see it. A dark-eyed minivan sliding up next to Lauren. She would have been too heavily pregnant to run. Angry hands reaching out, pulling her in. Denying anyone, everyone, the happiness of a family.

Julius Pollack, the bastard.

Fury twisted through Alice and she felt the muscle of his hatred. Felt him haul Lauren into the van. Felt the jostle of his flesh as he held her down. Felt Lauren's terror as a knife descended into her belly. Or had he shot her first? Alice felt Lauren's last living moments and saw through her eyes as she searched in terror for a soul in the face of Sal Cattaneo as he butchered her. The secret partner. They wanted too much, those two. They stole everything, from everyone.

Then, with sobering clarity, Dana corrected Alice's vision.

"It was an ice cream truck. Someone found it in an abandoned lot near Trenton."

A spiral of dizziness overcame Alice and she breathed deeply.

One, two, three.

How many times had she and Lauren and Maggie bought their children ice cream from those trucks? Nell had once admitted to Alice that she thought there was only one truck and it appeared at just the right moment. When she first saw the Mr. Frosty parking lot on Carroll Street, just past the bridge, her face startled into an odd, disenchanted expression. So there was no magic, just a lot of trucks.

Trembling beneath the blanket, Alice yearned for the feel of her children's warm, supple skin. The acrid sweetness of their breath. The chaos of their undisciplined joys. She wished Nell and Peter would rush into the room and cover her up.

Where were they?

She dialed Sylvie's cell number and listened to it ring.

Dana meanwhile bent down to pick up the peony pillow which had fallen out of the bag at their feet. She held the pillow on her lap, studying the intricate needlework, running her hand over its rough surface, turning it around to study it from different angles.

Finally Sylvie answered the phone. "I brought the children to Maggie's apartment," she explained. "It was closer. I wanted to get them out of the storm. Are you mad, Alice?"

"No, I'm not mad."

"Is everything okay?" There was a hardness to Sylvie's tone, a sarcasm that Alice didn't like. Sylvie was young; she didn't take things seriously enough sometimes. Which was why she was a babysitter, Alice reminded herself, dispelling the rasp of irritation.

"Yes, everything's okay. Listen, Sylvie, you don't have to bring them." She wondered if she had been asking too much of Sylvie lately, piggybacking her children onto Ethan's babysitting hours. "Mike's on his way home. I'll ask him to stop by and pick them up."

"I can hear the worry in your voice," Sylvie said. "Don't worry so much. It's unattractive, my mother used to say."

"He'll be there soon." Alice wanted to end the awkward call. She wanted the traffic jam that had ensnarled Mike to break up, release him. She wanted Julius Pollack locked in a cell. She wanted to close her eyes and escape today. She wanted her children.

"Bye, Alice," Sylvie said with a strange cheerfulness.

Alice pressed END and immediately called Mike's cell.

"Can't talk—traffic's moving," he answered.

"Pick up the kids on your way back, okay? They're at Maggie's, with Sylvie."

"Will do. You okay?"

"Fine." She would wait to tell him about the crime scene when he arrived.

"See you in a few minutes," he said. "I'm getting close."

She laid her head against the back of the couch and closed her eyes. Next to her, she could feel Dana pitching forward.

"Where did you get this?"

Alice opened her eyes to find Dana staring at the peony pillow.

"Judy Gersten," Alice answered. "She makes them."

"Them, plural?" Dana asked. "She's made others?"

"She does all that stuff. Needlepoint, knitting, sewing. It's all around her house and at work on her desk. She's says it keeps her busy. Sylvie finishes the pillows for her."

"What do you mean *finishes* them?"

Alice was surprised by Dana's sudden interest. "You know, backing, stuffing, all the finishing work. Then Sylvie takes them over to the Women's Exchange to sell them."

"Why?" Dana sat forward, holding the pillow on her lap.

"Just to help out, I guess," Alice said. "Sylvie's a part-time assistant at Garden Hill. Judy said the peony was Sylvie's idea as a tribute to Lauren. Lauren loved peonies."

"So you bought this?"

"No, Judy gave it to me. She *threw* it at me, actually. She said I should have it because I was Lauren's friend."

Dana held the pillow up for Alice to see. "Look."

"I know, it's beautiful."

Dana pointed at the lower left corner of the pillow. *"Look."*

Alice had never actually scrutinized the needlework; the large flower was captivating at a distance. She had come straight home with it, thrown it on her couch, headed straight for the newspaper. And then Julius decided to attack. The harder she looked at the pillow now, the more apparent it became that the background was not as simple as it appeared. There were two colors involved, not one as it first seemed, and in the corner where Dana was pointing, there was something else.

Alice held the pillow in front of her face. In the lower left corner, in a shade slightly darker than the background, were two tiny letters: LB.

Chapter 35

"Lauren's initials," Alice said. "Lauren Barnet."

"Where's this Women's Exchange place?" Dana asked. "I want to see the other pillows."

"But Judy said she made the pillow with Lauren in mind," Alice said. "That's why Lauren's initials are there, Dana. Don't you think?"

"No assumptions." Dana stood up.

"It's on Pierrepont Street in Brooklyn Heights," Alice told Dana. "Between Monroe Place and Henry Street, I think."

Dana left the pillow where it was. "When Frannie comes, tell her I'll be right back. And don't go anywhere, Alice. Got it?"

"Got it," Alice said, picturing herself, Mike, Nell and Peter running along the phantom beach. Air dry and light as cotton wisps. A placid ocean.

The uniformed officer by the door stood sentrylike with his hands clasped behind his back. Alice stretched out on the couch, pulled the blanket under her chin and closed her eyes. Mike would be back in Brooklyn any minute now. Pick up the kids. Come home. She wondered where Simon was and how he would react to the commandeering of his house by the police. Knowing Simon, it wouldn't faze him; anyone with the fortitude to love Maggie and, moreover, to live with her had to be even-keeled, as was Simon, reliably.

After a few minutes the front door squealed open and

Alice heard footsteps cross the hall to the living room. She opened her eyes: Frannie was talking to the front hall cop. Alice sat up, letting the blanket slide to her feet.

"Frannie," she said. "We've been waiting for you."

"I heard from Dana." Frannie crossed the room to Alice. "Pillow shopping, huh?"

Alice picked up the peony pillow from where it lay on the couch and handed it to Frannie. "Judy Gersten made it. When I told Dana how Sylvie finishes them and takes them to the Women's Exchange, she got pretty excited. Ran right over there."

"I didn't take her for a shopper," Frannie tried to joke. Her dark eyes shone, but she didn't, or couldn't, smile. "Sorry, it's been a rough afternoon. Dana's got good instincts." Frannie sat next to Alice on the couch and rubbed her face. "I could use some coffee."

"I'll make you some." Alice went into the kitchen and started a pot of coffee in the stainless-steel machine Maggie had bought when she lived here.

Frannie followed Alice and sat down at the large round table. "So, Dana told you we found the crime scene."

"She didn't tell me much, though," Alice said. "She said when you got here, you'd fill me in."

"There's a lot we won't know until all the evidence is evaluated," Frannie said. "That'll take a few days." She hesitated, glancing longingly at the coffeepot, which sputtered and steamed, filling the kitchen which a rich smell Alice remembered yearning for before this pregnancy.

"But?" Alice asked.

Frannie sighed. "But we learned a lot. It wasn't pretty, Alice. Are you sure you want to know?"

"I don't want to," Alice said, "but I need to."

"Okay," Frannie said. "Sit down, then."

Alice obeyed, installing herself on a chair across from Frannie.

In a deliberately calm tone, Frannie began. "There

was blood splatter on the interior side door, which tells us she was probably shot right away, just after she got into the truck. The C-section was performed right there on the floorboard, with a common kitchen knife. It was crude and slow, a lot of blood loss." Frannie watched Alice, pausing to let it sink in.

Alice nodded. "Go on."

"We found the knife and the tape that was used to close her wounds. If the doer was as messy as the scene indicates, we'll find fingerprints everywhere. The crime scene doesn't show a lot of experience or even much thought."

"But they've done this before," Alice said. "What about Christine Craddock?"

Frannie leaned slightly forward, her body language insisting Alice discipline her thoughts, drop her assumptions, really *listen*. "We never found Christine. Other than the attack on Pam Short, there is no evidence that the attacker has any other experience with violence."

"I watched Sal Cattaneo butcher a pig," Alice said fiercely. "He knows exactly what he's doing."

"Yes, he does," Frannie said, "when he cuts up an animal."

"I've seen Julius Pollack up close," Alice said. "He *is* an animal."

"Assumptions, Alice." Frannie's voice was steady. "Put them aside."

Alice heard the crying baby. Saw the video, the baby's television face. She nodded. Okay, she would put her assumptions aside; at least she would try.

"The biggest mistake a detective can make," Frannie said, "is to decide whodunit before evaluating all the evidence. We have evidence now. We finally have a crime scene. Only some of it is pointing in the direction of the Metro connection."

"Some of it," Alice said. "So it isn't a closed option."

"Everything's open right now," Frannie said. "Everything." She got up, found a mug in Simon's cabinet and poured herself some coffee. "Just remember that it's a puzzle. You collect all the pieces, which as you've seen can be a challenge. You put the pieces together. Then you look."

"Am I a puzzle piece?" Alice watched Frannie sip her coffee.

"It seems like it." She set down her mug. "But let's face it. We don't *know* who wrote that message on the window. It's convenient to think Pollack did it, but we won't know until we pick him up and have a chance to ask him."

"What about Ivy?"

"Her umbilical cord may have been cut," Frannie said. "Some tissue was found that might be leftover cord. If it is, if someone made the effort to tie the cord, it would indicate that whoever did this meant to keep the baby. That it was the motivation for the crime."

Who, Alice wondered, had wanted Ivy that badly other than Lauren and Tim? Was it *Ivy* the monster had wanted, or *any* baby?

"What about Pam?" Alice asked. "She was shot with the same gun."

Frannie took a long drink of her coffee, then nodded. "Yup. There's that."

Just then a small man with graying blond hair, one of the lab techs who had been working outside, came into the kitchen and knocked lightly on the archway's molding. Frannie twisted around to face him.

"Hey, Jerry."

"We're almost done here," he said. "We were able to lift one good print. Is this a rush?"

"Top priority."

"We'll take it over to the lab right now, ask them to skip it to the head of the line," he told her, "if they can."

"Thanks," Frannie said. "Call me when it's in. We want to run it through Printrak ASAP, see if we get a hit."

Jerry nodded and went back outside.

Frannie turned to Alice. "You've had quite an afternoon."

"We all have, haven't we?"

"Oh yes," Frannie said. "But in a way it's just the beginning. This is when we start to find out what's really going on. You should get some rest. You look wiped out."

"I'm waiting for Nell and Peter to get home," Alice said. "Mike's picking them up. I won't be able to rest until I see them."

"Why don't you lie down anyway," Frannie said. "I've got to make some calls, find out what's up with Dana, check in with Paul."

Alice headed over to the couch, feeling unbearably exhausted, as if her twins had quadrupled in weight in the last hour alone. She carefully bent down to pick up the blanket where it lay pooled on the floor, and had just tossed it back on the couch when she heard a commotion in the hallway.

Dana rushed into the living room and dumped the contents of two large shopping bags onto the floor. She had bought three more of Judy Gersten's pillows at the Women's Exchange, miniscule floral arrangements on pale backgrounds: rose, baby blue, dove gray. They all shared the immaculate needlework of the peony pillow.

Frannie bent down and picked up one of the pillows. She held it up close to her eyes, turning it slowly around. Then she held the pillow still. "ZL," she said, handing it to Alice. The pink-on-rose initials were almost imperceptible until you noticed them, and then they screamed.

Dana handed Frannie another pillow. "PS."

When they looked at the next pillow, with its blue-on-blue *CC* in the corner, there was dead silence. Finally, Frannie spoke.

"Lauren Barnet, Pam Short, Christine Craddock," she said. "It can't be a coincidence."

"Who's ZL?" Alice asked.

"Don't know," Frannie answered. "We'll have to find out."

"Judy Gersten," Alice said, vividly recalling the framed photograph in Judy's apartment of her and Sal

Cattaneo, pressed together, smiling like an old couple. Except he was married to someone else. "She's involved in this."

Frannie and Dana glanced at each other. *No assumptions.*

"Open them," Frannie said.

Alice hurried to the kitchen for a pair of scissors.

Dana started with the peony pillow, carefully slicing open the pillow's seam to reveal a neat track of tiny stitches. Dana continued to snip away until she had opened one side. Then she ripped apart the needlework canvas and velvet backing and peered inside.

"Can you bring me a clean sheet?" Dana asked Alice.

Alice went upstairs to the linen closet, found a neatly folded white sheet, returned downstairs and handed it to Frannie, who flipped it open and laid it on the floor.

Kneeling down, Dana upended the pillow's stuffing onto the sheet.

Masses of long brown hair tumbled out.

Chapter 36

"It's Lauren's hair." Alice knelt in front of the pile of long, soft hair. She wanted to reach her hand into this last bit of Lauren, but was she allowed to? Was it evidence now?

"Are you sure?" Frannie asked.

The officers and forensics techs who were still milling around turned quiet. Everyone knew that something had just happened. Everyone was watching them.

Alice nodded. She couldn't speak.

"Let's open the other pillows," Frannie said calmly.

Dana started in on one of the other pillows. ZL. Careful to follow the seams, she cut quickly and peered inside.

"It's white."

Frannie looked. "That isn't hair."

"It's some kind of foam, I think." Dana opened the CC pillow next. "More foam."

"What the hell is this?" Frannie was peering into the PS pillow. "It's gray."

"Looks like some other kind of man-made stuffing," Dana said.

"Get one of the techs in," Frannie told Dana.

As Alice kneeled in front of Lauren's chopped-off hair, it was all she could do to stop herself from weeping. The cacophonous pile of hair. The riot of hard evidence. Sickening detail. What would it tell?

Was there more than Lauren's hair in the pile?

Was Ivy's hair in there too?

Dana gently placed her hands under Alice's elbows and lifted her off the floor.

One of the forensics techs came in with a large paper bag. He gathered all the hair into the bag, sealed it and marked it with what must have been the code name for the case: *Mommy Killer.*

"Get it right over to Forensics." Frannie's voice cracked slightly, but she regained herself. "I'll call that guy who owes me a favor. I want DNA evaluation on every different hair strand he finds." Frannie got on her phone and started talking, her words blurring as a storm began to murmur through Alice's mind.

Nell and Peter.

"The babysitter." Dana's tone was soft, but probing. "Sylvie. What's her full name?"

"Sylvie Devrais," Frannie answered.

Where were they?

The front door squealed open and cracked shut. Footsteps hurried through the front hall.

"Alice!" It was Mike. Finally.

Alice faced the archway connecting living room to front hall. "In here!"

He walked in, looking hot and tired and almost crushed.

Why was it so quiet? Where were the kids?

"Didn't you stop at Maggie's?" Alice asked.

"No one's home," Mike said in a tone burdened by both certainty and plea.

"Sylvie said they were there. I told her you'd be stopping by."

"I rang the bell over and over. No one answered. I thought maybe they came over here."

"Maybe I misunderstood," Alice thought aloud. "Maybe she meant they were with Maggie at the store."

"No," Mike said, looking from face to face. "I thought the same thing. I called Maggie and she said she hadn't seen them. Ethan went somewhere with Simon this afternoon. Sylvie's only got our kids."

What was he telling her? It was *wrong*.

"Where are my children?" she demanded, turning to Frannie. "Where are they!"

A rivulet of sweat traveled Mike's jawbone as he too turned to Frannie for answers.

"Hello?" Maggie's voice called from the front hall. She rushed into the living room, black and white polka-dotted skirt flouncing around her knees. "Did the children turn up? Why are the police here? Will someone please tell me what is going on?"

"Mags," Alice said. "Sylvie said she was taking the kids to your place to get them out of the rain. I thought she had Ethan after school today. I asked her to watch Nell and Peter at the park for a little while—"

"Simon's taken Ethan to the dentist. Sylvie knew the plan."

Maggie's attention was snared by the window on which the words were still slightly visible. It took her a moment to decipher them backwards, then she read out loud: " 'Stop or they're next.' *They?*"

And suddenly Alice knew. *They* were not her unborn twins, but her Nell and her Peter. *Her babies.* Alice ran to the window and pressed her hands against the glass, clawing at the underside of the backward words. Screaming. "You fucking bastard!"

Mike followed her to the window and pulled her fist off the glass before it shattered. His face was rigid with anger. "I'm going out to look for them."

"Wait," Frannie said. She got on her cell phone and spoke rapidly with someone on the other end. "Sylvie Devrais. Is our guy still on her?"

"Your guy?" Mike glanced at Alice; he had to be thinking the same thing, that Sylvie was being followed just as Alice had been. Tested. Watched. If so, then had they all been under surveillance? Mike, Maggie, Simon, all the friends? Had Frannie thought all along that the killer was among them?

Had she been right?

"When?" Frannie asked.

An infinite beat of silence. Frannie's brow pinching over darkening eyes. The world ending. Or beginning. A suffocating transformation of time.

Alice stopped breathing. *One, two, three. One, two, three.* It didn't work.

"I can't breathe!" she whispered to Mike.

He turned around and stared at her as if she had spoken a foreign language.

"What?"

"I can't—"

"Did she have two kids with her, a boy and a girl?" Frannie listened a moment, then ordered, "Put an APB on Sylvie Devrais. And get an Amber Alert out on the kids. *Right now.*"

"I knew she was trouble." Maggie's voice snapped into the stunned silence that followed. "I just knew it. The little bitch."

Chapter 37

"I'm going out to look for them," Mike said again.

"I'm coming with you." Alice turned quickly to the living room's archway, the passage out of the house, toward her children. Then a spiral of nausea lassoed her and she stopped, bringing both hands to her forehead, resisting gravity.

"Alice?" Mike had his arm around her. "Sit down, sweetie."

"She better stay here," Frannie said, steering Alice to the couch. "Mike, you go ahead. I'm trying to reach the cop on Sylvie's surveillance; he hasn't been answering his phone, but when I reach him, he'll tell us where to look. Give me your cell number."

They traded numbers and Mike left. Alice sank into the couch, choking back the bile of her helplessness. She wanted to be with Mike out on the streets, looking, not sitting here. "I can't stand this," she cried. "We should have left town last week."

Everyone kept quiet; no one denied her that claim, because it was true. They should have left. They should have. And now it was too late.

It was the longest hour in history—a black hole for any mother; for Alice, a nightmare whose edges she had skirted blindly these past two weeks. She had never once feared for Nell's or Peter's safety. All this time, she had been looking in the wrong place. Making assumptions. Trusting blindly.

Sylvie.

How could it be?

Alice's mind swirled with numbers. Dates and times. All the hours she had entrusted her children to Sylvie.

But had she been completely wrong? Weren't Julius Pollack and Sal Cattaneo and Judy Gersten all somehow involved in this? Sylvie worked for Judy. Judy was close with Sal. Sal was Julius's secret partner. All the victims were involved with Metro Properties.

What other secrets bound them?

Stop or they're next.

Nell. Peter.

Stop what, exactly? Making trouble? Creating noise? Collaborating with the police?

And why, why, why hadn't the detectives told her the children may have been in danger? If they were having Sylvie followed, it was for a reason. The same reason they had *all* been followed.

The detectives knew all along.

It was one of them.

And they watched, and they waited, until something happened.

Alice sat on the couch with Maggie, frozen in the eddying coil of her thoughts as Frannie and Dana paced the living room, working their cell phones. Forensics was long gone to the lab with bags and slides of evidence. Photos to develop. Piles of hair and pillow casings to analyze.

Simon arrived into the chaos with Ethan, set him up in front of the TV upstairs in the family room, and joined the vigil in the living room. He sat next to Maggie on the couch, pressed against her, squeezing hands. Their comforting of each other comforted Alice. She wanted to be part of them, part of their passion, to be anyone but herself—because at this moment, more than any other moment in her life, she was completely alone. *Alone.* She was not part of Maggie and Simon's deep, if muddled, love; she was a woman, a mother, on the verge of unbearable loss.

Minutes dragged by until, finally, the first dribble of news came in.

"They've got Pollack," Frannie said. "He's cooperating. Dana, you stay here. Paul's coming in from Jersey; they're wrapping up the crime scene. He's meeting me at the precinct. The FBI's getting in on this. We'll have to debrief them."

Dana nodded, stopping in front of a long window, the butterscotch late afternoon drenching her in sun. She looked like a coin, Alice thought. Dark and golden and powerful. Flat. Unreal.

"I'll keep you posted." Frannie strode across the room, her worn black sneakers quiet on the wooden floor. "It shouldn't be long before we pick up Sal Cattaneo and Judy Gersten for questioning. And we'll start seeing lab reports. It's gonna be a long night." She paused to speak to Alice, Maggie and Simon, stunned observers surreally dotting the living room. "If we're lucky, we'll start to get some answers tonight."

How could *luck* still be thought to play into this mudslide of bad news? Alice wanted to reel the word back into Frannie's mouth. To stop her speaking altogether. To make her leave *now*. Get some answers *now*. There was nothing anyone could say to mollify Alice. Or one thing, just one: *We found them. All of them. Nell and Peter. Ivy.*

In the vacuum of Frannie's departure, Alice turned toward the windows. Outside, fistfuls of leaves gleamed with raindrops on the tall, old trees that shaded Clinton Street.

"What now?" Maggie asked.

No one answered. There *was* no answer. Or it was the same answer. *Nell and Peter. Ivy.*

Soon word came that Sal and Judy had been added to Frannie's collection at the precinct. Alice vaguely wondered how their presence would be handled with just one small interview room. Unless there were others, a labyrinth of cell-like rooms Alice hadn't been introduced to. A secret world in the basement. Or on a floor above. Alice didn't really know what went on in the Seventy-sixth Precinct. Or in the neighborhood. Or, for that matter, in the larger, mysterious world beyond her own. It was a secret world that had stolen her friend, and now her children. She closed her eyes and sank her head against Maggie's shoulder.

Suddenly a blinding light filled the living room.

"What the hell is that?" Simon sprung up and went directly to the windows. "Television reporters," he spat, yanking closed the voluminous curtains.

The room now was dark and Maggie got up to turn on all the lamps.

"I better make a statement," Dana said, "or they'll be on us all night."

All night, Alice thought. Would it be that long?

Dana called Frannie for approval and to discuss her statement. She would confirm the Amber Alert, but name no suspect in particular. "Under investigation," Dana said. "Got it." She disappeared outside for ten long minutes, then came back inside to join the wait. No matter how many seconds ticked by—seconds into minutes; a slow, torturous drip of time—the lights beyond the drawn curtains never dimmed.

In the wait, Alice's mind unhitched briefly onto a single possibility that she could see as clearly as that distant beach, as clearly as the faces of her children: had whoever killed Lauren and stolen Ivy also come here this afternoon to write a threat to Alice on Simon's window? If it had been Sylvie, had she detoured her escape for a bout of graffiti? Hailed a taxi and stopped here just long enough to leave behind a final threat? With Nell and Peter in the backseat, watching? They had always said Sylvie was so much fun. Did they have even a single inkling that, for the moment she left them alone, they should run? Had her beloved children squandered their single opportunity for escape?

What if Sylvie *had* put them in a cab? Already taken them far out of the neighborhood? With Mike circling the local streets in his pickup, spinning his wheels, tightening the noose of his panic while she sat here, helpless and useless, drowning in hers.

Alice shook her head in a futile effort to dispel such thoughts. She had been wrong before; she could be wrong now.

No assumptions.

One, two, three.

There was no more breath. There were no more thoughts. There was only time, long hard strands of it, tightening around her throat. And waiting.

Finally into the dread silence a cell phone rang—Dana's crescendoing chimes—and she flipped it open.

"We've been trying to reach you! . . . What? . . . You've been in the *subway*? . . . Where is she? . . . You what?"

Dana ended the call and faced the fragile group.

"That was Danny, your Andre Capa," she told Alice with a regretful sigh. "He lost Sylvie just outside Kennedy airport."

"She's taking Nell and Peter to the airport?" Alice stood up. The nausea came over her in a wave but she didn't care; she would dive into it, push against it, fly above it. She couldn't sit here another second.

Chapter 38

"Wait." Dana grabbed Alice's arm. "The kids weren't with Sylvie when she went into the subway. She was alone. Alice, they aren't with her."

"Where are they, then?" Her voice seemed to ping through the room. She didn't care how awful it sounded. "Let me go!"

"Come on." Simon stood next to her. "I'll go with you, Alice."

She flung the door open and held the railing as she ran down the front stoop. At the bottom step she felt her balance give way, felt herself toppling forward. Simon's hands caught her from behind, grasping an elbow and a shoulder, steadying her.

"Slow down," he told her. "Get your bearings."

The depth and authority of his voice stilled her certainty that she could fly up and over the rooftops and treetops of Brooklyn. That with enough velocity she could defy gravity. That with the superpower of her determination, her beloved children would appear in the distance, uniquely recognizable, shimmering with vitality, beauty, life.

But her body overrode her confidence, froze her in place.

"Let's go." Simon stood in front of her, holding out a hand. Alice noticed the scratched gold of his wedding ring. Had he never taken it off? "Come on now."

She stood up. A mere human. A mother, searching.

With Simon at her side she began to walk along Clinton Street in the direction of their old home.

"What are you thinking, Alice?"

"President Street." She stepped out of a patch of shade into an expansive pool of burning sun. Puddles of rainwater dotted the sidewalk; she walked into them, over them, past them. "That's the one address they have memorized."

They hadn't been at Simon's long enough to coach the children on his address, though they had already started learning the street number of the Third Place house. Why had she been so stupid, not training them for the present? Saturating them instead with assumptions about their future?

"Shouldn't we walk along Court Street?" Simon gently asked. She smelled his cologne in a waft of air, felt the steady warmth of his body as he kept pace beside her.

"Right," Alice agreed. "They might have gone into a store."

She had always made a point of taking them along on errands, as part of their domestic education. Urban survival skills involved levels of procurement: education, skills, money, apartments, goods. She had taught them to shop for quality and price. How to measure ingredients. Not to talk to strangers. She had taught them everything she thought they needed to know. But Nell, she remembered now, tended to scramble the last four digits of Alice's cell number, and she didn't know Mike's. *Foolish,* Alice chided herself now, walking along Warren Street with the bustle of Court on the near horizon; foolish not to have insisted both children know all the family phone numbers by heart.

Alice stopped in every store along Court Street, asking if two children, a little brown-haired boy and slightly larger peach-haired girl, had been in. *No,* she heard again and again. *What's going on? The police were just in here asking the same question.* Simon stayed on the street, eyes open, stopping any acquaintances. No one had seen them. They moved forward as quickly as Alice could; her body was leaden, hot, the twins already taking a stance against their older siblings, trying to hold her back. She could feel Simon's harnessed energy, nearly explosive, at her side.

Her skin bristled with droplets of sweat as she marched forward as quickly as her stubborn body would let her. They were getting close to President Street now. Close to their old home. *Oh, babies,* she silently wished, *be there, be there, be there.* They had never been outside her circle of protection before: home, school, friends, babysitter.

Sylvie.

The quicksand of dumb assumption.

Alice marched forward, grabbing deep into her lungs for breath.

"Slow a little," Simon beseeched her, laying his warm hand on her hot arm.

The orange DON'T WALK light at President and Court stopped blinking just as they approached the corner. A line of cars moved steadily toward the intersection. Alice crossed anyway. Crossed and turned onto President Street. Walked and walked until, just before the first park entrance, she saw Mike's hastily parked pickup truck angled next to a fire hydrant. The driver's side door gaped into the street.

In front of the pickup was a squad car, red and white lights revolving in silence.

Across the park a wail of sirens grew closer. Another squad car cut through the red light on Court Street and raced the wrong way onto President, stopping behind Mike's truck.

Alice and Simon broke into a jog.

The pickup's motor was running, but Mike wasn't there.

"Mike!" Alice screamed. Her voice seemed to bounce on pockets of humid air leftover from the spent storm. "Mike!"

"Alice!" Mike's voice sailed back at her.

And then a perfectly pitched duet, high and light as it floated out of Carroll Park:

"Mommy!"

Simon couldn't stop himself from bolting ahead. She ran behind him, gasping, holding her belly from beneath and running down the first path leading to the large central area separating the two playgrounds. Police were everywhere. Benches and asphalt and jungle gyms were drenched from the storm, but the sun was strong and neighborhood children had already gathered back for play under the wary gaze of their parents and sitters who must have been wondering why the police were crowding the park. A little boy zipped past Alice on a silver bike with training wheels. She stood in the middle of the playground, scanning the small bodies for Nell, for Peter.

"Mommy!" This time it was Peter's voice alone, and he was laughing. "We're right over here! Don't you see us?"

His little face was pressed between the iron bars separating the big kids' side from the central area. He was smiling at her. The bottom of his face was tinted green. Beside him, where he kneeled backward on a bench, Nell was pressed against Mike's side. Mike held a partially eaten puff of green cotton candy. Nell, whose mouth was clownish with a pink haze, turned around and waved. Mike now looked over at Alice, who came through the gate and nearly fell on her children with open arms.

"Sylvie brought them into the Autumn Café during the storm," Mike told Alice when she raised her head. His eyes were wet; he'd been crying, or making an effort not to.

The Autumn Café, just across the street on Smith. Where they had bought bagels and juices and coffees and muffins, and passed countless afternoons with their friends. The children had grown up in that place; they were known there, comfortable. Most of the college kids behind the counter knew Nell and Peter by name. Alice felt her lungs begin to inflate.

Standing beside the bench, Simon smiled at his reunited friends. "I'll call Maggie with the good news." He reached into his back pocket for his cell phone.

"She probably already knows," Mike said. "Frannie just called me from the precinct. She said we should take the kids back to Simon's. She's meeting us at the house so she can talk to them herself."

Alice was grateful and astounded by how efficiently the Amber Alert had worked. Yet it was a brand-new law. What would have happened to Nell and Peter just a year ago, without it? Would the neighborhood have been a strong enough net to catch them? Alice doubted anyone in the playground would have noticed they were alone; since they were such a common sight there, they might have stayed for hours, blending into play. And then what?

"Sylvie said she'd be right back." Nell shrugged her skinny shoulders. Her purple T-shirt, Alice saw, was wet all down the front. Peter's too. As if they had run headlong through the rain, led by Sylvie to a port in the storm.

"How long were you there without her?" Alice combed her fingers through Peter's hair, which had fallen into his eyes.

Peter shrugged. "I don't know."

"Didn't anyone ask you why you were alone?" She didn't want to ask specifically if the police had come into the café or just now found them here; she wanted, instead, for them to supply the details.

Nell shrugged again and took a nibble of her pink cotton candy. Alice never bought it for them; Sylvie must have given them money before leaving, and they had nabbed their chance for the forbidden treat.

"We went home after it stopped raining," Nell said. "We waited outside but no one came."

"We forgot!" Peter giggled. Meaning, they had conspiratorially *forgotten* they didn't live at the President Street house anymore.

"Then we came here," Nell said. "I made Peter hold my hand when we crossed the street, Mommy, so don't worry. Okay?"

"Okay, sweetie. Thanks."

Frannie wanted to have them driven back to the house in one of the many squad cars that now surrounded the park, but Alice objected.

"They're fine," she told Frannie on Mike's phone. "Let us walk home with them, okay? We all need to calm down for a few minutes. Please."

"We're going to have to question them, Alice."

"I realize that."

"I know it's hard, but try not to ask them too much. The more we can hear from them on the first telling, the better."

Chapter 39

Simon took the pickup to look for a parking spot so the Halpern family could walk back to the house together, a single squad car trolling just behind them. Hands linked, they moved slowly, four astride along the damp sidewalk. Though Alice sensed the rubber soles of her sandals hard against the cement sidewalk, she felt as if she was skidding; holding herself fast to this moment on earth was a discipline. Her body had turned gelatinous from the agonizing afternoon. Peter's small, damp hand tight in hers felt so fragile she could have wept. They had been abandoned for just under two hours. Abandoned in familiar territory, among familiar faces. But no matter how many people you knew in New York City, there were always strangers.

Yet strangers were not always whom you needed to fear.

At the other end of the family strand, holding on to Nell, Mike marched along with an energized bounce, still wound up from the chase. He was working hard to get the kids' minds off the fact that Sylvie had left them alone, and was telling them every knock-knock joke he knew. Their little voices tinkled on the damp air as questions lurched through Alice's mind. Why had Sylvie left so abruptly during the storm? Her sudden flight was so desperate. That she had taken care to leave the children somewhere familiar, where they were known, told Alice against reason that Sylvie cared about them. Though that thought sent shivers of disgust through Alice. How could Sylvie possibly *care*? She had sewn Lauren's hair into a pillow and embroidered her miniscule initials over Judy Gersten's handiwork, such a creepy taunt. Or had the two women worked together? But Judy in her drunken misery didn't seem capable of any strenuous plan. It had to be Sylvie who had killed Lauren. *Why* had she? Alice's head began to pound as they turned up Degraw Street toward Clinton. Why had Sylvie done it? Why had she stayed these past two awful weeks? Did it have something to do with Ivy? Was her plan incomplete?

Was Ivy still here in Brooklyn?

As they climbed Simon's front stoop, Frannie swung open the door, smiling hugely, with Dana at her side.

"Welcome home! I've got some popcorn and lemonade." She was Aunt Frannie now, suggesting the children change into dry clothes, waiting for them in Simon's kitchen, making them comfortable before beginning the debriefing.

"What a storm today, huh?" Frannie leaned forward, arms crossed together on the kitchen table. Her eyes stayed focused on Nell and Peter, offering full, irresistible attention. "What was it like being outside in the rain, waiting for your mom to pick you up?"

Nell grabbed a handful of popcorn and held it over her mouth, dribbling it in one piece at a time. "Sylvie's my favorite babysitter. She said I'm practically old enough to babysit too. She said today I got to practice babysitting Peter."

"It was fun!" Peter said. "We were big kids."

Bit by bit, Frannie teased out the story of their afternoon. Dana sat off to the side, taking notes.

The children remembered the first phone call, right before the rain. Alice remembered it too: turning to see Sylvie across the street in the park, answering her phone as Peter ran in front of her, hearing the first loud clap of thunder. After the call, she gathered them up and began to lead them toward the Court Street exit in the direction of Simon's house.

Then, her phone rang again.

After a brief call, she told the children to turn around and they walked in the opposite direction toward Smith Street and the Autumn Café. It was then that the sky opened up and they were drenched. Picturing the scene through the detectives' eyes, Alice now saw it: the café was half a block from the subway. Sylvie had needed to go somewhere quickly. But first she brought the kids to the café, told the girl behind the counter that she had to run out for a minute and would be right back. She gave Nell a ten dollar bill. Then she left.

As the details unfolded, something began to burn in Alice's mind.

Stop or they're next.

It had been written some time before she arrived home in the rain. If Sylvie *had* gone directly to the subway, she couldn't have written it. And if she didn't write it, who did?

Chapter 40

"Julius Pollack," Frannie said. "We got a print hit a little while ago."

"So it *was* Julius who wrote it!" Alice looked at Mike, holding his eyes a moment before turning back to Frannie and Dana. "Julius and Sylvie? Maybe Ivy *was* in his apartment for a while. Maybe it *wasn't* just the tape I heard."

"Whoa!" Dana held a palm flat to Alice, as if a gesture could stop the onslaught of forbidden assumptions. "We don't know anything about that right now, so back up and slow down."

"Dana's right." Frannie crossed her legs and cupped her palms over her top knee. "They're still checking the print against the crime scene."

But Alice couldn't slow down; her mind was flying. Had Julius and Sylvie both been involved in Lauren's death? It made sense, somehow: the older man, cynical and rich, and the naïve young woman.

Mike paced the kitchen with his fists clenched. "I'll kill him!"

"Shh!" Alice said. "The kids!" Maggie and Simon had taken them upstairs so they could play with Ethan in the family room.

Mike's skin blazed red; he looked as if he needed to explode but was imploding instead.

"I understand how you feel." The corners of Frannie's mouth dimpled with deep lines, instantly aging the young face. "But that's a job you won't have to do, Mike. If Pollack's guilty, believe me, the state and the feds will take care of him."

She checked her watch and drained her third cup of coffee, carrying the empty mug into the kitchen. When she came out, she announced, "I'm heading back over to the precinct. There's a lot to do. Dana's going to stay here."

"See ya later, chief," Dana said with a small salute as Frannie walked to the front door with one of the uniformed cops who had been on guard.

Frannie smiled, vanishing the shadow of years from her face, and she looked almost rested. "Nestor here's giving me a lift but Rula's still out front."

It seemed absurd to Alice that Dana would need to stay with them still—Sylvie was gone and Pollack was in custody—but she understood that what they knew was largely conjecture glued together with a few scraps of evidence. They didn't truly know what had happened, not today and not to Pam and not two weeks ago, to Lauren and Ivy.

By late evening—after a Thai dinner ordered in and two bottles of white wine Alice wished she could have shared—bits of news began to filter in through Dana. The first came when the four parents were upstairs getting their children to sleep. Alice and Mike snuggled with Nell and Peter in the guest room's double bed. Ultimately the kids would occupy their sleeping bags on the floor so Alice and Mike could sleep in comfort, though as far as Nell and Peter were concerned, they had the better deal. Maggie and Simon meanwhile put Ethan to bed together, comrades in life, apparently thrust past sex into each other's true graces by the shock of Sylvie's deceit. They were waiting in the living room with Dana when Alice and Mike finally came yawning down the stairs.

"She's done it!" Maggie spoke first, excitedly, with a tinge of anger in her tone. "She's slipped right out of our fingers!"

"Sylvie?" Mike asked.

"Seems so," Simon answered.

"What happened?" Alice addressed Dana, who seemed most likely to have a reliable answer.

Dana was sitting on the piano bench, legs crossed in the lotus position. "Frannie just buzzed me. We've pinned her down on the F train to the E to Jamaica. She caught the sky train to JFK, which is where Danny lost her. But now we've got an eyewitness who saw her at the Air France counter."

"She left the country," Alice said.

"Someone called her and told her the crime scene was found." Mike's eyes were bright in a face pale as clay. "That second call at the park today!"

"The call scared her," Alice said. "She had to leave."

"And so she's fled back to France," Simon added. "Where extradition is hard-proven."

Dana listened with a therapist's calm as the friends' guesswork unscrolled, but didn't say what she was clearly thinking: *no assumptions.* Alice remembered the core philosophy of this strange journey and stopped talking.

Assumptions were as lethal as doubt.

"Frannie and Paul are giving a news conference in a few minutes," Dana said, "if you feel like watching. You can get the facts."

They all went upstairs to the family room and turned on the television. Most of the local stations had gathered for a live news conference held by Detectives Francesca Viola and Paul Giometti of the Seventy-sixth Precinct. They stood together in front of the blue-tiled police station, facing the inevitable cluster of microphones and a bank of lights that blanched the night's natural darkness. They looked bone tired. Drained of their defenses, they stated the facts.

"This afternoon we issued an Amber Alert for two children who appeared to have been abducted by their babysitter in Brooklyn. The children have been recovered and are safe at home. The babysitter is Sylvie Devrais and she has not been found."

A picture of Sylvie suddenly filled the screen. Seeing her like this, as a suspect, stripped her of the sweet innocence Alice had always assumed for her. The detectives reappeared on the screen, explaining that Sylvie was also wanted for murder and that she may have had an accomplice.

"We have a list of suspects who may have helped Sylvie Devrais, but without hard forensic evidence"—Frannie paused on camera, her shrewd eyes blinking—"we won't make an arrest."

Alice read between the lines. Frannie had considered her words—*can't* became *won't*—free will substituted for helplessness. They were holding Julius Pollack at the precinct but they hadn't arrested him? Wasn't the print hit enough to get him on harassment and violating the restraining order? And what about Judy Gersten and Sal Cattaneo? Were the Three Musketeers of Brooklyn real estate all going to be questioned, then freed before hard answers were in hand? Either their lawyers were playing for time or the detectives were trolling for more action, setting traps. As Frannie spoke to the cluster of reporters, Alice knew the detective was calculating what she would put out to the media, as she had all along.

"I understand JFK's sealed off," another reporter asked. "No flights going in or out. How long will that last?"

"As long as necessary," Frannie said. Her tone sharpened to add, "We're looking for a murderer."

"What about Tim Barnet?"

Frannie's split second of hesitation told Alice something was up with Tim.

"Tim Barnet is one of many people we've been talking to," Frannie said, "but we have no reason to suspect him over anyone else at this point."

"He left town."

"We've been in close contact with him," Frannie said too quickly.

Had Tim's *guy* lost him too? Had Tim needed to get lost? Was Austin okay? Alice felt the first pulse of adrenaline that was always a precursor to insomnia. She wouldn't even try to sleep tonight, she decided. As long as Frannie was awake at the precinct, Alice would stay up too. Wait for news.

"What about Simon Blue?" another reporter asked.

"Oh, give me a break!" Simon howled, sitting between Maggie and Mike on the couch. "Have you poisoned everyone's minds, Maggie dear?"

Maggie gave Simon's leg a sharp slap, and laughed. "If only I could."

Simon and Maggie clasped hands and leaned against each other.

"Ms. Devrais worked for him," Frannie told the microphones, "so traces of her are all over his house, but beyond that we've found no evidence of his involvement in the case."

"Bloody right!" Simon called out to the TV.

"What about a money trail?" another reported asked. "How does Metro Properties tie into the missing women and babies?"

"Yes, we've looked at all the bank accounts of Metro Properties, as well everyone else who has come under investigation." A shaft of light momentarily blinded Frannie. She lifted her hand to shadow her eyes, and continued. "There's no indication that anyone received unusual amounts of money. There's nothing unusual there. Except"—she hesitated—"we haven't located any bank accounts for Sylvie Devrais."

"So the baby sale thing is—"

"We don't know," Frannie cut that reporter off. The whole issue of illegal baby sales clearly riled her. It was one hypothesis of many that had first been introduced, to Alice's knowledge, by Erin Brinkley in one of her articles. "We're looking at evidence, not taking shots in the dark."

"One more question—" a reporter shouted, but was interrupted by someone louder:

"What is the connection between Sylvie Devrais and Julius Pollack?"

Alice leaned in toward the television, listening closely.

Frannie's eyes narrowed. It was like she was standing in an avalanche of wild conjecture, fending off small bits while others flew by.

"None that we know of at this moment," she answered.

"What about—"

Giometti shifted in front of the microphones and said, "That's all for now."

Alice watched them turn around and walk back into the police station. She could almost feel the cool shade of the place, with its predictable comforts. The soda machines, ready to serve. The tables and chairs and dropped ceiling pocked with silver sprinkler heads. The fish circling in their illuminated tank. She wondered if the big fish had eaten up all the little fish yet, and if so, how it would survive alone.

Simon used the remote to click off the TV, then clicked it right back on. "Too wound up for bed," he said. "Let's see if Mr. TiVo did his job today." A few clicks and that afternoon's Red Sox versus Phillies game appeared on the television. Mike leaned forward, instantly glued to the game. Alice and Maggie looked at each other; clearly this was how their husbands were going to unburden their minds.

"I'll make us some hot milk, ladies," Maggie said. "I think there might be some gingersnaps too."

Dana stood up and stretched. "I'm heading over to the precinct," she said. "Rula's staked outside, if you need anything."

Mike pulled his attention away from the screen. "Does he do pizza runs?"

Dana looked at him and forced a wry smile. He forced one back.

"Honey, you're in Brooklyn. You can get a pizza delivered twenty-four/seven without police assistance."

Alice walked Dana to the front door while Maggie headed into the kitchen.

"Thanks," Alice said, "for everything."

"Just doing my job." Dana started to lean forward to give Alice a sisterly peck on the cheek—as if they were actually friends—but pulled back. She seemed embarrassed by the momentary lapse in professionalism. Instead, she put out a hand and Alice gave it a little squeeze.

Alice watched Dana walk down the front stoop. Detective Rula, a young Hispanic man in a gray sweatshirt and white Mets cap, appeared to doze in a dented Honda Civic parked at the curb.

Maggie had arranged two red ceramic mugs of hot milk and a plate of gingersnaps on the coffee table in the living room. Alice settled into the couch. She picked up one of the mugs and blew on her hot milk, watching a shiny skin congeal and wrinkle under her breath. It was still too hot to drink so she set it down and waited for Maggie, who had gone back to the kitchen.

Alice thought of Nell and Peter's two-hour absence today with immense relief and a shiver of fear that she felt would haunt her forever. But her children were safe now, home as it were; as close to home as they could get for the moment. Alice could almost smell their deep sleep, floating like a sticky-sweet cloud above the raucous din of the television one flight up. Beyond this room, this house, these people, the neighborhood slept soundly. Or so it seemed by the heavy silence outside. Alice wondered what she would find if she went out right now and walked the quiet nineteenth-century sidewalks. How many windows would be lit yellow, containing a fretful wakefulness? How many people in this city couldn't sleep?

She thought about flight. About staying and leaving. She and Mike hadn't had a chance to seriously discuss it, but they would. Later tonight or tomorrow morning. There were a hundred places they might go. Though admittedly, at this moment, she felt less determined to flee. She was so very tired.

"You know," Maggie said, flouncing onto the couch next to Alice. "I'm thinking Simon and I might just give it another go."

"Well," Alice said, wavering between her habitual diplomacy on this subject and a desire to say something mean and sharp to end Maggie's indecision, "you two are meant for each other."

"So." Maggie faced Alice. Silver moonlight shifted across the ceiling, shadowing her face. "Tell the truth. Do you think Tim's involved in this?"

Alice shuddered at that awful thought. "I don't want to think it," she said. "I *can't* think it."

Maggie leaned in. "But *do* you?"

"Maybe," Alice said, allowing that possibility to seep into her thoughts. "Do you?"

Maggie nodded decisively. "I always thought that man was too good to be true. He was too *easy,* do you know what I mean? Never a complaint. Perfectly devastated when Lauren died. But then he left town."

"He said he couldn't stay here anymore." Alice wanted to believe Tim wasn't capable of anything so horrible as what happened to Lauren. "It made sense, Mags, didn't it? Even you defended him at the time. He *had* to go."

"I've been thinking about it," Maggie said. "Simon stayed around when things got tough, and I really gave him hell."

"He stayed because of Ethan."

"Partly, yes," Maggie said. "But he also stayed because this is his home. Tim left because he didn't feel comfortable here. In this *place*. With *us*. Something else had changed. Don't you see it?"

Alice did and she didn't. If Maggie was right, then the detectives had been doubly right in thinking from the start that one of the friends had been guilty in Lauren's death. They had already connected Sylvie to the crime scene. Wasn't that enough?

If Alice had learned anything through all this, it was not to jump to conclusions. One thing she knew for sure was that people who cared about this case were burning the midnight oil. Frannie, Giometti and Dana were at the precinct right now, working shoulder-to-shoulder with the FBI. Police were swarming over the city all the way to Kennedy airport and beyond looking for Sylvie, hoping to pick up a trail that might lead to one lost baby girl.

Chapter 41

"What time is it?" Pam looked down at her body, which even beneath the white sheet showed that she had lost about twenty pounds. "Where am I?"

"You mean what day is it," Ray said, looking both enervated and wildly alert.

"No, Raymond," Esther corrected, "she means what *week* is it."

"I see Click and Clack haven't lost any love for each other." Pam winked at Alice, who had just stepped into the room behind Frannie and Giometti. She had persuaded them to let her come along in the hope that seeing her might help jog Pam's memory of the days just before her attack.

"Look at you!" Pam reached out to touch Alice's stomach. "Do you hate it when people do that? Maybe I *have* been here awhile; you look a size bigger. We had an appointment, I think—"

"We saw the house," Alice said, not knowing where to begin. The house was the last thing on her mind right now, after her children's recovery, after Pam's luminous eyes, her smile, her boisterous wakefulness, her life.

"Strange," Pam said somewhat wearily, but not without the verve that had made her voice so powerful on a good day. Alice felt a wave of relief, even joy. "Mom says I overslept but, to be honest, I don't feel that rested." She leaned back into her pillows. "Listen, people, I've got something I've got to say. Alice, you won't like it. Have a seat."

Ray immediately scraped a chair across the floor to Pam's bedside and gently guided Alice into it.

"It might interest you two coppers too." Pam winked, not losing a chance to dig in a proverbial elbow.

Frannie smiled. Alice only now noticed that Frannie's bangs had grown long in the last two weeks, touching her eyebrows, threatening her eyes. She needed a hair-cut, and some sleep, and probably a decent meal. When all this was over, Alice decided, she would invite Frannie over for dinner at the new house. Get to know her as a friend, fan what had sparked between them that first day on the playground when she was a local aunt out for a romp at the playground like everyone else.

"Go ahead," Frannie told Pam. She glanced at Gio-metti, who pulled his small notepad out of his shirt pocket and uncapped his pen.

"Too much talk could tire her out," Esther said, "after what she's been through."

"We'll stop if she gets too tired," Frannie said, "but this may be important."

"You hear that, Mom? It's important. So let me talk." Pam cleared her voice and was about to begin when Ray interrupted.

"You want I should take some photos?" Ray suddenly asked. "Document the conversation? I have my camera right here."

"You got it working?" Pam asked.

"Honey, I got you with every visitor, every doctor, every nurse. I filled an album already!"

"Not that tacky black and red one, I hope."

"Not that one. I bought something new, something you're going to love."

Pam and Ray exchanged adoring glances.

"That's okay," Giometti said, indicating his notepad. "This'll be fine."

Ray shrugged his shoulders and positioned himsel

against the wall at the head of Pam's bed, one hand resting on her shoulder as she spoke. She lifted her left hand to cover his, and began.

"Our sweet little Sylvie?" Pam said ominously. "An angel, she's not."

Everyone listened as Pam told them the story of what happened to her on the morning of her staged suicide.

"I was trying to find out who your landlord's partner was," she told Alice, "like I said I would. No biggie. I asked around the office and no one knew anything. Judy was gone for the day and since she's the boss, her files go back farthest, so I thought I'd take a look in her computer. I was poking around and I accidentally got into the network that links her up to her home computer."

"Accidentally on purpose, you mean?" Esther said. "Just like I taught you."

Pam grinned. "Judy works a lot at home."

"*Works.*" Ray rolled his eyes. "Drinks, is more like it. Pam's been carrying that office for years."

"Well," Pam continued, "so I was poking around a little and I saw a few very interesting things. There was a lot on Metro in Judy's home files, let me tell you, *a lot.* Turns out she not only does business with those jokers, but she's got a personal connection that's about as strong as it gets."

Of course, they had all figured by now that Sal Cattaneo had had an adulterous relationship with Judy, but in silent agreement they let Pam continue as if nothing had happened in all the time she'd been asleep.

"The partner," Pam said, "is none other than Sal Cattaneo, our local butcher."

They held their silence, allowing Pam the satisfaction of delivering a surprise.

"And my spinster boss, Judy, turns out not to be such an angel herself." Pam paused for dramatic effect. "Turns out Judy and Sal are an item. And they've been an item for a long, long time."

This *was* news to Alice. But possibly not to Frannie; her expression remained steady as she asked, "How long?"

"At least thirty years, the whole time Sal's been married. It started before he even got married. Judy's a real piece of work. She's got it all written down in her computer like it's some kind of heartbreaking romance novel. I couldn't stop reading once I started."

"Why should you?" Esther said. "She had it there for anyone to see."

"It was in her personal journal on her home computer, Esther." Ray clamped his lips tight; clearly he didn't agree with Pam and Esther's policy of random investigation.

"Anyhow, Sal was engaged to his childhood sweetheart, Angie, but he got involved with Judy when she was new to the neighborhood. That was when people who weren't *from* here were outsiders, big time."

"It still feels that way," Alice said.

"Oh no, honey, back then it was ten times worse. Judy Gersten was an independent woman, and she was Jewish, and she came all the way from Michigan. She was a *foreigner*."

"Hurry up," Esther said. "Get to the good part."

"You already know this story?" Ray asked Esther.

"No, I'm hearing it for the first time, just like you."

"Then how do you know there's a good part?"

"Because I know how to tell a story." Esther nodded. "And so does my Pammie."

"Will you two let me talk?" Pam said with a twinkle of love in her eyes for her husband and mother and their aggravating yet comfortable routine.

"So, talk," Esther said.

"So Sal's engaged to Angie, and along comes Judy Gersten, who opens up a real estate office on Court Street. An outsider. By now Sal's already started buying up neighborhood real estate. He likes Judy, so he gives her some of his business, then he gives her all of his business. Wink wink. By the time he hooks up with Julius Pollack, buying up tenement buildings together as Metro Properties, Judy gets a big chunk of their business. She's profiting big time from them. So the three of them, they're all getting rich together. And Judy and Sal? They're in love."

"But the guy marries Angie anyway?" Ray asks.

"You bet." Pam nodded with a wobble of skin that used to house her double chin. "Angie told him she was pregnant."

"But I thought Sal and his wife don't have any children," Alice said.

"They don't." Pam nodded decisively.

"She miscarried?" Esther guessed.

"Nope," Pam said.

"Just tell us," Ray said. "What happened?"

"Angie told Sal she was pregnant, but she wasn't."

"Why?" Ray asked.

Pam savored this moment, looking from face to face before telling them, "Because Judy *was* pregnant."

There was silence as everyone absorbed the information. Alice noticed that Frannie continued to look unperturbed. She had been questioning Judy Gersten at the precinct. Alice could picture it: Judy unraveling in the cold light of the interview room, rubbing the table's long, deep scratch with her fingertip, over and over, as if it were a thread she yearned to pluck from history and weave into a better past.

"It was nineteen seventy-three," Pam continued. "Abortion was legalized just that year. But Judy *loved* Sal—"

"Judy Gersten had Sal Cattaneo's baby?" Alice blurted out. "And he still married Angie?"

"Because he believed Angie was pregnant, and she was his designated wife, and that was how it was here back then. Before he even had a chance to find out she wasn't pregnant, and that Judy was going ahead with having her baby anyway . . . let's just say Angie's father didn't give him much choice."

"Wait a minute," Ray said. "Isn't her father Anthony Scoletto?"

"You got it." Pam took a breath. There was more. "You don't say no to the Scoletto family. And Sal probably loved Angie. They were children together, already family. So they married. And she never had that baby or any other baby. But Judy, she was independent, and she was angry, and she was in love, so she went ahead and had her baby."

"So where is it?" Ray asked. "It would be grown up by now."

"Thirty years old," Alice said, as heat fanned through her body. Her simple question to Pam—who was Julius Pollack's partner—had led to someone taking pains to try to kill Pam and disguise it as suicide. "Did Judy raise the baby?"

"She chickened out at the last minute," Pam said. "There weren't many single mothers back then. There wasn't even a word for it. Babies born out of wedlock were still called bastards."

Or *little bitches,* Alice thought, as it all came clear. She lowered her face into her hands.

"She gave it up for adoption. It was a little girl, adopted by a French family—father was a diplomat. They went back to France when Judy's daughter was still an infant."

Now Frannie's expression flinched, just slightly. But Alice saw it. So Judy hadn't confessed this part. Which meant she had wanted to hide it. But why?

"Judy tried to find the baby but she never could," Pam continued. "It caused her a lot of pain, and I think that's where the drinking comes in. Do you know, she still loves Sal and they still do business together? But he's still married to Angie."

"Go figure." Esther shook her head.

"Let me guess." Alice looked up. "Judy never found her daughter. But her daughter found her."

"Bingo," Pam said.

Pam's biggest mistake wasn't discovering the secret history of Judy Gersten and Sal Cattaneo, but tossing off a gossipy comment to Sylvie at the end of a workday. "What a day I've had," she had said to Sylvie as they closed up the office together the evening before the attack. "Please, whatever you do, don't tell me you were adopted." Sylvie had looked at her with such sharp surprise that Pam didn't pursue it, and she certainly didn't explain to the young assistant the details of their boss's past.

The next morning, Sylvie arrived unannounced at Pam's house, just before Pam was to have met Alice at the Third Place house.

"Judy told me to come," Sylvie said with her sweet smile.

Sylvie shared some coffee with Pam. Pam had planned on walking to the Third Place house, but Sylvie complained of having hurt her foot at the gym, so it was decided they would drive. They went together to the downstairs garage and settled into the car.

"Sylvie turned to me with the worst look on her face," Pam said soberly. "She had a gun. I told her she was out of her mind. Then she stuck the thing into the side of my neck."

That was the last thing Pam remembered.

They didn't stay long at the hospital after that. Pam was depleted by the conversation, and the detectives had what they needed. Alice kissed Pam on the forehead, promising to visit again soon. She smelled antiseptic now; Alice missed the baby-powder scent.

"I'll take your picture next time you come," Ray promised. "I'll put it in the album."

"Okay." Alice shook his hand, and hugged Esther. "Take good care of her."

"Why wouldn't we?" Esther offered a smile of yellowed, crooked, eighty-year-old teeth, which Alice suspected were all hers. "She's all I got, aside from Ray here."

Frannie and Giometti insisted on dropping Alice off at Simon's house. She rode in the backseat, watching scenes of the neighborhood flash by from the open police car window. The air was a weave of cool and warm breezes—the end of summer, autumn's approach.

They pulled up in front of Simon's house.

"Don't go anywhere," Frannie said as Alice stepped onto the curb and slammed shut the back door of the blue sedan.

Alice hesitated. "Is that an order?" She smiled as if she were joking, but they all knew she wasn't.

"Not really." Frannie leaned into the open window, eyes squinted, desperate for rest. "We might need you, Alice."

"But—" Alice wanted to argue that she was no longer needed. Sylvie had revealed herself. As had Julius Pollack. Somehow, they were both related to the crimes.

"Forensics analyzed the prints at the crime scene." Frannie's eyes were steady on Alice, doling out one crumb of information to pique Alice's curiosity, fuel her insomnia and glue her to *here*. "Sylvie's were the only match, besides about a dozen Mr. Frosty drivers, every one of whom we have tracked down and crossed off our list."

"Julius Pollack?"

"Nope."

"Sal Cattaneo?"

"Nope. And not Judy Gersten, either, in case you're wondering."

"So you're saying that Sylvie did this all alone?"

Alice stepped closer to the car, bending down a little to catch Frannie's eye, but the detective just shook her head. She had that *no assumptions* look on her face as she slid the stick shift into gear and drove away.

Chapter 42

The friends decided collectively to stay put, hold tight, and resume normal life; it would be best for the children and also for themselves. And so the next morning, Mike and Simon took Ethan, Nell and Peter to their respective schools. Mike then went to his workshop in Red Hook and Simon subwayed into Manhattan to teach a late morning class. Maggie and Alice had a few hours alone in the house before Blue Shoes was due to open at eleven. Two days had passed since Sylvie's great escape and one day since Pam's awakening. If anything was going to happen today, the detectives would know where to find them: at home or at work, pursuing the possibility of a regular day.

It was just past nine in the morning when the doorbell rang. Alice and Maggie, who were in the kitchen finishing their morning coffee and tea, looked at each other.

"Maybe we shouldn't answer it," Maggie said.

"It's probably just a delivery." Alice pulled her pink chenille robe closed over her massive tummy. "Unless," she smiled archly, "it's Simon's secret *lover.*"

"Or a mad killer, after you!" Maggie laughed her sharpest cackle, and both women flew to the front hall. Maggie reached the door first, glanced at Alice and turned the knob.

Standing on the front stoop was neither lover nor killer but a true surprise. Lizzie, in full California flower—tanned and wearing a pale yellow pants suit—

held out the morning paper as if she had simply stopped by to deliver it.

"Mom!" Alice shouted.

"Babydoll." Lizzie embraced Alice, who felt herself melting in her mother's arms. "How could I stay away?"

Alice wiped the mascara-tinted tears off Lizzie's cheeks. "They're okay," Alice said. "They're back at school. Everything's okay."

"How could everything be okay?" Lizzie composed herself. "That would be impossible, wouldn't it?"

Maggie picked up Lizzie's red suitcase from the front stoop's landing, carried it into the foyer and shut the door.

"Hello, Maggie." Lizzie offered a cheek and the two women did a double air-kiss. "How are you?"

"Addled, as usual. Men trouble, you know." Maggie offered Lizzie her most brilliant smile.

"So you're back with your husband, I see." Lizzie walked into Simon's living room and looked around. "Very nice. A little baroque, but basically I like it."

At the word *baroque* Maggie's eyes found Alice's and rolled dramatically.

"Actually Simon and I are not back together, not officially." Maggie joined Lizzie in the living room. Alice followed her mother and her friend, who had always managed to get along despite an underlying competitiveness; Alice hoped this would not be the moment it bred fireworks. "I decorated the entire house myself. Simon, of course, is free to redecorate, but I must say he hasn't changed a thing."

Lizzie peered up at Maggie through her calico-framed glasses, then broke into a wry smile and reached up to pinch Maggie's cheek. "It's gorgeous, *bubbelah*."

Maggie forced a smile. "Think I'll see if we have the makings of some real English scones. You must be starving, Lizzie darling. Shall I make you eggs and bacon as well?"

"Make for everyone," Lizzie said, plopping down on the couch and sighing deeply. "We'll eat together."

Alice sat with her mother on the couch, holding the

newspaper on her knees, still in its blue plastic sleeve. She was dying to open it, to learn Erin Brinkley's latest discoveries, but knew that the minute she did, the knot of anxiety that had taken up residence in her chest would instantly tighten. She and Maggie had deliberately avoided the paper all morning, and now here it was in her hands.

"How was your flight, Mom?"

Lizzie grazed the backs of her fingers along Alice's cheek. "How are you, babydoll? I've been so worried."

"I'm fine." Alice felt the crinkle of the thin plastic under her fingers. "Okay, it's been a nightmare. But it's over now."

"Let's hope." Lizzie yawned. "Any chance an old lady could get a strong cup of joe around here?"

"Coming right up, Mom."

When Alice returned to the living room five minutes later, Lizzie had removed her shoes and was stretched out on the couch, reading the newspaper. The blue plastic sat crumpled like an abandoned skin on the coffee table, next to the Metro section. Alice set down the mug of coffee and picked up the newspaper. And there it was, the latest.

In a lead article headlined FALSE IDENTITY STYMIES PO-LICE, Erin Brinkley claimed that Sylvie Devrais simply never existed. Another woman, Christina Dreux, had been given up at birth by Judy Gersten and raised in Paris by French parents, but there was no trace of Ms. Dreux having ever been in New York. According to her adoptive parents, Ms. Dreux had been a rebellious teenager who had left home at the age of seventeen, returning, humbled, after a year. Christina eventually trained as an obstetrics nurse but never worked as one. How she had earned a living was unclear. French authorities were in the process of reopening cold cases from the last decade, in search of missing pregnant women.

In "International Black Market for Babies," Brinkley revealed that the lack of a coherent database, linking missing babies and children internationally, created a huge loophole for traffickers in illegal adoption. Each case had to be investigated separately, taking large amounts of time and resources, and requiring a motivated investigator. Therefore, as soon as a baby or child crossed a border, it was nearly impossible to find him or her.

In "Slumlord Faces Grand Jury," Brinkley continued her exposure of Julius Pollack and Sal Cattaneo, citing individual cases of illegal evictions and the transformation of rent-regulated apartments into top-of-the-market cash cows. She also described the worst of the many harassment cases they had faced, making Alice shiver. Her encounters with him were nothing compared to what some of the other tenants had endured: withheld heat, deliberately broken windows, ignored rats.

Finally, in "A Secret History," Brinkley described the entwined backgrounds of Metro Properties and Garden Hill Realty, splaying open the long relationship of Sal Cattaneo and Judy Gersten. Erin had somehow gotten her hands on the photograph Alice had seen in Judy's apartment, and it accompanied the article. She wrote about Angie Cattaneo and the childhood romance that withered in a childless marriage. Finally, Brinkley tied in the other stories, with a long-lost illegitimate daughter returning to reap havoc in a scenario rife with opportunity for blackmail and deception. She brought it only as far as that, being unable to reliably demonstrate Sylvie's role, or lack of role, in the real estate angle of the story. But Brinkley made it plain what she believed, that Sylvie's goal was an age-old, lethal combination: revenge and money.

Brinkley couldn't print it outright in the newspaper, because the assumed conclusion of her long story relied so much on conjecture, but at the end of the article the implication was clear: Had Sylvie tried to destroy her birth parents by targeting pregnant tenants undergoing illegal evictions, then used her training as an obstetrics nurse to deliver the babies and sell them on the black market?

It seemed far too complicated to Alice. She didn't truly believe Sylvie could have lived among them for so long and undertaken such a dramatic series of crimes. A simplicity was lacking in the convergence of all the stories. Even after all Erin Brinkley's analyses, Alice wasn't fully convinced.

A phone conversation with Frannie later that evening confirmed Alice's skepticism. "Brinkley's a drama queen," Frannie said. "Sometimes she comes up with a good angle, but I'm telling you, other times we laugh at her around here."

"Have you met her, Frannie?"

"A few times. She's about twenty-four years old, shares a desk at the *Times* with another cub reporter. You know the drill. She's trying to fight her way up the ladder. Probably figures if she wins a Pulitzer Prize, they'll give her her own desk."

It made sense, the young, undisciplined reporter slipping guesswork into observation, keeping just this side of fact.

"There's always a story behind the story," Frannie said.

"Tell me the rest." Alice shifted on the couch, trying to get comfortable. Frannie's hesitancy on the other end of the line told her she wasn't sure how much she should say. Maybe she was sitting at her desk in the PDU, surrounded by male colleagues who would accuse her of gossiping. "Are you at work right now?"

"Actually I'm home," Frannie said.

"Good, then you can talk to me, Frannie. I've been part of this from the beginning. I was supposed to be the next set of initials on a pillow. It's part of my life story and I need to know."

On the floor in front of her, Nell, Peter and Ethan were building a city out of shoe boxes, blocks and Lego. Lizzie was on the floor with them, constructing her own corner of their empire. Alice vaguely watched them, her mind tuned to Frannie's voice.

"All right," Frannie said. "But I might give it to you

out of order. I've never had much trouble sleeping, but after the last few days I know exactly how you feel with your insomnia."

"Crazy," Alice said. "Myopic. Right?"

"Well, I'm not hearing things—" Frannie chuckled.

"Good try." Alice said. "I'm not one bit fazed. Go on."

"First of all, that *ZL* on the pillow? It panned out to nothing. No one with those initials came up missing."

"So there wasn't any other missing pregnant woman?" Alice asked.

"And there's still nothing on Christine Craddock. Zip. So as far as we're concerned, she's not part of this picture. All the stuffing in the pillows, except for Lauren's hair, was standard pillow foam."

"You were checking DNA for other hair strands in the peony pillow," Alice said, wondering if traces of Ivy's hair had turned up with Lauren's.

"We found Sylvie's hair, but that's no big surprise at this point; her prints were all over the crime scene."

"You mean Christina," Alice said. "I read the paper, remember?"

"It's a bad habit, Alice." Frannie paused. "So you know Christina Dreux was the baby Judy gave up for adoption."

"Was Erin Brinkley right, then?" Alice asked. "She *did* come back for some kind of twisted revenge?"

"That's what Brinkley wants all of New York to think because it makes such a good story, right?"

"It's kind of confusing, I think," Alice answered, watching the children run their little trucks along a road through their city.

"It's confusing," Frannie said, "because it's wrong."

Lizzie caught Peter's hand just before it knocked into the base of a tall tower.

"Christina Dreux was never here. Analise Krup was. She's a German girl who grew up in Paris. Her mother was a translator; it was just the two of them. Analise met Christina in nursing school and they became good friends. Christina decided to find out who her birth parents were and her father helped her. He's a diplomat, so he has access to all that information. Her parents respected her desire to know, and she found out, but decided not to act on it."

"But Analise did, right?" Alice asked.

"Right."

Nell stepped into the city and knocked down an entire neighborhood. Peter and Lizzie shrieked, *No!* but it was too late. Ethan immediately scrambled to rebuild.

"Her mother put us in touch with her therapist," Frannie said. "He said Analise is a classic psychopath. Do you know anything about psychopaths, Alice?"

"No, not really." Only what she had learned on television: that they were crazed killers, every one. Probably a simplistic assumption.

"Mostly they're con artists, manipulators, rarely violent. They blend in really well." Frannie yawned. "That's what makes them so dangerous."

Alice pulled the red blanket over her knees. It was starting to get cold.

"So this Analise," Alice said, "passed herself off as Christina pretending to be Sylvie?"

"Right."

"And Analise wanted to destroy Christina's birth parents by making it seem like they were killing tenants?" The convolutions were making Alice's head spin.

"Shh!" Lizzie shook her head at Alice and shifted her eyes to the children in a silent admonishment not to scare them.

Alice got up from the couch, slinging the red blanket over her shoulders. Mike and Simon were in the kitchen, so she went upstairs where she could finish the conversation in private.

"We don't think so," Frannie said. "We're not sure, but we think she might have come here to try to extract some money from them. You know, she would pretend to be Christina, work their heartstrings. But then her plans changed."

"Why?" Alice settled onto her bed in the guest room. Peter had left his Curious George doll on a pillow and Alice held its furry brown head against her chest.

"We're not sure," Frannie answered. "But she never asked them for money. She took information. She wove a pretty complicated cover for what she did to Lauren."

"You mean her change of plans was deciding to kill Lauren? And take Ivy?" It seemed incredible. *"Why?"*

"We don't know for sure at the moment."

But Alice did. Suddenly it was perfectly clear. Maggie was right, again. The *little bitch* had been in love. She wanted her man. But he was a devoted father and would never have left his children.

"Frannie?" Alice held Peter's doll tight under her neck, pressing her chin down on its soft head, bolstering herself.

"Say it, Alice."

"It was one of us after all."

Alice heard a buzzer sound in Frannie's background and a woman saying, "I'll get it." She realized she knew absolutely nothing about Frannie's life.

"Do you know where he is?" Frannie asked calmly.

Alice was momentarily shocked by the question. Did Frannie honestly think Alice would protect an accomplice to Lauren's killer? Lauren's worst betrayer?

"You're joking, Frannie, aren't you?"

"I don't really joke much."

"I've noticed that."

"Listen, Alice, I'm a detective. I have to ask."

Alice rolled over onto her left side to accommodate one of the twins, who had started to kick under her right rib cage. "If I had the answer to that question, Frannie I would tell you."

"I know you would," Frannie said.

Alice let it go at that. The truth was, she had no idea of what Frannie really thought of her. And it didn' much matter. Frannie was very good at her job, smar and determined, and Alice respected her even if sh hadn't made a new friend.

After that, minutes and hours and days slipped by. Nearly a whole week.

Tim Barnet and Analise Krup were hotly sought by every agency of law under the sun. And Ivy too. It was assumed now that they had her with them, hiding in some remote country. But wherever they were, how had they gotten there without a trace? And how had no one spotted them and sent word? Even if they were in a country with no extradition treaty, hamstringing the FBI, someone surely would have *seen* them. There were many calls, many sightings, but none were accurate. Were they too plain a family to notice—American father, French mother, little boy and baby sister? A psychopathic unit expert at slipping under the radar? And what about sweet Austin—how badly had they twisted his mind?

Alice tried not to cry now when she recalled the sight of Lauren's wrecked body. Once the floodgates opened, she couldn't close them and it all started again: insomnia, nausea, incessant trolling of the Internet, fruitless calls to Frannie Viola. Alice steeled herself against the memory of those wretched days in which she suffered the murder of her best friend and learned the awful truth of what could go on beneath the surface of a family's apparently happy life.

Six days passed with blissful uneventfulness, each calm hour a promise that the last one had been real. It was over, Alice thought; finally over. Until one afternoon—after a flash storm on the last humid day of a spent summer—when she returned alone to Simon's house for a few minutes before picking up Nell and Peter from school.

She knew it was inevitable the moment she heard his voice.

Chapter 43

"Shh."

The sound was distant, barely audible, like the crying baby who had haunted so many of Alice's sleepless nights. But this time Alice *knew* it was real.

She kept still a moment, then took a step across the foyer.

"Shh."

She stopped, listening carefully. "Simon?" She walked to the arched entrance of the living room. Outside, the sun was just beginning to split through a storm-darkened afternoon sky, sending tentative slivers of light over the gleaming ebony of Simon's piano, gently striping the slanted top.

"Alice, are you alone?" his voice whispered.

It didn't sound like Simon, but Alice *wanted* it to be Simon, *hoped* it was.

"Simon, is that you?"

"Are you alone?"

"Who's there?"

"Answer me."

He was sitting in the corner, blanketed in shadow. Someone hovered beside him, crouched down.

A shaft of broken sunlight crept slowly over the shadow that hid him. He leaned forward, with both palms open as if in offering.

Cupped in his hands was a small black gun with a curved white handle.

Alice stepped backward, shoving her hand into her pocket for her cell phone.

Beside him, the other person—who Alice now saw was not crouched, but small—became restless.

"Simon!" Alice called, hoping he was upstairs. *"Simon!"*

"Shh." He leaned fully forward now, green eyes glowing through the shadow. He was badly sunburned. "Simon isn't home."

"Daddy," a small voice whispered. "Please can I come out?"

Tim's right hand yanked the gun behind a cushion at his side, hiding it. "Go ahead."

Austin moved out of the shadow. He looked thinner. His face, neck and arms were mottled tan and red with sunburn. Hovering at his father's side, his eyes—a duller green now, Alice thought, and bruised with fatigue—sought Alice. Claimed her.

Ignoring Tim, she dropped to her knees and opened her arms; Austin fled quickly to her. She wrapped up his small body with her protection and love, holding tight.

"I can't believe it," Alice whispered into Austin's neck. She breathed in his cinnamon smell; breathed in Lauren. "I can't believe it's true."

"But it's what you always thought." Tim crossed his legs and leaned toward the right, making sure the gun remained completely hidden from his son.

"I never really believed it, Tim." She raised her eyes to his. Green. Damp. He had better not cry; she wouldn't tolerate that.

"But you thought it."

"I thought it against my will."

"It doesn't matter," he said. "Your instinct was mostly right."

"Mostly?"

He shook his head and glanced at the floor.

"Where is the baby, Tim? Where is she?"

His gaze fixed on her now, hardening with whatever determination had brought him here.

"At the funeral," he said, "I wanted to ask you something, but I didn't know how."

"I don't like this," Austin whispered in Alice's ear.

"Let Austin go upstairs, Tim," Alice demanded. She hated him. *She* would tell him what to do. If not for the gun, she would have taken the phone out of her pocket and called the police.

Tim nodded to Austin, who raced from Alice's arms and out of the living room. His footsteps thudded fast up the stairs.

"Why are you doing this, Tim?"

He shifted in the chair and reached beside him, his hand reappearing with the gun. Lauren had seen it. Pam had seen it. And now Alice.

Her phone. If she could just get her hand into her pocket before he shot her. Open up a line to someone who could serve as witness to her death. Not Mike; she couldn't do that to him. Frannie. Even Maggie. Someone.

"I don't want to do this." His face twisted into an ugly knot and he began, actually, to cry.

Alice's fear transformed to anger. What right did Tim Barnet have to *cry*?

She thrust her hand into her pocket and pulled out the phone, flipped it open and speed-dialed Maggie.

He stood up, hand gripping the gun. A click. Not loud. The trigger cocking. He raised the gun with a stiff, shaking arm and pointed it directly at Alice's heart.

"I just want to know *why*." Her voice cracked. But she was ready to jump into the wave of her ending; she was *not* afraid of this man.

He raised the gun higher and then turned it, suddenly, on himself.

"No!" Alice said.

She didn't care about Tim anymore. But Austin. He was upstairs. This would destroy him.

"Why?" Alice demanded.

Hand trembling, Tim pressed the gun into his temple. His finger began to depress the trigger.

But then . . . he stopped. Coward. *Do it,* her mind urged. *Do it, you bastard.*

Crumpling to the floor, he wept, pulling his hand away from the gun as if it were diseased and he couldn't bear to touch it.

Alice moved quickly to kick the gun away from him. It slid across the floor to the far corner of the living room, stopping next to a forgotten Power Ranger contorted into an impossible fighting pose.

She walked over to Tim and stood over him, feeling no sympathy whatsoever.

"Why, Tim? Why did you kill Lauren?"

"I didn't," he cried.

She felt like kicking him for that lie; even if he wasn't at the crime scene, he had still killed her. Alice controlled her anger, just as Lizzie had promised she could. To her surprise and almost pleasure, she felt capable of this moment.

"Why?"

He gathered himself off the floor and stood up, wiping his eyes on the back of his bare arm, slicking his skin with tears.

"Please, take Austin," Tim begged. *"Please."*

"What did you do with the baby?" Alice kept her voice cool, belying the heat that coursed through her body.

"Will you take him, Alice?"

"Yes. Now tell me."

He reached into his pants pocket and pulled out a folded, rumpled envelope. "This letter gives you legal custody."

She didn't know whether to hit him or laugh. Always the lawyer. Thinking of everything.

"My daughter is somewhere out there, somewhere in this world." Tim put the jackknifed envelope next to him on the floor. "We've been everywhere, looking for her."

Somewhere far away, Alice thought, somewhere hot. The sunburns.

The scorching beach materialized in her mind but she banished the image. She needed to stay present.

"How do you know she's out there, Tim?"

He shook his head mournfully. "I have to find her now." He got up and walked past Alice to the foot of the stairs. "Austin!"

There was no answer, though Alice suspected Austin had heard his father.

"I'm leaving now!"

Plain silence from Austin, resonating with banishment. Only five years old and he knew. He knew.

"I love you!" Tim called up the stairs.

He turned back to Alice, then shifted his eyes to the front door and seemed to will himself forward.

She walked over to the corner of the living room where she had kicked the gun. Holding the wall for balance, she lowered herself down. Flicked aside the Power Ranger. Picked up the gun. Turned to Tim.

"No," she told him. "You're not leaving yet."

"Alice—"

"Tell me why. Then you can go."

A hard, harsh sun poured through the window at the top of the front door, blanching Tim's eyes of color.

"I made a terrible mistake." His gaze fled to the door again, refusing Alice.

"You slept with her?"

He didn't answer.

She raised the gun on him and asked again. "Did you sleep with Sylvie? Is that what started all this?"

"Yes," he whispered. "I was never unfaithful to Lauren before. Sylvie wasn't supposed to fall in love with me."

Love. Alice wanted to scream, *That is not love.*

"Why didn't you just leave, Tim? Why did you have to kill her?" Tears engorged her but she stopped them from flowing out. She could hold them back until later. She had to do this now.

He shook his head. Bleached. Vacant. His forehead pleated with anguish.

"I told Sylvie I would never leave my wife. I would never leave my children." Finally, he looked at Alice. "I loved Lauren."

"Past tense," Alice said. "You said *loved.*"

"I didn't know until after it was over." His jaw tightened, he swallowed hard. Forced himself to say one more thing. "Sylvie did it herself, so she could have me and I could have my children."

Alice's hand began to sweat around the gun, the muscles of her inner palm were cramping, but she managed to keep it steadily aimed at him.

"Where is the baby?"

"Somewhere out there." His head tilted to the door. "I've been searching for her everywhere."

"But Sylvie stayed so long after . . . after she killed Lauren." The statement flew out of Alice and hovered between them. There it was, the simple fact. "Why didn't you just ask her?"

"She wouldn't tell me." His smile was a bitter contortion. "Unless I took her with me. She was waiting."

"She's gone."

"I know. I came back to bring Austin. He can't live this way." A tremor of shame passed over Tim's gaunt face.

"I should kill you."

"Let me find my daughter and then this will all be over. I promise you. Please, Alice, let me go so I can find her."

There was a sound on the stairs. Austin had come halfway down and was watching them.

Alice lowered the gun to her side, slipped it into her pocket.

"Her name is Ivy," she told Tim, just before he left.

EPILOGUE

Two years later

The minivan bumped and careened along Mexico's Pacific coast, heading south from Puerto Vallarta to Cruz de Loreto. The road had spiraled out of the town, with its tiered seaside villas, nearly two hours ago. Alice was beginning to worry. Lizzie hadn't mentioned the roughness of the terrain when she had given Alice, Mike and the kids their Christmas surprise. She had gone to the Hotelito with her new husband, George, on their honeymoon last spring and in her enthusiasm had booked the family vacation then; the success of her latest movie had afforded her such extravagances. It was supposed to be a luxury hotel with no electricity, fabulous food and candlelight every evening—a beautiful thought. And indeed, on the Web site, the *palafitas* with their thatched roofs looked heavenly. But the deeper into rural Mexico they got, the less comfortable Alice felt. The land was blanched dry from the heat. The houses, clustered together, were hovels at best. The occasional roadside restaurants were mostly rusted tin cans of buildings advertising beer and buzzing with flies.

Mike was sitting up front with their driver, Miguel, and so she couldn't read his reaction to the obvious isolation of this place. Years ago, when it was just them, the adventure would have thrilled her. But now she was a mother with five children. What if one of them got sick? Lizzie had said the Hotelito had access to medical care, but Alice saw nothing that indicated these tracts of sparsely populated, arid land were anything but forgotten third-world villages.

Nell, Peter and Austin, in the van's third row, seemed to love the bumpy ride. But the toddlers, in the second row with Alice, were looking a little green. Henry was fast asleep in his car seat, but Oscar was getting agitated; he needed a diaper change.

Alice hated to distract Miguel—she had noticed that every car and truck they passed had a cracked windshield, as did this van—but they were going to have to pull over. She leaned forward so he could hear her above the loud rumble of tires on the rocky dirt road.

"Excuse me," she said, knowing Miguel spoke fairly good English—he worked at the Hotelito and had welcomed them graciously at the airport. "We have a dirty diaper situation back here. Any chance we could pull over?"

Miguel twisted around, saw Oscar's pout and swerved to an abrupt stop in front of a broken-down shack with a hand-painted sign, CAFÉ. Miguel hopped out of the front passenger's seat and slid open the van's side door. The three older children immediately scrambled out. Mike stayed in the van with sleeping Henry, while Alice unlatched Oscar and grabbed the diaper bag.

Once outside the air-conditioned van, Alice was hit by the richly sweet country air. The humidity here was different than at home, where it settled into your lungs and made you suffocate. Here, it was heavily warm with light breezes that grazed your skin, circulating around you. All of a sudden, in this forgotten place, Alice felt elated to be so far from home.

Miguel had taken the big kids into the café and bought them orange sodas in glass bottles. They stood ten feet from a trio of Mexican children, the opposing sets eyeing each other until finally a boy reached into his torn red shorts and brought out a stack of Yu-Gi-Oh! cards. The gesture instantly broke the distance between them as the two groups nearly fell on each other.

"You see?" Miguel said, smiling. "Anywhere you go, kids find their way together."

"They should work at the UN." Mike had stepped out of the van and was standing near sleeping Henry.

Alice set Oscar down on his feet and he clung to her legs. Henry was the explorer of the two; Oscar mostly stayed close. There was a patch of grass at the side of the café that looked like as good a place as any to unfold the changing mat. Oscar laid himself down and lifted his legs; he wanted that diaper *off*. Alice changed him quickly, smiling and tickling his soft tummy. She swatted a fly from his face, set him on his feet and packed up.

Just then she heard the sound of a motor in the distance, getting louder, nearing the café. Behind the rickety building, she now saw, was a narrow dirt road that wound through a field and disappeared behind a hill. The motor puttered closer and Alice saw that it was a European car, white and dented. It was an old Saab, not the rough-riding vehicle she would have thought would best suit these roads.

Alice turned around to watch Oscar toddle in the children's direction. She caught Miguel's eye. He had noticed her looking at the incongruous car and with a self-forgiving smile said, "Gringos, like you."

Alice laughed. Yes, gringos like them. She turned back to watch as the car veered toward the café and pulled to a stop. Looking bored in the passenger's seat was a very tan woman with short black hair. She looked a little familiar, Alice thought—and then saw the man who had just stepped out from behind the wheel.

He was slight and lemony blond, his hair longish, curling behind his ears. Green, green eyes. A crackling tan. His attention snagged on the scene of the other gringo family.

The woman yawned, unlatched her door and came out of the car. She was wearing a black bikini top and long white flowing skirt that sat low on her hips. She had a ruby stud in her belly button. A tattoo bracelet encircled her ankle.

Behind her, asleep in the back of the car, was a little girl about two years old. Her head was turned away and Alice couldn't see her face—how she wanted to see that face!—but her brown hair was done up in two messy pigtails and the red birthmark on the back of her neck was as good as a face and a name. It was exactly Lauren's birthmark, in miniature. The maternal family birthmark common to every female in the family for three—now four—generations.

Mike stepped forward. So he had seen it too, all of it. Tim, Analise, Ivy. Standing right there in front of them, comfortable as locals in their sweaty, tanned skin.

Off to the side, Austin watched. He was seven now, lanky and confident. He dropped his soda bottle and took several steps forward across the dry, dusty ground.

Analise turned sharply to Tim, who directed her with a nod back into the car. Tim then walked quickly forward, kicking up dust with his woven straw sandals. His toenails were dirty. He stood in front of Austin, stared at him, then snatched his hand and tried to tug him toward the car.

"No!" Austin protested.

"Please!" Tim begged. "I can't leave you again."

Austin yanked his hand out of Tim's and ran behind Alice, who shielded him as Tim struggled to decide. But for Alice there was no decision; Austin was *her* son now. She would never let him go.

"On y va!" Analise called to Tim in French. Her tone was hard, free of the sweet, lilting accent she had mastered in Brooklyn.

Over by the van, Mike tried desperately to work his cell phone, but there was no signal this far along the map. Tim turned around and jogged back to the car, stirring up a cloud of dust. Mike threw aside his phone and chased him. Nearly there, Mike managed to grab the back of Tim's shirt.

"Stop!" Mike shouted. "Enough!"

Tim twisted himself free and Mike almost caught him again, but didn't. And so Tim slipped away into the essential inch of difference between capture and escape. He got back into his car, slammed shut the door and revved the motor, but before pulling out he paused to say something to Mike. It was a weird moment: Tim urgently speaking, Mike listening, both men pouring sweat and exhaustion and fear and rage and anguish, the remnants of their old friendship flying off them in broken bits.

It was just before the car began to move that Alice noticed Analise looking at her with cold, vacant eyes. At the snap of Analise's voice—*"Vite!"*—Ivy woke up in the backseat and turned around just as the old white car peeled onto the road.

Alice memorized her face. She was lovely. Round-cheeked, with Lauren's sandy brown hair cut in bangs above vivid green eyes.

Tim's eyes. She would see the world his way.

Mike pulled a scrap of paper and pen out of his pocket and wrote down the license number.

"I've got it!" he called to Alice as the car disappeared.

"You know these people?" Miguel asked.

"Very well," Alice said. "Is there somewhere we can make a call?"

By the time they got the café's phone plugged in and had established a dial tone, then managed a connection to the local police, who contacted Interpol, the FBI and ultimately Frannie Viola at the Seventy-sixth Precinct in Brooklyn, New York . . . by the time the local roads, highways and airports at Puerto Vallarta and Mexico City had been sealed . . . it was too late.

They were gone.

Later that night, lying in bed under a draping white mosquito net, Alice asked Mike, "What did Tim say to you?"

Hands clasped behind his head on the white pillow, Mike smirked. " 'I love her.' " He rolled over to face Alice. "Who do you think he meant? Ivy or Analise?"

"I'm not sure," Alice said. The cool humidity fast against her skin, she pushed off the white sheet and closed her eyes.

NOW AN ONYX PAPERBACK

"Strikes terror into a
lazy summer day."
—DONNA ANDERS,
Author of *Night Stalker*

FIVE
DAYS
IN
SUMMER

"Mesmerizing....Your heart will be pounding long after
you've turned the final page."—LISA GARDNER,
New York Times Bestselling Author of *The Killing Hour*

KATE PEPPER

0-451-41140-4

Now Available in Paperback

NATIONAL BESTSELLING AUTHOR OF *MONKEEWRENCH*

P. J. TRACY

LIVE

Live Bait

"AN ENTICING READ."
—*People*

SIGNET

SIGNET

Penguin Group (USA) Inc. Online

What will you be reading tomorrow?

Tom Clancy, Patricia Cornwell, W.E.B. Griffin,
Nora Roberts, William Gibson, Robin Cook,
Brian Jacques, Catherine Coulter, Stephen King,
Dean Koontz, Ken Follett, Clive Cussler,
Eric Jerome Dickey, John Sandford,
Terry McMillan...

You'll find them all at
http://www.penguin.com

*Read excerpts and newsletters, find tour
schedules, and enter contest.*

Subscribe to Penguin Group (USA) Inc. Newsletters
and get an exclusive inside look
at exciting new titles and the authors you love
long before everyone else does.

PENGUIN GROUP (USA) INC. NEWS
http://www.penguin.com/news